Only The Gods Decide

MIKE LLOYD

TRAFFORD

• Canada • UK • Ireland • USA •

© Copyright 2006 Mike Lloyd.
All rights reserved. No part of this publication may be reproduced, stored in a retrieval system, or transmitted, in any form or by any means, electronic, mechanical, photocopying, recording, or otherwise, without the written prior permission of the author.

Note for Librarians: A cataloguing record for this book is available from Library and Archives Canada at www.collectionscanada.ca/amicus/index-e.html
ISBN 1-4120-7675-7

Printed in Victoria, BC, Canada. Printed on paper with minimum 30% recycled fibre. Trafford's print shop runs on "green energy" from solar, wind and other environmentally-friendly power sources.

TRAFFORD
PUBLISHING

Offices in Canada, USA, Ireland and UK

This book was published *on-demand* in cooperation with Trafford Publishing. On-demand publishing is a unique process and service of making a book available for retail sale to the public taking advantage of on-demand manufacturing and Internet marketing. On-demand publishing includes promotions, retail sales, manufacturing, order fulfilment, accounting and collecting royalties on behalf of the author.

Book sales for North America and international:
Trafford Publishing, 6E–2333 Government St.,
Victoria, BC V8T 4P4 CANADA
phone 250 383 6864 (toll-free 1 888 232 4444)
fax 250 383 6804; email to orders@trafford.com

Book sales in Europe:
Trafford Publishing (UK) Limited, 9 Park End Street, 2nd Floor
Oxford, UK OX1 1HH UNITED KINGDOM
phone 44 (0)1865 722 113 (local rate 0845 230 9601)
facsimile 44 (0)1865 722 868; info.uk@trafford.com

Order online at:
trafford.com/05-2570

10 9 8 7 6 5 4 3 2

ACKNOWLEDGEMENTS

I found writing this book to be much harder work than I had originally anticipated. So I would like to thank my wonderful sister Janice, my mother in law Sheila, Marius and Debbie Potgieter, Lady Margaret Lilford, and my chum Mike Woodhatch for their many suggestions and constructive criticisms. Most of all I would like to thank my wife Jules for her considerable support during the writing of this my first novel. Without her help it would never have seen the light of day. I thank her most deeply.

I would also like to thank the Raytheon Aircraft Company for their permission in using the picture of the Beechcraft King Air C90B on the front cover.

ONLY THE GODS DECIDE

1

He wiped his sweaty face with a sodden handkerchief. Slipping the pack from his back he dropped it to the ground and stretched his arms wide to ease the stress of its weight from his muscles. Frowning he moved his head slowly from side to side easing the ache out of his neck and looked up and down the dusty track. A sense of weariness and isolation ran over him. He took a deep breath and let it out in a long sigh, pushed his hat further back on his head and glanced up at the clear blue sky. Twin white streaks of a plane's vapour trail scarred its way high across the heavens and he felt a touch of envy that the occupants must be sitting in cool air-conditioned comfort. He put his water bottle to his lips and finished off the last remaining mouthful.

That wasn't enough, so he bent down to open his pack to get at the second bottle and out of the corner of his eye noticed a movement in the grass. He closed his eyes in exasperation at his bad luck, and taking a long breath, he turned his head slowly. Five feet away was the biggest and ugliest Viper he had ever seen with its cold yellow eyes watching him angrily. It rose slowly swaying slowly side to side. It oozed malevolence.

He hated snakes especially Vipers. The bloody things made his blood run cold; they were unpredictable, tetchy and could strike without warning. Watching it carefully he bunched the soggy handkerchief in his right hand and then flicked it straight over the snake's head. The distraction worked as the Viper responded instantly, following the flight of the wet ball of cloth. Turning away and rising to its full height and in the blink of an eye it struck at the perceived threat. Frank had already unsheathed his machete in one smooth movement and now swiped at the Viper cutting it in two. He was a big man and could move quickly when he wanted to. Despite the heat he shivered at the sight of the thick body writhing in its death throes its evil head severed, falling to the ground.

He walked over and picked up the old handkerchief and carefully wiped clean the dark blue blade of the machete his hands shaking and then slowly slipped it back into its sheath at his hip. He leaned back against the boulder and slowly unscrewed the top of the second water bottle as he looked out at the endless expanse of Jungle remembering that day only a year ago when he had made up his mind to buy the old machete. For two weeks, and twice every day, he had walked past the old second-hand tool shop and had seen it; his eyes were attracted to it like a magnet. He smiled at the memory. It had sat in the window and fascinated him, almost talking to him and he had wanted it but couldn't understand the reason for the attraction. Eventually, he had given in to the impulse and had bought it even though he had no need for it, after all what did he need a machete for? The machete however had been the catalyst. As soon as he had unsheathed it in his shed and cleaned, caressed and oiled the cold blue steel the idea had begun to form. He wanted to explore the pyramids of Central America. He had always wanted to from a child. Anyway, it was perfect timing, his wife had just walked out on him after almost twenty-three years of marriage. He smiled again to himself at the memory, "Good God, was that really a year ago?"

As long as he could remember he'd had a fascination for the ancient civilisations of South America and photographs and stories of the old Aztec and Mayan ruins that lay mostly undisturbed deep in the jungles of Central and Southern America had intrigued him. In those quiet moments that one gets sometimes, he had promised himself that one day he would come and have a look at these phenomena. He wanted to see and feel the history of the ancient peoples who had inhabited that area for over two thousand years. To see the pyramids and to get a taste of the continent. He never thought this dream would come true but he had made it happen and he had his ex-wife to thank for that. If she hadn't walked out on him he would still be sitting in front of that bloody television, vegetating, probably watching a football match bored out of his skull.

He was getting a taste all right and had begun to feel that what he was doing was a particularly stupid thing for a man of forty-seven to do. He had been walking for almost four hours in a 90-degree heat without a stop, but he was keen to get home, he'd had enough of sleeping rough and being wet and hungry. On top of it all he was afraid of snakes. Scorpions were bad enough but snakes were the pits. Big ones like this one made his skin crawl. Taking a mouthful of water from the water bottle, he swirled it around his mouth and spat it out. He grimaced and wiped his mouth with the back of his hand, the water was warm and tasted like dishwater.

"Christ, what wouldn't I give for a cold pint of beer?" he said out loud. He fantasised at the thought of how nice it would be if he was in a bar in Rio instead of here, with air conditioning keeping him cool, a long-legged blonde by his side and a cold lager sliding down his throat. The thought of it made his taste buds salivate. Several times over the last few days he had caught himself talking in this fashion. It was definitely a sign of oncoming senility but quite comforting. It was time to go home. He pulled his map from his backpack and checked his position. About another twenty-odd miles and five hours of hard walking and he should reach the village he was aiming for. "There by supper time if I get my finger out," he thought.

He didn't hear it coming and the sudden roar of an aeroplane flying low overhead made him jump. He ducked down instinctively it was so low. He had been miles away, daydreaming, and the plane seemed to come from nowhere. It was gone from sight in an instant and he heard it drop down into the valley to his right. As far as he knew there was only jungle down there and certainly no landing strip. He waited to hear the crash. But he was wrong because the plane's engines slowed in tempo eventually dropping to a tick over and then stopped. "There has to be a landing strip down there somewhere, and if there is, there's people, and if there are people there's water, food and company." he reasoned.

Heaving his pack back onto his back and collecting his rifle he set off at a sharp pace disregarding the perspiration running down his body and, after no more than half a mile, found a well-used track leading down to his right. "Very well used too, a lot of trucks have been travelling up and down this track."

He was curious and wary at the same time. What on earth was a plane doing landing down here? It wasn't good to get into trouble here in the Jungle when you were on your own miles from anywhere. It was either Jungle bandits, drug smugglers, or a mixture of both. Either way he should keep his nose clean but his curiosity got the better of him. Unslinging his rifle from his shoulder he hesitated for a moment pondering on the potential problems that could lie ahead. Then he shrugged his shoulders as though making up his mind and tucked the gun into the crook of his left arm with his right hand caressing the trigger guard. He started walking slowly down the track keeping to the edge in case he did run into trouble. He had walked down the steep track for only ten minutes when the crackling sound of gunfire close by made him stop; startled. His hackles rose and he went down onto one knee. He listened carefully and could make out small arms fire as well as rifle. After only a few minutes the firing stopped and he could hear shouting.

"Now what the hell is that all about?" he said out loud. He needed to see what was going on and looking around he saw several large outcrops of the same colour rock as he had leaned against only a few moments before. Dropping his backpack and slinging his rifle over his back he eased himself up the nearest clump. It was some thirty feet high but it was still not high enough for him to see anything. The jungle canopy was well over 90ft but it did allow him to look around. Another enormous clump of rock rising high into the sky, some fifty yards away through the jungle looked to be just right. It had to be twice as high as the one he had climbed and with luck should give him a good sight of the valley. Sliding back down, he collected his pack and eased into the thick undergrowth making his way to the large rock formation.

Breaking through into the clearing he was shocked at the size of the rock. It reared out of the jungle floor and towered high above him in the rough shape of an eagle's beak and looked as though it broke through the canopy of trees. He didn't have a good head for heights anymore but he thought it would be ideal and should allow him to see the whole valley. Opening his backpack he rummaged for his binoculars, another handkerchief, and three magazine packs for his rifle. Hanging his binoculars around his neck he stuffed the magazines into a pocket, slung the rifle across his back and putting its telescopic scope into his right thigh pocket he set out to climb the rock.

More sporadic gunfire broke out which lent urgency to his climb. The rock was craggy and shards cut his hands. The going was easier than he thought it would be and after a hard and sweaty ten-minute climb he found himself above the trees and he could see clearly into a long wide valley some two hundred and fifty yards away. It must have been over a mile long and about two hundred yards wide. Strangely it was almost treeless, simply covered in long yellow grass. He was closer than he originally thought. He stood wiping the sweat from his face and examined the extraordinary scene that lay before him. The gunfire was now constant and in the distance sat the aeroplane and some twenty or so RVs and lorries. Puffs of smoke drifted up from a group of people huddled around two of the lorries in particular and they appeared to be shooting down the valley, almost towards him. "It looks like a bloody film set but it can't be. Not down here surely?"

Scanning the valley through his binoculars he wondered what the hell they were shooting at. Then he saw them. Eight or nine men were moving slowly and carefully through the long grass towards the RVs and they were using their rifles in a slow but steady fire rate.

Frank realised that the scene evolving in front of him was for real and looking at the situation from his vantage point he thought that if it was for real then the group of people by the vehicles stood no chance. Scanning back to the line of advancing men he suddenly realised who and what they were. Jungle bandits. These guys were not nice people to know. He watched the scene for a few moments knowing that something had to be done. He didn't want to get involved; it was nothing to do with him and yet he couldn't just sit and watch people being slaughtered and the people at the end of the valley would be slaughtered without a doubt; and not nicely either. From what he had heard over the last few weeks the men would die slowly and eventually, after some time, once the men had had their fun the women would die. A frown creased his forehead and he shook his head. God damn it, he had to do something. He sat down on the rock, put his binoculars carefully to one side and unslung his rifle. He flicked his Stetson back off his head, wiped his face with his handkerchief again and caressed his pride and joy, a Remington 700 bolt-action rifle. He quickly wiped down the barrel and made sure his spare magazines were full. He had scoured all the gun merchants in Rio for two days looking for just such a model and after careful thought had bought this one. It was second-hand and had obviously been well used but interestingly enough it had also been very well looked after. Frank had fallen in love with its menacing dark blue looks and gleaming well oiled mahogany finish as only men can with guns especially as he had been able to keep himself fed with the small game he had been able to shoot with it. It was a beautifully balanced gun, chambered for .235 Winchester cartridges, which carried quite a punch even at long distances. As a bonus, the previous owner had fitted scope mounts. He settled himself down into a prone position and fidgeted his body until he was comfortable, his body forming an inverted Y, his legs splayed. He then eased the scope from its hiding place in his thigh pocket and slid it gently into position on the rifle. Tightening the knurled holding nuts he flipped off the lens covers and dropped his right eye to the rear of the scope. The valley sprang into life in front of him through the powerful lens but was slightly fuzzy. He gently eased the focus control and the bandits loomed into view looking as though they were walking only a few yards away from him. They were continuing their slow but relentless progress towards the group of people by the wagon's smoke wisping up from their rifle barrels. The scope gave him the distance, 310 yards, and he altered the sights accordingly. He was zeroed in. He eased his laying position on the rock overhang and put the spare magazines close to his right hand, checked around him, and took another look at the battle going on in front of him.

He felt a surge of excitement, which he hadn't felt for a long time. Nervous sweat ran down his armpits and the little finger on his right hand twitched uncontrollably, just as it used to. He smiled to himself at the memory. He could clearly see the people at the campsite even at that distance and counted more than twenty in total with almost half being women. The group were in serious trouble and knew it. He could almost see the frightened expressions on the women's faces. By the look of it there were about four men shooting. The others were helpless. They had no other weapons. The bandits were continuing to make their steady and determined progress and, as he watched, three broke away to make a flanking movement down the left-hand side of the valley.

There was nothing else to do but to even up the situation otherwise there would be a massacre and it would not be a fun situation if those women fell into the bandits' hands. He had heard what they did to white women. "Better to give the little shits a scare and take those three out first," he thought. "Just like old times." He wiped a trickle of sweat from his brow that threatened to drop into his eyes.

Adjusting the scope carefully until their figures were sharp in his lens he tracked the three bandits, picking out the leader. "Wind and elevation Frank my boy, wind and elevation," he said to himself out loud. He gently squeezed the trigger. The leading man's head burst like a ripe melon from the impact of the bullet travelling at 2500 feet per second and before he had dropped Frank had worked the bolt ejecting the empty cartridge and, hammering in another round, had focused on the next man. He was swearing quietly to himself as he had aimed for the first man's torso. Too much elevation, he wouldn't make that mistake again, it was much too messy. The second man had been looking elsewhere when his friend was hit but he sure heard the crack of the rifle and he stopped, looking around, startled at the different sound. He gaped at the gruesome sight of his friend's bloody corpse falling headless to the ground. He and his other colleague froze at the horrifying sight. That was a bad move as they both made a perfect target. Frank watched through his scope as the man turned his head and then shot him high in the chest. The man did a slow pirouette as the high velocity round hit him and then he crumpled like a puppet; his heart and nervous system destroyed in the fraction of a second. It was like shooting turkeys in a barrel. The third man, realising at last that he was under fire, threw himself down into the long grass but Frank could still see him from his high vantage point twenty feet above the jungle foliage. Aiming carefully he squeezed off another round but saw a puff of dust rise no more than two inches from its target. He frowned, too much elevation again. He was out of practice at shooting at such long distances. The man however rolled rapidly to his right; he must have been frightened out of his skin. He jumped to his feet leaving his rifle behind and set off at a dead run as though the hounds of hell were at his heels to re-join his now stationary companions. Frank could clearly see his mouth opening and closing as he shouted to his colleagues as he ran. Tracking him through his sights he carefully squeezed off the last bullet in the magazine. For Frank it was pure magic. The man, shot through the side chest, his heart and lungs torn apart and collapsing from the shock of the impact, carried on several paces as though nothing was wrong but then his legs went and he tumbled to the ground rolling and rolling, eventually coming up against one of his horrified colleagues, dead.

Frank allowed himself the luxury of a grin. To hit a running target at that distance was exceptional and as an ex-professional it gave him much clinical satisfaction. He didn't allow himself a second thought about the fact that he had just killed three men. That would come later. A memory flashed through his mind for a millisecond. His grizzled old Flight Sergeant saying "Wherever you see a threat to yourself or your colleagues, don't hesitate to remove that threat using whatever means necessary." Frank shook his head in amazement. He hadn't thought about that wonderful old git for more than twenty years. In the meantime all shooting had stopped now as the bandits looked around them to see where the rifle fire was coming from. Even gunfire from the group of trucks had stopped. They had also seen the three men die.

Frank wasn't worried about that; he was too busy changing magazines. With a fresh one in the rifle, he re-focused his sights on the remaining bunch of agitated bandits. Then they spotted him and five rifles pointed up to his position on the rock and let go. Bullets pinged and whined off the rock. Frank wasn't worried about that either; they would take a while to get the distance where he was located on the rock whereas he was already zeroed in. He quickly snapped off two more shots, just to put a scare into them more than anything else. He didn't feel that more killing would achieve anything except to remove what threat there was left. If they persisted then he would kill them. As it was those shots with the dust spurting up at their feet was enough. That was it; they turned as one and ran for the cover of the jungle. He tried a little fancy shooting wanting to take one of their hats off but missed. The crack of his rifle however lent a sense of urgency to the fleeing men as they crashed headlong into the jungle. He heard faint cheering from the group of people further down the valley.

It wasn't a time to hang about. These Bandits were not very bright but they were cunning, which was worse and you have to second-guess people like that or you die very quickly and Frank had no delusions about what type of death he would suffer if they caught him. It would be a slow one that's for sure. The primary factor was that they knew where he was but he didn't know where they were now so it was time to leave. Slipping his remaining ammunition into his pocket, he draped his binoculars around his neck and slipped the rifle over his back before climbing back down as quickly as he could. He hated that. Climbing down a steep cliff is always so much more difficult than climbing up for some reason and it took him another ten minutes. Heaving a sigh of relief at getting both of his feet back on sound ground he slung his pack back onto his back, took another swig of the brackish water from his bottle, and set off to find his way to the valley.

He broke out onto the valley floor ten minutes later; more by luck than judgement onto an expanse of knee-high grass. In the distance about half a mile away he could see the plane and people who were now milling about the RVs and trucks.

He stopped, hesitating on the edge of the jungle. For sure the bandits would still be around, watching from the cover of the jungle. Watching now, curious and careful; watching to see if there was any opportunity of continuing with their original plan and also curious as to who had killed their colleagues. Wanting to have their revenge. Frank checked the distance from where he stood to the R.V's. Must be about another four hundred yards of open grass. There was nothing else to do but run for it. He unslung his rifle from his back and checked that it had a full magazine and slipped on the safety catch. He took a deep breath and broke into a fast trot with his pack banging his back and his machete slapping his leg. He put his head down and went for it. He was a big, powerfully built man; just over six feet tall and after six weeks in the jungle he was a trim and muscular sixteen stone. His long strong legs had always been his biggest assets, the result of a lot of cycling in his youth, and they had made him a force to be reckoned with on the rugby pitch during his late teens and early twenties, enabling him to outrun many a full back. When he wanted to Frank could be very fast on his feet. When he was much younger he could do the one hundred yards in eleven seconds, but that was a long time ago and at this moment in time, with his advancing years and all the kit he was carrying, he was content just to hack it at a medium pace. Even so his long legs covered the ground quickly.

The hair on his neck bristled as he waited for the expected crack of a rifle but there was a deathly silence. He passed by two of the grizzled remains of the bandits he had shot. He was too busy trying to get his breath to worry about them but he did scoop up one of their rifles. Gradually the voices of the people in front of him went quiet and there remained only the hum of the generators and the rasping sound of his breathing. They had stopped what they were doing and were now watching him trotting towards them. He couldn't shout because he was saving his breath but he grinned to himself. He obviously looked unfriendly and suddenly appearing like this from nowhere running towards them must be alarming them especially just after the fire fight.

He realised that he must look a bit rough but that wasn't his main concern right now. He put all his concentration in just breathing hard. He hadn't washed for three days, and was carrying three weeks' growth of pepper and salt beard on his face. What with that and his long dark curly hair sticking out from under a wide-brimmed sweat-soaked Stetson, wearing dirty khakis with a large Bowie knife on one hip, a machete on the other and carrying two rifles plus the rucksack on his back, he did indeed look a bit rough and dangerous.

As he closed on them, two men broke out of the group and walked towards him, each one breaking out pistols from hip holsters. He didn't like that at all.

"That's not very nice," he thought. He stopped; breathing hard, sweat pouring from his body in the noontime heat. He dropped a rifle and slapped at the flies that swarmed around him and raised the other rifle in the air. He was less than fifty yards from them.

"Hold it right there boys. I'm not here to give trouble," he shouted. "I'm the good guy who was shooting up the bad guys just now."

"Stay where you are mister and put those guns down," one called.

"Oh, for Christ's sake," he thought. "Not fucking likely, our little friends might be back any minute so like it or not I'm coming in," Frank shouted.

"Let him come on in," said a voice from the group of silent spectators.

They holstered their guns and fanned out letting him through. He shouldered his rifle, and carrying the other, broke back into a trot until he was level with them and then he slowed to a walk carrying on past without giving them a single glance. He estimated that there were about twenty or so people there as he had thought.

"Hi there," he said with a grin as he walked up to the main group of men, stopping to lean on his rifle and gasping for breath still, "any chance of a cold beer?" Sweat was pouring off his dirty face like a river.

A tall blond-headed man in his late thirties with typical English aristocratic features and that slight red flush in his cheeks which is common to that breed stepped forward out of the group and put out his hand.

"Good afternoon, my name is Ian Crompton," he said in a beautiful modulated English accent. "I'm the Director and these are my colleagues." He gave a slight shrug as he waved his hand in an arc. "Actors and film crew actually. So, you are the fella who saved our bacon. Nice shooting old boy." He turned and shouted, "Someone get this man some water, fast."

Frank flinched at the "old boy" bit but smiled and said. "The name's Frank Blake."

Crompton took Frank's hand and shook it vigorously at the same time thanking him profusely on behalf of all his people. "Hear Hear," echoed from some of the men who had grouped around him curious as to who this stranger could be who had, without a doubt just saved their lives. A young man ran up with a large bottle of water, which Frank took gratefully. He put his head back and poured the contents down his throat with a large amount of it running over his face and down his neck and chest. It was cold and tasted like nectar. He listened to the man Crompton who was giving instructions to some of the men to go and collect the weapons and ammunition from the dead bandits.

A tall extremely good-looking blonde broke out of the group of women standing close by and strode over to them; her whole body was screaming rage and indignation. "Ian, we have all had it and so have I. I'm fucking out of here. That was ridiculous and damned dangerous. You never said anything like this could happen. We could have all been fucking killed or worse. I'm out of here. Get that bloody pilot over here now and tell him we are leaving. Look what you have done to Liz and the rest of the girls. They are terrified."

She was obviously upset and very angry. All of this was spoken with a very broad Australian accent. Frank leaned against a water bowser and watched this little episode with amusement. The woman noticed Frank looking at her with a grin on his face.

"And what the fucking hell are you grinning at?" she shouted at him, completely ignoring the fact that Frank had probably just saved her from being raped and tortured. Frank didn't answer. Shrugging his shoulders he turned his attention to his gun. "One hell of a woman that is," he thought.

The man next to him excused himself to Frank and walked off with the woman trying to calm her down.

Frank spun around as he heard some shots ring out. "Don't worry, the boys are just making sure that those bandits you shot are dead," said a big tall man who had walked over. "That was nice shooting by the way; we were watching you up on that rock. That must have been around three hundred yards and you only missed once as far as we could tell. Where did you learn to shoot like that?"

"Oh about twenty years ago and I had forgotten I could quite frankly. I suppose it's like riding a bike. You never forget, but I missed twice actually." Frank looked at the man, he was very familiar and then he realised. "Hey, you're Kurt Younger the film actor aren't you?"

The man laughed. "Sure am!" Before Frank could say any more the actor was interrupted by two of the film crew and taken away. Frank dumped his backpack, sat down on the ground and started to clean the rifle. Crompton came over having pacified the women, and Frank looked up at him.

"Any chance of getting a wash around here Ian?" he asked. "I badly need one. I'm starting to smell."

"Of course old boy. Jennie," he said turning to a very pretty dark-haired girl standing next to him. "Show the man where he can clean up." Turning back to Frank he said, "When you are ready we can have a chat. We need to get those bodies out of the way first before they start to smell, so we shall all have to do a little digging first." He looked hard at Frank. "I would like to thank you for risking your life Frank. Taking those chaps out saved our bacon we know that. Frankly we were getting worried. The consequences of what might have happened do not bear thinking about. Anyway, we all want to know what the hell you are doing out here miles from nowhere so get cleaned up and we can have some dinner and talk it over."

Frank couldn't help but be impressed. The man acted as though he had done this sort of thing all his life and as though he was a Major in the army; he was so relaxed and controlled.

The pretty girl with blue eyes, short dark hair and great legs all tucked into an open neck shirt, shorts and boots came over to him grinning and took his hand. She was only about 5'6" and had to look up to Frank towering above her. "They all wear the same bloody clothes," he thought looking around. The group broke up under the director's orders and started tidying up the camp. The girl took him towards one of the trailers chattering all the time and giving him little upwards glances as she did so.

"What are you really doing here in this wilderness and on your own?" she asked.

"I'll tell you later over a beer if you are interested in the ramblings of an old man." he grinned back.

She laughed. "That's a date. There are showers in there," she said pointing to a long trailer van. "I'll come back for you in fifteen minutes. By the look of it your clothes could do with washing as well. If you wait a second I'll see about getting you something to wear until yours are dry. One of the native women here will do your clothes for you for a couple of dollars."

"That's sounds good to me. See you later," he said.

The shower water was ice cold. "God that's good," he thought. He washed the grime from his body and noticed for the first time several small cuts and bruises. "Better treat them before I do anything else," he thought. Small cuts fester in the jungle and if not treated quickly can turn into a problem. He then wet shaved and brushed his hair. Looking into the mirror he saw the good-looking strong tanned face of a man somewhere in his early forties grinning back at him through wide set dark blue eyes. His nose showed that it had been broken once and there was a slight scar running from his lower jaw halfway up his right cheek but it was not too disconcerting. If anything it added character to his face. "Not bad for a forty-seven year old," he thought. His dark hair was starting to thin a little at the temples and had the beginnings of grey starting to show. He was definitely going grey around the sideburns and he badly needed a haircut.

He dried himself and moved out of the shower. A figure shot out of the room, the door to the trailer banging. He laughed. Obviously he had caught the native woman as she was leaving the clothes. He picked up the shirt and two cans of beer rolled out from under them.

"Great God Almighty, that Jennie is a darling woman," he thought.

He broke open the top of one and poured the cold contents straight down his throat. It didn't touch the sides. It was the best thing he had tasted in weeks and he gasped wanting more. He quickly finished the second can as well. He put on the clean clothes. The girl was a good guesser and they fitted him perfectly. Feeling a lot better he left the tent to find the young girl waiting for him. She looked up at him and then looked around him.

"Where is that dirty old geezer who went into the van then?" she said with an innocent look on her face. She spoke with a London East End accent but there was a touch of class training in there as well somewhere.

Frank played the game. "He's still in there but he told me that there was a good looking young woman out here waiting for him so I thought I would come and check you out myself," he said.

She looked straight up into his eyes for a moment, smiling, and then slowly looked him up and down.

"Well, you do scrub up well don't you? I would rather have a drink with you than that scruffy git so let's go."

She tucked her arm into his as she led him towards the main group of people. "I have to say that I was very impressed with the way you shot those nasty people at such a long distance. I heard the men talking afterwards and they were impressed too. They also said that you had the look, whatever that means."

He looked down at her pretty face. "What it means is that when you are dealing with people who have no regard for your life, or anyone else's for that matter, then you give no quarter otherwise whoever 'they' are won't take you seriously. You have to make an immediate impression otherwise you can die very quickly. All I did was to make that impression and those who managed to escape got the message. So, your name is Jennie?" he asked changing the subject.

"And your name is Frank?" she countered.

"What's going on here then?" he asked. "I can see that you are filming but what's it all about?"

"We're filming a 'David Schnell' story. We have the usual hunky male hero and two beautiful women who fight for his services, naturally. Frankly the script at the moment is rubbish and the girls can't act to save their lives but it will sell, no doubt about it, because of the names involved."

"Who are these two women? I have already met the hunky hero Kurt Younger. "

"Oh, you will meet them tonight at dinner. Kurt is all tanned rippling muscles and no brains but big box office and then you have the tall delectable models Josie Sales from Australia and the dark and sultry model Liz Hunt from England. The girls hate it here because of the flies, snakes and scorpions. This appalling heat is getting to everyone and we are all getting ratty. We have all agreed that we need to get out of here as quickly as possible and without a doubt this episode has clinched it. The filming is nearly finished anyway. They have finished with the girls who will definitely fly home tomorrow, but there are two more days to go before we finish entirely. Perhaps that will all change now, I don't know."

The thought crossed his mind that the plane could be a quick way out. "Would there be space in the plane for another?" he asked.

"But you're my Tarzan," she laughed. "The intrepid hunter, traveller and saviour. Don't say you want to get back to civilisation quickly and leave all this beautiful jungle and heat, especially as we have only just met."

He looked down into her laughing eyes and realised she was flirting outrageously. He had been away from civilisation for only a short while and yet his communicating instincts had already slowed dramatically.

"Listen," he said, "I don't have to tell you that three weeks in this heat at my ripe old age is bordering on the excessive. I've had it with sleeping up trees and not getting my morning cup of tea. I miss my soft bed and morning shower."

"I can't wait to get out either," she said. "I like the idea of the shower and soft bed too. Come to think of it, I will be back in Rio myself in three days and will be staying at the Sheraton. Why don't you give me a ring and come round?" she said. Her eyes were dancing and her cheeks were pink.

He looked down at her and found his eyes wandering to her breasts.

He liked what he saw. Her mouth was slightly open and a small red tongue flicked across her lips. She was watching him. "Christ, she's not much older than my daughter," he thought. "But there again, what difference does that make."

"If you can get me on that plane we have a date for sure. I'll take you out and give you such a good time you will never forget it."

"I'll bet you would too" she said her eyes still dancing. "I'll see what I can do."

Ian Crompton was standing talking to a group of his people and Frank joined them.

"Hi Frank, you look better. I would like to introduce you to Kurt Younger who is the male lead in our film." The big guy turned and took Frank's hand.

"It's all right Ian, we have already met," said Kurt. "Pleased to meet you anyway Frank; very interesting introduction!"

Frank liked him instantly. If Kurt had no brains as Jennie said then nor did he. The man had a straight gaze and when he smiled his mouth and eyes did too. There was humour there and he looked like the sort of man to have around when in trouble.

"Pleased to meet you too," Frank said. "I'm going to have to tell you that I am a huge fan of yours and have seen all your films, good and bad. By the way, unlike other male stars, you look much better in the flesh than you do on screen."

Kurt laughed. "There have been a fair share of bad ones I have to admit," he said. "And you are very kind. Listen, we are going to have dinner now. Please sit next to me and we can talk."

"He can't do that because he is sitting next to me," Jennie said.

Frank answered that he would be happy to sit between them.

2

TABLES WERE BEING PUSHED together and food was being professionally prepared and laid. Several fires were lit in the gathering dusk and were spaced around the eating area. Lights were strung and the whole scene began to have a party feeling. All thoughts of the remaining bandits returning seemed to have disappeared but they decided to play safe by having three guards patrol the area for the rest of the night on a rota basis.

He found himself sitting next to Kurt and Jennie as previously arranged but the surprise was Crompton sitting opposite with two beautiful woman either side of him. Frank was introduced to Josie, the tall blonde who had given Crompton the verbal lashing, and Liz. Josie was completely natural with no apparent hang-ups and full of questions. Frank remembered having seen her in the newspapers many times, of course, and had read that she had married only a few months ago. Liz, he noticed, gave him a long hard intense look and then seemed to ignore him being more interested in a small skinny man sitting by her.

Frank looked at the people around him as they ate and chatted away and thought the whole thing surreal. No more than a couple of hours ago they were in a fire fight; at risk of being killed and mutilated. Now here they were chatting away about mundane things and their work just as though nothing had happened, despite three men lying dead in their graves half a mile away. He had never experienced anything quite like it before; well not for some time he reflected.

He looked up to find Josie fixing him with her beautiful green eyes. They were wide spaced, very large, and had a slight Eurasian look about them, which was almost hypnotic. She was indeed a very beautiful woman.

"You are very quiet Frank. We know nothing about you so how about telling us all exactly what the hell you are doing in this God forsaken jungle."

This was obviously a subject they were all interested in as everyone stopped talking and looked at Frank with great interest. Yes, indeed was the thought that ran around the table, what was this chap doing all alone out here in the jungle?

"It's no big deal. I'm just here on holiday," Frank said quietly.

"Bollocks," said Josie. "I don't believe that for a second. You appearing, just when you were needed most is too big a coincidence." A murmur went around the table. They obviously agreed with Josie. He found Crompton looking at him particularly keenly. "Are you with the CIA or something Frank?" asked Josie. He was amazed at her directness and almost open hostility.

Frank felt exasperated and looked Josie straight in the eye. "No Josie. I'm not with the CIA, MI6 or any other funny bunch. I'm just Frank Blake, a normal bloke on holiday doing something that I have always wanted to do and that is looking around a few pyramids. Is that all right with you?" He asked. "In this instance I just happened to be in the right place at the right time. Perhaps you should reflect on what might have happened if I had not. I am just pleased to have been of help. Anyway, if you are really interested I'll tell you what I have been doing."

"I am sure everyone would like to hear that Frank," said Kurt glancing at Josie. "Pay no attention to her she's just a little shook up that's all. Come on, Frank, what have you been up to then?"

"OK, at the risk of boring you all to tears, I'm sure you know most of the stories about the Aztecs and Mayans and if you do please bear with me, it's just that for more years than I care to remember I have been fascinated by both of those civilisations and have devoured any and every book I could find on them. It always struck me as odd how such clever people developed their civilisation to such a very high degree with no contention until the Spanish struck. For instance, they would still sacrifice to their Gods and yet they had a finer measurement of time mathematically than we have today. Also, how did they build those enormous artefacts and to such exacting tolerances? The best engineers in the world today couldn't do that with the same materials. And we think we are superior. Also, there is the fact that the Mayans, as a race, disappeared almost overnight. What happened to them is a whole story in itself. Well, a theory really. I could go on but any of you who might be interested should read up on them. There are many books on these two quite incredible civilisations they were fascinating people. There are also many heavy theories as well. So that's why I'm here."

"Very interesting Frank," said Crompton, "Now why didn't we think of something like that?" he asked, looking round the table. Before anyone could answer Josie asked "So, where is your wife while you are doing all this then and what does she think of you swanning around the jungle getting lost and killing people?"

An embarrassed silence fell on the group.

Frank paused and then frowned. He raised his eyes slowly from the table and looked directly at Josie until she broke eye contact. The sarcastic content of Josie's questions was beginning to get to him and what he really wanted to do was to tell her to simply fuck off. She was just a little too pretentious for her own good he thought.

"She doesn't know where I am because I didn't tell her. She left me a while ago for another fella," Frank replied.

"I'm sorry to hear that Frank," she replied apologetically. Frank was surprised at the almost gentle way she spoke and the immediate change in attitude. "Maybe there's hope for her yet," he thought.

"It's OK, don't worry about it. I hear it happens all the time" he said.

"Has anyone got a spare bed that Frank can use for tonight?" Ian asked changing the subject and looking around the table. "He is our guest after all and we must ensure that he is comfortable after living rough for so long."

"There's another bunk in my trailer," said Jennie quickly. All eyes pivoted to her but she didn't flinch. "What do you think Frank?" she said leaning against him, "Would you be OK sleeping with me." Everyone laughed.

"Just as long as you don't try to abuse me I think I can handle it," Frank replied, grinning.

"I think he could be more than a match for you Jennie," laughed Josie. "You want to remember that he killed three men this afternoon so don't bite off more than you can chew, if you know what I mean."

Jennie raised her eyebrows in innocence. "I don't know what you mean at all Josie. I am a good girl and wouldn't dream of laying my hands on such a gorgeous guest. I am sure Frank would behave like a gentleman. Wouldn't you Frank?"

Frank turned and looked into Jenny's laughing blue eyes. He said nothing for five long seconds and her eyes slowly grew larger. "OK, Jennie," he said eventually. "I promise to be a boring gentleman if I must." And he turned back to give a wink to Kurt who burst out laughing.

"Ian," Frank said. "If there was any chance at all of getting a lift back to Rio with the girls tomorrow it would be appreciated. Obviously I will pay the going rate. I have badly mistimed this little adventure and I should really be getting back to my business in England if it's still there."

"I think that should be all right," said Ian, "I'll check with the pilot later and let you know. You can actually do me a favour Frank when you get back. Go with the two girls to the British Embassy and tell them what happened down here. They will no doubt communicate with the Brazilian authorities who will probably send out the army to check things out. Better be safe than sorry."

"That's fine, I'll do that for you," Frank said.

Someone mentioned the gunfight with the bandits and the men started to talk avidly about it and how quickly it was over. One member of the camera crew wondered what the repercussions would be for having killed three of the bandits. Ian thought that there would no doubt be an investigation by the Brazilian Police but that shouldn't cause them too many problems. The police would probably be quite happy that the bandits had been virtually wiped out. The members of the crew also felt a lot better now that they had more weapons having collected the rifles and pistols from the dead men. This conversation was obviously going to run and run.

Jennie decided to call it a night and, getting up from the table, made her excuses to leave. "I'm bushed. Goodnight everybody," she said. "Frank, that's my trailer over there, the blue one. Make yourself at home when you are ready."

"Sure Jennie." Several others also made their excuses and left.

He tried to start a conversation with the sultry Liz but she was too much hard work and seemed to be carrying a huge chip on her shoulder. She was a renowned worldwide black beauty and had the world at her fingertips; but something was not right there he thought. There's no fun in the girl whatsoever. Josie was the exact opposite. Cracking dirty jokes like a man but looking totally fabulous and wrapping every man around her little finger. Throughout dinner she had been trying to get a rise out of Frank in a nice way and had bridled at first when Frank responded back but she quickly realised he meant no harm by his remarks.

She cocked her head on one side and looked at Frank after he had made one of his one-liners. "I'm glad you found us Frank," she said. "I have to say your old-fashioned charm is much appreciated and something the younger generation could learn from." There was much laughter from the other men at this comment.

"Thanks for the back-handed compliment Josie. Well, I am going to crash," good night everybody."

"Hope you are able to get a good night's sleep," said Josie to more laughter. Frank grinned.

He made his way to the van and, opening the door, went in. It was dark except for a low light down the end. He moved along the narrow corridor and entered Jennie's bedroom. She was reading and put the book down as he entered.

"Hi" he whispered.

"Hi yourself," she whispered back and she moved slightly.

The sheet slipped to reveal her breasts but she made no move to cover herself. Instead she watched him. He looked down at her for a moment and then smiled, "You are a very beautiful young woman and I'm sure I will kick myself in the morning but I am simply going to wish you a very good night. Sleep tight."

He turned and made his way down the small corridor to the second bedroom.

* * *

Frank woke with a start to the sound of loud banging on the door of the trailer. Someone was shouting his name. At first he didn't know where the hell he was but he touched the girl's warm body by accident as he moved to get up and remembered. He rolled out of the bed and stumbled naked to the door. Looking at his watch it said it was only seven in the morning. Opening the door he looked down on one of the film crew.

The young man looked in amazement at Frank standing there naked. "Mr Crompton asked me to tell you that the pilot will be taking off in an hour. Some problem with the weather and he wants to get up above it before it gets to Rio. The girls are also getting up now," he added.

"Thank Mr Crompton for me and tell him that I'll be there in fifteen minutes," he said. He went back into the bedroom and started to look for his clothes.

"Where do you think you're going?" she was standing in the doorway with her dressing gown hanging loosely from her shoulders.

He turned and looked at her. "I'm afraid I've got to go. The plane is taking off in an hour," he said.

"Well that leaves us plenty of time and I promised you a treat so get yourself back down here."

She grinned wickedly and took hold of his hand. There was no way he was going to get away from this determined young woman.

3

ON REACHING THE PLANE he found the pilot checking the engines. He was a large florid-faced man with thick hairy arms dressed in dirty jeans and a tatty checked shirt. The man reeked of whisky and body odour, and he was chain smoking. "Not exactly the sort of person that fills you with confidence," Frank remembered the way the plane was flown into the valley the day before and reserved his judgement.

The girls hadn't turned up yet. Frank climbed inside the plane and packed his backpack away with his rifle and machete in the rear. The plane was filthy with all sorts of debris on the floor including straw and two broken pallets. It looked as if the pilot had been transporting pigs or something similar. He threw the pallets out of the door and kicked out the other rubbish scraping it out with the side of his boot.

Climbing back out, Frank walked around the plane and found the pilot with an oilcan in his hands still checking the engines. "How long will it take to get to Rio?" he asked.

"Between two and three hours depending on the weather," the pilot replied. Frank almost gagged. He had got too close and was nearly knocked over with the pilot's bad breath. The pilot glanced at Frank. "You that fella from the jungle yesterday? 'cause if you are I would get your arse out of here if I were you. If them bandits decide to come back and get hold of you then…" He didn't finish the sentence appearing to be bored with the conversation but he gave Frank another sidelong glance and fished into his overall pocket and pulled out a small dark coloured bottle. He slowly unscrewed the top all the while looking up into the hills and then put it slowly to his lips and took a long mouthful of its contents.

Frank looked up at the hills too and wondered what this filthy old drunk of a pilot knew. "Don't you worry old man; I'm coming out with you now."

The thought of spending two or three hours in such a small plane with this man reeking of whisky and BO was not a pleasant prospect. "Can't go to the loo or take a stroll down the aisle. Just hunched in a small seat. Well at least it will cut a week off my time down here and anyway I'll soon be in a comfortable hotel room and civilisation," he thought.

A team of four men began loading film gear into the rear of the plane together with a couple of crates of canned food that were not wanted in the mess. It was all equipment that they didn't need now and it was a good opportunity to move it back to their base. The two girls appeared with two men staggering under boxes and suitcases.

Frank heard the pilot curse under his breath. "Jesus Christ, Look, there's only room for two suitcases each and hand luggage," the pilot said to the two girls.

Immediately an argument started with Liz resorting to shouting and swearing but the pilot didn't budge.

"Either leave all that stuff behind or stay behind yourself. I don't give a damn which" he shouted into Liz's face. "It's make your mind up time because I'm taking off in five minutes." With that he climbed into the plane.

"Fucking bastard," Liz screamed at the pilot. She was incandescent with rage. "How dare he talk to me like that? I'll fix him."

Josie spoke quietly to Liz and then turned to Frank. "Morning Frank, look, there is a spare seat with the pilot. I think under the circumstances that it would be a good idea if you sat with him and Liz and I will sit in the back."

"Morning Josie "Frank replied and glanced at Liz. What a nightmare, he shrugged his shoulders in resignation. In a couple of hours he would be well rid of the lot of them. "I'll do that now. Let's go." He climbed into the plane and squeezed himself into the tiny cockpit and into the co-pilot's seat. The pilot was already there and ignored him as he checked his instruments. The smell from the pilot was overwhelming in the confined space and Frank opened his side window for some fresh air. "Well that's just great," Frank thought. "I'm flying with a drunk and at 8am in the morning for God's sake."

The girls had also taken their seats. Ian Crompton poked his head around the rear door. "Nice to meet you Frank," he called, "I'll probably see you in Rio in three days if you are still there. Give me a call if you are. I'll be staying at the Sheraton along with the rest of the crew whilst we complete things."

"Will do," Frank yelled back, "and thanks for looking after me." With that, Ian waved a hand and disappeared shutting the rear door at the same time.

The pilot glanced back at the girls to ensure they were belted in but didn't say anything. Frank glanced back at Josie who regarded the pilot and raised an eyebrow at him whilst holding her nose. Frank grinned and nodded. He returned his gaze to the pilot's actions.

The pilot eased both engine starting levers open. The two engines slowly started to roll and very quickly roared into life. Frank watched everything avidly. He had done some glider flying but had never sat inside such a small cockpit before with all the associated maze of instruments. This particular instrument panel looked as though it had seen better days. In places there were wires hanging down. He wasn't impressed.

Once the engines were howling to the pilot's satisfaction and he had tapped a few dials, he waved to the ground crew who removed the chocks from the wheels. The pilot increased power and the plane rumbled over the grass down towards the end of the valley quickly picking up speed.

"Is everyone belted up and ready?" the pilot shouted. Both girls shouted "yes" from the cabin behind them.

The plane turned and, engines roaring began its run down the grassy strip. Frank waved to the blur of faces as they swept past and watched everything with great interest. The pilot was actually very good and he lifted the plane off the ground with ease. They were climbing away out of the valley in seconds.

"Is this plane your own?" he shouted at the pilot above the din of the engines. The pilot couldn't hear him through his headset so Frank tapped him on the shoulder and indicated that he wanted to talk to him. The pilot rummaged around under his seat and produced another headset. He plugged it into the instrument panel and handed it to Frank to put on.

Frank repeated the question once he had the volume tuned. "Yes," replied the pilot "I make a good living by renting it, and myself, to people such as that lot back there. I'm very busy."

"What is this plane?" asked Frank.

"It's a Beechcraft," the pilot replied. "She's actually a "King Air C90B." That's the model type see, one of the most successful planes in the world. Thousands sold probably. This one has seen better days but still goes. This model isn't made anymore. Not that attractive, unlike the new ones, but she's a good packhorse. Tough as old boots. We've flown a few miles together we have, and she has never let me down."

The pilot lapsed into silence so Frank gave it up as a bad job and relaxed as the plane banked onto its heading. He loved flying and if he had his time again would liked to have been a pilot. "There's still time," he thought. "I can maybe stay over here for another two months and take my licence." He was sorely tempted.

His mind drifted back to this morning. He smiled to himself feeling smug, the girl had been a very willing sexual partner and they had made love three times before eventually falling asleep. "Not bad for an old boy," he thought. Jennie had really given him a treat this morning and, despite the fact that time was pressing, had expertly brought him to a climax very quickly with her mouth. She had obviously done that before too. He decided that he would contact her again as soon as she arrived in Rio and have some fun. The motion of the plane and the drumming of its engines were very soporific. It didn't matter whether it was a train, bus, taxi or plane; he was always asleep within five minutes.

***

Frank awoke with a start. The plane was rising and falling violently. He looked around him. The sky was dark with rolling black and grey clouds stretching up to the heavens and rain lashed the windscreen. They were obviously in the middle of a storm.

"What the fuck is happening?" he shouted to the pilot. He was shocked to see that the man had a bottle of whisky in one hand and was flying with the other. There was a stupid grin on his face. Looking at his watch Frank realised no more than an hour and a half had passed since they took off.

"Tried to go around the storm," the pilot shouted back. "Too big and I can't get above it either so we will just have to fly through it. Better put your belt on again mister and check that the girls are belted up too. This is going to be a bumpy ride."

There was a scream from behind as the plane plunged down for a moment only to soar back up just as quickly. The plane was acting as though it was on a roller coaster ride and the engines howled. Frank was checking that the girls were OK when there was an enormous flash and a bang. The plane lurched over sideways but straightened up just as quickly.

"What the hell was that?" Frank asked

"Been hit by lightning," laughed the pilot looking at his instruments. "No bloody compass any more or radio by the look of it. Most of the damn instruments have been fried and read zero." He was flicking switches and tapping dials.

"This is really bad," Frank thought to himself. No compass and no radio. "How are you going to keep a heading?" he shouted to the pilot.

"I've got a magnetic compass here," he said pointing to his side of the cockpit. "But it's unreliable. Hasn't been swung since I've been flying this crate. We will just have to trust to luck that it's correct."

"I think it could be said that I have just jumped out of the frying pan into the fire. Nothing underneath but dense jungle and nothing up top except storm, lightning and winds. Should have stayed on the ground and walked out" he thought.

They flew on for another twenty minutes. Sheets of rain crashed against the window shield to the point where he could see nothing most of the time and great crashes of thunder assaulted their eardrums. Frank had never been in such violent weather and nor had the girls by the sound of their screams. Even the pilot was now very quiet with occasional bursts of swearing. The plane felt and behaved as though it was a feather being blown by a light wind and Frank marvelled that it kept going at all. What really worried him was that there appeared to be no parachutes. Frank's heart was pounding and his chest felt tight. He was beginning to feel frightened. "No, frightened is not the word I'm looking for. I'm bloody terrified," he thought.

Again there was another tremendous flash and a bang, lightning zigzagging across the sky. The girls screamed. The plane lurched violently again and seemed to hang on one wing tip for a long while before slowly straightening out.

"The auto pilot was slow recovering that," thought Frank and when he turned around from watching out of the window he went cold with horror. The pilot was slumped over the controls. He heard Josie screaming "What's wrong with the pilot Frank?" He leaned over to lift the him upright but was restricted by his harness.

"Josie, get up here and give me a hand," Frank shouted. The plane slipped into a shallow dive. He released his belt and began trying to lift the pilot. "He weighs a bloody ton," he thought. He couldn't budge him. As soon as Josie arrived they both heaved and pulled the pilot upright.

"He's passed out, drunk as a skunk." Frank was frantically trying to hold the plane on an even course with one hand and holding the pilot with the other.

Josie was pressing one hand against the pilot's neck. "There's no pulse, Frank," she shouted.

Frank said nothing. The plane was now all over the place.

"We will have to get him out of his seat and lay him in the aisle some how" he shouted. There was only room for the two of them and the dead drunk pilot. Gradually they pulled him out of his seat. Liz joined them and together they heaved him into the aisle by the rear seats all of them trying to hang on for their lives at the same time.

"Look after him," Frank shouted to Josie and he quickly jumped back into his seat and settled the co-pilot controls into his hands. "Priority," he thought, "let the autopilot fly the plane straight and level." He watched the horizon indicator but it didn't straighten out level. It continued in a shallow dive.

"Can you fly this thing Frank? Are we all right?" Josie called. He could hear the terror in her voice. He could also hear Liz sobbing and crying behind them in fear.

"Never flown one in my life but I did a lot of gliding once. I think the principle is the same. The bad news is that either the autopilot has given up the ghost or somehow it's been knocked off. Either way I will have to take control," he replied. "She's flying in a circle but I'm not sure of anything really. At least we are flying level now but in which direction we should be going is anyone's guess." He looked at the magnetic compass, which was swinging all over the place, and he hadn't noticed in which direction they had been flying anyway.

Josie climbed into the other seat. "He's definitely dead," she said. "Looks to me like a heart attack." She was silent for a while. "What are we going to do?" she whispered. She was close to tears and terrified. They were flying completely blind into lashing rain and winds. He looked at the altimeter, at least that was working, and it read 3,000 feet.

"Must climb higher," he thought. "Mountains around here are at least 4,000 ft high. Must climb higher. We were flying at 8,000 ft before all this started." He slowly pulled back on the yoke and increased throttle. He watched the height indicator slowly rise. He levelled off at 8,000 ft and eased back a little on the throttle.

"Ladies, we have a major problem here. We don't know where we are. We don't know which direction we are flying. I can't contact anyone because the radio is out and I am not a proper pilot. I can, however, keep this thing in the air for a while but at some stage we are going to come down and that's going to be crunch time." They flew on in silence for a while with each of them deep in their own thoughts. A thought struck him.

"Hey Josie, do you or Liz have your phones with you?"

"Mine's in the back. Hold on I'll get it," Josie said.

He felt that the sky was brightening slowly and the rain was definitely easing. The plane became much more stable.

Josie returned and sat back in the second seat and Liz appeared at the doorway. "What are we going to do, Frank?" she said. She looked terrible. Her eyes were red from crying and her hair dishevelled.

"Get ourselves out of trouble somehow. Josie, is your phone a sat phone otherwise we are wasting our time because you won't get a signal out here without a sat?

"Yeh, bought it last month because I wanted to be able to contact home from out here in this bloody jungle."

See if you can raise one of your friends in Rio. Anyone will do. We need to tell them our problem and get them to tell the airport controllers. They might be able to help me."

Josie punched in a number but there was no reply. She punched in another number and waited. "Jack," she called, "can you hear me? Jack, it's me, Josie. I'm in big, big trouble." She quickly told Jack the story. He said he would get onto the airport and tell the authorities to phone her right back.

"Thank God for that," Frank thought. Even Liz smiled through her tears.

The rain eased and they could see that the clouds ahead were breaking with blue sky showing in many places.

"Look," Frank said. "Blue sky, enough to make a Chinaman a pair of pants. We will be all right now." It was an old joke but the two girls smiled.

He spoke too soon. The right engine coughed and he felt the plane lurch. It coughed again and started to stutter and miss-fire badly.

"What the hell?" he shouted. "Both of you get in your seats and belt up. Josie get onto that man again and tell him we have a bigger problem." He checked the fuel gauges. They were showing empty. His heart sank into his boots.

"Holy Mary of Jesus, we have no fucking fuel girls." What he didn't know was that he had reserve tanks and should have been switching over to them.

Liz wailed in despair. "We are going to die. We are going to die."

"Oh, shut the fuck up Liz," cried Josie, "What can we do Frank?"

"I honestly don't know. Try the phone again, Josie."

Josie dialled her friend but the phone was engaged. "He must be on the phone to the airport," she cried.

The starboard engine stuttered and coughed again, returned to normal and then stopped completely. The plane lurched violently with the drag of the propeller and Frank had to correct it.

The other engine missed a beat, faltered, and then picked up again. "We are going to have to go down before we fall out of the sky. Josie, get back up here and help me find somewhere to land," he shouted. They were into bright sunlight again but all they could see below was endless green jungle with a few small mountains pushing up out of the trees. Josie joined him in the cockpit.

"I'm going lower so that we can see better so hold on while we dive girls," he said. The remaining engine missed a beat again. "Please don't stop," he thought. He looked at the fuel gauges. They were hard on zero and not moving, they were running on air.

"Look over there," Josie cried. "Is that a patch of grassland down there or what?"

Frank eased back on the remaining throttle and let the plane slip into a shallow dive losing height rapidly until they were down to two thousand feet. Turning the plane gingerly he saw the patch of grassland over the left wing looking like an island in a patch of dark green trees. It looked odd. Mottled with trees, it was a strange shape. The engine coughed with its note rising and falling twice again.

"We are losing it, and we are losing height. I can't hold her," Frank shouted. "Whatever that is down there we are going to have to land on it. Josie, tell Liz to tighten her belt as much as possible and to put her head in her hands, then you do the same."

"Can you land the plane Frank?" she asked.

"I've never landed a prop plane like this before, but I have gliders a hundred times. Anyway, we have no other choice so I'm going to have to learn fast. She just has so much drag with the stalled propeller."

He lined up the nose with the strip of grass. It was definitely shaped oddly he thought. "OK, what do I do now? Drop the undercarriage first and reduce speed, keep the nose up and hold it above stall. It's a piece of cake." As the undercarriage went down the remaining engine missed, picked up, coughed and spluttered for a moment, steadied and then stopped abruptly. There was silence except for the sound of the wind whistling past. The plane lurched, the nose dropped, and the plane started to drop like a stone.

"Shit, it couldn't last until we landed could it," he shouted to no one in particular. "Oh no it had to die on me just to make life even more fucking difficult. Josie, get hold of that green lever and push it forward until it reads twelve degrees."

"What for?" she shrieked above the noise.

"It drops our flaps and slows us down," he yelled back.

The sweat poured down his face and his body shook with both excitement and fear. "Fuck it, how the hell did I get myself here," he thought. "If I don't get this exactly right I'm dead." He prayed silently to his mother. He often talked to her in times of extreme stress it sometimes helped.

The small strip of grassland was rushing towards them.

"It's too damn small to land on, I can't land on that," he shouted. They were still falling too fast. "Another six degrees," he yelled at Josie, and then the field seemed to disappear.

It was one of the few times in his life when he completely lost it and panicked. His eyes went wide, his hackles stood on end and starting to hyperventilate he gasped for air. He felt as though all his muscles were failing. "What the fucking hell?" he shouted.

He then realised they were falling into a valley which dropped sharply and to the right. He was running out of time. Fighting desperately with his limited ability to keep the plane from stalling out of the glide, he followed the valley down. The plane was sinking like a stone, shuddering and shaking violently in the beginning of a stall and the controls felt heavy and unresponsive. He was all over the place and almost out of control swinging left and right and finding it almost impossible to fly a straight line. Frank was simply terrified.

"We're going in too fast." He yelled.

A huge shape appeared out of the jungle in front of them as if by magic and Josie screamed. Frank was about to wrench the yoke control with all his might when the plane banked sharply to the left and then back to the right. For a fraction of a second he thought, "That's odd, what the hell was that?" The girls were screaming their heads off. They flashed past the huge dark monolith. He just had time to re-align the stricken plane for the grass ahead of him. It was coming up fast when he saw the remains of a broken plane to his right on the ground.

"Poor bugger," he thought."

The plane was falling towards the grass and was almost out of control. "Shit, I'm coming in too fast," he felt elated, excited and felt that he was almost in control of himself at last. "Got to keep the nose above the horizon, just hope to hell that the ground is flat and even," he thought.

"All the flap you can give me, Josie," he yelled. The plane was shuddering violently and felt nose heavy. His arms ached with the effort and the sweat was pouring off his face. Suddenly the plane felt light and positive, and holding off, seemingly on its own it gently dropped down towards the grass. It landed with a bump and bounced back into the air.

"Shit. Don't fuck it up now Frank," he shouted.

Josie was now sitting bolt upright in her seat shouting excitedly, "Get her down, Frank, get her down, get her down!" The steering went light again and the plane dropped smoothly and almost flew itself back down onto the grass. It bounced a little again and stayed down. He thrust hard on the brakes and gradually the plane skewered slowly to a stop in long grass.

They sat in silence. The only sound was a ticking from within the cockpit. He looked around trying to trace the sound and saw that the ignition lights were still on. He lent forward wearily switched off both engines ignitions and shut the throttles.

"I'm alive. I don't believe it but it's true. I'm alive," said Josie in amazement. "Christ Almighty mate, I was sure that we were going to die and then I felt everything was going to be all right, simply unbelievable. What do you think, Liz?" she said to her friend sitting behind them.

Liz was sitting slumped in her seat with her eyes closed; tears were forcing their way out from under her eyelids and running down her cheeks. Her face was contorted like that of a child who has been severely reprimanded. Her shoulders were shaking as her hands moved to release her seat belt.

"I never, ever, want to go through that again," she said. She opened her beautiful eyes and turned to look at Frank. "I never thought we would make it either. I'm totally and completely exhausted. Frank, you have saved our lives, my life. How you did that I just don't know. I shall never, ever fly again. I have to say, Frank that I thought you were just a normal arrogant male pig when you came on the set yesterday, posing with your gun and stuff. From now on, man, you are my number one person. I'm never going to be able to repay you for getting us down here safely but I'm sure going to try." A small smile broke out on her tear-stained face.

"Blimey," said Josie. "Hey Frank, Liz never talks to anyone for longer than one sentence at a time. That's praise indeed."

Frank had turned around facing both of them releasing his seat belt. His face was dripping with perspiration and his hair hung down over his eyes. At that moment he looked a hundred years old. He wiped his face with his arm.

"You're embarrassing me girls but thanks for the kind words," he said grinning, "We're not out of the wood yet so don't count your chickens. We have to get home somehow. Thanks both of you for staying so calm. By the way, please accept my apologies for swearing so much on our way in. I don't normally swear like that."

"Bloody pom to the very end. Forget it," said Josie, "At least we are alive. OK if we get out and have a look around, Frank?"

"I would suggest that you find your kit in the back and put on some boots," said Frank. "We don't know what's out there in that grass OK? So just be prepared."

The girls undid their seat belts and started to rummage about in the back of the plane while Frank scrambled over the dead body of the pilot. He climbed out of the cockpit and slid down to the ground from out of the side door.

The grass came up to his knees. He looked slowly around him. They were in a deep valley about one mile long and half a mile across with massive walls either side rising to over 300ft. It was very similar to the one they had left early that morning.

It's quite a beautiful place," he thought. A pyramid made of a very dark coloured stone dominated the valley and it had been built at the entrance where the cliffs rose above them. It looked very impressive and beautiful and yet he had a strange feeling about the place. Otherwise, everything was quiet. The end of the valley where they had stopped ended with a rock face rising vertically above them. A small waterfall cascaded down it.

He looked hard at the pyramid. "So that's what we nearly hit," he thought.

The girls joined him in looking in awe at the pyramid that dominated the valley and rose high into the sky.

"The first thing we ought to do is get that pilot out of the plane," he said. "If he is dead then we have to bury him. If we don't he will be stinking in no time in this heat."

After a struggle, they managed to lift the pilot out of the cabin. He was indeed dead. Frank looked around him. "We will take him about a hundred yards away and bury him over there," he said pointing to low brush. Sweating and panting they dragged him over to the brush. Frank went back to the plane. He searched for the emergency toolbox and found it in a small compartment behind the front passenger seat. He also found two torches, some candles and flares; a hand held compass and the statuary Red Cross kit plus a folding shovel.

Frank told the girls to go and sit in the shade of the plane's wings whilst he set about digging a shallow grave. He worked slowly in the heat; sweat pouring from his face and body. Liz showed concern by coming over to him every ten minutes with his water flask. Eventually he finished and rolled the body into the shallow grave. The girls came over while he said a few words over the body; he then covered it with earth and put a marker by the grave. They walked back slowly to the plane.

"It might be a bit callous just burying him like that but there's not much else we can do. If we ever get back we will have to try and let his family know what happened," Frank said. "Josie, can you keep his wallet and stuff and be in charge of it?"

"Sure, Frank," she said.

"OK. I'm going over to that waterfall to clean up and shower off. When I get back we should see if we can get any reception on your phone Josie." Frank said.

Fifteen minutes later he was back. He started to walk in small circles tramping down the grass around them.

"What are you doing for heaven sake?" said Liz.

"I'm thinking," he said "and while I'm thinking I'm going to flatten this damn grass around the plane in case snakes, or anything else that might be around, creep up on us. I have a phobia of snakes in particular. So you can both give me a hand while we think of a way out of here."

"They will be searching for us won't they, Frank? " asked Liz.

"Of course they will," he said. "That call you made will have alerted them. The only thing I don't know is how long we flew in the wrong direction or even which direction we were flying in. We could be anywhere within a 1,000 square mile area. They will fly a set pattern until they have covered every area along the route we were supposed to have taken but even then, will they see this valley? That's another question."

They were silent for a while as they walked around the plane flattening the grass in an ever-widening area.

"OK that will do," he said. "Let's unload the stores from the plane and see what we have."

There were two large crates of surplus tinned food, three crates of camera and filming accessories and a crate of surplus bedding as well as General spare crew clothing.

"God is good to us," he said as he opened the fifth crate. It was full of kitchen cooking utensils including two gas bottles with cooking plates.

"Well I'm amazed, it's as though they knew we were going to crash. We have everything we need to last us for a while. The only thing we don't have is water and that's over there," he said pointing to the waterfall.

"I'm not drinking that," said Liz, "Heaven knows what's in that water. I'll be ill."

"No worries, Liz, all we have to do is boil it and it will be fine. Basic Boy Scout stuff really. Now, I'm English and the first thing English people do when they have a problem is to have a cup of tea. I want you girls to get out one of those gas bottles and see if we have any tea or coffee in the stores. I'll go and get the water."

The girls agreed to his simple plan of action, pleased to have something to do to take their minds off their predicament. Frank walked over to the plane and searched for his gun and pack.

"Here's the tea," he said laughing as he pulled out a crumpled carton of tea bags from his pack and threw it at them. "Basic survival stuff when you are in the jungle on your own," he said in way of explanation.

He set off across the valley to the cliff and waterfall at the end with two of his water cans and three others from the stores. "We're not set up too badly," he thought. "Some good stores, sleeping bags and water on tap. We can last quite a while as long as none of us get sick for any reason. We were lucky to survive that flight let alone the landing."

He reached the waterfall and filled his cans from the pool. The water was crystal clear and he risked a mouthful. It tasted cool and sweet. What a shame to have to boil it he thought but better to be safe than sorry. Lying on the ground he lowered his head into the water letting it cool and refresh him, washing away the stress of the day. He rolled onto his back letting the sun dry him and looked up into the cloudless sky. He thought about his family and friends who would be missing him by now and how worried they must be. The thought of having to be responsible for the two girls depressed him, having said that, he found both of them interesting.

Josie was the strong one mentally. She was a tall girl, willowy like all models with long strong legs and small breasts. She was a beauty with classic looks, high cheekbones; large, wide set green eyes that looked at you directly and a large, generous mouth, which smiled easily. Her manner, most of the time, could only be described as 'laddish.' She liked to be one of the boys and she could drink as well as the next man, which obviously stemmed from her upbringing on an Australian bush farm living with her four brothers. She was comfortable in the company of men. Her blond hair, normally hanging long and loose was braided into a sensible pigtail.

On the other hand, Frank thought Liz was a mess mentally. Not quite as tall as Josie, only 5' 7." She had large brown eyes below a high forehead with a pert nose and a large-lipped mouth, which betrayed her ancestry. Her breasts were on the small side in common with most models and her black skin shone as though it was oiled. This, together with her long mane of jet-black hair and perfect legs, had made her into the premier black model throughout the world. When she wanted to she could make men's jaws drop with her long swaying cat-like walk. Her main problem was her attitude. Having been brought up in a single parent family, she never knew her father and she lacked the strength of character that Josie had. She was completely the opposite of Josie and was never friendly to men, preferring the company of women. Frank recalled that it was well documented that she was a lesbian.

"Oh well, it's not all bad," he thought. "Probably every man's fantasy really, crash landing with two of the most beautiful woman on the planet. Not mine though; it's just all a bloody nuisance." He climbed to his feet and set off back towards the plane. He could just see it above the tall grass and he thought of the crashed aircraft he had seen as he flew into the valley.

"I'll have to look at that tomorrow. If the crew died I'll have to bury them. I wonder if any survived and what happened to them?" He shivered at the thought of hitting the pyramid at that particular moment. It had been so close. "That's something else," he mused. "It could be a great place for the mobile if I can get to the top of it and get a signal. I'll do that in the morning as well." As he walked he remembered the strange way the plane behaved as it came into land, almost as though it flew itself. " But that's nonsense," he thought.

As he arrived back at the plane he found the girls crouched over the flame from the cooking plate of the gas bottle. He realised that the evening was closing in on them.

"OK. Let's have a cup of tea to keep ourselves warm and then we can work out where we are going to sleep tonight." he said.

"We have already worked that out, Frank," said Josie. "If only we could get the back seats out of the plane we could all sleep in the back now that the crates are out. It's going to be a bit tight and probably bloody cold."

Frank squinted at the plane. "That problem is easily solved," he said. He made the tea from the now boiling water and took a sip.

"Yuck, no sugar but good though," he said as he took another sip. "I'll just have to learn to appreciate tea without sugar." The liquid ran down his throat and warmed him. "Not bad at all," he said. The girls grinned at him over their mugs.

"I never thought I would appreciate a cup of tea so much," said Josie.

"Me neither," said Liz. "I could really do with a large gin and tonic though."

Frank looked at his watch. "In an hour or two it's going to get cold and dark so let's see if we can get those seats out."

He undid the bolts holding the rear two seats down with a spanner from the tool kit and the girls helped him out with them through the side door. They left quite a reasonably sized area. Climbing inside the plane, the two girls started to arrange the bedding. It was getting dark quickly and they worked by the light of one candle.

"Try and zip all three bags together somehow because, whether you like it or not girls, you are going to have to sleep with me. Our combined body heat will keep us much warmer than if we sleep on our own." he said.

"I'm surprised at you Frank," said Josie laughing. "And I thought you were a gentleman."

"Well, I will be fulfilling a dream but frankly all I want is to keep warm." Frank laughed back.

They kept their clothes on just removing their boots and climbed into the bedding. "Christ, it's hard," said Liz. "I'll never be able to sleep."

"Complain to the management in the morning," said Frank. He lay there for a moment. "I'm famished," he said. "I'm going to get a can of beans. Either of you two fancy anything?"

The girls shuddered. "You aren't going to eat a can of cold beans, Frank," Liz said.

"Nothing wrong in that," said Frank. "They can be really tasty cold when you're hungry."

Opening the side door, he jumped out of the plane and found the crate of tinned food. He quickly found a tin of beans and opened it. Climbing back into the plane he closed the door behind him and eased himself down next to Josie. Resting on one elbow he proceeded to feed himself with a spoon from the can. Josie watched him in the candlelight. "OK" she said after a while, "Let's have a mouthful." He carefully passed a heaped spoonful to her and fed her. She munched away thoughtfully.

"Disgusting," said Liz. "Josie, how could you?"

"Mmmmmmm, they aren't bad," said Josie.

"If you want any more you can get your own can," laughed Frank as he settled himself down. "I think it's going to get really cold in here very shortly, with the plane being metal but it's better than being outside. I suggest that if we start to get too cold we simply put more clothes on."

"Or we simply snuggle up to you, Frank, because you're such a lump," said Josie moving against him. Liz got up to put her coat on and got back into the bedding saying nothing. Frank did his usual trick and fell asleep in seconds only to be awoken by Josie a short time later shaking him.

"Frank, I'm freezing," she whispered to him. "Can you cuddle me, please?" He turned and put his arms around her and she moved up tight to him.

"God, that's so much better, thanks Frank, its so damn cold. I can't help thinking that this is a crazy country. Boiling hot in the daytime and freezing at night," she said. They lay for a while getting warmer and she moved against him. He couldn't help himself. He started to get hard. He was lying in bed with a very beautiful woman, albeit fully clothed, and he had his arms around her; his body reacted as it was programmed so to do.

"Is that what I think it is?" she whispered in his ear.

"Sorry," he said, "Pay no attention. He has a life of his own and has been getting me into trouble all my life." She giggled quietly but said nothing. Her breathing slowed and steadied as she fell asleep.

He lay staring at the deck head in the flickering candlelight thinking about the last two days and wondering if he would ever see his family again. What had happened to him today he would never have considered possible in his wildest dreams. Life had played one of its strange tricks and had chosen him as one of its pawns in the big game. He was now responsible for the lives of two beautiful women but that didn't worry him particularly; it was how he was going to get them back to civilisation that worried him. He felt sure that the authorities would by now be aware of their plight and would just possibly start to widen their search areas. If they did then they would be found and that was all there was to it. Alternatively, they might have flown too far off course and nobody might think of searching this particular area and then they would be missed. It didn't bear thinking about. His only hope was contacting the outside world in the morning with the mobile but that was a long shot. Even if he could make contact he had no idea where they were. Anyway, by now Reuters had probably picked up the story that the two actresses had gone missing and it would be international news. If his name had been added to the story then his children would be frantic with worry. If the full story of his killing of the bandits came out, and it probably would, then that was most certainly going to be a problem for him when he got back, if he got back. He didn't want the world to know about that one. It could cause all sorts of old wounds to pop to the surface especially if certain people got to hear about it. It was all a bloody mess.

He lay thinking and making plans for the next day well into the night until the candle finally spluttered and died. Still thinking, he continued staring into the darkness.

4

HE AWOKE TO FIND sunshine pouring in through the side windows of the plane. He had moved over during the night and all he could see were two tousled mops of hair poking out of the bedclothes. The inside of the plane was now actually quite warm and snug.

He eased himself out of the makeshift bed. The girls grunted almost in unison but carried on sleeping. He quietly opened the plane's door and let himself drop to the ground. Putting on his boots he looked around. The sun's rays were just starting to penetrate the valley and the mist was slowly rising. "I need firewood if we are to conserve the cooking gas," he thought and looked at the jungle that ran in a thin line around the edge of the valley.

He collected his machete, rifle and backpack and set off. He quickly covered the ground to the woods and started to look for light brushwood. Collecting the driest kindling wood he could find he also added as many small logs as he could carry. He carried everything back to the plane. Glancing at his watch he realised it was still only 8.30am. He made three more trips. There was only a narrow strip of woodland around the edge of the valley, about thirty feet deep at the most, and in some places hardly any. It was on the last trip whilst rummaging around for the firewood he came upon an area where the rock face showed. As he started to walk across to the woodland on the other side he noticed a darker area to the rock face, and through scrub and bushes, he noticed the mouth to a cave. He veered across to it, more out of curiosity than anything else, as it flashed into his mind that it might be better for them to camp there. The mouth of the cave was almost fully covered in low brush and bushes and up close it turned out to be quite large once he had cleared some of the brush aside. It was about eight feet to the ceiling and about the same wide, but as soon as he entered it the ceiling dropped rapidly. He had no intention of going deep into the cave, his fear of snakes being paramount, but he thought he could come back later with a torch and have another look. Then he noticed the cans.

There were six 'jerry' cans stacked against the inside wall. All the paint had peeled off them and they looked old and rusty but there was no doubt about it - they were 5-gallon petrol cans. He dropped everything he was carrying and with his heart beating with excitement he crouched by the cans, picking up each one in turn and shaking it. They were all empty; he was very disappointed. Looking around him he saw there were also some wooden boxes, which had almost completely rotted away. They were empty also. By the look of it the cave roof dropped so quickly that it had no more depth than about twelve feet. There was nothing else there.

"This place must have been used for storage of some sort but by whom?" he thought.

Gathering up the wood he had been carrying he set off back to the plane and put it with the other firewood he had picked up earlier.

He was still restless and looked down the valley where he could just see the tail fin of the crashed plane. "It can't be far and I could be there and back in thirty minutes," he thought. "I'll let the girls sleep on. It would be interesting to know what happened to the crew."

He set off down the length of the valley carving his way through the long grass eventually arriving at the crash site some thirty minutes later. He stopped. The shape of what was left of the plane was familiar. He frowned to himself trying to remember then the realisation shook him to the core and he stared in disbelief. It was the look of the engines and cockpit that did it. He wandered around the broken plane, which had broken into two distinct pieces. The cockpit was still intact with the main body together with one wing and engine. The other broken wing and engine lay approximately one hundred yards away towards the pyramid.

The fuselage was painted grey but there was no doubt in his mind as to what it was. It was a Second World War German Heinkel bomber. He had seen so many photos and film of this plane both in books and on the television. But, it was so old. "It must have been here at least fifty years," he thought.

Out of the corner of his eye he noticed something in the grass, he moved closer. Partly hidden by the grass was the skeleton of a man. It was obvious that he had been thrown out of the plane on impact. The man had not been wearing a jacket, only shirt, trousers and boots and there was not much left of them. There was no sign of identification except for a strangely shaped metal object hanging around his neck. Frank bent down to have a closer look. It was quite an extraordinary piece of neck jewellery as far as that type of thing went. About four inches long and quite thick, Frank imagined that it must have been quite heavy. He frowned. What was this man doing carrying such a heavy piece of personal jewellery as that. It looked as though it was made of stainless steel, as it hadn't rusted at all. He thought he would leave that for the time being and come back and have another look later. He walked over to where the wing had been wrenched from the fuselage and carefully climbed in the plane and then into the cockpit, which was virtually intact. He wasn't too happy thinking that there might be snakes around. They liked this type of environment.

In the pilot's seat there was another skeleton but this one was wearing a peaked cap that had fallen jauntily over the side of the skull, a black leather jacket in remarkably good condition, shredded trousers and boots. It was the strangest sight he had ever seen, a skeleton sitting in clothes, very weird. The pilot had obviously strapped himself in before the crash and looked as though he was still flying the plane. Although the jacket was a little battered it was still in good condition, the rest of the clothes were in tatters. "I'll have that jacket," he thought. He squeezed himself into the cockpit from behind and sat next to the dead pilot. Gently prizing open the jacket he was shocked to see that the pilot was wearing a pistol in a shoulder holster. Frank eased the pistol from its holster and looked at it. He recognised it as a Walther P38 automatic usually used by the German Wehrmacht during the Second World War. It was in amazing condition having been virtually cocooned by the jacket and the holster. He put it on the cockpit floor. He searched for the man's wallet and found it. He also put that on the floor. Frank gritted his teeth and gently eased the old jacket off the skeleton and then removed the holster. He noticed with surprise that the man had something wrapped around what remained of his waist with a buckle at the front.

He undid the rusted buckle and, pulling gently, eased a long thick pouch from around the skeleton's waist. It came away with ease and looked like a money pouch but wasn't. It was made of a thick waxy cotton material and well strapped. Holding it in one hand Frank picked up the wallet, jacket and pistol and jumped back out of the cockpit. He knelt on the ground and started to undo the waxed thongs that were wrapped around the pouch. He opened a small area and gasped at what he saw. Shattering shafts of light exploded as the sun caught its contents.

"Diamonds," he exclaimed his eyes wide with amazement. "Bloody great big ones too." He opened his handkerchief on the ground and poured out some of the contents of the bag. They spilled out, all about the same size, about half an inch in diameter, circular in shape and each one as big as his thumbnail. They were all cut the same way and when the sun caught them the effect was stunning. He glanced around him to ensure no one was watching and felt foolish, as he knew full well that no one was around. He sat cross-legged on the ground staring at the diamonds as they lay glittering on the handkerchief in the grass. He picked up one and rubbed it on his sleeve. The bloom went and the sun's rays caught, bursting light all around; he gasped at the beauty of it.

The implications and the opportunities of the find roared around his brain. "If I get out of here, several problems could arise," he thought. "How do I get these diamonds back to civilisation without being found out and what am I going to do with them when I do get back? Who the hell did they belong to? This is like winning the lottery, but then again, when we get back, if we get back, the story will get out that we found this plane. Somebody will surely know that I found it and will assume that I found the diamonds. That's if they are still alive and knew they were on the plane in the first place." His brain was in overload and he couldn't answer his own questions.

Looking down at the diamonds he mused. "You, my little boys, are going to make my life very complicated I'm sure." He carefully opened the pilot's wallet. There were a few German Deutchsmarks of a type he had never seen before, but that made sense if they were wartime. There were also two letters, which fell apart when he touched them. Then he found the pilot's identification: 2nd Flight Officer Uben Flugen Marine, Hans Mauber stationed at Schleswig in Schleswig-Holstein, Germany, dated 26th February 1945.

Maybe the diamonds were payment for flying the plane into this valley, but more likely, Frank thought, he had stolen them from somewhere. Stuffing the pouch into his own pack he eased his way back into the main cabin. He looked around carefully his hackles now well and truly erect and laughed at himself and his fear. It was quite dark and he couldn't see too well so he aimed a kick at the side wall. His leg went straight through the rotten wooden shell. He kicked again to make a larger hole. He could now see into it quite clearly. Two skeletons were piled in one corner near to him, their uniforms hanging off them in tatters. They had obviously been thrown together in the crash and their skulls grinned back at him. Large wooden boxes of a type similar to those he had found in the cave were everywhere especially around the corpses. It looked to Frank as though the boxes had broken loose on impact and simply crushed the two men. He looked closer; they were German officers but what rank he could not determine. He continued to look around and saw what looked like two bundles of rags lying up against the bulkhead of the plane.

He stared at the bundles feeling sick. Something told him to leave them alone but his curiosity was up now and greed had taken over. Drawing his machete he moved forward slowly and bent to slide it under the first bundle. He flicked it aside and nearly died of fright. Hissing and spitting, three very large vipers reared to their fullest height and stared at the intruder who had dared to disturb them. Frank backed rapidly towards the rear opening of the plane but stumbled as his legs, weak with fear, tripped over one of the wooden crates. He now presented less of a body mass to the snakes as he fell on his back in a cloud of dust and dirt and two of them came for him. Frank yelled in fear and fright as he struggled to his feet but they were on him in a flash. He rolled fast on the filthy floor of the plane never taking his eyes off them for a second and swiped at the nearest viper with the machete as it lunged for him with its fangs bared and its cold evil eyes determined to punish him.

Frank's luck held as his wild swing sliced the first viper in two but the second one was more of a problem. The nearest thing to it was Frank's boot and that was what saved his life. The snake hit it with all its force and sunk its powerful jaws into the toe of the boot. The steel toecap broke the snake's fangs and temporarily stunned it. Frank swung again and the snake was dead. Shaking with fear he stumbled out of the plane and ran for thirty yards before he stopped. Leaning on his knees he fought to catch his breath shuddering in fear and loathing at the thought of how near to death he had just been. He looked around him and sat on one of the boxes until his racing heart slowed. He brushed the dirt and dust from his clothing and thanked the Gods for saving him from a death that he feared more than anything.

Gradually his brain began to shake off what had just happened and he reasoned that maybe, just maybe, the other snake might have left the plane but he wouldn't bet on it; and then there was the second bundle to be taken care of. There were probably more of them under that one as well. Thinking about the cabin he felt that something wasn't quite right there somehow. The thought flitted around his brain but wouldn't surface. It would come in its own good time. That had been quite the worst moment of his life and he wanted to burn the damned plane but the girls would be interested in seeing it. Looking around him he remembered the skeleton and he got up and walked back to where it was lying on the ground. Obviously it had been thrown from the plane on impact and died instantly. By the look of the position of the head he had broken his neck. All around the skeleton were more large wooden boxes with rusting metal straps around them. He counted six.

He walked over to one of the boxes lying in the grass and struck the lock hard with the butt of his rifle. The lock broke on the first hit. He eased the box upright and used his machete to prise open the lid. He sat down hard on the ground before his legs gave way. He counted twelve large gold bars stacked together inside. He shut the lid again and sat on the box, his brain racing. This was all getting too much.

What the hell had been going on here? A German aircraft flying with at least two German officers maybe three; and full of gold, crashing in the middle of the Brazilian jungle, near to a pyramid? All very strange he mused, especially as it was fifty years ago. He looked again at the pilot's wallet, 1945, near to the end of the war. Mmmmmm, maybe they had done a runner from Germany and had decided to land and stay in Brazil, as some of them did, but why here? Frank looked up at the pyramid standing there. "The secret is inside you, isn't it?" He thought.

He stood up and walked right around the plane and then stopped and sat on the original box that he had opened and looked at the scene in front of him. He laughed quietly to himself at the irony of the situation. He could well be rich beyond his wildest dreams right now, but within a short period of time could be staring death in the face through starvation. Shrugging to himself, he prised open the box again and lifted out one bar. He shut the lid and put the bar in his backpack.

He got up off the ground and stared at the huge monolith of the pyramid, which stretched up into the sky no more than three hundred yards away. "No, I'll leave you for now. Better get back to the girls and get some food inside us all. Then I'll show them all of this." He realised that he was talking to himself again. Slipping his pack onto his back he started the walk back to the camp. He walked with his head down thinking and was therefore startled to hear his name being shouted. He looked up to see the girls jumping up and down by the plane waving their arms.

"What the hell is the problem now?" he thought. "Bloody women." He quickened his step. The two girls ran up to him both talking at once and asking where the hell he had got to.

"Listen to me for a minute you two idiots. First of all I'm not going to leave you so don't worry your heads about that. And secondly, one way or another, I am going to get you out of here. Thirdly, we are going to have some breakfast and some tea and coffee and then I am going to tell you a story. Liz, I want you to go over to that tree line and find some more wood. Josie, you start getting some breakfast together and I'll light the fire."

"What shall I make for breakfast," asked Josie. Liz was already heading obediently for the woods.

"Rummage around in the food crate and get out whatever you think we will like. We need some plates, so get to it." She sidled up to him and put her arms around his neck and kissed him. "Oh, I love it when you're so manly" she joked.

Frank frowned in embarrassment. "Just do as you're told young lady and make me my breakfast," he said peeling her arms from around his neck and grinning. "And don't forget you're married either." Liz brought back an armful of wood. He lit the fire and pushed on some of the logs that he had brought out from the woods earlier. Josie opened up a stale loaf and a tin of marmalade and Frank started to toast the bread over the fire.

The girls began to discuss how long they would be there and asked Frank directly what he thought. He had no illusions whatsoever. They had flown for a good sixty minutes in heaven knows what direction. The search planes would in all probability check out their original route and then work on an ever-widening pattern over three to five days. After that the searching would stop on the assumption that they had crashed into the jungle and were dead. He could not tell the girls that though.

"I reckon that we will be found within five days," he told them. "Until then we will just have to survive the best way we can. We have to look out for each other and support each other whenever we get depressed. This is survival time girls. This isn't a game. This is the real thing. Make a cock up out here and you'll die. Fashion, make-up and who's singing the latest hot music and all the rest of the stuff you do on a day to day basis back home, means diddly squat out here." The girls looked at him wide-eyed in silence.

Frank pulled the dead pilot's pistol out of his pack and began to check it over. "Where did you get that Frank?" said Josie.

"I'll tell you later," he said. "Now listen to me. Your personal hygiene is very important out here. You have to look after yourself and if you cut yourself let me know. Think twice before you do anything such as going for a walk and ask me if you aren't sure. The majority of the time I want us to stick together and somehow or other I will get you out of here even if it means walking."

Josie said, "Frank, you said you had a story to tell us. What is it"?

"Let's clear up the breakfast things and pile everything back in the plane first." he said killing the fire. They spent another ten minutes doing so.

"OK ladies, if you think you are rich, think again. You know I talked about seeing a smashed-up plane when we came in here. Well, that's where I have been. I went over to it this morning and guess what I have found." He turned and pulled out the gold bar from his backpack. He had covered it in an old shirt. He laid it down in front of them and they moved forward expectantly.

"What is it Frank?" said Liz in a hushed voice. Frank pulled back the shirt with a flourish.

"GOLD," he said, "loads and loads of bloody great gold bars. They are scattered all over the grass back there."

"How many are there?" Josie cried excitedly.

"Well, if you have a spare moment or two I thought we would wander over there and count them, but there is a problem." he said.

"What the problem?" asked Liz?

"Well, there are a few skeletons over there which you won't like at all and maybe something else in the cabin. I'll tell you all about it on the way over."

As they walked towards the crash site, he explained to them what he had found. He also explained briefly how it was widely known that the Nazis had secretly moved enormous amounts of gold and treasures, ravished from the European countries they had occupied, out of Germany during the last months of the Second World War, and then, via submarine, shuttled it to South America. Frank believed that this plane had probably been ferrying three such people and their loot when they flew into the same valley, but they had made the mistake of hitting the pyramid.

"The question we have to ask ourselves is why did they choose this place?" He said.

They arrived at the crash site and the girls shuddered at the sight of the skeleton on the ground and the one in the cockpit. They re-opened the box Frank had opened and marvelled at the sight of the gold bars just laying there.

None of them had the nerve to venture into the broken rear cabin leaving that for another day. Liz had an idea.

"Frank," she said looking around. "This plane didn't burn when it crashed. Do you think that they ran out of fuel as we did or do you think that they were simply trying to land here? Maybe there is some fuel left in the plane."

He looked at her in amazement. "Liz, where on earth did that come from? Let's have a look."

"Well, I'm not stupid you know," she replied tartly.

Frank walked around the hull until he found the fuel filler cap in one wing. Using his knife he tried to undo it but the knife would not move it. He took his machete from its sheath and banged the filler cap several times with the hilt. He then jammed the tip of the blade in the slit and gave it a wrench. He felt it give a little. He repeated the process with the girls hanging over his shoulder. The filler cap moved a bit more and then freed itself.

"That's not bad after fifty years," he thought.

He spun the cap free and there was a loud whoosh as the tank equalised itself. Josie handed him a long stick. Tearing off a piece of his shirt he wiped the stick carefully until it was as clean as he could get it and then stuck it down the fuel pipe and felt it hit bottom with a hollow boom. He then withdrew it. He looked at the stick for a long moment hardly believing his eyes, "Bloody hell, I don't believe it." He sniffed the fuel on the stick.

"It smells OK," he said. "Liz, you're a bloody marvel. There's fuel in this tank all right but its fifty years old. I have no idea if it will work but it's worth a try. By the sound as I undid the fuel cap the tank was probably airtight and if that is so then the fuel should be O.K. Maybe a little depleted but O.K. I think somehow we have to get it out of there and re-fuel our plane with it. We will have to think that through but I think we should leave that 'til the morning. I tell you what we should do. Let's tidy up all these boxes and stack them by the plane for now."

The girls agreed and working as a pair they excitedly collected the boxes and dragged them one by one and stacked them neatly together a few yards away from the broken airplane. They took their time doing this as the boxes were extremely heavy. There were over a dozen boxes in all. Exhausted, they sat and discussed entering the broken hull with Frank.

"We do have a problem here. There is no point in trying to get more gold out of this plane because we couldn't carry it all anyway. I'm sorry to be negative but if that fuel works and we get our plane started and get out of here we still don't know where we are and we certainly can't take all of this gold because the weight will hold us down. Now I really don't know if I can fly our plane out of here. Because of the short take-off area I don't even know if I can even get her up out of this valley. The climb is so steep we would need to be very light indeed. Let's think this out a moment. We get the plane started and stripped of everything we don't need. When we get out of here which way do we go, and will we have enough fuel to get there?"

"If this was a German plane and they were planning to land here for some reason surely they would have had a map. If they did it must be up there by that pilot," Josie reasoned.

He looked at them in amazement. "Why didn't I think of that," he said and promptly climbed back into the cockpit. After a few minutes searching he found a weather-beaten brown leather pouch down by the side of the skeleton of the pilot. He carefully picked it up expecting it to fall apart any second. He climbed back out from the cockpit and sat down on the grass with the girls. The buckle on the pouch was rusted solid so he cut the strap, folded back the flap, and peered inside. Deciding to play safe he turned the pouch upside down and three documents fell out. Each was covered in waxed paper. The first one did indeed turn out to be a large-scale map of South America; and in particular Brazil. A flight plan had been drawn on the map starting at the coast and ending in the middle of the jungle with a circle. They decided that the ending and turn around point must be where they were.

Frank was very excited. "Let's get back to our plane, have some lunch and a cup of tea and I will try to work out what heading we will need to get back to Rio."

"What about the gold?" asked Liz?

"It's been here for fifty years I am pretty sure that it won't run away now," he said.

They walked back to their plane discussing the merits of leaving the gold and what to do with it. Liz was very quiet. "What's troubling you, Liz?" asked Frank.

"I'm trying to work out how much all that gold is worth. We found a dozen boxes on the ground. There must be another dozen in the plane. Each box holds twelve bars so at even $200 to the ounce there must be about three million pounds worth back there."

"Yes, but unfortunately we wouldn't get that ourselves even if they have such a thing in this country as treasure trove as we do in England. We would probably get some sort of percentage eventually because every European country will be claiming that the gold was stolen from them," he said.

"That's not fair," said Josie.

"No, but that's life," said Frank philosophically. He said nothing about the diamonds.

They arrived back at the plane and the girls set about sorting some food for their lunch. It was now very hot indeed and Frank stripped off his shirt and sat in the shade under one wing of the plane leaning back against the wheel. He put his sunglasses on against the glare and sat thinking. "Within three days my world has been turned upside down. One minute I'm walking along a dusty mountain track going home and the next I'm fighting bandits and then finding dead Germans in a plane full of gold and diamonds." The thought he had inside the hull flashed through his mind again and then was gone. He shook his head trying to get it back but it was gone. He continued to muse for a while as to how fate could change life in an instant. "So many questions, and anyway, why did fate choose me? I'm just an average bloke." The question went unanswered.

The girls brought over the food. Corned beef sandwiches in stale bread.

"Sorry, that's all we could think of," said Josie.

"It will do," said Frank taking a swig of his tea. "Thanks for the tea. What would I do without my cup of tea?" The girls were standing between him and the sun so he couldn't see them clearly until they sat down beside him in the shade. They had stripped off as well, down to their shorts.

Liz saw the look on his face. "Don't get any fancy ideas mister," she laughed. "We envied you taking of your shirt so we did as well. Besides, bras are horrible in this heat and we know you will be asleep in a minute anyway."

"Ladies, you are absolutely right. We aren't going anywhere in this heat so wake me in a couple of hours, please," he said. "When it's cooler we can start getting the fuel. That's going to be hard work but we have plenty of time and we don't have anything else to do at the moment do we?"

He closed his eyes. That thought raced through his brain again like a ghost. "I've seen something that's worrying me but I'm buggered if I know what it is," he thought. Thoughts and sights of the day flitted briefly and the soft drone of the two girls talking softly sent him on his way.

* * *

He found himself standing at the bottom of the pyramid looking up at the top. A female voice was calling softly to him. It seemed far away but slowly came closer and closer. He knew this voice. It came from far in his past and he began remembering emotions he had felt at that time but could not pin a name to that so familiar sound. The voice continued to call his name gently as if it wanted to talk to him.

"Who are you?" he called.

"Don't you remember me, Frank?" it said. The voice was now so evocative and familiar, and at the same time frightening, that he could feel his heart hammering.

"I know you, but your name is eluding me. I know that we once knew each other but I can't remember the name. "Who are you?"

"Oh Frank, I'm disappointed in you. Wait there," it said.

He felt a presence come down at him from the monolith; he could see it as well as feel it. The presence wrapped itself around him like a cloak and then hovered in front of him in no particular form, simply, a grey swirling cloud.

"Hello, Frank," it said and gradually the form of a beautiful blond young girl began to materialise in front of him, hovering just off the ground. Dressed in jeans and an open neck shirt he recognised her instantly.

"Sandy," he gasped. His mind reeled at the sight of a girl that he had first known when he was ten years old at school. He had worshiped this girl into his teens and had at last convinced her to be his when they were both eighteen. They had an affair, the power of which had swept them away for six months until she had told him that her parents were moving abroad and that she had to go with them. The last time they had been together was on her last day in the country. They had lain in each other's arms under the shade of an oak tree by the side of a cornfield under a hot summer's sun; both crying their eyes out, and promising undying love forever. The next day she was gone and he never heard from her again.

He had pestered her friends endlessly asking them to tell him where she had gone but no one knew and no one ever heard from her again either. He had often thought of her over the years. She was his first true love and he had often wondered what had happened to her. Now she was standing in front of him.

"You do remember me then," the young girl said.

"How could I ever forget you? You were my first love, but Sandy," he said, trying to concentrate on the vision in front of him. "You are still eighteen, how can that be. I am now forty-seven years old and so should you be."

"I will always be as you last saw me Frank. My, you have grown into a beautiful man, tall, strong, and so handsome. Your hair is just starting to go grey and it suits you." There was a hint of wistfulness in her voice. "I did love you so, Frank. I was so pleased to see that it was you when you flew into the valley. We made sure that you landed well and you no doubt felt that, but didn't understand. I will look after you as best I can while you are here and when you leave. However, I have come to warn you, Frank. Do not disturb the pyramid. You may take the material things away with you that are there but do not disturb us. What you see in front of you is beyond your comprehension even to an intelligent man such as you. Trust me. I will do my very best to protect you but I can only do so much."

Frank looked at the vision in front of him and smiled. "I hear what you say Sandy and will try to understand. Why have you never tried to contact me when we loved each other so much?"

"I can't explain that now Frank. I was simply not allowed to and we quickly became deeply involved here. That's all I can say. It's so nice to see you again Frank." Again there was the sound of wistfulness in her voice. She appeared to wipe a tear from one eye. "You must go home though and as quickly as you can. Do not stay here for long or you could be affected by our emissions. God go with you and please, don't ever forget me. I will be with you now for ever."

The vision slowly disintegrated back into the grey mist and then left him, swirling back up to the monolith. He found himself overwhelmed emotionally and he slumped to the ground. Old emotions buried deep within swept over him in great waves and he found himself sobbing uncontrollably. He knew he was acting like a child but he could no more control it than fly to the moon. After a few moments he found the strength to gather himself together and standing up he looked back up to the pyramid, wondering.

* * *

Josie, gently shaking him, woke him.

"Come on Frank, wake up" she was saying. She had put her shirt back on but the first thing he noticed was that she had no bra on. His eyes lingered on her beautiful breasts as he tried to focus from the sleep. Josie was deliberately still leaning over him watching him with laughing eyes. He shook his head to clear it of the disturbing dream. "Was that just a dream or what?" he thought.

"I'm seeing double trouble," he said. Both girls laughed.

"We found some big saucepans in one crate. Will that be OK to carry the fuel, Frank?" asked Liz.

He put the dream behind him and concentrated on the job in hand. "I have a better idea than that," he said, and told the girls about the cave he found earlier and the cans. "If we can clean them up they will do just fine," he said. "How we get the fuel out I don't know but I will think of something."

It was much cooler than earlier on with the time being about four in the afternoon. They set off for the cave to get the cans and had only gone a few yards when Frank stopped dead in his tracks. The elusive thought crystallising in his mind with stunning force.

"The seats," he exclaimed. "The bloody seats!"

The girls had stopped too and were looking at him. "What on earth are you on about Frank? What do you mean?" said Josie.

"The bloody seats in the crashed plane," he said. "There were four seats in the back of the plane but we have only seen three skeletons. They would not have put four seats in if they were only carrying three people because of the gold. We are a skeleton missing!"

"Are you sure?" said Josie.

"Well, think about it. You saw into the plane as well as I did. Did you see three skeletons in there or only two," he asked.

"Two," the girls chorused.

"Right. I can't settle until I solve that problem so the fuel will have to wait. Let's get over there," he said. They walked quickly over to the crash sight again saying nothing to each other. Everyone was thinking.

"We will split up but keep in sight of each other," Frank said. "He must be out here somewhere. Josie, you take to the left of the plane. Liz, you search on a line towards the pyramid and I will search out to the right. Let's go."

Frank beat a wide path towards the pyramid and could see the other two doing the same. They walked for half a mile, seeing nothing, when Liz gave a cry.

"Frank, Josie, look!"

They both ran through the long grass to Liz. They were now almost at the foot of the pyramid towering above them. Liz pointed up the steps that rose upwards towards the first level. There, seemingly hanging on the steps, right on the last one before the first level, were the white bleached bones of a skeleton gleaming in the fading sun.

5

THEY STOOD MOTIONLESS LOOKING up at the skeleton. "So, there was another one after all," said Frank.

"I'm thinking something more explicit," said Josie "but can't say it, but it's two words and one begins with F and the other is Hell."

They looked at one another. "That is spooky," said Josie. "What on earth possessed him to crawl from the plane crash up to there?"

"Whatever it was we haven't the time today to explore the situation. What I propose is that we leave this to the morning when it's cool and fresh and get some stuff together so that we can be ready for any eventuality because I have a sneaking feeling that we are going to find something up there." He was thinking about his dream.

"What sort of thing, Frank?" said Josie.

"I don't know but this whole scene is worrying me. Something big was going on down here. I think that plane was actually trying to land here and but for the accident we would never have known that they had been here at all. Unfortunately the pilot clipped the pyramid and that was it. Having said that however why were there never any more flights in? Was it just this group who were ferrying the gold and why were they all together? I think the answer is up there somewhere," he said pointing to the pyramid. "And I'm not going up there until I'm fully prepared."

The girls were disappointed but could see the logic.

Forgetting all about the fuel, the three of them walked slowly and silently back to their own plane in the afternoon heat.

They sat down in the shade of the wing again and discussed the situation. Liz, normally just a listener, could not stop talking about the day and what had occurred.

"Beats modelling and filming into a cocked hat" she said. "This is all so exciting. Crashed airplane, dead bodies and gold, it's all so spooky.

There we were making a film about this sort of thing but it was not half so exciting."

"Ah, but that was about a desert island, Liz, not about here in the Amazon jungle. And we were dealing with drug dealers in the film whereas here it is Nazis from the Second World War."

They talked over their situation for another couple of hours until they realised the sun was beginning to set. "I'll light the fire again so that we can have a hot drink before we settle down," said Frank.

"That was so cold last night, Frank, can we have the gas heater on for a while in the plane this evening?" said Josie.

"I don't have a problem with that just as long as we restrict it to an hour. That should warm the place up and we'll wear more clothes as well. It will all help," he said. "I'll tell you what we also forgot to do today in all the excitement. We forgot to try to get your mobile to work, Josie. I'll try it in the morning."

After having some tinned fish and some soup, they settled down in front of the open fire, each of them deep in their own world.

Frank looked at Liz. She hadn't spoken for some time. Tears were falling slowly down her black cheeks again. He moved over to her and put his arm round her shoulder. "What's the problem kiddo?" he asked softly.

"I'm frightened, Frank. I don't think anyone will ever find us and we can't get the plane out of this valley. We will die here the same way as those others did. I want to go home Frank and to be with my parents and partner. I miss them and they must be absolutely destroyed thinking that I am dead somewhere in the jungle. I just want to go home. I don't care about the gold, I just want to go home," she repeated.

Frank and Josie consoled Liz until she stopped crying. "What did I promise you Liz? I promised both of you that I will get you back home and I will. We already have a strategy and it will work. Do you trust me Liz?" he asked.

"Yes, Frank, but it's just that we are hundreds of miles from anywhere and all this frightens me. I'm not used to it, Frank, and nor is Josie despite the brave act she puts on."

They cleaned up their patch, put the fire out and went into the plane and to bed. This time the girls asked Frank to sleep in the middle so that they both could cuddle up to him. Within a very short period of time they were all asleep.

Frank awoke slowly. Josie had one arm thrown over him and was gently snoring into his left ear. Liz was laying in a similar fashion and was also gently purring. It was a bright clean new day and Frank watched the shafts of sunlight appear through the windows of the plane.

He lay there relishing the peace and quiet thinking for some time about his dream. It had been so vivid and was still with him. Perhaps she had contacted him deliberately through his dream or was it just a dream. No, it was real, he was sure of that. How extraordinary, if this was all true that Sandy may have ended her time here in this wilderness and jungle where he might end his. She had said that she had helped him to land. He remembered when he was gliding the plane in that his hands had felt that they were being guided. What about when the pyramid appeared? The plane had flipped left and right on its own, there was no doubt in his mind about that. No, that must have been an illusion surely although there was no other explanation. He knew that he could not have done that on his own. No way. "I can't fly a plane with that type of skill," he thought. "At best, and with all the luck possible, I would have broken it up on the pyramid or on landing." He vowed to himself to do as she had asked.

The diamonds, though, were another matter. Who had given them to that pilot and why were they strapped around his waist? How was he going to get them back to England? Then there was the problem of selling them and hiding the money from the Inland Revenue. Should he take them to Switzerland? Where was the best place to sell them and get the best price? Again, there were so many questions that he couldn't answer right now.

"First, I have to get out of here," he thought. He worried about that for some time as well. There were several facets to the whole thing. Probably the first was to wait and see if they were found. Second, explore the pyramid if they could get into it. Third, to try and get a phone call out and fourth see if the engines of this plane would start with the old fuel from the German bomber.

He began to fidget, wanting to get on with the day. He glanced at his watch. It was only 6.30 am. "I'll sleep for another hour then get up," he thought.

He awoke to find Liz digging him in the ribs. "Come on, Frank, get up it's nearly ten o'clock." Frank cursed. "Damn it," he said. "I was awake at 6am this morning and then fell asleep again and you girls are worse than useless," he stormed.

"What's your hurry, sweetheart? You are in bed with two wonderful women and all you want to do is get up," laughed Josie yawning and stretching.

"You know damn well that this day is important and there are a lot of things to be done. Now you can die here if you want but I'm not going to and if we want to get out of here we have to shift arse, to be crude, and get moving. Now let's get going," he said.

Without looking to see the effect of his words, he threw off the bedclothes and got up. Moving to the door he opened it and jumped out.

"Sod them," he thought. "Stupid bloody women, they have one thing on their minds all the bloody time." He was angry with himself at having wasted so much time; he had been sleeping just as though they were in a hotel.

Liz followed him out of the plane, doing up her shirt watching him as he started a fire. "What's got into you, Frank?" she said. "You are normally so easy going."

"I can't believe that we have wasted so much valuable time. For all we know there might have been a search plane-flying close by. Have you no sense of urgency here?" he asked her. Josie now jumped out of the plane and walked over to the two and heard his last remark.

"I'm sorry Frank, we didn't think. Please forgive us. I don't like it when you're angry. It feels like you are against us and this is a bad enough situation as it is. We really need you Frank and won't sleep in like that again we promise" she said tears welling in her beautiful eyes.

Frank got up, looking at the two of them. They looked like naughty little three-years-olds who were about to get a smack.

"Come here," he said opening up his arms wide. The two girls ran to him putting their arms around him and hugging him tight, burying their faces into his chest.

"I told you I would look after you and I will. I'm only really angry with myself for wasting so much time." he said. "Now let's get some food inside us, wash up and get on with what we have to do." When they had finished they all walked over to the waterfall, stripped off and washed themselves without the remotest embarrassment.

While they were drying themselves and dressing Frank said, "Earlier this morning I was thinking of our priorities. We should first get a phone call out because we haven't heard a plane yet. We should make that our priority. However, I'm fascinated with the situation up there," he said, pointing at the pyramid, "and I want to know if we can get inside and, if we can, what's in there."

Frank was sitting on the ground putting his boots back on and Josie came over and stood in front of him, her hair was wet and bedraggled, her shirt still sticking to her damp body emphasising her pert breasts. She put her hands on her hips and put her legs wide apart. She looked down at him with her wide set green eyes flashing, grinning, and knowing full well that she looked simply fantastic even without her makeup.

"Well, shift your butt old man and let's find out the answer," she said.

Frank wanted to make a grab for her but knowing she was only teasing, left it. She had read his mind anyway and had moved out of immediate range still grinning.

"Why don't you two just behave?" laughed Liz, who could see full well what the two were up to. Frank grumbled something about 'bloody women' again but pulled on his shirt and they made their way back to the plane chatting together happily. Frank filled his pack with torches, food, water and a small crowbar from the tool kit. They then set off for the pyramid.

They started to climb the steps moving slowly in the mid morning heat until they reached the skeleton some one hundred feet above them. Whoever it had been had been pretty tough. Frank examined the skeleton's frame. He had broken his right leg, left arm and his collarbone. He pointed it out to the girls.

"What possessed him to crawl all that way in that state?" he asked aloud almost to himself.

Liz leaned forward. The skeleton had one arm stretched out in front of him. "He's got something in his hand," she said. They all leaned over and Frank prised open the bones. The object fell from the fingers; it was the same as that found around the neck of the skeleton in the grass.

"What on earth can that be?" Josie asked.

Frank picked it up and studied it carefully. "If I didn't know better, I would say that it looks to me like some sort of key," he said. He turned around and looked at the pyramid in front of them. They were on a small plateau area of the pyramid. The area was about ten feet wide and obviously ran right around the pyramid. In front of them there was a recess in the steps.

"Who ever that was, he wanted to get in here, and I reckon that this was his key."

"I think that's a doorway of some sort," he said pointing to the recess. This pyramid was somehow different to the others that he had visited in the jungle. The stonework didn't look so old and it was almost a deep purple in colour. It was a lot smaller too. "All very odd," he thought.

Followed closely behind by the girls he walked to the recess with the metal object in his hand. He brushed the surface of the stonework with his hand working from the top towards the bottom. Halfway down in the middle of the stonewall he disturbed some dust hanging to the stonework. A small slit appeared. "Is that a hole?" asked Josie.

Liz was very nervous. "Shouldn't we go back and think this out?" she said, "I have bad vibes about this."

"Hold on for just a minute," he said. "Just let me try this thing in the slot. I want to know if we can at least open this door, if that is what it is." He tried the metal object several ways before it suddenly slid effortlessly into place. He pushed the key further in and nothing happened. He tried to slide it to the left and nothing happened but when he slid it to the right there was firstly a loud click and then a long sighing sound.

"Get back," he said. Silently the huge door started to slide on its own to the right as they staggered back into the open and eventually stopped when the door had obviously completed it journey.

They moved back to the opening, choking on the dust raised by the enormous stone door. They attempted to peer inside. Frank switched on his torch. The sight that glowed in the shadows raised the hackles on their necks. As Frank swept the inside of the chamber with the torch beam it showed row upon row of the same black crates as they found at the crash site. More gold. The crates were piled six high in places and two and three deep. Paintings were stacked everywhere. Other crates with stencilled writing in German were neatly piled against the walls. The room was large but not enormous, as he had expected. As the dust settled they gingerly moved inside. "This place hasn't been opened in years," Frank said, choking on the dust. Everything was covered in cobwebs.

Josie seemed overwhelmed. "Bloody hell, this is fantastic. Frank, this is a treasure cave. Look at this painting. It's a Rembrandt and this one, Frank; look at the names on these pictures." She could hardly control her excitement. "Good God, Liz, we will never have to work again. There must be millions and millions of dollars worth of stuff here. We will be famous." She started to dance around. "What a story. What a story" she laughed. "Just wait until the newspapers hear about this."

Ever the realist, Liz said. "We have to get out of here first." But she was excited as well.

Frank walked over to a row of larger boxes near the wall. He smashed down on the lock with the butt of his rifle and lifted the lid. The two girls were peering over his shoulder and both gasped at the sight. Jewellery of every description gleamed in the torchlight. They both started to run their hands through the rings and necklaces when Frank stopped them.

"OK, ladies. Now we know. This was probably one of the Gestapo's secret South American stores for some of their bounty from Europe. However, they lost out big time. Let's just remember that all of this stuff belonged to people at some time or other and was stolen from them. Just imagine the misery and deprivation behind every article that you see here now. Think of all the deaths that were involved in the taking of this stuff. It doesn't bear thinking about." He stood up and pointed his torch at other boxes nearby. BELZEC was stencilled on the sides of a few of them. "Oh, no," he groaned. He walked over and again smashed his rifle butt down on the clasp of one and lifted the lid. It was full of gold teeth. "I thought so," he said. "Do you realise what sort of horrors lay behind all this. Frankly, I want none of it. I will take a reward for finding it but I want none of it. It gives me the shivers. Let's go back outside and think about what we have here."

They turned to go and their world changed forever. Hovering in front of the door was a white luminous cloud. As soon as Frank's eyes fixed upon it he felt his legs crumble beneath him. Trying to call out to warn the girls only a small croak came from his mouth, his vision blurred and he slumped to the ground unconscious.

He awoke to find himself laying on a hard wooden bed and his brain slowly came alive. It ached. He lay still looking at the ceiling and suddenly pictures materialised in front of him showing himself and the two girls climbing the Pyramid and entering. Frank shook his head unable to make any sense of what he was seeing and tried to rise but he seemed to be tied to the bed although looking down he saw there were no ropes or ties. Frank was a reasonable and practical man and when faced with any type of problem usually took a step back and weighed up the situation before acting. In this case he had no option. He relaxed back onto the bed and took stock.

The last thing he remembered was seeing that misty white shape at the door's entrance and feeling an instant and almost overpowering feeling of danger, and yet here he was laying seemingly held invisibly and yet alive and feeling O.K, except for the headache. He turned his head to his right and he could see Josie laying in the same fashion but with her eyes closed. He called her name but there was no response. He could just see Liz held in a similar fashion the other side of Josie. He called her name also but again there was no response. He seemed to be able to move his head with ease so he looked to his left and started. The white misty cloud was no more than a few feet away and he had the absolute knowledge that it was watching him.

It made some noises and then a cough and several squeaks in various octaves and then: "Do not be afraid, are you hungry, thirsty?"

Frank looked at the cloud in stunned silence and then replied. "I don't think I am afraid and no, I am not hungry, thank you but some water would be good." His mouth felt like the bottom of a birdcage and his head hurt like hell.

A square object about a metre cubed slid across the room materialising from nowhere. A pitcher of water and a glass goblet was on top. It stopped by his left hand. He made to move his left hand to reach for the water and discovered his hand was free. He poured the water into the goblet and drank spilling some onto his chest. He put the goblet back and rested his head all the time watching the cloud. It stayed static. This was surreal; he felt he must be dreaming because this type of thing just did not happen. Yeah, that was it he was dreaming and in a minute he would wake relieved and laughing about it with Liz and Josie. He dug the nails of his left hand into his palm and felt the pain. No way, he was awake. In that case what the bloody hell was all this about? The white cloud continued to watch him, motionless. He felt like laughing out loud, this was Dr Who time and was only seen on television, this simply could not be real. Except that he couldn't move and that cube definitely slid across the floor on its own. He glared at the cloud and then had an idea. Before he could say something the voice spoke.

"I shall get her and you can speak."

No, no, no, no, that couldn't happen either, he had just decided to try something and ask if he could talk to Sandy, was that a long shot or what? Before he had been able to say anything at all it had answered his unasked question. Almost immediately Sandy slowly appeared by his side still dressed in the same clothes as the dream.

"Hello Frank, sorry to give you such a shock but you have brought this upon yourselves." She hesitated and turned away as though listening and then said "they have asked me to explain everything to you. That is indeed a great honour Frank. They don't do that sort of thing but appear to see something in you about which we will talk later. Firstly me, yes I do exist but not in the fashion that you understand. My father and I were recruited all that time ago. We have worked for them ever since and will do so for ever or until we are not needed. This is their pyramid Frank as is all that is within it. They have no name that I am aware of and yet their powers are quite beyond your imagination. More of that another time, at the moment you successfully passed their first test and found your way into the pyramid. Only one other man has ever done that and he is laying on the steps of the pyramid outside as a warning to others. They are impressed that your logic and your enquiring mind enabled you to find your way. But, because of your curiosity, you are now in their hands so to speak and you can be assured that your future will be very interesting indeed."

"You are kidding of course, I don't know what the hell you are talking about Sandy, and none of this makes any sense. I'm talking to what can only be a spirit and also looking at a white cloud that can speak! If all this is true and this isn't a bad dream what do they want with me and are they going to harm us?" Frank asked.

"You were guided to us Frank. You don't have to believe that but you were. My Masters want you to work for them out in the world of Earth. There are a lot of things they need to know and the fact that you are a grown man and relatively free of any ties except your own family means that you could move about freely. Riches can be yours with ease but the penalty you pay for that is that you gather information for them. You will not be gathering information in the way that you know or think you know but they will simply record and analyse everything you see and hear. If you agree to this you and your friends will be set free. The girls will not remember anything and you will only remember a few selected items. Over and above that they will condition you shortly. It will be quite painless Frank and will not harm you."

Frank thought for a moment. "If everything you say is true Sandy then what about that fella outside? It doesn't look to me as if your chums aren't harmless."

"Yes, Richard was a big disappointment. He was recruited many years ago when quite young. He had tremendous potential, very bright, inquisitive, but born at the wrong time and in the wrong country. We looked after him during your war so that no harm came to him but he became greedy and the goods in the room downstairs are a testament to that. He turned into something quite unacceptable and not at all what my Masters wanted. He became useless to them so they completed his journey, let him bring his goods to us here and then his life was "finished." My Masters are ruthless when it suits them."

Frank was quiet for a while then turned and looked at the white cloud that hovered behind the vision of Sandy. He didn't like the feeling that he got from it, it was a primeval feeling, and he felt completely useless, felt threatened and frightened. He wasn't used to the feeling of not being master of his own destiny. He was a prisoner of a force that was beyond his understanding and he needed to know more. If he was going to die at least he should have some knowledge of what was about to kill him. "Who are they Sandy, what do they want and why are they here?"

"Enough." The white cloud spoke with a hint of impatience and then began to transform gathering density and form then suddenly it was the object of a tall Monk in a brown habit. The face was of an old man, tanned, full and rounded with even white teeth a high forehead beneath a bald head and a strong nose and full mouth. The deep blue eyes sparkled almost as though the man found the situation amusing, there was a smile hovering on the man's lips.

Frank was adjusting to the situation. "Good morning, at least it's kind of you to show yourself rather than hovering there like a puff of smoke." He was pleased with himself being able to be sarcastic under the circumstances.

The man's eyes did not change. "For your information, and the question that is in your mind, you are quite right, this is not my true form. You wouldn't like that I know, but it is more acceptable to you Earth people. Your questions are tiring my pupil, she is not used to talking in this way so I will let her go and rest." He didn't turn away for a second but Sandy suddenly disappeared without a word. The smile was still on his lips.

"There is no reason for me to explain myself to you Frank but as I want us to be friends I will. My colleagues and I are not of this planet you call Earth. We are a much older race than you. As a comparison I would put us as three thousand years in advance. You are in your early development and we are here to watch you. We stay for five hundred of your earth years at a time and have done so since the beginning of your early development. Sentinels if you like. We find the Earth race still primitive yet quite interesting, still barbaric in most countries with what we find is a horrifying degree of savagery. A miscalculation was made many years ago by us in your development which has left the human earth race with a brain quite capable eventually of great potential and sophistication but unfortunately, in some instances still unable to suppress that primitive savagery and hate that is a throw back to your early past and it is this that we believe will bring about your eventual destruction. That brings us to yourself Frank. We have recruited a number of human earth men and woman working for us throughout your planet. Not many but a few and they are in all stations of your societies and countries. They have to be replaced on a regular basis because your life spans are so short. Your effective working life for us is only 100 of your earth years, not very long at all." He continued to smile down at Frank but Frank had the distinct feeling that the man had gone away for a moment.

"Yes, hmmmm, we need more people and we have chosen you Frank to help us. We need an increasing presence out there in your world, observers if you like, and we have been observing you ever since you landed here in this country. We have gone over your past and you suit the situation perfectly. We track quite a lot from here and know much from your television and radio but we have discovered that it is imperative to actually have people on the ground so to speak. That way we can really find out what is going on in your development. In return we will help you personally; with financial reward and material comforts. We also understand your emotional needs and feelings and the fact that you need physical well being and health. We understand all these things. These you will have together with longevity of life simply by being you and for travelling your planet. You are an excellent specimen of manhood Frank but you will not live beyond 57 earth years. That is programmed into your physical being. We have read you. We will extend that life for many more years than that. We can do that, obviously. In fact you will not appear to grow much older at all and your appearance will simply slowly age as against the rapid deterioration that would be normal. That is what you will receive for helping us. I have already taken that you accept. You do not have to talk Frank because, as you have already discovered, I can read your mind. But have caution, I warn you, we do not suffer disloyalty nor do we accept greed and avarice. We can kill you in an instant if need be, or alternatively cause you extensive, terminal and extremely painful harm, it is up to you. We have found it wise to warn you humans of the consequences of deceit. You are still barbaric and mutinous and we find the majority of you have little or no morals or ethics. We cannot teach you these things, you either understand them or you don't. In your instance Frank we believe you do but we have been mistaken before as you have seen outside. He is left there as a reminder.

In essence Frank help us and we will help you. You are not under any pressure to do so. Say no and you will wake up outside this place with no memory of our conversation. Say yes as I think you will and we can continue."

Frank studied the figure in front of him and thought. He really had nothing to lose, after all what was being asked of him, spy on his fellow human beings? Was that so awful or immoral? After all these beings were doing that anyway. He had a thought.

"If I accept how do I report to you?"

"You don't, we will see everything through your eyes Frank, and you will not even know we are there. You will be a transmitter if you like; do you understand what I mean?"

"Yes. So I will not have to do anything or say anything just observe wherever I am is that what you mean?"

"Yes, that is what I mean."

Frank was finding it difficult to think knowing that whatever this figure was it was watching him thinking. Very tricky, he couldn't see any problems though only benefits but there again he wasn't the deepest thinker in the world so any deep and moralistic principles that some others might have were certainly not in his agenda and anyway if he agreed it would enable him to carry on with his life and resume doing whatever he wanted to do. Besides, with the diamonds he found he would indeed be financially secure if only he could get them back home and sold."

"One last point. You will be given certain abilities, nothing extraordinary; a sharper memory for instance, a little more strength, certainly faster reflexes and perhaps sharper coordination between eye and hand. In other words your physical being will sharpen and revert to your earlier age of twenty earth years. If you like we will tune you in a similar fashion to the way you earth men tune racing cars to get a better performance. Yes, that is a good analogy. I am sure you understand that Frank. Yes I thought so. I emphasis that we will not interfere in your day to day life, it will be up to you how you conduct yourself and live your life but you will certainly be able to utilise the profits from the goods in the attached chamber once you have been able to remove them, Again you will have to use your ingenuity to do so, we will not help you there either but under no circumstances will we allow other than yourself and friends to descend into this place. We will not hesitate to destroy anyone that enters or tries to enter. Do not under estimate our abilities Frank. That is all."

"I agree, what will happen to my friends here?"

"The figure slowly turned and drifted over to the two girls who were laying unconscious. "They will awake with you outside, they will remember nothing, and you Frank, on the other hand, will remember most of the things we have discussed. Discuss this with no one, we will talk again Frank via my trainee Sandy, she will be your guardian and your contact. Good luck, we look forward to working with you."

The figure smiled at Frank and slowly evaporated until there was nothing to show he had been there. Frank felt a weariness grow over him and a desire to sleep; he succumbed to the overpowering feeling and closed his eyes.

6

Frank found himself outside the pyramid door with the key in his hand, just as before, and the girls were chattering behind him just as before. He still had a headache.

Frank never had a headache and this was a bad one. He thought that if they had been messing with his brain this was probably the consequence. He sat down in the shadow of the wall and the girls followed suit chattering excitedly about what they had just seen. He let them chatter on as he thought about what he had just been through. He looked out across the Jungle and took a long deep breath. So, his life had changed course once again. Whatever had just happened he decided had happened, or had it? Maybe he was losing the plot and had just had one of those strange moments that we all get once in a while. Perhaps it was the effect of seeing all that wealth in the pyramid. Whatever, he decided to simply carry on as normal because he was a practical man. He took another deep breath and turned to the girls.

"Hold on girls, let's think this one through." He stood up and walked back into the cavernous room and looked at the awesome sight in front of him. The wealth stacked in boxes in front of him was almost unimaginable. What a challenge he thought getting this lot back to England. How the hell were they going to do that? He walked back into the sunshine and sat down with the girls again. They were now silent.

"What the fuck are we going to do with that lot Frank?" asked Josie in her usual eloquent manner.

"Listen, I'll tell you what I think. When we get back, if we get back, and tell everyone about this place it will be inundated with treasure hunters within day's, Governments and looters all trying to get in on the action. We have the key. No one can get in without these keys. That means we do have some control over this situation. I suggest that we somehow get the gold from the plane up here and lock it in with the rest.

Then, when we get back we negotiate with whomever until we get the deal we want. We have to stick together on this one. I sincerely believe that they will try to split us up and turn each against the other. But if we stick to our guns maybe we will get something out of all this." He waved his hand at the open door. "What do you say?"

The girls looked at each other and then at Frank.

"I can't believe what we have here. This is all just like a dream. I trust you, Frank," said Josie. "I have only known you for a few days but I trust you. What about you, Liz?"

Liz looked at Frank. "I didn't like you when I first met you Frank. I thought you were a cocky little shit. But I was wrong. I like you and I trust you as well. You're quite right of course, the human misery that lays behind all that stuff in there is beyond our comprehension. If we start to think about it ..." She stopped talking and they all stood looking at each other. "I'm with you Frank, we do what you suggest."

"OK. No one is rushing to get us out of here so I think the next thing we do is make the call. Then we can set about getting the other gold up here and shutting the place up again. It's time to get your mobile out, Josie."

Josie stood up, took her mobile phone out of Frank's pack and switched it on.

"No signal, Frank, " she said.

"We will have to climb higher then," he said.

They climbed another hundred steps up the side of the pyramid until they came to another small flat area. There was another door there too.

We shouldn't actually have to do this with your type of phone Josie so what's your signal now, Josie?"

"I still don't have one," she said her voice croaking.

Frank took the phone from her and switched it off and then on again, it was showing that the battery was half charged.

"What the hell is wrong with it Frank? It was working OK on the plane."

"I don't know." Frank said quietly. "It's just not picking up the satellite signal. Let's go back to the plane.

They went back down to the next layer. Frank walked over to the door of the pyramid and inserted the key again. The great stone door slid back into place with a "whoosh" and he wondered how that operated.

Their mood had now changed and they walked down the steps and through the long amber coloured grass back to their plane in silence each deep in their own thoughts.

Frank thought that there was no reason for the phone not to work and decided that perhaps Sandy and her people had decided to keep them here for a while. That was a bit ominous if they had decided that but it was out of his control. Best make the most of the situation until something positive happened but how to keep the girls spirits up was going to be the problem.

"Listen, I really don't feel that good and could do with some serious shut eye. It's not like me but it's probably a reaction to all that's been going on so if it's all right with you I'm going to have a quick shower over there and then get my head down."

"The girls looked at him with concern. "We'll have a cup of tea ready for you when you come back Frank." Josie said.

They watched him walk off to the waterfall and talked over the day. The both knew that their lives depended on Frank without a doubt and although they wanted to get on and get things sorted they obviously had to fall in line with what Frank wanted to do.

In the meantime Frank stood naked underneath the waterfall and thought long and hard about his day. In reality he didn't know what to make of his experiences. He definitely felt strange in himself and this blasted headache was unusual to say the least but as to the rest, was it possible that the human race was being observed on the quiet by beings from another planet and why anyway? He hadn't asked that question and kicked himself for not doing so. Christ, if this was true and the world found out then total chaos would reign. Everyone would panic, markets would crash and goodness knows what would happen. Maybe some governments in the world, the USA for instance do know about this and aren't saying. It was all a bit of a responsibility but then again was it? He simply had to get on with his life and leave it at that and if his body clock had been tinkered with then great. He didn't have a problem with that.

He looked around him and over to where there was a large rock on the edge of the small pool. "Let's see how strong I am then." He thought. Under normal circumstances there would be no way he would attempt to lift this rock at his age. Ten years ago, but not now. He squatted down and clasped his hands around the rock, bent his legs, straightened his back and lifted. The rock came out with a rush and he stood up holding it tight to him. "Christ, I can do it after all." He thought and carefully dropped it back in the water. He looked at it for a moment and lifted it again. Once more it didn't feel that heavy although his brain told him it was. He lifted it higher and threw it. It landed ten feet away from him and he laughed out loud. "Christ, that's amazing." No way on earth had he ever been able to do that at any age.

He went back under the cascading water for a while and then walked back into the warm sunshine and dried off. So, he was stronger then and therefore things must have happened to him. That's why he felt a bit strange. He began to walk back to the plane and bent down to pick up another small rock about the size of his fist. He turned and threw it at the fir tree that stood by the lake about sixty feet back. With unerring accuracy the rock struck the trunk of the tree with a loud 'thwack'. Frank smiled to himself with a childish glee. He had always wanted to be able to throw things like that and even at forty-seven it gave him a great feeling. "Small things please small minds" he thought.

Arriving back at the camp he squatted down and drank the welcome tea the girls had made for him; and then excusing himself he climbed into the plane and, taking off his boots, fell asleep on the bed, exhausted.

* * *

He awoke to the smell of cooking. He looked around him and smelt the girls and the early morning, He rolled over and put his boots on and climbed back out of the plane.

Josie was by the fire with a pan of beans bubbling and he could see Liz coming back from the lake.

"Morning dozy head" cried Josie. "Man can you sleep, do you realise you have been asleep for almost sixteen hours."

Frank looked at her in amazement, "You're kidding, sixteen hours, never." He looked at his watch, she was right, it was now almost 9am and he had gone to bed about four in the afternoon yesterday.

"Morning Frank" called Liz; Frank smiled at her and asked if he could have some of the beans. He was feeling very hungry and his headache had gone. In fact he felt good.

The girls looked hard at him and Josie smiled. "Well it must have done you good old man because you are looking great, in fact you're looking amazing for your age."

Frank admitted to feeling good and asked what they had been doing.

They chatted happily for a while and he asked if they had heard any planes but they said they hadn't.

"In that case let's try your phone again Josie." She passed him the phone and he switched it on, immediately a signal appeared and the girls, who were peering over his shoulder shouted with glee.

"That's it then, I'll do a number recall and see if we can raise that friend of yours Josie." The phone rang for a while and then a man answered it.

"Hello, Jack, it's Frank Blake here, Josie's friend." There was a loud exclamation and Jack started to shout questions until Frank had to tell him to stop. "Jack, no questions now but we are O.K, that's all you need to know short term. You have to get this right first time because we haven't much battery strength. Are you able to take this call OK now? Right. Tell the search people the following." Frank explained what had happened on the plane and the time involved. "They will have to widen their search pattern because we have not heard a single plane," he said. "We are in a deep valley with a pyramid at one end. Tell them we have flares and we will send one up every few minutes when we hear a plane. Tell everyone we are all well. I'm going to have to switch off now, because I want to conserve the battery. Tell them not to give up because we are OK for the moment. If they need to contact us, you have the number. We will switch back on in an hour for five minutes OK? Cheers for now."

Frank switched off the mobile and looked at the girls.

"That guy is going to be one hell of a frustrated person but I had to conserve the battery. We have a chance, ladies. We are going to get out of here." Josie did a little jig on the spot grinning all the while at the other two.

"Christ mates, I'll soon be back with me husband and a long hot bath and cold wine and loads of sex." She flopped to the ground panting with her long legs thrust out in front of her. In her head Josie was already home.

Frank laughed and they chatted on speculating as to the effect that phone call would be having on their friends and loved ones.

They were all gently dozing in the heat when Frank awoke with a start. Someone had just shouted his name out loud but the two girls were still dozing. He was sure that someone had just shouted "Frank" very loudly but decided that he must have dreamed it. Looking at his watch he realised it was just a little over the hour.

"Josie, wake up and switch on your phone. Here, give it to me," he said.

He grabbed it from Josie, saying sorry at the same time, and switched it on. Almost immediately it rang.

"Hello," he said.

"Is that Frank Blake?" said a voice.

"Yes," he said.

"Right. Listen to me Frank. This is the American Ambassador to South America speaking. We are all very concerned about the three of you and are doing our best to co-ordinate things this end to find you quickly. I have General Rodriguez Lomax here who is in charge of the search. He will ask you a few quick questions in an endeavour to speed things up."

"Mr Blake. This is General Lomax. We know your original heading. When the pilot died, did the plane swing left or right? Please try to remember, this is very important."

"It definitely swung to the right, General," Frank said. "How far right I can't remember but once I regained control I brought it onto a level heading and maintained that heading as best I could. You already know for how long. I would estimate that we are about two hundred and fifty to three hundred miles off our original course. That's only a guess of course."

"Have you any fuel at all?" asked the General.

"No, we landed with the engines dead."

"Did you use your reserve tanks?" he asked.

Frank went silent for a second. "Reserve tanks? We have reserve tanks?"

"Of course you have reserve tanks. You will have about an hours flying with them." He explained where the switches were. "Can you fly the plane?" he asked.

"I am not a qualified pilot if that's what you are asking, but I have done some hours with a glider, and I could probably take off," Frank said his brain still in a turmoil about the reserve tanks. He then remembered something from the flight plan of the dead German pilot but decided to hold his tongue.

"General, we have found some fuel which is obviously very old. I can't go into detail but would it work if mixed with the reserve tanks?"

"You have found some fuel. How did you do that?" said the General. "Well, anyway, yes, it probably would but it would be pretty poor quality but O.K. if it had been sealed in an air proof container or tanks. Do you intend to fly out because if you do, let us know and we will pick you up on radar and guide you into another airport with our fighters?

Frank looked at the girls and repeated what the General had said.

"Give me your number, General, we will phone you tomorrow at this time and let you know our decision," he said. "Battery is getting very low. Talk to you then," He took the number and switched off.

"Why didn't you tell them where we are?" said Liz eyes blazing. "If you had done that, they would have been here within a couple of hours and we would be home for tea. What are you playing at Frank?"

"I was thinking of the gold," he said. "If they find us now, they find the gold. If they find that everything here goes out the window. We will be the losers. Let's go back to our plane and talk this through. If you want I can easily phone them tomorrow and tell them to come and get us. It's that easy, now you know that."

Liz came over and sat down in front of him looking him straight in the eyes. "What is it you want to do, Frank?"

"OK," he said. "First I want to say that I feel a real fool. If I had been thinking clearly I would have realised that the plane had reserve tanks. I'm a complete bloody idiot. I don't know where we would have ended up if I had switched over the tanks, maybe we would have crashed anyway. Who knows but I do feel a bit of a fool. Sorry about that." The two girls said nothing and Josie just shrugged her shoulders. "Anyway, look, I'm going to be brutally honest. You two girls are millionaires in your own right. Because of your beauty you are able to demand enormous sums of money when modelling and acting. I am at a later stage in life and for one reason or another I have no money, well not much anyway. I see this as an opportunity to provide myself with enough to have a comfortable retirement if I need one. You wouldn't do too badly either. If we let them fly in here I reckon you can say goodbye to any really good money and we could well end up with a pittance as a finders fee. If we fly out ourselves with a couple of gold bars, show the media and pump it all up, the three of us would make millions. Think of the situation for a minute. I'm making this up as I go along but think about it. We fly out ourselves and get guided to an airport within our flying range. The media will be waiting for us. The coverage will be fantastic and will go all over the world. Two famous models survive terrifying ordeal and find a German Second World War treasure trove. What a story. We could syndicate it and maybe have it made into a film. That's the dream and this time it would be a true story. You could see the headlines. Your personal reputations will go up to an incredible high. I must admit mine would as well. Then again, mine would be starting from zero anyway. The alternative is to let them come and get us tomorrow. Some of what I have said would still happen but think of the effect we would have if we flew back ourselves. Just think about it."

Both of the girls had listened to him in silence.

Liz said. "All that's very well, Frank, but we could crash on take off or landing. You admit that you can hardly fly. I vote for getting picked up. That's the surest way of getting back."

"I hear what you say Liz and it does make sense. But it's not the dramatic way, it's not the exciting way, it's not the 'living life to the full way'. My God, can you see their faces if we flew back ourselves? The whole world would be at our feet. We could feed them such a story that hasn't been heard for years and will never be heard again. Nobody would ever forget the day that Josie Sales, Liz Hunt and Frank Blake flew back from the dead with GOLD bars on board as well as treasure. Can you imagine the media's faces when we show them the gold bars? Can you imagine it? We would dine off this story for the rest of our lives." Frank had got carried away but he meant every word.

There was a silence for a moment, and then Josie said. "Yeah, Frank's absolutely right Liz. I vote we fly back ourselves. Let's do it, this could be the biggest thing that we ever did or will ever do Liz."

Liz looked at both of them. Frank and Josie had flushed cheeks and their eyes were bright. There was another silence for about ten seconds as they all looked from one to another.

"All for one and one for all," she said quietly.

Frank and Josie whooped and both jumped on Liz rolling her on the ground, reducing them to hilarious laughter.

Frank sat up. "Right, this evening we start to get those boxes of gold up to that storeroom. We retrieve the other key and bring back down the skeleton on the pyramid and put it near the crashed plane. We tidy up so that nobody knows where we have been. In the morning we start to transfer the fuel to this plane. When we have finished we will tell them that we are about to take off. We will then be in God's hands, ladies."

Taking some rope from the plane they later set off for the crash site. Roping three boxes together all three set off for the pyramid. When they reached it they set about climbing and hauling the boxes up to the first level. Once there they operated the door again and slid the boxes in. By the time they had been back and forth three times the girls were worn out and exhausted. Frank felt fine and smiled to himself at the change in his fitness. They kept three bars back to take on the plane and completed the task of transferring all the gold.

Soaked in perspiration they carried the skeleton back down to the crash site and laid it on the ground near the cockpit. Breaking some brush they swept the pyramid steps until it looked as though nobody had passed that way for years. They carefully did the same around the crash site. By this time it was very late and the light was failing.

Totally exhausted, they walked slowly back to their plane again. They fortified themselves with more tinned food and tea and then bathed themselves in the cold water of the waterfall. Once refreshed they found their way back to the plane and sat and talked for a while before climbing inside again to go to bed. Frank climbed into the pilot's seat and looked at the controls, familiarising himself with them and going through the starting procedure in his head memorising the throttle controls. He got up and looked down the valley at the pyramid the other end.

"As soon as I get up enough speed I have to get her up and climbing at full boost," he thought and at the same time retract the undercarriage. The less drag the better."

He checked the transfer fuel switches from the reserve tanks and wondered why he had not noticed them before. "I'm no bloody pilot, that's why not," he thought. Taking off his boots he climbed into the sleeping bags with the two girls.

"We have to get as much fuel as we can in the morning. Early start ladies. I want to be up at six and I want the two of you up as well. We will operate a shuttle system for the fuel. I will show all that to you in the morning. Good night ladies."

The girls said goodnight and he felt Josie cuddle up to him behind whereas Liz turned on her side and wiggled her bottom into his lap. "Yeah," he thought, "this will be some story all right."

He was woken at four in the morning by the sound of rain. He had not experienced rain in the jungle for over two weeks and now it rained and rained hard. He shook the girls awake.

"What's the matter?" slurred Josie.

"Listen to that," said Frank. "If it carries on like that you can forget about taking off today or being rescued if it comes to that. Nothing's going to fly in that rain, what a bummer." He was very disappointed.

Josie grunted and rolled over. "We can have a bit more sleep then can't we Frank " she asked and was instantly asleep again.

Frank lay awake thinking. He thought of his children who by now must be very worried indeed. They would have heard that he was missing, and know that he had been heard of again but no one would know exactly where. Because of the international reputation of the two girls what had happened to them was probably running on all the major television news programs round the world. Christ, that would mean millions of people would know what was happening and speculating. He thought that the newspapers would be having a ball. And what about his business? How was that standing up to the fact that he still had not come back? "They will just have to cope somehow until I return," he thought. "If I can get some money for these diamonds then the problems in that respect will be over." He felt some guilt about not telling the girls of the diamonds. His mind returned to the problem of getting the diamonds out as he drifted back into sleep. He woke up again later with the two girls snoring gently and the rain still pounding down. It was remarkably snug in the plane and he loved the sound of the rain beating down. He moved onto his side and looked straight into the open eyes of Liz just three inches away.

"Thought you were asleep," he said.

"I was thank you very much," she said quietly. "It must have been you moving which woke me. What's the time anyway?"

"I think it's around 9.30am but it really doesn't matter because we aren't going anywhere. We might just as well stay in bed because there's nowhere else we can go, not if we are going to stay dry. So, are you going to tell me your life story, Liz?"

She yawned and stretched herself, like a cat. "I'm single, 26, black and considered to be very beautiful and very good at what I do i.e. modelling. Acting I'm not so sure about. I'm also rich and a lesbian, anything else you want to know?" she said arching her eyebrows.

"She tries to come over all hard but she is just a pussy cat really," he thought.

Frank stepped right out of character and the words just popped out of his mouth before he could stop them. "No chance of a fuck then?" he said, grinning. Despite herself, Liz burst out laughing, her voice taking on a deep timbre, low and happy.

"For God's sake Frank, grow up," she said but he knew she had found what he said to be funny.

There was a nudge in his ribs. "You never ask me that," said Josie in a voice thick with sleep.

"Too afraid of what you might say, anyway you're a married lady," he answered and they all laughed.

"That I am," she replied, "That I am. He must be very worried about me."

"I was just thinking the same about my kids," Frank said.

"I know your wife left you, Frank, but have you got anyone else in your life yet?" It was a typical Josie question. He was beginning to understand how she ticked.

"Yes and no really," he replied. "Several possibilities, but no one to really take my breath away as yet. I must admit it would be nice to be in a loving relationship again, and a steady routine. I'll look into that when I get back." Breaking the mood he said, "Anyone fancy some tea 'cause I do?" He slid out of the bed, lit the small gas ring and put on the saucepan of water. There wasn't a lot of room in which to move so he opened a window in the cockpit for some fresh air.

"As soon as it stops raining we get the fuel and then throw everything out of here except for some food and water. This plane has got to be super light on take off."

"What, all my clothes?" said Liz. "Yes, if you want us to get home," he said.

The two girls lay in the bedding chatting to each other while Frank busied himself with making the tea. "No food unless you want cold baked beans or cold corn beef. That's the choice, I'm afraid." Both girls shuddered and simply asked for tea.

The rain poured down for the rest of the day and evening but stopped around midnight. They passed the time sleeping, talking and singing songs to each other. By the end of the day the place began to smell a little and Frank had to wedge open the door to let in some fresh air. The night passed in fitful sleep for all three of them.

The next morning arrived bright and beautiful and they all woke early. By six they were out of the plane and washing. They then had some breakfast and started the re-fuelling of the plane. Frank managed to use a metal tube from the German bomber as a pipe. He sucked until the fuel started to run and poured it into the old fuel cans that had been cleaned out. He had also made a funnel for the girls to use when pouring the fuel into their plane. Liz volunteered a pair of her tights, unused, as a filter for the old fuel.

He showed them how to carry the cans by sliding a strong branch through the handles so that they could both carry them together. By ten o'clock the girls were exhausted and pleaded for a rest.

"Please can we have a break, Frank?" they pleaded. "We are getting dizzy going back and forth. How much longer do we have to do this?"

"Until we can't draw any more fuel out. Liz, you're practical. I'll take over and you pour the fuel. I'll show you how."

"Frank, shouldn't we contact that General and tell him our progress?" asked Josie.

"I've been thinking about that," he said. "They will be waiting for our call. I think it's safe to assume that we are going to take longer than we thought to get all this fuel out and that it will take the rest of today at this rate. I'll go and phone him in a minute to say, barring accidents and rain, we will attempt take off in the morning at around 9am. That will give the grass and ground some time to dry out. I'll make sure we both have the same time. If we are successful in getting out of here and we climb to 8,000ft they should pick us up on their military radar as soon as we pass 5,000ft. I have my own compass in my backpack and also the manual one the pilot had. They are both correct to each other within a few degrees. I checked that the other day. I know roughly the heading we should be on from that German map and then it's plain sailing."

As the girls continued the gruelling job of re-fuelling, Frank climbed the pyramid and made the call.

Within three rings a man's voice answered the call.

"It's Frank Blake," he said.

"Wait one," said the voice "I'll get the General"

Within a few seconds the General came on the line. "I was about to re-launch the search for you Frank," he said. "What's been happening?"

"It rained all day yesterday and we couldn't do anything," he replied. "We are re-fuelling now which will take all day. I intend to attempt take off in the morning at 9am. What do you make the time?" They synchronised watches. "I will climb on a heading of 12 degrees to 8,000ft, God willing, and await your fighter escort."

"I have all that. Will you contact us by your phone in the morning when you are up?" he asked. Frank looked at the battery state of the phone. It was very low. "I might have enough battery for a thirty-second call and that's it," he replied.

"One last thing" the General said. "I have been talking to the experts about this fuel. We feel that it will be of a very poor quality but being mixed with new fuel should almost balance things out. After you start the engines check your engine gauges to ensure that they are warmed up. Apply full brake and then give the plane full throttle. You are taking off on grass and will need all the speed you can get. When your engines reach two thousand revs let go the brakes. You must have your flaps in the take off settings. When you reach 90mph pull back on the stick gently. Keep the throttles wide open on rich mixture and get your undercarriage up. After a few minutes you can ease back on the mixture settings to normal. Have you got all that?"

Frank's brain was racing. "Yes, anyway I have to go. Hopefully I will call you in the morning. If you don't hear from us you'll know something has gone wrong. Then you can send the search planes. Send them on a heading of 270 degrees. I estimate we are about 280 miles down that heading, out."

He switched off the mobile and scrambled back down the pyramid and then ran over to the crash site. The girls were still re-fuelling.

They worked until sunset. "Let's pack it in now," said Frank. "We've run out of time. If we haven't got enough fuel now it's too bad." They were covered in sweat, dirt and fuel. Deciding to clean up they walked over to the waterfall and stripped off together and scrubbed themselves clean.

"Hey, you girls don't look too bad in the nude," Frank said.

"Well, you could do with losing some weight old man," replied Liz. Josie laughed. "He's not so old that I wouldn't say no to," she said.

"Listen, children. You're both only just older than my daughter so stop misbehaving or I'll give your backsides a tanning," he said.

"No, no, no Frank. That would take a man," said Liz. Then, seeing the look in Frank's eyes, she screamed and scooping up her clothes started to run back to the plane with Frank in hot pursuit.

"I'll give you such a tanning the likes of which you wouldn't have had since you were a kid," he shouted. She was fast and he could have easily caught her but just kept behind her and she was laughing. When they got to the plane she stopped and turned, completely naked in the low light and threw her head back laughing with excitement.

"OK, so you're faster than me," he gasped.

He looked around. "Where is Josie?" he asked. There was a scream from the direction of the waterfall and the sound of running feet. Frank grabbed his rifle, slamming a round up the breach and knocking off the safety catch as he did so. Both Frank and Liz were naked. Frank started to run towards the waterfall shouting Josie's name. She screamed back in reply. "Help me, Frank, help me!"

He could see her now. She was running fast towards him along the track they had made through the grass. Behind her he could see dark shapes closing in on her. She looked back and screamed again but kept running. Christ she was moving. Frank stopped. Dropping to one knee and taking aim, he fired at the fast moving shapes and saw one fall. Before he had time to slide the bolt and push another round up the spout, the others veered off and disappeared into the darkness. Josie rocketed past him and jumped straight into the plane. Liz followed immediately. Frank slowly eased himself back to the plane keeping a hard watch out. Nothing moved. He climbed back into the plane, closed the door and started to put his clothes on.

"What the hell was that all about?" he asked Josie.

She was lying on the floor gasping for air and sobbing with fear, with Liz bending over her. Josie was only partially clothed but had managed to put her shorts on, her shirt was badly torn.

"I don't know, Frank," she said. "One minute you two had taken off and I was just starting to put my clothes back on when I smelt something. I turned around and there they were right behind me, just standing looking. I couldn't see their faces because of the hoods they were wearing and they were a bit small and smelt horrible. As soon as I screamed one tried to grab me but I managed to tear my shirt away from him, or it, and I took off. I can't tell you the relief I felt when I saw you Frank. I saw the flash of your gun but never heard a thing. One of those things was right alongside me. They appeared to be able to run faster than me, no that's not right, they seemed to float, anyway, I heard him cough and he went down, brilliant shooting, Frank."

Liz was quickly getting dressed. "Who are they, Frank?" she asked.

He had a pretty good idea who they were but wasn't saying. "Look, ladies, I don't know diddly squat about these things. All I know is what I saw. And I did hit one. Whatever it was, neither of you is going out there tomorrow until we are good and ready to leave. Liz, do you know how to handle a gun?"

"I've fired a shotgun, Frank, but that's all."

"OK. I'm going outside to have a look around. Liz, here is the rifle. All you have to do is point and pull the trigger. You have three shots left. Keep your finger off the trigger until you get serious." Frank pulled on his shirt and shorts and slipped on the holster for the pistol. He slipped out the magazine and checked the 9mm rounds. He then slid his machete into its scabbard and checked the gun's safety catch. "I'm going to be out there for about fifteen minutes. If anything tries to get in, with me not here, wait until you see whoever they are and then fire. Shut the door behind me."

The girls looked at him in alarm.

"You're not going out there, Frank, are you?" said Josie.

"I need to know what the situation is. I want to see the one I knocked down" he replied.

Liz pulled him around so that he faced her. She was only twenty-eight years old but her face was set and very serious. "Frank, please be careful, I'm not being melodramatic but, if anything happens to you what will we do?"

"Thanks, Liz. If anything happens to me, you get straight up that pyramid in the morning whatever happens and phone the General and tell him to come and get you all right? Now shut the door behind me."

He kissed the two girls and before they could stop him, dropped out of the side door into the blackness. He heard the door shut behind him. He squatted on the ground for a few minutes letting his eyes become used to the dusk.

"Just like the old day's," he thought. Frank had served seven years in the RAF Regiment as a regular airman, rising to Sergeant, like his father before him. During the last four of those years he had operated within a small unit of twelve specially selected men, integrating with other Special Forces of Her Majesty's Government in various theatres of the world. He had never had to kill anyone face to face, instead he had discovered that he had an aptitude for long distance shooting and had specialised as a sniper. Killing someone at long distance anaesthetised the horror of killing as far as he was concerned. He felt nothing when doing that. Killing someone up close however was a totally different matter. That would be difficult for him. He had been taught how to look after himself in a fire fight and how to shoot. He was a very good shot, a complete natural with any type of gun.

He moved quickly out of the light coming from the plane and into the darkness with all his old training coming back as though he had never been away. He was just twenty odd years older that's all. He went fifty paces and then went down onto his stomach laying still, listening. He was already breathing hard. He wasn't used to running bent over double.

In fact he wasn't used to running full stop but still felt good. Nothing moved. Although it was now dark he found he could see quite well. "Well, well." He thought.

"Those things, whatever they are, are from the bloody pyramid I'll bet a pound to a penny but what the hell are they playing at? And they moved without making any sound," he thought. "And they could move fast. Josie wasn't hanging around and they were able to keep up with her quite easily. Which means, they can come at me without a sound, and very quickly if they want to. Better keep the old peepers open, my son. Mother, wherever you are, I need some help down here now," he prayed.

Getting to his feet he moved towards the sound of the waterfall. He swept the area bending low and jogging quickly. It was a killer running like that and he stopped twice to get his breath back. "If they are around they must be busting their sides laughing at me running around gasping like this," he thought.

After he had covered the whole area from their plane to the waterfall he had nothing to report and there was no dead body.

"I know I hit one," he thought. "But where the hell is it?"

He rested for a bit in the rocks by the falls. It was almost pitch black when the clouds hid the full moon but occasionally it would break through the cloud and the valley would light up. He sat and waited for this to happen. When it did he scanned the whole area. There was nothing. He put the Walther P-38 pistol back in its holster and pulled out his machete. He waited for the moon to come out again. There was still nothing to be seen.

"With all this bloody grass, I'll never see them," he thought. He moved away from the rocks and looking around him walked slowly back towards the plane; all the while swinging the machete gently back and forth. That weapon gave him immense comfort. It was beautifully balanced and razor sharp. "The perfect weapon for a situation such as this," he thought. The feeling of being watched was as strong as ever and goose bumps went up and down his arms, and ran up his neck into his hair. That used to happen too.

Sandy's voice whispered in his head. "Sorry about that Frank, some of our helpers here became curious. It won't happen again." Frank didn't acknowledge her voice and just grunted. Life was just getting trickier but he wouldn't say anything to the girls, they would think him completely loopy. He got to the plane, and knocking on the door, called out. "It's OK it's me, Frank. Let me in."

The door opened six inches and all he could see was one of Josie's eyes. "Come on stop messing about Josie," he said. "Let me in." She swung back the plane door and he jumped in. She banged it shut behind him.

"Well?" said Josie looking at him with wide staring eyes.

"Nothing," he said taking off his kit and knife belt, "Whoever or whatever they were, they have gone. I need a cup of tea. You haven't thrown out the little cooker, Liz, have you?"

"You're amazing Frank Blake," she said. "We are probably about to die and all you can think of is a cup of tea. OK. I'll make you one and I'll have a bloody cup of tea as well. What about you Josie?" She nodded her head.

While Liz busied herself doing this they talked over the situation.

"I'll stand guard tonight for two hours and then each of you do the same so that at least we get some sleep. We are going to need it. This plane is ready to rock and roll I hope, so, first thing in the morning come seven o'clock I fire up these damn engines and we get the hell out of here."

They drank their tea, relishing the warmth that it gave them and then the girls settled down for the night talking quietly to each other until they fell asleep. Frank moved into the cockpit and sat looking at the controls thinking of the morning and what he had to do. He went through the sequences as best he could.

"If I have ever needed you, Mother, it's now," he said aloud to himself. "You got us in here safely. Please help us to get out. Just put your hand under the plane and lift her out of this damn valley."

Despite his age it still comforted him to talk to his mother. He chuckled to himself at what people would think if they found that he did this. The instances of men praying to their mothers in times of extreme stress and danger are well documented. He sat thinking of his family, his brothers and sisters and his children.

"I wonder what they are thinking about all this mess?" he thought. "They're probably worried sick, and wondering if they will ever see me again." An indescribable feeling came over him. It started at the top of his head and rolled down through his body. He shivered and smiled to himself as he looked out through the windows into the darkness. He felt safe and strong and that something, or someone, was looking out for him.

He lifted his rucksack onto his lap and pulled out the key studying it. It was the weirdest shape and yet very light being the size of a small spoon. It could easily be carried around the neck as one of the dead Germans had. That was the strangest thing. What story lay behind those guys and their efforts to get out of Nazi Germany as the war was ending? What sort of story could be told about that? Intriguing stuff.

Before he realised it, his shift was up and Liz took over. They talked for a short time and then he settled down next to Josie. He put an arm around her; she said something in her sleep and moved against him. In his usual way, he was asleep in seconds.

Josie was shaking him awake. "It's six o'clock, Frank, come on wake up dozy head." He shook himself. "What happened?" he asked. "You were supposed to wake me for my shift at 3am."

"We decided to let you sleep as you have to fly us out of here. Anyway the night was quiet and nothing happened so get your butt into this flying seat mister and let's go," she said. Her face was set and serious.

He stretched and slowly climbed out of bed. Looking out of the cockpit windows he could see the suns rays just starting to come down the valley. The sun was rising fast and mist covered the valley floor.

"I can't take off until the sun burns this mist off so there's time for a cup of tea." He grinned at Josie but she just shook her head in exasperation "Also, I want to wipe my face over and dump everything out of this plane that's not necessary. So I will do that if you girls get the tea on."

"What about the call to the General?" asked Liz?

"Oh Christ, I forgot all about that," said Frank. "Josie, give me your phone.

Josie gave him the phone and told him just to do a number recall.

He opened the door, stuck his head out and looked around slipping on his holstered pistol and his machete as he did so. All was quiet so he set off at a sharp trot. There was a surreal feel about the valley with the tail fin of the crashed Heinkel sticking up out of the mist, which lay across the valley floor in front of him. Arriving at the base of the pyramid, he began his slow climb up the steps; he sat down and did a number recall as suggested by Josie.

A female voice answered almost immediately. Frank told her who he was which she already seemed to know. He explained that he had no battery left and asked her to tell the General that they were about to take off at least an hour earlier than scheduled. He made her repeat the message and then rang off.

When he arrived back at the plane, he found that the girls had begun to unload everything that wasn't essential, piling it all into a heap about fifty yards away from their take-off track. When they had finished, they helped him put only one of the pair of seats back in the plane. They wouldn't need two.

"Just carry what you need," he thought for a minute. "That's strange, that's almost exactly what our pilot said to you two before he took off." They stopped what they were doing and walked over to where they had buried him.

"No doubt someone will come back for you chum and, with any luck, very soon," Frank said over the grave.

"I'm going to start the engines and run her down to the end of the valley over there." He pointed to the cliff at the end of the valley. "I'll turn her round there and I will then have the full length of the valley to get up." They looked down the misty valley to the vast monolith at the end just over a mile away. The valley was really a dogleg with the pyramid at the bend. The remainder of the dogleg rose rapidly to normal ground level.

They walked back to the plane and warmed themselves with tea. Frank was hungry and settled for toast and beans. The girls simply had toast. The mist had almost cleared by the time they had tidied up and cleared everything away. The sun was well up and felt warm. It was going to be another hot day. It was a good time to take off. The cool air would give the engines more power. Frank looked around him, making sure that they had not left anything on the ground that might get in their way as they took off.

He was the last into the plane. Josie had settled herself into the co-pilot's seat without comment and Liz had already strapped herself into her seat. Frank poked about and ensured the three gold bars were tied down together with his rifle and rucksack. The diamonds were carefully tucked up safely inside. He climbed into the pilot's seat.

7

"ARE YOU LADIES READY?" he asked.

"I've got butterflies in my tummy," said Josie looking out of the cockpit window.

"Is it bad luck to wish everyone good luck?" asked Liz. No one answered.

Frank looked at the instrument panel. "When I say raise the undercarriage Josie, that's the lever I want you to pull and you're to pull it instantly is that OK?

"Yes, Frank," she said.

"Also, I want you to read off our speed from that dial there every ten miles an hour until we are airborne OK?

"Yes Frank" she answered.

Frank glanced at her. She was as white as a sheet and looked how he felt.

He turned the ignition switches on and heard the electric pumps priming the engines. He waited for the ticking to stop. He turned on the rich mixture, set the throttle open a quarter and fired the port engine. It whined over slowly, caught and burst into life with a roar that startled everyone. It quickly settled into a steady beat. He did the same with the starboard engine, which duplicated the first. He let the engines run until their gauges showed a steady temperature and then gently opened the throttles. The plane slowly heaved into action and quickly built up speed so that Frank had to throttle back a little. They trundled down the three hundred yards to the end of the valley and he turned the plane with the brakes until they were lined up for take off straight down the valley.

"Yeah," said Josie in a broad Australian accent. "It's as though you have been doing it your entire life mate."

Frank smiled. He felt anything but confident.

"OK. Here goes nothing. Let's go home." With his feet pushing and holding the plane on its brakes, he opened the throttles full. The engines roared to a howl and the plane lurched, like a dog on a lead, wanting to go. He gradually released the brakes and the plane shot forward accelerating with the speed of a motorbike. "Ground speed, Josie?" he cried. He fought to keep the plane level because of the un-even surface of the valley floor.

"Christ, everything's happening a bit quick," he thought. " 40, 50, 60, 70."

"I'll hold her down until 100," he thought pushing hard forward on the stick; he could feel the plane beginning to come alive. "80, 90 100, 110," Josie screamed. He eased slowly back on the yoke and the plane leapt into the air. All he could see was the great monolith speeding towards him at frightening speed.

"Gear up, Josie," he shouted "Gear up!" Out of the corner of his eye he saw her lean forward and pull the lever. The plane was rising and climbing with the speed of a fast lift.

"Come on, baby climb!" he cried. "Mustn't stall," he thought, "keep her rising nice and steadily." He pushed harder on the throttles to ensure they were fully open and almost casually moved the yoke to the right so that they would miss the pyramid. He instinctively knew that they would miss it now. They were already higher than the top. He was still climbing hard when he heeled the plane gently onto its left wing tip to follow the valley, as they climbed over the top of the pyramid.

"Look at that Frank." Josie said quietly.

He glanced quickly over her shoulder and for a brief second saw it. The top of the pyramid was open.

He blanked it from his mind concentrating on keeping the plane climbing steadily. The engines sounded rough when he realised he was still on rich mixture and he quickly leaned forward and flicked the two switches back to normal. The engines settled into a much happier note and he watched the speedometer settle on a steady 150 knots. "That's good enough for me," he thought. "Just keep climbing at that speed baby."

"We're out of trouble, ladies. Josie, please pass the compass that's in my top shirt pocket. Hold it nice and steady away from the instrument panel and give me a reading."

"Thank Christ for that," he heard Liz say from the back. "Bloody unbelievable. What a buzz that was. Hey, what was that all about back there as we came over the pyramid?"

Josie, concentrating on the compass, told her what they had seen.

Liz went quiet. "What does that mean then?" she said eventually.

"We don't know and frankly we haven't got time to think about it right now. What's our heading Josie?"

"320 degrees, Frank."

"I'm going to turn to our right slowly. Shout when we get to 30 degrees, OK?" He started the slow turn, at the same time continuing to climb.

"You're coming up to 25, 27, 30 degrees," she shouted. He straightened the plane on the new heading, checking on the horizon indicator which was one of the few instruments still working. He pulled the throttles slowly back to three quarters and levelled out the climb a little. The plane settled back to 130 knots.

"We're now at 2,500ft," he said to them. "I imagine that they might pick us up at around 5,000 to 7,000 ft. We will have to wait and see what happens then." He patted the instrument panel. "Well done my beauty. Josie, any power left in that mobile of yours?"

Josie pulled the phone out of her pocket and switched it on. "Nothing Frank, absolutely nothing, it's dead," she said.

* * *

The General was standing in the control room with his President and three Ambassadors. The English, the American and the Australian Governments were all represented as well as senior Army officers, Josie's husband and senior press editors. This was a very important moment and the attention of the world was on these men in this room. The attention of the international press was overwhelming especially now that they knew that Josie, Liz and Frank were trying to make it back on their own and that they were very much alive after all. The story had grabbed everyone's imagination and the excitement waiting for the next contact was immense.

"As you can see gentlemen, we are scanning the skies for them now. It is still early and I don't expect to see them for half an hour so, perhaps we should go and meet the press for ten minutes and bring them up to date with what is happening," said the General.

Ever since the word had gone out that the three were alive, the world's media had gone berserk. Two of the world's most beautiful and well-known women were not dead after all. Speculation had been enormous and the pressure to find them immense. The General had played a very clever game with both diplomats and the media in fending off their recommendations by saying that it was the request of the three that they try to make it back on their own. He was laying his future on the line. If anything happened, and he felt that it probably would, his career was finished. At the same time he had felt an affinity with the man Frank Blake. He would have wanted to do the same in his place. Fame and glory was there for the taking for a brave and resolute man. He felt thrilled to be part of the scene. He was also very worried.

They walked into the room reserved for the press and the place erupted. He sat down with his President and the three Ambassadors and called for silence.

In front of the hushed throng, nearly 150 strong from all over the world, and whirring television cameras he said. "Ladies and gentlemen, at this point in time I can only tell you this. Frank Blake, who as you know is with Josie and Liz, has told me that they were going to attempt to fly out from wherever they are. That they now had enough fuel, and don't ask me where they got any because I don't know, and that they were going to give it a go. The ladies by the way also confirmed that they wanted to do it this way. We had offered to send in the helicopters but they refused. Frank Blake said that they would take off at around nine o'clock. As I understand it, they have taken off an hour early. On that basis my staff have informed me that providing they make it on an average climb rate they should start to show on our radar screens fifteen minutes from now. So, that should be 8.15am our time. At that point we will scramble two fighters to intercept them and guide them home."

As soon as he paused, everyone started to scream questions. He politely answered each one for a few minutes. The Times correspondent from London called.

"How can you reconcile the fact, General, that you are allowing two internationally famous ladies to be flown by an individual who can, on his own admission, hardly fly a plane and who certainly has never had any instruction?" There was overwhelming agreement from the rest of the press.

"Sir, this individual, as you call him, managed to remove a dead pilot from his seat when flying at God knows what height, and in a raging thunderstorm, take over the plane, suffer total engine loss and land the plane successfully in what must have been the most stressful of situations in an area not known for having flat green fields. The ladies have the utmost faith in him apparently. Anyway, we will soon know."

As the press erupted again, an army officer burst into the room. Everyone stopped talking and looked at him.

"General, Sir. We have them on radar, 300 miles out heading this way," he shouted.

Pandemonium erupted as the press fought to get out of the room to the phones. The General slowly got to his feet with the Ambassadors following him.

"Get the fighters in the air" he ordered the officer who promptly saluted and shot out of the room.

"Let's go, and watch the action gentlemen." He put his arm around Josie's husband's shoulder.

"It looks as though she is coming home safe, son," he said. Tears welled in the young man's eyes. He felt his own eyes prick a little but he quickly swallowed, blinked and marched off to the radar room.

* * *

Liz unbuckled her seat belt and joined them in the cockpit. "It's lonely back there," she said, "and I'm missing all the action."

"You just hold on tight because it's a little bumpy," Frank said. They were now at 7,000 ft and still climbing nicely. "I reckon that they will now have us on radar. Can you imagine what's going on back there? The press must be going mad. Your husband will be there waiting too Josie and will know that you are almost home safe."

"It's all down to you, Frank."

"No, it's been a team effort. We've helped each other"

Josie laughed. "You're dead right there mate, all for one and one for all, for ever."

Without doubt her accent seemed to be getting broader the higher they flew. They continued to climb until they reached 8,000ft at which point Frank levelled out the plane. He watched the speed rise to 170knots. While the girls chatted as only women can he mused on the last few days. So many unexplainable events had transpired that it seemed to have all been a dream and yet he knew it hadn't been a dream, well at least most of it hadn't. He wasn't too sure about his own dream and the strange "shadows." The events inside the pyramid and the conversation with the 'Monk' were to him deeply disturbing and he wouldn't and couldn't allow himself to think about those particular events at this time simply because it was all so improbable. Yet there was no doubting what he had seen, heard and felt. Some time soon he would have to sit down on his own and work through the sequence of events in his own mind and try to make some sort of sense out of it. If necessary find out from experts as to whether he and the two girls had gone temporarily insane or whether the events did actually happen. Yes that was the way to tackle it. Leave it all to later and blank it right now. There were more important things to do.

His mind flicked to lighter things. His life appeared to be changing rapidly; in fact it had changed dramatically he thought. Two weeks ago he would have laughed in the face of anyone daring to suggest that he would shortly kill three men, let alone fly and land a plane dead stick, and have a hidden fortune in gold and diamonds. A few months ago he had been Mr Joe Average, moderately well off with three kids and a small business back home. He'd been relatively happy with his lot, as are 90% of the male working population. All ambition had been ground away by the boring schedule of climbing out of bed to meet the deadline of joining that horrendous queue of cars on the main orbital trunk road. Doing the same thing every morning, of getting the paper and stealing fifteen minutes at work to read of the rich and famous in another world, and simply doing the same routine every single bloody day; seeing no way out, just doing what he had to do to survive and provide for his family. The usual humdrum of every day life had slipped the years away until he was suddenly forty-seven years old, divorced, and wondering in stunned amazement at what the hell had happened to him.

The great thing about this holiday was that he had purged his ex-wife out of his system. In fact he hadn't thought about her for days, which was a good sign, and then his life changed out of all recognition. He thought that if he let his mind dwell on all that had happened recently he would go mad. It simply didn't happen in real life but what was it his father used to say. Truth is stranger than fiction and you just couldn't have made this up. People wouldn't believe him, and if this had happened to someone else and he read about it even he would have laughed in disbelief. But it had and here he was calmly flying a plane with two very attractive women on board, and an unknown amount of wealth in diamonds hidden away in his pack.

He wondered what his kids had been thinking. They must have heard one way or another that he was missing and had probably thought the worst. Their old fashioned normal dad. They hadn't understood from the very beginning his desire to go off to Central America. It was the usual thing. It was all right for them to back pack off around the world. It was generally thought the "thing to do" among the young set but their dad? No, not their dad that was too embarrassing. Now their fears would have been confirmed and the first thing he would have to do when and if they landed OK was to phone and talk to them. He wondered how they were coping with things. No doubt they had been in touch with their mother, bloody woman!

He glanced at the two girls who were continuing to talk animatedly now that they knew they were near home. He was pleased that they had accepted him as their mentor and friend even though they lived in a different world. He couldn't imagine them even glancing at him once if they had met under normal circumstances. As it was, they were great girls and had relied upon him completely through the ordeal of the last few days. The three of them had been through a lot and yet they had held it all together. Frank didn't consider himself stupid and he knew this little adventure was going to end shortly but not before he had rung the maximum out of it, by God.

There was no going back now and without a doubt his life had changed forever. The world press and general media would see to that. In fact he knew that his ego was expanding by the minute and he smiled at the fact that he was aware of that. He was going to have to put on a totally different personality to his real one. They would want someone a bit wild, a bit crazy and loud, someone larger than life. Well, he could handle that and if that was what they wanted then that was what they were going to get. Where it was all going to take him he had no idea but the prospect was exciting. He shivered; someone had just walked over his grave.

"Frank, look out of my side of the plane," said Josie, breaking into his thoughts.

Frank leaned forward and looked. There, no more than three hundred yards away, were two army jet fighters flying alongside. The pilots were waving. The girls got very excited and were waving back wildly. One jet flew a little closer and indicated were they OK? The girls gave the thumbs up sign. The pilot indicated that it would be about ninety minutes before they reached their landing site and advised them to follow what he did. The whole episode took several minutes as the girls tried to guess what he was trying to say.

They took advantage of this time to work out their strategy when they landed. They agreed to take a gold bar each in their pack and when the opportunity arose to tell the media what they had found.

"We have to stick together like glue for the first couple of days while the news media and the Brazilian Government settle down," Frank said. "Then I guess they will want me to guide them back to the valley." The girls agreed to let Frank do the talking.

"I can't wait to see my husband again," said Josie. "He must just be frantic so the sooner we get all this out of the way the better because we will be shooting off for a couple of days if you know what I mean."

They laughed and fell silent for a while, each deep in their own thoughts about their lives ahead and what the next few days and weeks would hold. Each one of them making plans and thinking about how happy they would be to be back with their various friends and families.

Frank was getting tired now with concentrating but the girls were having a great time flirting with the pilots. They both got up and started to put on their make up. They kept it simple; just the same they still managed to look stunning. They discussed at some length what they should wear until Frank said. "Ladies, I thought I told you to chuck out your clothes."

"Well, we thought that if we did get back, Frank, that we would have to look our best regardless," said Josie. Liz nodded vigorously.

"May I suggest ladies that you just wear what you have on? You both look great. Tanned limbs everywhere and torn and brief shirts and shorts. I reckon a bit more cleavage would not go amiss. Show them loads of boobs and their eyes will pop out." The girls grinned and each undid another button on their shirts. He looked back at them. They had changed their footwear to trainers. He shook his head in despair. They had smuggled aboard spare shoes with them for goodness sake.

The jet pilot indicated that they should start to lose height down to 5,000ft. Frank pulled back on the throttles and watched as his height started to fall. He adjusted his throttles so that the fall was gradual.

"You will have to get back in your seat and strap in, Liz. You too, Josie," he said. "We must be getting near."

The girls chatted away excitedly.

"Where the hell is this airport?" Frank said. "Josie, ask that pilot how far we have to go. Our fuel state is not so good.

"He is indicating another twenty five miles, Frank, and that you should be dropping to 3,000 ft now."

"Josie, this time I am going to need you to help me lower the undercarriage and drop the flaps. That's the lever for the undercarriage and that is the flaps. You see you can drop the flaps by degrees. We will first drop the undercarriage. Let's do that now."

Josie pulled on the lever and the plane immediately lurched. They were going too slow and the plane started to stall. Frank increased power a little. "Come on, baby, behave yourself," he said to the plane. "Don't let us down now." He was sweating profusely and Josie looked at him.

"You OK, Frank?" she asked.

"You could say I'm a little stressed," he said. "Can you see the airport yet?

"The pilot is indicating ten miles and that you should be going down a little more," she said.

"Drop the flaps, Josie, ten degrees and let's see what happens," he said. She did so.

The plane was starting to move all over the place and Frank tried desperately to calm it down. "Hang loose," he thought, "treat it gently and it will fly down on it's own." He lightened his grip on the stick and the plane steadied.

"There it is, Frank," Josie cried excitedly, "look over to the right a bit."

It was a hot, hazy day and the ground could just be seen through the blue haze. But he saw it now all right. Main runway right in front of him with others going off at all angles. The jets could not fly this slowly and peeled off waving good luck. Josie waved back.

"A little more flap Josie," Frank called. He felt the plane stagger a little and increased power a fraction.

"This is too easy," he joked. "A bit more flap Josie." They were now only a couple of miles out and lined up perfectly when he realised that he was probably too high. He reduced speed and felt her drop and immediately had to boost speed a little. "There has to be a happy medium somewhere," he thought.

"Full flaps, Josie, and let's get her down." Josie looked at him with wide eyes and pulled the flap lever all the way down. The plane slowed dramatically and Frank boosted power again to hold it in its descent.

"Josie, call my speed out to me all the way down until we touch," he shouted above the noise of the wailing engines. "Hey, look at all those fire engines out there. Have they got that wrong or what?"

Josie didn't answer and Liz had her head in her hands.

* * *

He let the plane float down the last twenty feet on its own. Josie shouted out the air speed as he controlled the drop with the throttles. It felt as though he had been doing it all his life and then the wheels touched and stayed down. He immediately shut the throttles and eased on the brakes until he was almost standing on them. Fire engines were racing along either side with their crews waving excitedly.

He had almost come to a standstill when a car shot out in front of them with a sign on the back saying 'follow me.' They followed the car slowly with no one saying anything. They were all emotionally drained and exhausted.

"I think we have been here before," said Frank. They were being guided towards a parking bay when Frank simply stopped the plane, shut the throttles and switched off the engines.

Liz was repairing her make up quickly. "God, it's so good to be back safe," she said. "Thanks Frank, I love you."

Josie broke the tension by laughing and saying, "You've made a conquest you bloody Limey. In fact, you've made two. I love you too."

He looked at both of them. "And I love you two, too," he said. "They can park this bloody thing themselves. We'll get a lift back. Let's get the gold. One each and put them in our packs. Don't say anything to anyone yet until I give the word." The girls undid their seat belts and without saying a word jumped up and grabbed their belongings. Frank had hardly got out of his seat when the cabin door burst open and a screaming horde of journalists and media people began shouting questions.

A squad of soldiers quickly arrived and pushed everyone back.

"Look out ladies, here come the big brass," Frank said. He strapped on the dead pilot's old shoulder holster and gun and buckled his knife around his waist. He humped his backpack onto one shoulder and jumped down from the plane with his rifle over the other shoulder. The shouting and cheering was deafening as he held each girl's hand and raised them in the air as they slowly got out of the plane with their bags. The girls were laughing and playing to the crowd and the cameras. They looked fantastic.

Frank felt a hand on his shoulder and, turning, looked into the dark brown eyes of a grey haired, ruggedly built man, about his height and in an army uniform.

"You must be Frank Blake?" he said.

"And you must be the General?" Frank replied.

"Welcome home Frank, fantastic landing, you had us all going there for a while. Introduce me to the ladies, will you."

After the introductions they were whisked away by car to the airport buildings much to the annoyance of the waiting crowd.

In the VIP lounge Josie's husband leapt out of the crowd and flung his arms around her. They were introduced to the President who appeared taken aback by the attractive girls but not for long who, recognising they had made a conquest, played the game for all they were worth and flirted with him outrageously. Josie's arm remained firmly around her husband's waist all the time. He looked totally bemused and could not take his eyes off his beautiful wife.

With so many people milling about, all wanting a piece of the action, Frank decided that a quick chat with the General and the President was urgently needed. The Secret Service minders were watching him continuously and looked extremely nervous about his rifle and pistol and several times asked him if he would like them to carry them for him. Frank knew that if he gave them up for one moment they would disappear permanently. Anyway, he wanted to keep them for a certain reason. He was working out a plan in his head.

He approached the General and took him aside.

"General, the girls and I want to speak to you and the President in private right away. We have something of enormous importance to tell you. Can you please arrange it, as we want to get to a hotel as soon as possible? We're absolutely shot. We also need to arrange a press conference today because they are not going to go away until we do."

"I thought you might have something to tell us. There have been some strange things going on and I would be interested to have some answers. I'll talk to the President now, if I can pull him away from the girls. He's positively drooling over there. Wait here and I'll see what I can do." The General moved over towards the President and whispered in his ear.

As soon as the General had left him Frank was surrounded by people all trying to talk to him at once. Five television crews were trying to shove their lenses into his face and the flashes from the press cameras were dazzling. A very tall, handsome and distinguished looking man closed on him.

He held out his hand and Frank took it. Almost for a laugh Frank gave him the Masonic signal and wasn't surprised to feel it returned. They smiled at each other. The man spoke.

"My name is Sir Anthony Graham. I'm the British Ambassador to Brazil. You have given us all quite an interesting time Frank. I can't remember when I was last so excited. You do realise that the whole world wants to know the identity of the man who has rescued these beautiful ladies don't you? I want to tell you, before things get out of control, that I am at your disposal dear boy. This is my card and I have been given instructions from London to give you every assistance possible, and I mean every assistance. Call on me at any time if you find you need help." He raised one eyebrow and Frank knew exactly what he meant. He looked up into the tall man's eyes. He was struck by their steel grey colour and their intensity.

"I am about to go into a meeting with the General and the President on a very important matter concerning our time away Sir Anthony. If I could ask you to get in touch with me as soon as we get to an hotel, I expect you will know which one they are taking us to, then I will fill you in before we go into the press conference.

"Is this more excitement Frank?" said Sir Anthony thoughtfully.

Frank smiled up at the older man. "I'm afraid it is Sir," he answered. People heard what he had just said and questions were being screamed at him. He just kept saying to everyone that all would be explained at the press conference.

He could see the General was watching him and now waved him over. Frank gathered up his equipment and, smiling at everyone but saying nothing, he worked his way over to the General and the President who was now watching him very intently. The flash of the cameras dazzled him and hurt his eyes. He let out a piercing whistle and the girls turned, looking at him in surprise, as did everyone else. He beckoned the girls over to him.

"We are going to have a quick chat with the General, some of his chums and the President," he said winking at them. They knew exactly what he meant.

"Lead on, Sir," he said to the President.

They were guided into a large room obviously used as a boardroom and for meetings, and everyone sat down, the two girls and Frank sitting together. They were making a bit of fuss because of their heavy packs. Josie's husband gave them a hand and made a comment about how heavy they were.

With everyone seated the General leaned forward on the table supporting himself with his elbows. "Well you three, welcome home. I have to say that you have given us a bit of a bad time. First of all everyone thought you were dead and then, from nowhere, you come alive again. Frank, we haven't got a lot of time because we need to get you all to an hotel as you have requested and then you need to get some rest before the press conference which I would guess should be held in about four hours. So, tell us all."

Frank stood up. "Gentlemen, what we have to tell you is nothing less than momentous." He had their full attention immediately and the room went quiet.

"I'll be as brief as possible. As we were running out of fuel, Josie found a valley for us to land in. After we had landed, and that's another story in itself, we noticed that another plane had attempted the same feat and had crashed. When we had sorted ourselves out we decided to check this out and when we did we found boxes strewn everywhere. In those boxes we found these." He looked at the two girls and nodded. They all took out their gold bars and put them on the table.

Sharp intakes of breath rolled around the table. The gold bars gleamed against the dark rosewood of the tabletop and seemed to have a presence of their own.

"Not only that gentlemen. I am certain that the plane is a Second World War German Heinkel bomber. There were five skeletons laying about both in and out of the body of the plane. This is the dead pilot's gun," he said placing the Walther P-38 pistol on the table. "They were all wearing what was left of German Nazi uniforms. We obviously concluded that the plane had therefore been there some sixty years."

"How much gold is there?" The General asked quietly.

"I am saying here and now that the three of us are claiming everything we discovered as treasure trove. However, it doesn't stop there. I'm not going to tell you how we made the discovery but we do have to tell you that we found their main horde in a cave. In that place we have discovered a treasure trove, gentlemen that includes many rare works of art and so many boxes of gold and heaven knows what, that we cannot possibly guess the value of. We wish to announce this at the news conference later today and we want to say that you have agreed to mount a mission to bring the treasure back to Rio for evaluation." He sat down. He felt close to total exhaustion but he had to carry this through.

The president looked at Frank. He was now masking his excitement with the ease of a professional politician.

"What an incredible story Frank. What an incredible roller coaster ride of emotions you have put us through since you all disappeared. I am not sure that it would be wise to tell the press of your find but if that is the wish of the three of you, and you feel that you must, then I cannot in all honesty see how we can stop you. Of course the legality of your claim on the treasure will have to be explored in depth. I am quite sure that if what you say is true, and that it is Nazi gold, the claims as to who actually owns it will come from every corner of Europe. That I am sure of and then, of course, there is the fact that it has been found on our soil."

He looked at the two stunning girls and then turned back to Frank. The room was as quiet as the grave. Nobody moved or said a thing. There was a long pause. The President then spoke again carefully choosing his words.

"May I suggest General that you concur with our heroes' request? I would suggest that you lose no time in organising the removal of the treasure from wherever Frank, Liz and Josie have hidden it because I think you have hidden it, haven't you Frank?"

Frank smiled at the president. "You bet, Sir." There was a ripple of laughter around the room.

"I thought so. I will leave it to you all to organise this at your leisure and will talk to you again on your return. Obviously I would like to see what you have found. In fact, I can't wait." The President stood up and so did most of the people in the room. He looked at the three and smiled. It was obviously meant to be genuine but the end result was the equivalent of being smiled at by a wolf before being eaten. Frank felt the menace and made a mental note not to trust this man as far as he could throw him.

"I would like to say that you are like a breath of fresh air blowing through my life. I wish I could have been with you on this great adventure. Whatever happens I wish the three of you well and look forward to seeing you again soon." With that he nodded and left the room with his staff and guards.

Frank and the two girls rose and packed away the gold as the General came around the long table towards them.

"Have I introduced my husband, James, to you yet, Frank? In all this mad panic I can't remember," said Josie.

Frank turned to look at the young man who still had that bemused look on his face. The boy, for that was what he was to Frank, stuck his hand out.

"Sir, I want to thank you from the bottom of my heart for bringing Josie back to me. If what you have just said is true then I would really like to come on the expedition if you don't mind."

Frank smiled up at the lad for he was very tall. "I'm six feet two so he must be around six five I should think" thought Frank. He was so typically American school from his crew cut hair and his sincere attitude. He was a good-looking lad with very broad shoulders and tanned handsome face. He vaguely remembered Josie saying that he played American football at a very high level. Josie was obviously in love with him.

"Your wife is a very special lady James, with many talents." He glanced wickedly at Josie who was blushing to the roots of her hair. "Of course you can come with us if only to keep her out of my hair." They laughed.

The General had arrived at their group and had heard the last part of the conversation. "Frank, let's get things under way. You all want some rest. While you are doing that I shall be organising the trip back to wherever it was you were. I think this will take a couple of days so we will provisionally pitch for the 18th. Two days from now. That should give you time to recover from your escapades. So let's get you to your cars. They should be ready and waiting for you outside the main doors. My staff tell me that there is an enormous crowd outside including the media. My soldiers will make a corridor for you but I want you to briefly tell the press that you will be holding a press conference in four hours time at 2pm. Is that OK?"

Frank looked at the two girls who nodded. "That's fine by us, General," said Josie. "Let's go." They picked up their packs and Frank shouldered his rifle, put the pistol back in its holster and shrugged his pack onto his back. Putting his faithful old hat back on he said, "OK I'm ready."

"You look as though you are going to war Frank," said the General, laughing.

Frank glanced at him and said. "I think I am, General," and walked ahead of the girls through the door.

As soon as the doors opened the soldiers leapt ahead of them pushing, shoving and beating a way through the throng of shouting screaming people who were all trying to touch the three of them. Frank turned and put his arms around the two girls' waists and they marched together laughing towards the main doors. That picture was destined to be on the main pages of all the world's newspapers the next day. The press were screaming questions at them so they stopped when they got to the doors. Frank climbed on top of one of the baggage trucks and waved for quiet. The television cameramen aimed their lenses at him.

"Ladies and Gentlemen. Josie, Liz, and I want to thank you all for giving us such an amazing homecoming and reception but we have to tell you that we are totally exhausted. We badly need some rest and a wash and brush up."

"They look OK to me," said a wag from the audience and everyone laughed.

Frank looked at the two girls smiling up at him. "They do, don't they," he said. "I want to tell you people of the media that we will be holding a press conference in four hours time. General Lomax will tell you where. You had all better be there because you will hear a story that will amaze you. We have a story to tell that will rock your socks off. More I cannot say right now so see you then and thanks once again for your patience." With that he jumped back down to the girls and, amid howls from the press, were escorted out of the building to the cars.

A long white limo was waiting for them and they climbed in after putting their packs carefully in the boot. Josie cuddled up to her man. Liz and Frank simply sat exhausted. Frank leaned forward and pressed the bar button. As the car moved off a tray of glasses and bottles swung out from the front seats.

"Bottles of Champagne, no less," said Frank. "Right, we will have one of those to celebrate." He promptly opened one and poured four glasses.

"Here's to us," said Liz. "And to all that follows. All for one and one for all eh?" The four clinked their glasses together grinning at each other like idiots.

"That's a bit corny but it does apply to us doesn't it?" asked Liz. Frank nodded wearily.

They chatted happily all the way to the hotel. On arrival they signed in and put their gold bars in the hotel safe and Frank asked the manager to put his guns away safely. The manager could not believe his eyes at the sight of the gold and the fact that this now famous group was staying at his hotel. They asked the soldiers to stay and look after them until after the press conference. The Sergeant in charge told them these were their orders anyway and that it was a pleasure. His eyes travelled to the girls and Frank could understand what he was thinking.

The foyer of the hotel was now packed with people trying to see them and the soldiers hustled them to the lifts.

"Right, we're off," said Josie hanging onto her husband. "See you downstairs in what, three and half hours?"

"Wait until I phone you, Josie," Don't tire yourselves out too much. Try and get a little sleep children," he joked.

Liz went into her room with a mumbled "See you later."

Frank looked around his room. Whoever was organising this had done them proud. A large sumptuous bed beckoned him but he felt that a bath was in order first. He hadn't had a bath for, he couldn't remember how long. He slid into the deep warm water and relaxed. He couldn't think any more and he quickly slipped into a deep sleep. He awoke slowly to find himself lying in cold water.

"Stupid sod," he thought. He was always doing this. Falling asleep in a hot bath was what he had done all his life. He climbed out, vigorously rubbing himself with a towel then wandered into the bedroom. Liz was asleep in his bed. He stood looking down at the contrast of her dark skin against the white sheets. He peeled the sheet back slowly to find her naked. Sliding into the bed he covered them both with the sheet, rolled over and instantly went to sleep again.

His sub-consciousness woke him two hours later. Slowly surfacing he realised where he was. Reaching out a hand he touched Liz's thighs.

"You can pack that up for a start," she mumbled.

"Thought that would wake you, dozy head," he said. "What are you doing here anyway?"

"I was lonely so I thought I'd sleep with you." She giggled. "The sight of you laying in the bath will be one I will take to my death bed. You were all shrivelled," she laughed.

He lifted up the sheet and looked down at himself. "Well I'm not now," he said. Liz lifted up the sheet as well and looked down at his erect penis.

"Don't be so disgusting," she said," and dropped the sheet back. "Can't believe a man of your age would get a hard on just because he's lying next to a beautiful hot bit of black pussy like me."

"Now you're being disgusting," he laughed and climbed out of bed. "It's time we got dressed and down to the press conference."

Liz heaved herself onto one elbow and the sheet fell back from her body. "A look of amazement came across her face."What now?" she said.

Frank had reached the bathroom and looked back from the door. "Yes now, so shift that black arse and start to get dressed." He shut the door laughing just as a pillow hit it.

He didn't have to worry about Josie. She was knocking on the door ten minutes later. She was on her own.

"What are you doing here, Liz, and where is lover boy?" asked Josie.

"It's not what you think, Josie. I was just lonely, that's all. Hey, remind me later to tell you where I found Frank earlier on. You will just die. Where is your man then?"

"On his back, exhausted," she answered. "Are we all ready?"

Frank came out of the bathroom. "Hail the conquering hero," cried Liz. Frank gave her a sharp look.

"Let's get down to the foyer and collect the gold and get this show on the road."

The girls chatted happily in the lift going down to the reception area. Three armed soldiers were still escorting them. Frank had left his rifle in his room.

As they exited the lift they were met by one of the General's aides who described the room in which the news conference was to be held. "You are to be there in fifteen minutes," he said.

By the time they had collected and signed for their gold it was time to make their way to the conference room. They entered through curtains to find the room crammed with cameras, spotlights and people. The noise rose to a crescendo on their entrance. The General was waiting for them and escorted them to the raised dais, which had the regulation table and four chairs. Microphones had been laid out seemingly in their hundreds on the table in front of them.

"Hell, I'm nervous, Frank. What happens if I say something wrong?" said Josie.

"Just be yourself and take the lead from me," he said. The three of them sat down at the table with Frank in the middle.

Questions were immediately being asked at such a rate and volume that it was simply a babble of sound. Frank raised his hands and waited for them to be quiet.

"Ladies and Gentlemen, good afternoon. We have a story to tell you and not much time to tell it in. It would be appreciated if you would simply let us tell you our story in our own way, and when we have finished you can ask questions. So if you want to hear it you had better shut up," he said sternly. He had forgotten that the television cameras were turning and that the world was watching and listening. He had little experience of talking to large groups of people and wasn't at all comfortable with it. The sight of all these people hanging on his every word made his stomach churn and yet he knew how important this press conference was to all of them.

Frank was an average sort of guy, with an average education but his size and body language gave him a presence and normally when he spoke people listened. At times, he could be shy to a fault and yet at others, very strong mentally, and very determined. He had realised at an early age that the lack of a university education did not necessarily mean that the good things in life could not be achieved. Working for someone else would always mean that his opportunities would be limited. Working for himself, the opportunities were endless. This he had done for the last twenty years and it had made him extremely self-reliant and it had imbued him with considerable self-confidence.

As he started to talk, so the audience became quieter and quieter until the only sound was the scratching of pens and the whirring of the cameras. These hardened and experienced media people had not heard a story like this for a long time, if ever at all. He explained in detail how the pilot had died at the controls and how he had to take over, finally landing the plane with no power left in the engines. He told how they survived for the five days, and how they eventually found the German bomber. At this point, he was interrupted again and questions started to fly at him. Once again, he warned them to let him finish the story. When it came to the gold the audience gasped as one. The girls and Frank put their bars on the table and everyone stared as though they had never seen gold before in their lives. He talked for another fifteen minutes explaining how they found the treasure 'in a cave' and how they had felt when they saw what the treasure consisted of.

When he mentioned this there was an explosion of questions. He ignored them and insisted that he wanted to finish the story first and they could ask questions afterwards. He gave brief details of some of the artists and their paintings and also spoke of the vast quantities of precious stones and plate. He spoke without interruption until he finished with their arrival at the airport. He said nothing about the diamonds, or about the silent running figures or their fears of the pyramid.

There was silence for a moment and then the questions exploded.

"Jon Lineman from the French Bulletin, Mr Blake. This treasure, is it your opinion that it had all been stolen by the Nazis during their occupation of Europe?"

"Yes it is, Jon. The most horrific thing of all, as far as we three are concerned, is the certain knowledge that a considerable amount of this treasure was stolen from Jews just before and certainly after they had been killed. There will have to be a plan, instigated by someone, to ensure that most of this treasure is returned to the dependants of these people. That's our view anyway," said Frank.

"Frank York of The Mail, London. May I ask a question of the ladies? Ladies, the whole world is staggered by what you have gone through and yet, if I may say so, you look better now than before." There was much amusement from the other members of the media. "What would you say were the most terrifying times?"

Josie lent forward to the microphone. "Sleeping in the plane with Frank. He could snore for England."

The audience erupted with laughter.

"No seriously, I can only say what I felt, I don't know about Liz but when we realised the pilot was dead and we were flying into the storm with someone who was not a qualified pilot, that was a very, very, scary moment. The other was when Frank said we were out of fuel and we could not see anywhere to land except for jungle. I was terrified at that point too and seriously thought we were all going to die. That was it for me."

All eyes turned to Liz.

"Quite frankly I was terrified the whole time and screamed and cried a lot. I'm telling you all here now, that it was simply very frightening. I was at a disadvantage because I was sitting behind them and couldn't see much and could only hear what Josie and Frank were saying, but that was enough, and the way the plane was rising and falling so violently, well, it was just too much. Josie was up front with Frank and when the second engine went out and Frank was trying to glide it in, well, I was not happy then at all either and really felt that we were going to die. Frank was swearing a lot but he did apologise afterwards."

"New York Tribune. Who first discovered the gold?"

"I did," said Frank. "The girls were still sleeping but I had seen the crashed aircraft as we were trying to land in the valley. So being an early riser, and as they were both snoring," (both girls hit him) "I decided to walk over to see what it was all about. At first I was only interested in the dead pilot. His skeleton was still at the controls of the aircraft. I examined him and found this on him." He rummaged in his pack and brought out the Walther P-38 in its holster. There was a gasp from the audience. He pointed it into the air. "I haven't tried the ammunition yet," he said and laughed as everyone ducked. "Don't worry, I won't," he said.

"You'll all have to forgive him because he is quite mad," said Josie. They were beginning to enjoy themselves.

A girl from the media spoke. "Jennie Collins from Los Angeles News. We are all very interested to know how things went at night. Josie. How did you sleep and in what?" There was a rustle from the audience. This had obviously been a question everyone wanted to ask. The girls played it to the full.

"The first night was very cold and Frank told us to wear as much clothing as possible. We had taken the seats out of the back of the plane and that left quite a cosy area," said Liz. "We zipped the sleeping bags together and just cuddled up under them. Frank told us to do that and it was a very good idea because we shared our body heat. It was still very cold though."

"Of course we knew what Frank was up to." There was considerable laughter from the audience. "He insisted on sleeping between Liz and me to ensure that he had two warm bodies to cuddle up to him. I think he was the warmest person on the plane each night." Josie said. "And yes, we did keep our clothes on all the time. She paused and then said. "Except, of course, when we showered under the waterfall each morning and evening."

"What happened then?" asked the girl from Los Angeles.

"That's for us to know and you to wonder about," said Liz to laughter all round.

All eyes turned back to Frank.

"Gerhard Gleist from Berlin. Mr Blake, your story is quite astonishing. One minute you are walking on holiday in the jungle, killing bandits we understand, and the next you are crash landing a plane that has no fuel, then you are sleeping with two of the most beautiful woman on the planet and finding gold and treasure. Not only that, you bring them all back safe and sound. You are a hero and a very brave man in everyone's eyes and yet we know nothing about you. Can you tell us something about yourself?"

"Gerhard, that's for another day," Frank said. "I will tell you this though. If there is such a thing as a guardian angel, then mine has been working overtime over the last week or so. Yes, I have been living every man's dream and nobody would believe it if the script had been written for a film. They say truth is stranger than fiction. I think I have covered every emotion it's possible to cover, including great fear, more than a couple of times. I do have to admit to being physically drained at the moment but nothing a few days sleep won't cure. As for me as a person, I'm just your average forty-seven year old business man."

"That old?" quipped Josie to more laughter.

"I have been very lucky and instead of winning the lottery I have had the privilege of living with these two very naughty girls for a week and finding treasure. It's been an interesting time!"

The questions carried on for another five minutes until the General walked onto the stage, holding up his hands.

"Ladies and Gentleman. I am sure you will understand if we bring this meeting to an end now. Our heroes are exhausted and need some time to recover." He held up his hands again as the clamour for more started. "I'm sorry but that's it. We may do another conference when we recover the treasure, which incidentally we will do within the week. See you all then." He turned to the three at the table. "Come on, you three, let's get a drink."

"I'm with you there, General," said Josie.

"So what's the next move then, General?" asked Josie. They were in the bar and being protected from everyone by soldiers.

"We have five Chinook helicopters and will have them ready in a couple of days. You will obviously come with us to show the way and show us what you have done with the loot won't you Frank?" he said.

"Of course General" Frank answered smiling at the man.

"The press conference, by the way ladies, went very well indeed. Several agencies are after you all for your own stories already. I don't know what you want to do about that."

"We are going to talk it over, General. The girls have their own agents who will insist on doing their negotiations. I will have to appoint one to do mine. There are several areas we need to sort out but not right now. I need another few strong beers and then some good food. Where would you suggest I go to get that then, General?" he said.

Josie's husband turned up and was allowed through to his wife.

"We have things to do if you know what I mean," said Josie, "so we will see you later. Frank, if you want to talk to me about stuff, this is my mobile number. She gave Frank a card and looked up into his eyes. "Keep me abreast of the situation, won't you," Frank nodded. Josie looked at him for a moment longer and tears came into her eyes. She glanced at her husband and said, "Excuse me a moment, Richard." She walked up to Frank and put her arms about his neck and kissed him full on the mouth in front of everyone. Frank was rocked to his socks but instinctively put his arms around her and squeezed her. The media were still watching everything from a distance and cameras flashed and whirled. Still holding him she said. "I have had one hell of a time with you and Liz, Frank, which will last me all my life. I want to thank you for bringing me back home safe and sound." She released him and stood back wiping the tears away from her eyes, smearing her make up and smiling. "Thank you, you pommy bastard." She said the last five words in her broad Australian accent and then turned, and putting her arm around her husband, hurried off with her head down.

"That girl has balls, General," said Frank.

"I have no doubt at all about that, Frank," he replied.

Frank turned back to Liz who was also wiping her eyes. "What are you going to do until we get back, Liz"?

Liz looked up at Frank. "If you don't mind, can I have some lunch with you. My parents are flying in within the next few hours so I have some spare time and we can talk over what we should be doing. Is that all right Frank?"

"Sure," he smiled down at her. Looking at the General he said. "Sir, I will be here for a while if you need me. If I disappear, simply leave a message at reception and they will ring me."

"I think you should still have my escort for a couple of days until things cool down. Is that OK with you?" the General asked.

Frank and Liz agreed to that and they decided to stay at the bar for a while and asked if there were any bar snacks they could have. These were brought to them.

Several drinks later they were both leaning on the bar feeling very good indeed. Liz looked devastating showing off her black skin in a white blouse and trousers. Her blouse seemed to Frank to be showing more and more of her small but beautiful breasts the more they drank.

Liz was now almost leaning on Frank and was whispering to him. "Frank, you are leering at my breasts again. If you really want to see them why don't we go up to my room and finish what we started earlier. I'm feeling very horny."

"But you don't like men," he slurred back.

She looked at him. "I like you and that's all that matters, isn't it?"

Frank put his arm about her and turned to signal to the soldiers. "Get us out of here, Sergeant," he said and grabbing his pack they made their way to the lift.

They said nothing until they went into her room and then as the door closed Liz launched herself at him. Burying her mouth on his she tore at his shirt and trousers. Frank lifted her up and walked through to her bedroom and slowly lowered her onto the bed with his mouth still on hers. He undid her blouse and she pushed her breasts at him. She had no bra on. He lowered his mouth to them as she prised off his shirt and trousers. Reaching down she put her hand around his erect penis and held it gently all the while massaging it. He moved his mouth back to hers and sliding his hand down inside her knickers cupped her with one hand and gently caressed one breast with the other. Releasing him she lifted his head from her mouth and looked into his eyes for a moment.

"I have difficulty doing it with a man Frank but I want to do it with you." She kissed him, thrusting her tongue into his mouth. Still keeping her eyes open and still kissing his lips, she whispered, "Ever since we landed in the valley I have had an ache in my loins for you, mister. Now get rid of it please. Please love me, Frank." This last sentence was uttered with a sound he recognised. It was the sound of a soul desperately searching for someone to trust and to love and to take care of her.

He put his arms around her and kissed her for a long time as he ran his fingers slowly through her hair and down her long back. He whispered back to her. "Relax with me Liz, trust me." He began doing the thing he loved to do. He slowly removed her knickers and as he did so she opened her legs for him. Looking down at her beautiful face and into her lustrous deep brown eyes, then down further at her beautiful black body, he was amazed at the hunger he felt for her. Her hips were moving slowly and she was thrusting her breasts at him, watching his eyes roam her. She was his for the taking and he decided that he was going to take his time with her.

They drifted off into their own world of mutual gratification, both of them needing this closeness and physical love at this time and both sensing that each was willing to give to please the other. It was several hours later, still with their arms wrapped around each other, that they lay in the darkness talking quietly of the recent events and of their lives.

"I'm very thirsty, Frank, is there anything in the fridge; like champagne?" Liz eventually asked.

"I'll have a look," he said rolling slowly out of her arms and stumbling over to the drinks cabinet in their room. Opening it was like opening Pandora's Box. It wasn't a small fridge. It was full size and stuffed full of delicious snacks as well as alcohol. He opened a bottle of Moet, grabbed two glasses and took over to the bed a pack of smoked salmon snacks. Liz put on a low light and they both blinked at each other smiling, as their eyes grew accustomed to the change of light. He poured a glass each and they sat on the bed drinking slowly and munching the snacks.

"I can't think of a nicer way to spend an evening," he said. "By the way, Liz, that last trick you pulled on me, where on earth did you learn that one at such a tender young age? That's a first for me and I have been around the houses a few times."

"What's your problem? You liked it, didn't you?" she laughed.

"Yeah, I certainly did. I'm logging that one away for another day, that's for sure. When is your partner flying in by the way?"

"I'm sorry, Frank," she said, "She's coming in tomorrow afternoon. That was the first flight she could get. We have been together for three years now and I really do miss her." She moved over and put one arm around his shoulders holding her champagne in the other hand. "I needed this tonight, Frank, and want to thank you now in case we don't have the time in the morning. Thanks for looking after me so well over the last five days. I know I have said that before but I just wanted to show my appreciation to you and I did need some loving and to be held tonight. If that's being selfish I can only say I felt that you needed that as well. I don't have any regrets about doing this with you because we have become so close. For the first time in my life I have found someone of the opposite sex with whom I can talk to and relax with without feeling any pressure of having to take it further if I don't want to. I know that sounds crazy, after what we have done tonight, but I knew that you wouldn't make a move on me unless I let you and that gives a girl a good feeling. As you have found out, I like to be in control."

Frank kissed her and, finishing off the champagne, rolled onto his back. "Be in control some more then."

* * *

He awoke with a start and, looking out of the window, realised that the day was well advanced. The voice had shouted at him again startling him. This time it cried his name with a note of urgency. "Frank!"

He lay back in the bed and looked at Liz's tousled head on the pillow next to him. He was about to wake her when the voice came again, louder this time. He recognised the voice. He sat up on the edge of the bed shaking his head. He noticed a white slip of paper on the floor by the door and walked over and picked it up.

Slowly opening it he read the contents.

"Bastards," he cried and stormed back into the bedroom. Liz heaved herself onto one elbow blinking. "What on earth is going on Frank?"

"The bastards are double crossing us Liz. They have sent helicopters into the valley. Somehow they have found it. How did they do that? Get dressed now. We need to sort this out, fast."

Liz moved quickly grabbing her dressing gown and making her way to the bathroom; she stopped and turned back to him. "How do you know all this Frank? You haven't been out of this room. I didn't hear the phone ring either."

He walked over to her and put the slip paper in her hand. "I have a phone call to make."

Liz read the few words on the paper. "I don't agree with the instructions but we are going now for the treasure." It was unsigned.

"But who is it from Frank and what does it mean?"

"That's from General Lomax I bet a pound to a penny but he couldn't sign it could he? It's that double crossing bastard of a President that's who's ordered this. I saw a look on his face when I first told them about the treasure. Damn, I should have realised he would pull this trick but I was so tired." He searched through his wallet and found the card he was looking for. He made the call. The British Embassy answered. "Sir Anthony Graham please. Would you tell him it's Frank Blake on the line and that it's extremely urgent."

"I'm terribly sorry," said a snotty male voice," but he is having his breakfast at this moment in time and it's quite impossible to interrupt him. May I suggest that you phone back later?"

Frank lost it. "Listen to me you pompous little shit. Get him on the line, now! And I mean now or I will personally come down there and shove my fist up your arse and pull whatever it is you have for brains back through it. Is that quite clear?"

There was a pause. "Perfectly," the voice answered primly and then there was silence for a short while.

"Hello Frank," said Sir Anthony, "What are you doing shouting and frightening my staff. His voice suddenly changed. "Is there a problem?"

"Yes, Sir Anthony there is a problem. I have just been informed that the General has jumped the gun and has found and landed in our valley, and right now is probably searching for the treasure one week before we were supposed to do it together. Now, we left a few surprises and he will be coming back with his tail between his legs and possibly quite frightened. Before he does that I need to talk over the situation with you, please, if possible."

Again, there was a pause. "Of course we will help you, Frank. Come over in an hour and bring the lovely ladies with you. In the meantime I will talk to London and get some advice on how we can help you. See you later, dear boy, and don't worry."

"Thanks, Sir Anthony," he said as the phone went dead.

Liz came out of the bathroom moving fast. Her face was thunderous. "If you're right, Frank, they are bastards. They are trying to jump the gun and grab all the glory and all the loot." She stood still, completely naked, in the middle of the room drying her hair. "How are we going to stick them Frank?" she asked.

"We are going to see the Brits at the Embassy and see what they can do for us." He picked up the phone and dialled Josie's number. The phone rang for some time and then a muffled male voice answered.

"Hi, James, it's Frank. We have a major problem brewing and I need to talk to Josie right away. Is that all right?"

"Sure," said James. "What's up doc?" said Josie coming on the line. Frank told her. "We're with you in fifteen minutes. Don't you dare go to the embassy without us." She said and hung up.

He watched Liz getting dressed, she grinned at him. "What have you got up your sleeve, Frank?

"I'm thinking of "the shadows" Liz and that Pyramid. I'm sure that the two are linked and if they are then something is going on there that may well kick back on the General when he lands. I think we were just lucky and got out of there at about the right time. I have a feeling that he is going to get one hell of a shock out there and will be coming home with his tail between his legs, that's for sure."

Liz was half way through pulling a shirt over her head when she stopped. She looked quizzically at him. "You're hiding something from us Frank and I don't like it. Nor will Josie when I tell her. You are going to have to tell us. We will make you."

"OK. I'll agree to that but we will talk more about that later." There was a knock on the door and Josie walked in with her husband. "What's all this about then?" she asked." I'll explain on the way," he said.

They clattered down in the lift and were storming across the foyer when there was a shout. They stopped and turned around, suddenly realising that their armed guard was not there. Three men walked quickly across the foyer towards them. "Frank, Josie, Liz. What's going on then?" Frank recognised them from the press conference. They were correspondents from The London Times, and the New York and Californian papers. This could be really helpful he thought.

"We're going for help. General Lomax, or his President, have double-crossed us. He has already gone to the treasure site without us and is probably right now trying to steal it" Frank could feel his anger rising again and felt Josie's hand on his shoulder. "Well, he is not going to get away with it if we can help It." He said and they turned and hurried out of the hotel.

"Wowee," said The Times man. "I think there's another story about to burst here boys. George, you follow them and see where they are heading. We will start to make enquires this end to see if what Frank said is true. If it is, then I wouldn't like to be in the General's shoes."

The foursome took a taxi to the embassy. On the way the girls asked Frank what he was going to do.

"Now that the President has shown us his true colours we have to find a way to get the treasure out ourselves. How we do that I can't imagine at the moment because it would mean privately hiring helicopters and personnel, and then again could we trust them? With what's at stake we would probably have our throats cut. That's an exaggeration but could easily be true. I think Sir Anthony might come up with the answers. What do you think James?"

"Don't ask me, Frank, I'm completely out of my depth here. I suppose it's either the Americans or the British who will help us at the end of the day. Let's wait and see what happens here."

The guard on the gate had obviously been warned of their imminent arrival and waved them through without stopping them. They were ushered through the reception area and into Sir Anthony's office. He was sitting there, Noel Coward style, in an elegant ribbed brown and gold dressing gown.

"Sit down, dear people. Would you like tea, coffee, breakfast anything?" He ignored Frank completely and attended to the girl's comforts fussing around them in his slippers whilst barking out instructions to his staff and ordering food and drink before turning to Frank, who was still standing up and restless.

"Sit down, Frank, for heaven's sake and do try to relax," he said. "Now. I have had a talk with the Foreign Secretary and we have discussed your situation at some length." The two girl's jaws dropped open and they sat straight up in their chairs with James nearly spilling his tea.

Frank stayed slumped in his chair watching Sir Anthony from under his eyebrows. He glanced at Frank and then addressed the girls.

"Yes, he is an old friend and I thought that I should discuss the situation with him directly as there are a number of quite tricky problems here that we must consider. Obviously we cannot, under any circumstances, offend the Government here. They are our friends despite what you might say. On the world scene they are important to us and Great Britain must not be seen to condone any action that might jeopardise our relationship with Brazil. At the same time we would not be averse to having the treasure arrive in England. Now, that is one scenario. I have to advise you, however, that some friends in the Foreign Office have informed me that there are already several Governments and certain organisations showing considerable interest in what you are doing. We know of at least three making serious plans to intercept you with the intention of removing the treasure from your possession for their own use or possibly to abduct you for ransom. I have also been informed from the very highest level that the CIA is very active in that area right now. The Israelis, Russian Mafiosi and, interestingly, some members of the old IRA, are all intending to be major players and are in all probability making their plans as we speak. Certain factions in the Middle East; well-known Muslim extremists, are also showing considerable interest. The CIA are the most advanced as you would expect. What you have failed to realise is that through announcing your exciting find to the world you have now put all of your own lives at risk. Quite a naïve thing to have done actually but you weren't to know that, of course."

He turned and looked at Frank who looked and felt as though a horse had kicked him in the nether regions. The girls looked frightened.

Sir Anthony added. "We believe that the General realised this and with his President's recommendations and approval, launched a quick strike to prevent anyone else having a go themselves. By the way Frank, the Foreign Secretary and his advisers are curious as to how you knew so quickly that this had happened. Can you throw some light on this?"

Frank was studying his fingernails. "I can't tell you right now Sir but you could say that I have someone on the inside who is one hundred percent loyal, and who will tell me what is happening on an ongoing basis. He looked at the girls. "I'm sorry girls, I had no idea that I might be putting your lives at risk. I was so blinded by the thought of all that money that I didn't think there could be any risk." He looked at the Ambassador. "What would you suggest we do, Sir?" he asked. I bet you know exactly what to do you crafty old sod, he thought to himself.

"I have to tell you Frank that we will want to know more about your friend. He, or she, could be very handy later. The suggestion that has come down to me from the Chiefs of Staff is the following. We launch four large helicopters, probably Chinooks, from one of our aircraft carriers. Coincidentally we have one that is fraternising with the Yanks off the coast in the Gulf of Mexico at the moment. Not too far away fortunately. Flying below radar we would be able to go to wherever this treasure is and with your guidance, remove it all back to the carrier pronto and carry it all back to dear old Blighty double quick. The General will, of course, eventually realise that the treasure has been removed and be upset. We will throw a few red herrings about to confuse him and anyone else that might be looking, particularly our friends in the CIA. The trouble is that the CIA will have recorded our movements by satellite and eventually pick it up. Hopefully it will be too late by then. We will vehemently deny any involvement, which they will accept, of course. That's international politics. Frank will materialise with the good ladies, and the treasure, in England and eventually put it up for auction. You will tell the world that you have asked, say, Christies to oversee the operation regarding the valuation and auction of the treasure. I am waiting to hear from them as we speak. They will hold it all in their vaults for safety. As far as the world media is concerned, the story would be that having being crossed by the President you obtained private help and removed it all yourself. The President will endeavour to push for international legal entitlement of the treasure but we believe that he wouldn't stand a chance bearing in mind where it came from in the first place."

They all looked at Sir Anthony in amazement. "How on earth did all that come about in an hour?" laughed Josie.

Pleased with their approval, Sir Anthony beamed at the two girls. "Just experience, ladies, and good contacts. Now you three, you will want a little time to decide what to do and whether this is the correct avenue for you. Secrecy is the keynote here. Without doubt your rooms are bugged and are probably being videoed. Josie shrieked at this news and her husband looked shocked. Liz wasn't at all comfortable with that news either bearing in mind what happened earlier. Frank couldn't have cared less. As far as he was concerned there were greater issues at stake than his bedroom antics.

"You are quite OK in here as this room is my room and is constantly swept. I will leave you for fifteen minutes while I change. Talk to you all later then." He got up and strode quickly from the room.

Frank was horrified about the whole episode. "I simply can't believe I was so stupid," he said. "I was thinking down such a narrow avenue and now we have the whole bloody world after us. I have to ask you ladies, is it worth it? I will go along with whatever you two decide. The thought of the CIA, Israelis and 'Uncle Tom Cobbly and all' coming after us is enough for me to want to go into hiding for quite a few years."

"We found it Frank, it's ours. After all we went through we deserve to be rewarded by someone for finding it. I say let's do what Sir Anthony recommends and get it all back to England. What do you think Liz?"

Liz didn't answer for a while. Everyone was quiet, waiting. Liz looked at Frank. She could see the torture he was going through in his mind. They were good friends now and she could read him. At the same time she loved him like an old lover and respected him. She knew he needed his ego boosting after those traumatic words of Sir Anthony. Josie was headstrong and impetuous. It fell on Liz at twenty-eight years old to be the mother figure to both of them at this point in time. She chose her words carefully.

"Josie is right Frank, it's ours. You took us into that valley, guided us to the treasure and got us back. Surely you realise that it is yours as well, almost by right really. You deserve a percentage as well as us. Quite honestly, when dealing with such large sums of dosh as we are about to we will need to get the very best advisers. I think that's priority. The British Government can be quite devious as well as anyone else but, if we are smart, then we can still hold our own. I say let them go get it on the understanding that you go with them Frank. We can go to the ship and stay there until we get back to England. That way we will be safe from these other weirdoes who could be after us. When we get back to England we will do as he says and get Christies to value and auction it, and take it off our hands. We can then get on with our lives and wait for the commission." She stopped and looked at the two of them. "How does that sound?"

Josie punched the air and cried "Yeah, Liz. Jesus Christ I have never ever heard you talk for so long. Yes let's do it. It makes sense Frank. You know it does."

Frank got up from his chair, walked over to Liz and bent down and kissed her hard on the mouth. When he finished he lent over her looking down into her eyes. "I said it once before in the valley and I say it again, you are one smart broad. Everything you say makes sense. OK. Let's do it then. James," he said talking to Josie's husband, "Can you see if Sir Anthony is ready?" James walked to the door and opened it. The Ambassador was talking to several people in the main hall and looked up as the door opened.

"We are ready, Sir," he said.

Sir Anthony came back into the room. "He walks just like a cat," thought Frank. "He is so smooth, a professional politician. I like him but wouldn't trust him as far as I could throw him." Frank vowed to keep a very sharp eye on the situation in future.

"We have agreed to go along with your plan, Sir. We would all like to be transported to the carrier and to go back to England on it. I suppose that you would wish to drop us off somewhere before we land so that we are not seen being transported by yourselves. That's fair enough. We can work on that. We are prepared to swear that the English Government was not involved in this operation and that we organised it all ourselves because we feared for our lives. We could in fact spread that with the press tonight. Would you agree to that Sir Anthony?" he asked innocently.

"That is excellent, No 10, and the Foreign Office will be pleased. Now, it would be better if nothing was said to the press quite frankly but that of course is up to you. I anticipate that if what you say is true, Frank, the General will be back in two hours. By that time you should all have disappeared. Right now the aircraft carrier HMS Burma is on its way to a rendezvous point twenty-odd miles off the Brazilian coast. We need to talk now, Frank, to get some idea of logistics for the pilots as to how far inland they have to fly. How many men we will need to collect the treasure and how many troops to defend us."

"I can give you co-ordinates when we get to the ship, Sir. Obviously we wish to protect this information. We have agreed that I go with the expedition. You will not need any troops in support, Sir. Twenty or thirty strong men with lifting gear will do."

"Err, wait a minute." Josie took Frank aside. "What about those weirdoes who attacked me in the valley Frank?" she whispered. "Shouldn't we say something about them?"

"Not right now, Josie. I did think of saying something about them at one stage but I have a feeling that they may be a card that we can play later." He winked at her. "Never show all your cards at one time Josie, we are playing for big stakes here with very serious players. Right, I suggest that we go back to the hotel, collect all our gear, and the gold, and have you pick us up in unmarked cars in one hour, Sir. Is that OK?" Everyone agreed.

Back at the hotel they made their way via the back entrance to their rooms. Frank scrambled his backpack together making sure that the diamonds were well stacked away at the bottom. Just in case he was being watched he resisted the inclination to examine them. They congregated at the reception desk with Josie offering to pay the bill for the four of them. As she was doing so, the three members of the press walked over and addressed Frank. "You appear to be in a hurry all of a sudden, Frank," said the man from The Times. "Going somewhere?"

"Yeah, we're going somewhere all right, we're getting out of here," he replied. "This is going to be your lucky day boys. Here's an exclusive. We have just been informed, by very reliable sources, that there are several international organisations showing an unhealthy interest in us, and the treasure. So, as you can imagine, we don't wish to be kidnapped and tortured. We have therefore decided to go into hiding until the problem has been resolved. You can print that."

The three press men looked startled. "Who are you talking about Frank? Can you give us any further information as to which organisations you are talking about? Are you talking Mafioso, individual countries or what?" one of them asked.

Frank saw a TV team coming over towards them. He didn't want to get involved in that scene. "Use your imagination guys. Who do you think? We are talking about millions of dollars here and there are any number of international organisations of a certain type who would dearly love to be able to add our findings to their pot, so we are gone. OK? We are not going to be picked up by strange people and forced to divulge where the treasure is. That's if the President hasn't got it already." A British Navy Captain approached them and caught their eye.

Frank and the girls gathered up their gear. "See you in a few weeks," he said to the press and cameras as they walked out of the hotel. The press followed them sensing a new story, shrieking and screaming questions at them, which they ignored. The four threw their kit into the car and climbed in. The car sped off.

"Well, you certainly put the cat amongst the pigeons there, Frank," said Josie. "They won't rest now until they know exactly where we are. His 'nibs' won't be at all pleased."

"The story isn't finished yet, what's that expression? It's not all over 'till the fat lady sings,' ain't that right? Hey, when you first met me did you think that all of this would happen? Come on girls, you're having the time of your lives. You might die tomorrow but think what we have been doing and there's a lot more yet," said Frank.

Frank's enthusiasm was infectious. Liz looked at Josie and her husband. "He's completely off his rocker you know" she said nodding at Frank. "Who wants to be a model and actress when we can be doing this instead. Life will never be the same again," she laughed.

"Hold on everybody, we are being followed and we will have to shake them off," said the Naval man.

The driver accelerated and the car shot off at high speed. Within a few minutes and after driving down several side streets, he was happy that they had shaken the followers off. They drove for just under an hour into the forests and eventually arrived in a clearing some fifteen miles from Rio. A helicopter was waiting for them with its engine running and rotors turning. The girls were very excited and ran doubled over for the helicopter with the men following along behind carrying their gear.

The crew of the chopper helped the girls climb aboard and guided them to their seats. They then went back and sorted out Frank and James. They asked politely if they could look after Frank's rifle. Frank let them store it away with all the bags.

They wasted no time taking off and within an hour they were flying low over the sea heading due east. The helicopter made such a noise that they all wore helmets and Frank retired into his own world. He mused on what had been happening to him and tried to envisage how everything might turn out.

"Financially independent. I wonder?" he thought to himself. "What's that going to take? If I make say two or three million pounds out of the diamonds and my percentage of the treasure that would have to do but I would have to be careful. Better than a kick in the balls, I suppose. The trouble is two million pounds just doesn't go anywhere in today's world. A good car, a better house and a million in the bank would just about be it and would probably see me through if I were really careful. But, there lies the rub doesn't it? I'm not careful. The answer to all this my boy is a really good financial adviser. I shall have to look into that as soon as I get back to England, that's for sure."

Shortly after, looking out of the side window Frank saw the aircraft carrier. It was enormous. Painted battleship grey it contrasted with the beautiful azure sea it rested on. Within a few minutes the chopper landed safely aboard and they were disembarking. They were escorted to their cabins watched by a curious crew. Frank felt relief at being aboard and safe from the unknown. The Navy Captain poked his head around his door.

"Two things, Sir," he said. "We are keeping hold of your rifle until we land, if you don't mind. We don't like passengers having guns on board which I am sure you will understand. I have been asked to advise you that we will be collecting you in about two hours for talks about your trip back to the mainland. I should get your head down until then, Sir. You will find drink and snacks in the refrigerator for your comfort. See you later. If you need anything use the phone and dial 9." He nodded politely and, shutting the door, he withdrew.

Frank sat on the bunk thinking again. He lifted his pack onto the bunk. Undoing the straps he rummaged around and withdrew the diamond pack. It was a long time since he had looked at them and he gently poured a few onto the blankets. They gleamed in the lights of the room. All of the stones were at least fifty carats and seemed huge to those he had seen in shop windows. He didn't know much about diamonds but knowing that even tiny ones cost a $1000 upwards he realised that each one must be close to $300,000. Soberly he calculated that just the few laying in front of him represented almost a million dollars. "I must be carrying seven or eight million dollars worth of diamonds in this pack," he thought. "That throws my calculations out a bit. That was definitely my lucky day when I found them around the pilot's waist." He scooped them up and gently poured them back in the pouch. He then put the pouch deep in the backpack again. Lying back on the bunk he let himself drift off into a restless sleep.

* * *

"We must be quite near to where we picked them up on radar General," the pilot said over the intercom. General Lomax was sitting up front behind the flight crew in the lead helicopter with some fifteen highly trained support troops strapped in behind. There were three other helicopters in the fleet all flying line abreast one mile apart and each one at four thousand feet. All were endeavouring to find the valley that Frank and the girls had flown out of. His instructions from the President the evening after the press conference had been brusque and simple.

"General, it is our duty to find this treasure and I order you to assemble an expedition right away. Find it and bring it back to me. If it is on Brazilian soil it belongs to the State. Do not return until it is in your hands. I am relying on you completely, General, to bring the treasure back without fuss. I particularly do not want the press to know that we have done this so the operation must be carried out in the utmost secrecy."

General Lomax had no doubt about the President's real intentions but thought it worth a shot. "Shall I ask Frank Blake to accompany us to guide us there" he asked innocently.

"Are you mad?" the President screamed at him. "The treasure is ours by right and I want it. Do not even consider discussing this with them. Just do as you're told and get it." He knew the President of old and to even consider arguing was probably to welcome termination of his position in the Government and possibly his disappearance either into obscurity, or worse. He felt very uncomfortable about the whole situation. The least he could do was to leave an unsigned note for Frank.

They flew for another thirty minutes scanning the ground for a sign of the valley but there was nothing but jungle spreading for miles in every direction. The radio crackled into use. "Blue three here. We have something on the starboard quarter at two o'clock. Am descending to have a closer look. Do you see it blue four?"

"Yes, we do blue three," came the reply "We will follow you down."

"General Sir, it's definitely a valley and by the looks of it there is an enormous pyramid at the entrance. It must be the one."

"Proceed into the valley and land, Blue three and four. We are following you. Did you hear that blue two?" He received acknowledgement and they turned to follow the two specks in the distance. They flew down into the valley and the General immediately saw the remains of the old crashed aircraft as Frank had described. Blue three and four had already landed by the site with their troops spilling out of the aircraft. His helicopter followed suit and he was out onto the ground quickly. Calling his officers together from the other aircraft, he discussed the situation with them.

"I think they must have discovered a cave or something very similar somewhere in this valley and therefore I want you to deploy your troops to scour every inch. We have about five hours before dusk so I suggest that you also set up camp near the crashed aircraft and arrange for us to camp here for the night. Should we not discover the treasure site tonight we must in the morning."

His officers, knowing what was at stake, dispersed to their platoons which quickly divided the valley into areas and they set off to explore in the late afternoon sun. A group of four started to set up the camp and began to organise food for later.

The General walked over to the crashed German plane alone and immediately saw the skeletons on the ground. His skin crawled at the thought of how long they must have lain there. Looking up at the cockpit he saw the pilot still sitting there as Frank had described. "Where have you hidden the gold Frank?" he thought. "What have you done with it?" He looked around the valley and wondered what he would have done in Frank's position. He turned to look up at the pyramid and the answer came. At that moment shots sounded over to his right then he heard shouts. Continuous fire started and then abruptly stopped. There was silence.

He started to run back to the campsite, pulling his radio at the same time. "Major, Major, what the fuck is going on?" he screamed. "Sanchez here Sir. I don't know, General. That was Finez's group and they were about three hundred metres away but I can't see them because of the grass. Hold on, Sir, I'll try to call them." He called for Finez but there was silence. He called again and as he did so there was an enormous explosion close to the camp. The General was knocked off his feet by the force and thrown several metres. His head was spinning and he was confused. "I'm under fire," he thought. His professional training kicked in and he rolled for some cover in the long grass. Looking up over the grass he saw that one of the helicopters had burst into flames. He stayed where he was and called Sanchez back. "Major, I want you to explore and find out if any of Blue platoon are still alive. Report back to me."

"Right away General. What's going on Sir? My troops are worried."

"Frankly, I don't know. Carry on, Major. The sooner we have some answers the better." A scream started from the camp and ended suddenly in a gurgling sound. There was another scream and a voice shouted out. "Look out General. They are coming your way." He rolled fast to his left and drew his pistol. "Not good news getting separated from my men. Should have known better," he thought. Getting to his feet he orientated himself and set off at a stumbling run for where he knew Major Sanchez to be.

"Crump..." That was the sound of a second helicopter going up. He knew that. He was not fit and was panting desperately. He hadn't run in years and the sudden exertion was almost too much. A figure ran out in front of him, indistinct and fuzzy, and he let go at it with his pistol. The figure disappeared only to reappear to his right. He fired off three more shots at it. They must have missed because the figure kept pace with him but now there were three more. He had covered nearly one hundred metres when he crashed to the ground. A hand was stuffed over his face. "Quiet, General," someone whispered in his ear. He realised that he had stumbled into one of the platoons and relaxed. He opened his eyes and recognised one of the group. Two more came running in and joined them. Then Major Sanchez rolled through the grass and joined them.

"What the hell is going on Major?" the General asked.

"We are under attack, Sir. By what or by whom I have no idea. All I know is that I have lost more than half of my men. Both of the other platoons are probably gone and two of our helicopters are blown up."

"Booom," another helicopter erupted in flames to their right. "There goes another, General, this is serious Sir. We have to get out of here, now! We don't know what, or who the hell we are fighting." At that moment the remaining helicopter started its engines. They all looked at each other. "General," said Major Sanchez, "we have to get to that chopper now before he leaves us stranded. Can you make it?"

"If you guys give me a hand, I can," he said rising to his feet. Two soldiers put their arms about his shoulders and they set off at a dead run.

"Any Blue platoon survivors to the chopper now," screamed the Major as he set off after them. There was no sign of anything except dead bodies as they ran hard for the helicopter; its engines were now running.

They hurtled into the cleared area where the camp had been. All the soldiers detailed to set up the site were dead. The pilots of the remaining helicopter spotted them coming and started to hover just off the ground. They plainly didn't want to hang around. The group scrambled into the chopper with six other soldiers appearing from nowhere. Their faces were white with fear.

The General ran to the cockpit. "Get out of here fast," he shouted to the crew. The pilots needed no other bidding and the chopper heaved itself into the air and climbed rapidly away.

"There is no sign of anything out there," shouted the Major above the din of the engines. "By the look of it, Sir, everyone's dead." Hanging on tight the General leant out through the door opening and scanned the valley. There were dead bodies everywhere but no sign of attackers. Eighty per cent of his men were dead and there was no indication of who had killed them. He put on a helmet and pressed the transmit button. "Captain." "Yes, Sir?" came the reply. "Head back to base Captain, as fast as you can go."

The chopper climbed at full power out of the valley and steadied on its climb to operational height and heading. General Lomax slumped to the floor and exchanged looks with his men. Running from the unknown had etched fear into all their faces.

* * *

In a bunker, three hundred feet down in the Appalachian Mountains, in the United States of America, twelve men and woman were grouped around a large plasma television screen. The valley was showing on the screen with the helicopter climbing rapidly out of it. The satellite camera showed every detail including the dead bodies laying on the ground and the three destroyed helicopters. The picture clarity was stunning.

The head of the CIA, Lieutenant Colonel Frank Rogers Jnr., stood staring at the screen. "What the hell happened there gentlemen?" he said quietly. Turning to his team, he said, "Did any one of you see exactly what went on there, anything at all?" Everyone was standing still and staring at the screen hardly able to believe what he or she had just seen.

His assistant, and PA, Libby Miles was the first to speak. "I'm sure I saw some shadows moving around Sir but it might have been my imagination as it all happened so quickly."

A young Navy lieutenant backed this up. "Yes Sir there seemed to be a lot of very wispy shadows moving about very fast. Or I think there were. Jesus Christ those guys didn't seem to stand a chance. But there didn't appear to be any gunfire aimed at the Brazilians Sir that's the strangest thing."

"Replay that tape now," he told the projectionist. Thirty seconds later they were again watching the helicopters land and the troops disembarking and spreading out; moving towards the valley sides. The pictures were of a very high quality and he could even see the General moving over to the old crashed aircraft. At the height of the short battle he could just make out shadowy figures. He turned to his second in command. "What are they?"

"Never seen anything like it Sir. Can't even see what type of weapons they are using, if any at all. "Freeze it there," he commanded the operator. "Now blow that up as far as you can go." The operator enlarged the screen by 300 per cent and panned in to one of the figures. At that magnification there was nothing to see except a slight discoloration. The operator panned back until the shadow slowly formed but again there was no discernable shape except for a blurred image of a face under its hood.

"The strange thing is that they just seem to run the soldiers down." The second in command said this slowly. "Almost driving over them, and when they do, look, the soldiers die." It's the same with the helicopters, look." They were watching the play back in slow motion. The sight of the helicopters exploding and bursting into flame was a spectacular sight.

"I want a complete study done of that scene and some answers pretty damn quick. I'm not sending in my men until we know what those things are and how to counter attack them." The CIA Chief Executive turned and slowly walked away to his other meeting; thinking deeply. "What the hell are those things?" he said to his PA. She shrugged her shoulders. "What ever they are, they have to be got rid of before we can send in our team to get the treasure, Sir," she replied.

An Air Force messenger came hurrying up to them and the PA took the envelope. She passed it to the CIA Chief. He looked at the markings on the front.

'IMMEDIATE. FOR YOUR EYES ONLY."

He raised his eyebrows and opened the envelope.

It said simply. 'Subjects have disappeared completely, stop. Intelligence is that the British have them, stop. Am using contacts to confirm rumours, stop. More later. Stop.'

"Damn it to hell, it's the Brits again. You have to take your hat off to them. They've moved like greased lightning. I should have remembered about them. Slippery as a 'barrel load of eels' they are." He paused and studied the letter again not really seeing it. "Use all and any satellites possible that can scan the ground over Brazil and bring me all the information you think may be involved with this situation. I think I will have a word with the President about this." He continued on to his meeting.

* * *

Captain George Wellesley leaned forward, his elbows on his desk and his chin jutting forward. The responsibility of HMS Burma, a 20,000-ton British aircraft carrier and nearly one thousand five hundred men and women was his and he was angry. As he saw it his beloved ship had been requisitioned to baby-sit some bloody members of the public and to initiate some sort of stupid plan to collect some sort of treasure trove from the middle of the bloody jungle. To top it all he had just been pulled out of a very pleasurable exercise with the American Fleet in the warmth of the Gulf of Mexico, which he had been thoroughly enjoying.

He scowled at the British Ambassador to Brazil who was sitting opposite him. His two top officers also sitting in on the meeting flinched. They knew only too well what their Captain was like when he got into one of these moods.

"I fully understand what you are telling me and what our Government wants me to do but honestly Ambassador the cost of doing what you ask will cost millions. What am I supposed to tell my crew? That they are to sit on their fannies for three weeks while we run this fella around the South Atlantic? Has the Prime Minister honestly tried to cost this whole escapade out? What on earth can this treasure be worth for God's sake to take the principle British Aircraft Carrier out of a very important exercise with our premier NATO partner to do this junket?"

The Ambassador chose his words carefully. "The Prime Minster and his Cabinet believe that this is a very important situation and that the eventual rewards for our country will prove this exercise well worth while. Besides, it is thought that eventually the prestige of our country will be enhanced to a very high degree if we can pull this off. And, if we are successful and everything works out well, it won't do your career any harm either. For a while your ship and your name will be at the centre of the Government's attention. That can't be bad, Captain Wellesley can it?"

The Captain was quiet for a while as he pondered the pros and cons of the situation. "Tell me Ambassador, this man Blake, what's his background and how has he managed to suddenly become such the centre of attention that the British Government is prepared to go to these enormous lengths to assist him?"

"From what information I have received from England and from my own enquires, it would appear that the man is either quite an exceptional human being or just plain lucky. I'm not sure which at the moment. He was educated to an average standard in one of our state schools, nothing exceptional there, and joined the RAF when he was eighteen. He decided that the RAF Regiment was for him and it wasn't until he had been in for three years that he changed direction. He volunteered to join a small elite operational squad of fourteen men that was being formed, which was to liaise frequently with, err, other special branches of the armed forces. The hierarchy of the RAF, being a jealous bunch, had decided that the Army and the Navy had their Special Forces branches and therefore it was decided that the RAF should have theirs, to be called the Royal Air Force Special Services, RAFSS for short, a bit of a mouthful I know but there you are. His speciality appeared to have been as a sniper as he was proved to be quite gifted with the ability to handle a rifle shooting long distances. He proved that point two weeks ago when rescuing an English film unit in the Brazilian jungle which was being attacked by bandits. He shot three of them, the bandits that is, apparently in spectacular fashion from a range of some three hundred yards, killing them all. Over twenty people from the film group witnessed the scene and have verified what happened. I talked to their director, strangely enough the son of a friend of mine, who was very impressed and said Blake was very cool and matter of fact about it as though it happened every day of his life. They wanted to ensure that it was noted that they were all extremely grateful for what he did and expressed their opinion that if he had not turned up when he did they would undoubtedly have died, or worse, at the hand of the bandits, as we know."

"Interesting," said the Captain.

"Yes, we thought so too, especially when you consider that he hadn't done anything like that for some twenty odd years. Anyway, to continue, he left the services after seven years, four of which had been in the Special Services squad in which he served with some distinction in several areas of the world's trouble spots rising to the rank of Sergeant, the top rank possible in that type of group. He retired from the RAF at twenty five I think it was and was held in high esteem by his commanding officer. As I understand it, he was commended three times for bravery during action, Very unusual, as you know Captain. He married and started a small business selling computers but has concentrated on software over the last few years. His income has been moderate and his business has run smoothly for those twenty-odd years during which time he had three children, two boys and a girl. He divorced his wife last year, reasons for which are a bit hazy; anyway he appeared on holiday in Brazil apparently doing the pyramid tourist thing when he came across this little episode with the British film crew. He cadged a flight out of there with the two girls and the rest you know. The pilot had a heart attack during a storm, Blake takes over, runs out of fuel, manages to find the only bit of open ground in five hundred square miles of impenetrable jungle. He lands the damn plane successfully, finds a fortune in old Nazi treasure, and Bob's your Uncle." The Ambassador took a sip of his wine, his mouth having become dry.

"Even more interesting. This report we have just received about General Lomax and most of his men being wiped out is very unsettling, what does Blake know about this? Why weren't he and the girls troubled while they were in the valley? There are too many ifs and buts about the whole thing, too many coincidences. Nobody has that amount of luck, do they? It just does not add up." The Captain glanced at his officers for help. They simply shrugged their shoulders.

The Ambassador took another sip of his wine and rolled it around his mouth thoughtfully. "As I understand it the Government is uneasy about it all as well but have decided to go along with the man. I must admit I was impressed with Blake when I first met him at the airport. He's strong mentally, there's no doubt about that, and he has a habit of looking you straight in the eye in a disconcerting manner. Between the four of us, I can tell you that he is a brother Mason. He gave me the sign. I must admit to being surprised when he did so. It was the last thing I expected. I think we should get him up here and have a chat. See if we can prise the truth out of him. Get the girls up here as well."

* * *

Frank woke to the sound of banging on his door. "Wake up Sir," a voice called. "You're wanted in the Captains quarters in fifteen minutes. Please be ready Sir."

In exactly fifteen minutes Frank was being escorted by two very large, silent, marine troopers decked out in white uniforms and with pistols on their hips. Frank glanced at them and thought they would be a real handful. They marched ahead and behind him; he felt like a naughty boy at school being taken to see the headmaster. He was ushered into the Captain's cabin to find both of the girls sitting there in jeans and tee shirts looking stunning. The Captain, the Ambassador and two senior naval officers were all dressed in their best whites.

Holding out his hand the Captain came forward and introduced himself to Frank. He deliberately gave no recognition. "Huh huh, I'm in for a grilling here," Frank thought.

"Good afternoon, Frank, welcome aboard Her Majesty's Ship 'Burma' I'm Captain George Wellesley and I'm in charge of this vessel and all that goes on within her." Frank said hello, shook the man's hand in return and sat down next to the girls who both kissed him in greeting.

Frank studied the Captain. He was a tall man, the same height as Frank with a long handsome tanned face, high cheekbones and widely spaced bright blue piercing eyes, which seemed to lock onto yours and didn't let go until he was ready. He had a wide mouth with a mean look about it. Strangely, for a Navy man in such a high position, although he talked with the confidence of a good education, there was still the soft burr of a Scottish accent. His voice and the way he controlled his movements were indications of a man well used to dispensing orders and expecting obedience. The Captain busied himself by ensuring everyone was well watered. The Ambassador spoke first.

"I have rather good news for you. Her Majesty's Government has agreed to go after your treasure and to bring it back to this vessel for safe transportation to England on the understanding that Great Britain is never mentioned in connection with this exercise. Do we all agree on that?" he queried. Everyone nodded in agreement. "We have the go-ahead from London. Incidentally, before we go further, we have been informed that your General, Frank, General Lomax, has just had a severe shock and has returned to Rio with only a few of his troops left. The others, apparently, have been wiped out. They are minus three helicopters. Now before we start Frank, we have to say to you that we find this extremely disturbing as I am sure you can understand."

Frank had to suppress a smile. He glanced at the Captain who was studying Frank intensely.

The Ambassador continued, "You did say that you had this covered somehow Frank, and forgive me if I have this wrong, but I recall that you said that there were some surprises that the General would come up against. Well these are some pretty serious surprises if he loses almost fifty men. What happened out there Frank?" He felt the girls move uneasily next to him.

Frank was quiet for a minute. "In all honesty Sir I am at a loss as to how to tell you about this valley." He got up from his chair and shuffled about for a little while. He looked and felt very uncomfortable. They all waited in silence. "The best I can do for now is this. I did say that I had someone on the inside in the General's team. Well that was a lie. Something happened when we were there which we don't want to go into right now but I believe that the valley has it's own protection system but for whatever reason I do not know." Everyone looked startled and the girls broke their silence.

"We knew you were up to something Frank the day after I was chased," said Josie. She turned to the Captain and the Ambassador. "One evening Frank and Liz were fooling around and left me by the waterfall where we had been bathing. I was starting to get dressed when I felt someone watching me. I turned and saw several shadowy figures just standing there a few feet away looking at me. I screamed my head off and ran like hell for the plane, still screaming for Frank and Josie. These figures kept up with me with ease. In fact one was along side me and he seemed to be just floating. Frank heard my screams and shot at them. The one alongside me coughed and went down. The next thing I knew I was in the plane with Liz and Frank. Later on Frank slipped out into the night to have a nose around. He came back after about an hour saying he couldn't find anything, not even the body of the one he shot." She wanted to say about what she saw when they flew out and looked at Frank. He gave a slight shake of his head knowing what she wanted to say.

The Captain had been following the conversation with his eyes locked onto Josie. He now turned to Frank.

"You obviously know something, Frank, which could very well affect the outcome of our trip. Did you know that the General would meet these, what shall we call them, shadows? and why did they not harm you and the girls when you were there for five days?"

Frank was now half sitting on the Captain's drinks sideboard. "Yes, Captain, I had a pretty good idea that they would give the General some trouble. What I do know is that the pyramid has its own defence force." There were murmurs all round when he said this. "Fortunately, whoever 'they' are looked kindly on Josie, Liz and me, and never appeared to want to interfere too much in our day-to-day life there. I believe we were not perceived as a threat. I also believe that we can go back at any time we want and remove the treasure as long as that is all we do. I am afraid anyone who wishes harm to the pyramid will die Sir. It really is as simple as that. Whoever the shadows, as you call them Captain, are they have capabilities far beyond ours. You do not have to fear them as far as our expedition is concerned and as long as our people behave themselves and honour their situation."

"Do you really expect us to believe that rubbish?" the Captain asked.

Frank looked at the man. "Try going in there without me," he said.

The Captain walked over to Frank and stood about three feet from him. "Don't you threaten me mister," he said in a loud voice glaring at him. "This is the British Government you are dealing with here. You don't threaten or blackmail Great Britain. Now tell us the truth and let's have less of your nonsense."

Frank looked calmly at the Captain who had gone red in the face. "As I said, Captain, try going in without me, you will lose everyone. Do you want to give it a try? Do you want to lose men as the General did? Wouldn't that be a waste of time and personnel?" He was mocking the Captain and the Captain knew it. They stood face-to-face glaring at each other but Frank felt the cool one.

"So don't call me a liar," said Frank calmly. "I don't give a monkey's fuck as to who you think you are and who you represent. Just don't try to patronise and bully me, or the girls. We won't stand for it."

An extraordinary thing happened. Liz jumped up and moved to Frank's side. Her eyes were flashing and she almost, but not quite, bared her teeth in anger. "Josie and I know Frank. You don't. If Frank says that's what is happening in the valley then that's what's happening. If you guys don't believe it then don't go. Drop us back on the mainland and we will hook up with someone else."

Frank put an arm around her slim waist and she leaned against him. He felt good. They both looked at Josie who also moved over to them. "I agree. If that's what Frank thinks then that's fine by me," she said.

The Ambassador moved in to calm things down. "I'm sure that we all want the same things Frank. The Captain has to be sure that his men will not be under threat and he needs more concrete evidence than what you are giving that's all." He was curious himself anyway.

Frank continued to bluff his way out of trouble. "Do you really think that I would deliberately set out to harm our own troops who were going to help me remove the treasure? Do you really think that I would go back into that valley if there were any possibility of harm coming to my friends or me? Of course not. I can only repeat myself; they will not be under any threat whatsoever as long as they all behave themselves and as long as we don't disturb the status quo."

"All right then." The Captain was now in control of himself once more. He hadn't been spoken to like that for years and he didn't like it. "We will have to respect what you say. My recommendation is that we leave at first light and fly in with four of my Chinooks with thirty men and you, Frank. Hopefully we can load the treasure in three to four hours and get the hell out of there. My biggest fear is that America will be watching us and will try to interfere. We will have to take that risk. I suggest that you have an early dinner and that you get some rest. You will need to be ready and on main deck at 4.30am, Frank."

Frank agreed and turned to thank the girls for their support. Liz whispered to the other two. "All for one and one for all." They smiled at one another.

"You two go and enjoy yourselves. I'll do what the Captain suggests and get an early night"

"Do you want me to come with you Frank?" whispered Liz into his ear.

Frank looked at her and nodded. "If you like."

The men stood up as they left and they were escorted back to their cabins. The escort stopped at Liz's cabin. She looked at them. "I'm with him'" she said nodding to Frank. No expression whatsoever showed on the escort's face. "Yes' Mom'" was all they said as they moved onto Frank's door. He opened it and went in with Liz closing it behind him. "That will give them something to talk about," he laughed.

"That's for sure. Now let me give you something to smile about too," she said moving into him.

They lay afterwards letting the air conditioning of the cabin cool their bodies. He couldn't help but stroke her beautiful black breasts and stomach. She lay watching the contrast of his tanned hands moving over her body.

"You know Frank, if someone had told me three weeks ago that I would be making love to a man within such a short space of time and be enjoying it I would have laughed in their faces and taken the bet."

"Don't question it, just enjoy it," he said.

They continued to talk until the daylight passed into night. Both were so comfortable in each other's company because there was no judgement from either side and also they were friends. The friendship could turn into raging passion whenever it needed to, which they both found extremely satisfying.

Frank woke again to the sound of insistent knocking. He glanced at his watch and saw that it was only 3.45am. He rose and opened the cabin door. "Time to rise Sir bearing in mind the early start," said the marine.

He thanked the sailor and headed for the shower.

Liz was still dozing and answered a muffled goodbye to him when he left. He was escorted to the galley and given a huge breakfast of tea, cereal and fruit juice, scrambled eggs and bacon with toast. As soon as he was finished he was again escorted and he eventually arrived on deck to find a busy scene with the helicopters already running their engines and soldiers crouched ready to embark. A young officer noticed Frank and walked over to him carrying a helmet. "Morning Sir, I'm Major Ian Evans. I understand that I'm to be advised by you as to how we operate this mission. I have been fully briefed by the Captain who has advised me of possible problems, if you know what I mean." He looked meaningfully at Frank.

Frank nodded to him. "I know what you mean Major, you will be all right, trust me." He was strapping on the German Walther P-38 and found himself being watched by most of the soldiers and the Major. He removed his grubby Stetson and put it in his backpack, which he shrugged over his shoulders. There was no way he was going anywhere without his diamonds. "May I see that?" said the major pointing to the Walther P-38. "Sure," Frank said handing over the weapon.

The Major hefted it in his hand feeling the balance. "Is this the real thing Sir?" he asked.

"Yup," said Frank. "It's at least sixty years old and still in beautiful condition. I found it on the body of the dead pilot from the crashed aircraft, which you will see later. Most of the German officers in the Second World War had these; they were standard issue and ultra reliable. This one still works well even after all that time. Shall we go?"

The Major turned to his troops and waved them to the choppers. The racket was deafening. Frank felt more excited and alive than at any time in his life. He was virtually in charge of over thirty trained assault troops and four Chinook helicopters and they were going on a mission. He hadn't had power like this even when he was in the RAF. He walked over to the leading chopper with the Major escorting him thinking "It can't get better than this."

On getting into the leading chopper a crewman fixed his helmet and switched on his radio. Almost immediately the pilot came on. "I'm told that you have a vector and distance for us Sir."

"Wait one," Frank said. He fumbled in his shirt pocket and took out the papers he had been working on. "OK. Your vector is 205 degrees and your distance should be 330 miles, give or take a couple of miles."

"Roger that Sir. All aircraft, you have heard the heading. Let's get to it. We will be flying below 100ft and keep an eye out above for bandits, out."

The chopper clattered into the air and turned onto its heading. Frank looked out of the side door, which was open. He was shocked to see how low they were flying. He settled himself down and closed his eyes. In a few seconds he was asleep.

Someone was shouting his name and shaking him. He opened his eyes to see the Major with helmet on and his face blackened. "ETA, according to your figures Sir is ten minutes. The pilot would like you to join him to confirm the valley is the correct one." Frank moved up into the cockpit and plugged his helmet in. They studied the terrain for some ten minutes with Frank becoming more and more uneasy when there was a shout, "Port side at 11 o'clock Major."

Everyone turned and scoured the horizon. There indeed was a patch of light green in a sea of dark green, and looking a strange shape.

"That's the one Major all right." How could he ever forget his first sighting of that valley at a time when he was running out of fuel? At the time it felt like seeing Shangri La. He felt a deep excitement churning his stomach over at seeing the valley again when a voice boomed inside his head. The sound level was so loud for a moment and then receded to a more reasonable level as though someone had turned down the volume.

"We have been waiting for you Frank. There has been some trouble here but it is quiet now. We know that you have come for the treasure and we have been watching you since you left your ship. I have been asked to say that it would be appreciated if you could finish what you have come to do and to leave as quickly as possible. It's becoming nothing but a source of irritation to us. We are also being scanned from the sky. Even now Frank you are being watched." There was a pause as though she was listening to someone else. "Yes I will ask him. Frank would you like us to stop the eyes in the sky from watching you?"

He put his head in his hands and thought. "Yes please Sandy." There was no answer but he just hoped that she had heard him. What was that all about? Did he really hear that message or was it the remnants of his dreams? It couldn't possibly be for real. Christ if people knew he was hearing voices, and he was hearing voices. He felt confused and he put his head in his hands again.

"You OK Sir?" the Major was watching him with some concern.

"Sure Major. Let's get to it. Land as close to the base of the pyramid as possible."

"Jesus Christ, Major, come and look at this," cried the pilot suddenly. The chopper crew and the Major gaped at the view as they circled the valley. The other pilots came on over the radio. "Hey, what's been happening here skipper? Is it OK to land? There are bodies everywhere and look at that. Is that burned out choppers or what?"

"Wait one," said the leading pilot. He turned and looked at the Major. "What the hell is going on here Sir? I'm not that happy about going down in there. Somebody's already tried by the look of it. Should we get confirmation from base?"

"Negative," said the Major. Just hold station for a minute." He went aft to where Frank was standing looking out of the window. "What's all this Sir?" he said pointing at the scene of devastation below. "My boys are a little worried."

Without looking at the Major Frank said. "Your men will be perfectly O.K. Major. Tell your men they will be protected and they have nothing to fear. Go ahead and land and I will talk to them." The Major relayed the news to his pilots.

All four aircraft clattered down into the valley and landed. The troops piled out and formed their respective protective rings around their individual aircraft. They were all looking at the crashed and burned aircraft and the dead bodies lying all around. Frank climbed out of the helicopter and took off his helmet. He pulled the battered old sweat stained Stetson from his pack and put it on. He walked to the pyramid and climbed several steps and turned around. The Major was right behind him.

"Call the men over Major but leave the pilots in their cockpits." The Major gave Frank a sharp look, walked down the pyramid steps and spoke to his men at each aircraft. He came back with the men filing along behind. Frank waited until they were all grouped at the bottom steps.

"Men, don't worry about what you see here. It's not your problem and you won't be affected. The treasure is in this pyramid and I have the key." He raised it in the air. "It's your job to get it out of there and into the choppers at the double. Do not touch anything else except the treasure or we could be in trouble. Major, may I suggest that your troops line up the steps forming a chain so that everything can be passed down from up there easily. You and I, and four others, will go into the pyramid to remove what we find there and pass it down. OK?"

The Major was visibly sweating with a film of perspiration across his forehead and his top lip. He was only thirty-eight years old and although experienced in combat had never experienced anything like this. This was the unknown and nothing can terrify like the unknown. None of his training had prepared him for anything like this.

"Yes Sir" he answered. He gave his orders to his Sergeants and Corporals and the men began to form a line up the pyramid.

"Pick four men, Major and follow me." He stopped. "I want you to ensure that there is a Sergeant at the beginning of the chain and at the end. I want to ensure there is no pilfering, if you know what I mean. I also want an inventory made of what we have loaded. Is that understood Major?" Oh, and by the way, ensure we have plenty of torches and lights up there please."

"Yes Sir." The Major replied.

Frank slowly went up the steps to the first level and approached the door. He knew there were several troopers following close behind him watching, fascinated. He could imagine the conversations in the Sergeants mess later that night and the stories they would have to tell for the rest of their lives. He approached the recess where the door was. It looked as though nobody had been there for a thousand years. The girls had done a wonderful job covering their tracks. He even had to brush away sand from the keyhole.

The Major came panting up the steps with three more troopers, each was carrying armfuls of high-powered torches. He rushed across the levelled area not wanting to miss anything.

Frank turned the key unit and pushed sideways. Again there was the sound of rushing sand and the massive stone door slid slowly to the right. There were gasps from behind him. He handed out the torches and moved into the vaulted room. The designated men and the Major moved in behind; they stayed close to Frank.

"OK Major. Get your men to work," he said. The men, including the Major, were standing and staring with their eyes almost on stalks at the array of treasure lying in front of them illuminated by the torches. "For Christ's sake get a move on men" he shouted at them.

Galvanised into action the Major lit four lanterns and then directed his men in the removal of the boxes of gold.

Frank moved over to the paintings. They were in superb condition with many still in their original packing. "These alone will be worth millions," he thought. "Heaven knows what the eventual total will be." The day before he had asked the girls to contact Christies in London and ask for a team of people to stand by to assess the treasure. The director had been sworn to secrecy and told that Frank would contact them again as soon as the treasure was safe. Christies were not told where the treasure would be, but to 'just stand by.'

Quickly the men developed a rhythm and everything began to move swiftly. Frank found that he could lift a full box of the gold fairly easily but only did it once. The looks of the troopers when they saw him do it stopped him from repeating the action. He gave himself a small smile of immense satisfaction realising that indeed he had amazing strength but it wasn't a good thing to show it off with these guys. They worked for three hours loading the helicopters far below until the Major, now soaked in perspiration, pleaded with Frank for his men to rest. "Let them have half an hour Sir so they can grab a drink and something to eat. There isn't a lot left but they will be able to work faster if they have a break now." The Major was looking hard at Frank. "You look extremely fit Sir if I may say so. You haven't even broken into a sweat." Frank shrugged his shoulders and walked outside joining some of the men on the levelled area. They sat down and broke out rations and water, and rested in the hot sun with perspiration drying rapidly on them. The men below were chattering constantly about what they were doing, with the information coming down to them from the men working in the vault.

"I've never seen anything like it Sir," said the Major. "How on earth will you ever be able to value it all? I counted at least two hundred boxes of gold alone let alone those other boxes and the paintings. You have some of the most famous artists of all time there. Was all this looted from Germany then Sir? We couldn't help noticing the German swastika flags of course."

"Too many questions Major. Sorry but I don't have all the answers yet. I suspect that this was one of the main warehouses for the Nazis escaping from Europe as the war ended and that those organising it died in the plane down there," he pointed down into the valley at the crashed Heinkel. "I also suspect that the survivors have been looking for this stuff ever since and could still prove troublesome if we don't get our finger out let alone countless other organisations who would dearly love to get their hands on it as you can imagine. Loading it on board is not the end of the matter. We have to get it back and I have to tell you that, without a shadow of a doubt, we are probably being watched by satellite right now."

There was an uncomfortable murmur from the men around him. "I suggest that you pass it on down the line that everyone should keep their eyes peeled for trouble, particularly from the air. At the slightest sign we will abandon what we are doing and get back to the choppers fast."

The Major got onto his portable radio and started talking rapidly to his pilots. He was asked a question and passed it onto Frank. "They are asking how long will it be before we finish Sir."

Frank stood up and walked back into the vault looking around him. "Maybe half an hour," he thought. "About half an hour Major if we get back to work now. Let's finish it."

The word had got out to the other troopers in the line and, sweating profusely in the heat, they re-doubled their efforts. Within twenty minutes the last box was being passed back down the line and Frank and the others swept the area with their torches. Only the flags remained. Frank walked over and tore one down. With the others watching he folded it and put it into his pack. Out of the corner of his eye he saw a sparkle. Pointing his torch he saw a small pile of stones that glinted in the light. He walked over to them. Lying on the floor he found a handful of diamonds and emeralds that had obviously fallen out of one of the boxes. Picking them up he was aware of the men watching him. He walked over to them holding the precious stones in his cupped hands. "Let's go out into the light," he said.

Standing at the top of the level with the group of about ten men around him and with the rest of the troopers watching, he said. "Your help today is appreciated more than I can say. Your Government will eventually take their fair share of all this and you will never see a penny. I might not either." There was laughter at that. "I have just found this handful of diamonds and emeralds lying on the floor in there and that's the last of it. You deserve a bonus for sweating your guts out today helping me to get this lot back."

"What I am about to do is completely illegal so it's going to be down to you as to whether or not you allow anyone else to know about this. I am, therefore, going to give this bunch of diamonds to the Major as a gift from me to you guys with instructions to ensure that the proceeds are evenly distributed amongst you. How he goes about cashing them I don't want to know. As far as you are concerned you have never seen them and know nothing about them. Write down a list of every man present today, including the helicopter crews and the Major will make sure you get your share within six months."

Frank turned and looked at the Major who looked shocked. "Are you prepared to do this, Major?"

"Of course I will Mr Blake, you are very generous and the men will appreciate it I'm sure, but if it ever gets out my career and the careers of the other men here today will be finished."

Frank was silent for a while gazing out over the vast green jungle stretching out in front of him. "All right Major, I will sell them for you chaps and get the cash equivalent. Give me a while and I will see what I can do. But I will get the money back to you I promise, is that, OK?"

"That's very fair Sir," said the Major and the men around him murmured their agreement and thanks.

"Right that's settled. Pass that back down the line and let's go home." He turned the key and the great door rumbled back into place.

A cheer went up from the men that echoed around the valley bouncing off the walls. Everyone began moving swiftly back to their respective helicopters which were now running up their engines. Within ten minutes the choppers were taking off in line astern; clattering noisily and slowly out of the valley with the vast weight of the treasure distributed between them. Most of the men looking back at the carnage left behind were thanking God they had emerged safely. Many of them were thinking of what must have happened in that valley. They would all have amazing stories to tell their families and children in years to come

Frank looked back down the valley as they rose into the late afternoon sun. "One day those men should be buried Major."

"Yes, Sir, I was thinking the very same thing," the Major replied.

Frank settled himself down in the cabin. He put his helmet back on so that he could stay in contact with the pilots while he concentrated his thinking.

"Goodbye Sandy. Thanks for your help. Maybe we will meet again one day."

For a while there was silence except for the clattering of the helicopter engines. Then, did he imagine it or was it real? There seemed to be a reply run through his head. The voice said softly:

"Maybe we will Frank maybe we will." As he drifted off into an exhausted sleep he thought that he was definitely going loopy.

* * *

The CIA man and three of his staff hurried to the Operations Room. The operations executive met him at the door. "We have just picked up a fleet of four large helicopters heading for the valley Sir. We think they have probably come from the British aircraft carrier HMS Burma but we can't be sure. They are flying very low, probably to avoid the Brazilian Radar but they are definitely on a heading for the valley."

"What's their ETA?" the Chief asked.

"We estimate about twenty minutes Sir. What would you like us to do?"

"Well we can't scramble fighters. The Brazilians wouldn't like that at all. We could try to intercept them when they come back and force them down somewhere but I think that wouldn't go down too well with the Brits. That's if it is the Brits." He pondered for a while. "Could we launch a force of our own to the valley now and intercept them do you think"?

"We would never make it in time Sir. We might if we could get some paratroopers out there within the next three hours, but by that time they might have been and gone. Besides Sir, there is the problem of that unknown force out there. Could we be sure that we didn't suffer the same fate as the Brazilians?"

"You have a point," said the CIA chief. "It's interesting to ponder on the fact, ladies and gentlemen, that the Brits, if it is the Brits, must know about the massacre and if they do how come they are going in? How come they think they can do better than the Brazilians?" He paused, thinking. "No, they know something. There's no way they would go in with such a force knowing what happened to the Brazilians if they weren't sure that it wouldn't happen to them. They know something that we don't, very interesting indeed. We can only wait and see."

They continued watching the progress of the helicopters. As they approached the valley the screens suddenly went blank. The CIA man roared, "What the fuck has happened?" There was total panic as frantic efforts were made to restore the picture. "We have lost all contact with the three satellites Sir."

"Well get it back and fast," he roared again. Despite every effort it was impossible to regain the links until some five hours later when, for some inexplicable reason, all screens came back on. The questions raised were never ever properly answered. There was by then no sign of any helicopters. The valley was empty except for the carnage of the previous expedition.

The CIA man looked at the screens and the images from the valley. "It's too late, they have been and gone. If it takes me the rest of my life I'm going to find out what went on down here today."

* * *

The Captain watched the radar screens with his usual intensity. Standing along side him Liz and Josie hopped from foot to foot waiting uneasily. Suddenly four blips came up on the screen at maximum range and at the same time the voice of his radar chief came on. "We have picked them up Sir, seventy miles out. They are flying low and quite slowly." The tannoy on the bridge came alive.

"Exercise air fleet four zero, zero in bound. All operational staff are in good condition. Exercise completed as designated." This was the code name for the operation and the code for a satisfactory completion had been given.

The Captain smiled at his crew on the bridge. "What does that all mean?" asked Josie."

"It means, dear lady, they have the treasure and they are all safe. They are about thirty minutes from landing. Now if you will excuse me I will arrange for their reception."

Dancing up and down the girls whooped and threw their arms around the Captain. He extricated himself grinning broadly. "Get these mad woman off me!" he commanded his crew in a joking manner. "Lieutenant Rogers, escort these ladies to the flight deck so they can welcome their hero home."

All four helicopters swept in low towards the carrier and flew in line astern along the length of the main deck. The ship's crew were yelling, waving and cheering. They peeled away and landed back on the carrier each helicopter sweeping in from behind and landing in its allotted place. The troops disembarking from the planes were grinning from ear to ear in anticipation of many free drinks that evening as they told their stories.

The girls ran towards the leading chopper and, as Frank emerged looking gaunt and tired; they engulfed him with their arms and kissed him, at the same time throwing questions at him. "Yup we have all of it, can you imagine?" he said to them smiling.

It was the next day when they were requested to attend the Captain in his cabin. At midday they joined him.

"I wish to say this to you. I am in charge of a warship and what is happening right now is normally out of my remit. However, I have been thrust into the middle of all this and have to do as my masters bid. I have, therefore, been having lengthy discussions with London" he began. "The Foreign Office is most perturbed about us having stolen, that's their word not mine, this treasure from Brazilian soil despite the fact that it was a direct order from the Home Secretary. There's obviously a conflict between the Home Office and the Foreign Office but that is not our concern right now."

"President Ramirez is apparently incandescent with rage that his expedition failed so spectacularly. General Lomax has disappeared. Assassinated we believe. The President's Secret Service has been making extensive enquiries as to the whereabouts of the three of you and believes that you have launched your own expedition. Beyond that he is just guessing right now but, nonetheless, he is very angry and could prove to be a threat to you all later. That's one factor. The treasure is being crated and should be ready for transportation very shortly. That's the second factor. Now, how do we protect you three and get the cargo back to England? We have decided therefore to put the following to you."

"We propose that we fly you two girls by helicopter and land you safely but secretly in Barbados where you will be looked after by the British Consul and then you will be put on the first flight straight back to London. After that you would be on your own. As for you and the cargo

Frank, after retrieving our helicopter from Barbados we intend to sail on down to the Falklands. A cargo jet will be waiting to fly you and the cargo back to England."

"Once back home we suggest that you all hold a press conference stating that you have personally retrieved the treasure, that it will shortly be going up for auction, and that you have nominated trustees who will negotiate with anyone who feels and can prove that any of the treasure may have been stolen from themselves, or their families, during the Second World War."

The faces of the three were getting grim. Liz said. "By the sound of it this could all go on for years and years with claim and counter claim costing thousands and possibly millions of dollars. By the time the British Government, trustees, lawyers and others have had their bit we will be left with very little. Where's the fairness in that?"

"Not my problem," said the Captain brusquely. "You know my orders. After that, you are all on your own, but the Government will be advising you along the line of course. They will talk to you in greater detail when you get to London. They will make contact with you apparently. So, that is the reality, what do you think?"

"We would like to talk about this in private Sir, if you don't mind," said Frank.

"Don't be too long in making up your mind," said the Captain. "I'll be back in fifteen minutes." He left the room.

"OK, girls, what do you want to do?" asked Frank.

They were both silent and looking at each other. Eventually Josie said. "It sounds like a stitch up to me Frank but what other options do we have? It has all got so bloody complicated. I thought that all we had to do was get the treasure back and sell it and that we would end up very nicely off thank you very much. Now, all I can see is the Brazilians coming after us all the time wailing 'You pinched our treasure' and thousands of unknown people all saying 'It's ours.' It's just a bloody mess."

"I agree," said Liz. "Let's do as he says. At least that way I can be back in London quickly. I have a lot of long term and ongoing engagements to do. My agent must be going potty."

"Well, I haven't got anything to do so I might as well stick with it. I quite expect that my business has gone bust by now and I will have to attend to that first," said Frank.

Liz looked at him. She hadn't thought about how he made his living and that this whole episode must be causing him big trouble financially.

She had an idea. "Frank, we are friends aren't we, and the best of friends at that?"

Frank, wondered what was coming next. "Sure," he said.

"As you know Frank, I'm very well off and my agent has made me a millionaire a couple of times over. I don't really need all this treasure stuff although it would be nice if it comes off. I already earn about three million dollars each year so what the hell. If it would be of help, what I am prepared to do is loan you three hundred thousand dollars to tide you over until you start to get some money back from the treasure. At that point you can pay me back. How's that?"

Frank was stunned. "Liz I don't know what to say," he thought for a while as the girls watched him. "I do have a problem financially right now and probably need to bail my business out of trouble. I will gratefully take up your offer. If you get your agent to draw up the contract, and as long as it's reasonable, I will sign it and pay you back within an agreed period as you have suggested. Thanks Liz, I can't tell to you how much that gesture means to me."

"You can try later" she laughed and Josie joined in the laughter too.

They called in the Captain and agreed to his offer.

8

TWO WEEKS LATER FRANK landed on an RAF base in Norfolk and, after supervising the unloading of the cargo, was whisked off by a smartly dressed young man who introduced himself as Richard Clark from the Foreign Office. Frank was taken to an impromptu Customs and Excise office. The only question asked by the very pretty, sharp-eyed, Customs lady was whether he had any weapons on him. He looked over her shoulder to where two men in suits stood watching him intently, one with silver hair and the other quite young. "They know all about me I guess," he thought. "Let's see what exactly they do know." "I have a Remington high velocity rifle with scope and a couple of magazines plus some ammunition, a 9" Daniel Boone knife and a machete all of which I would be loathe to give up. At one time or another in the last two months any one of those saved my life," he told her looking straight down into her brown eyes.

Her eyes wavered a little under his gaze. She had obviously been given some sort of orders but her training was giving her trouble. She wanted to jump at this man and demand a strip search he was so bloody arrogant. At the same time he reminded her of her cinema hero Harrison Ford. She swallowed. "I am afraid I will have to take your rifle Sir, as you obviously don't have a licence to hold it here in England. The knife and machete we will note. Please advise us every two months on this telephone number as to where you are in case we wish to talk to you about them later." She paused as he reluctantly gave up his rifle and ammunition. He went to put on his backpack.

One of the men walked over. "We understand that you also have a 9mm Walther P-38 pistol Sir," he said. The young blonde boy shuffled uncomfortably next to him. Frank turned and looked at him with one eyebrow raised.

"It is illegal to hold a firearm in this country without a licence Sir.

Therefore, if it is still in your possession, it would be appreciated if you would give it up now," said the man in the raincoat.

"Who are you then?" Frank asked.

Frank felt Richard's hand on his arm and for some strange reason he felt himself slipping into a foul mood, getting angrier by the second. An intense feeling of irritation ran across his shoulders and down his back, it was utterly illogical but he wanted to hit something. He hadn't had to deal with unnecessary authority for ages and the sudden introduction to this type of aggressive behaviour, after all he had just been through, was, to put it mildly, too much. He knew he was being stupid but everything was suddenly boiling inside him and he wanted to let rip at something or somebody. This fella was right in the firing line. The man had cold eyes and was very cool. He was obviously experienced at dealing with people like Frank. He also had authority on his side. He believed that he could handle any problem.

He was wrong. "Never mind who I am it's none of your damn business," he said. "Come on, Mr Blake. We know you have this weapon so hand it over."

Frank could feel the frustrations and angst of the last few weeks boiling over and there was nothing he could do about it. He was going to pop and almost with relief he gave into the feeling. Without taking his eyes off the man's own he riffled through his pack and slowly withdrew the Walther P-38. Its highly polished gunmetal blue barrel gleamed dangerously in the overhead lights. In the blink of an eye he leaned over the counter and put the gun in the man's face at the same time cocking the mechanism.

"Oh, this one you mean, Officer?" he said and stupidly pulled the trigger. The man's eyes flicked shut and then opened wide at the sound of the snap of the hammer hitting nothing but steel. But he didn't move a muscle. He had badly misjudged his opponent. His companion's hand shot to his own gun under his armpit and pulled it. Aiming straight at Frank he shouted. "Put that gun down Sir, now."

Frank pushed the agent violently into the customs girl and, all in one movement, shoved the gun back into his rucksack. He felt the initial rush of hot anger easing and he fought to control himself. He could feel the control pouring back into his brain and he shivered. He had never done anything as stupid as that before in his life and was appalled but at the same time felt very pleased with himself. He smiled sweetly at the second agent who still had his gun pointed at Frank, ready to fire, and who was giving him a final warning.

The young man by Frank's side spoke quietly. "Gentlemen stop this right now. Mr Blake is under the protection of the British Government and will need a gun to protect himself from certain factions who are showing an unhealthy interest in him. It has therefore been decided at a high level that he should keep this gun. Is that understood?" Both of the agents were glaring at Frank. Frank continued to grin at them. The older one said angrily, "You had better watch your step mister. Now that we know all about you we are marking your card." Both agents turned and walked away.

Richard turned to Frank. "If you don't mind me saying so that was an extremely stupid thing to do. You need men like that on your side not against you. They can be very dangerous people if they want to be and you have made an enemy. I can only give you so much protection after that you are on your own."

Frank didn't answer. He was becoming bored with the whole situation. The fact that he was now going to be in touch with Government circles at the highest level held no interest for him. The whole episode had become far too complicated. He was a simple man at heart with normal tastes and had no real aspirations over and above just being comfortably off and being free to do the things that he had always wanted to do. Secretly he had been considering selling the treasure at auction anyway and handing over the proceeds to the Brazilian Government less an appropriate commission for him and the girls and letting the Brazilians sort out the problems that would follow. The alternative would be to do the same with the English Government. After all he had enough diamonds in his backpack to solve all his financial problems for years to come. That was another thing. He needed to disappear for a few days to Amsterdam to find the best place to move them and to arrange transfer of the monies that would arise from their sale. There was a lot to think about. "I'll take it one step at a time," he thought. "Treasure first, diamonds second, the money for the troops third."

"I need to get some clothes. I seem to have lost everything somewhere down the line," Frank said to Richard. He had borrowed clothes on the boat but those, and his bush kit, was all he had. Everything else had been left behind in Rio.

"I need to get you to London as quickly as possible, you look fairly acceptable as it is so you can get kitted out when we get there," said

Richard. They argued about this for a while but the young man was adamant.

"I need to stop at the first bank you see," he said to the driver. "I need to get some cash. My wallet is absolutely empty."

"It's all motorway now Sir until we get into London so you might just as well wait until then."

Frank gave up and went to sleep.

He awoke slowly and noticed that they were now in a heavily populated area. Gradually his brain cleared from the fug of sleep and he realised that they must be in London. He glanced at the boy sitting by his side. He was wide-awake. Frank kept quiet until they arrived at the hotel in Knightsbridge by idly watching the traffic and pedestrians. He was trying to adjust to seeing so many people so suddenly.

When signing in at reception, Frank was given a note and some very curious looks. When asked about his luggage he said, "This is my luggage" holding up his backpack. He was then shown to his room with Richard in tow.

"You're not going to sleep with me as well as watching over me are you?" he asked.

The young man blushed and told Frank that someone would be down in the lobby at all times should he need help of any kind and that he would be back in the morning. He then left.

Frank sighed with relief; he was alone at last and back in London. He opened the note, which was from the two girls telling him to contact them as soon as he was settled. Just to comfort himself he pulled the pouch from his pack and poured the diamonds onto his bed. He looked in wonder at their brilliance. Up until now he hadn't had the time to actually count them. On the boat he had been worried that someone might walk in on him at any time. Privacy had not been available there at all.

He counted exactly one hundred stones from the pouch found on the dead pilot and some forty much smaller stones found on the floor of the pyramid. "I wonder what the story is behind these little babies?" he thought. "What a story they could tell if they could talk." He did some calculations; if he only managed to get £100,000 for each of the stones from the pouch then it would still be around ten million pounds. "That will do nicely," he thought. He put his own back in their pouch and the others in his spare handkerchief. After having a shower and a shave he looked at himself in the mirror. His hair was far too long now not having been cut for almost five weeks but he slicked it back and tidied himself up with the razor. He dressed again in the navy trousers, bush shirt and boots. "I look ridiculous," he thought. He really needed to sort himself out now. It was after three o'clock in the afternoon so if he wanted to kit himself out he had to do it now. Shouldering his pack he wandered back down to reception.

"Could you please put this somewhere safe?" he asked the receptionist innocently.

"Of course Sir," said the pretty young lady looking at him. She seemed to hesitate for a moment. "Mr Blake," she blurted, "Are you the man who saved the lives of Josie Sales and Liz Hunt? You are aren't you because I recognise you from the television. Oh, I thought that was so romantic and brave."

He said answered "yes" because he thought that it would get him better service.

"I haven't any clothes with me as you can see. Lost them all somewhere between Brazil and here," he said to her. "I'm just going to pop out for an hour to sort things out, OK?"

"Yes, of course Sir. If we can be of any assistance?" she paused "just one moment Sir." She walked smartly off to a small office to the side. He watched her bottom as she walked away and realised he was being watched himself by the other receptionist. She had heard the conversation and smiled at him. He smiled back.

"Wonder if I can spot the Government man?" he thought. He turned and, leaning against the counter, casually looked around the foyer. He spotted him straight away sitting on a side chair with a newspaper. "He's seen too many damned movies," he thought. The foyer was packed with tourists, mostly Japanese, coming and going in large groups.

There was a tap on his shoulder. He turned to find the young lady standing there smiling at him with an older man in a pin stripe suit. "Mr Blake, Sir, this is my manager, Mr Crouch," she said.

The manager was a short man dressed impeccably in a charcoal pin stripe suit; blue shirt and what looked to Frank like a British regimental army tie. He stepped forward taking Frank's hand, shaking it vigorously. "Mr Blake. I've heard all about you of course and saw your interview on television recently. I'm proud to have you in our hotel. What a time you had and so exciting. I was absolutely enthralled by the whole thing and all that treasure, my goodness." He looked Frank up and down. "Yes indeed, most exciting."

"Queer as a nine bob note," Frank thought.

"Well, I understand that you are in need of a few things?" the manager said "Yes, mmmmm," he said, looking Frank up and down again.

Frank explained that he had just arrived back in England, had lost his entire luggage and only had the things he stood up in.

"We would be only too delighted to help you Mr. Blake. May I suggest that we provide you with a driver and take you over to Harrods? We do run an account there and I can phone ahead to arrange for personal service. I'm sure they would be delighted to solve your problem, especially when they know who you are. Of course you will receive preferential rates and anything you want can be purchased there, I am sure," he said smiling.

Frank raised an eyebrow,

"Oh but yes, of course," answered the manager the smile going from his face. "We would be only too pleased to look after the bill for you as well Sir."

Frank smiled and thanked the Manager for his courtesy and generosity and promised that he would do his best to ensure their hospitality became known. He meant it.

Within half an hour he was being ushered into Harrods by two security guards as though he were royalty. He liked the experience. "Well, the trip has been worth it just for this," he thought. People were looking at him and he began to realise that he was perhaps a little famous after all. One of the guards started to talk to him as they made their way through the various departments to the men's outfitting section.

"Couldn't help but recognise you, Mr Blake," said the guard. "When we heard that you were coming over, Brian and I" he nodded to the other guard, "we said 'Christ Almighty, it's that bloke who disappeared for two weeks with Josie Sale and Liz bloody Blake. You do know, of course, Sir that's the dream of every red-blooded man on the planet, don't you?" He started to whisper. "What were they like Sir, in the flesh so to speak? My God what bodies they have on 'em. I'd have done anything to have been in your shoes Sir."

He decided to have a bit of fun, after all life was serious enough as it was right now and he had no one to talk to anyway.

"Well, at first I didn't think about it a lot because we were too busy trying to stay alive but it did strike home when we settled down for the first night and I realised I was laying next to two of the most beautiful women in the world and again next morning when we washed under a waterfall. There were no secrets held back then, if you know what I mean."

He looked at the two guards who had their mouths open.

"Bloody hell," said the first guard. "Just wait until I tell my mates tonight. They won't believe it. You must be just about the luckiest man alive Mr Blake." They had arrived at the men's department. "We will just hang about Sir until you are ready to leave; that's our orders."

"Fine," said Frank.

A smart young coloured man approached him. "Mr Blake?"

"Yes," said Frank.

"My name is Jacob and I have been detailed to look after you. Where would you like to start"?

For the next two hours Frank had the time of his life. Not having to worry about the cost he simply bought the best of everything. Deciding to start from scratch he bought enough clothes to last him for the next two years.

He decided to return to the hotel wearing a black leather jacket with a light blue shirt and dark blue tie, black trousers and black leather shoes. The quality was simply superb and he felt a million dollars.

He thanked Jacob for his time and asked whether the rest of the clothes and luggage could be sent over to his room at the Hilton. He suddenly realised that he had no cash on him and told Jacob so. He felt embarrassed. Jacob smiled at him and said it was perfectly all right as he understood in the circumstances.

The first guard came up to him. "They do have a bank here Sir. I'm sure they could help you."

"Lead on my man," said Frank laughing. The guards guided him to the bank as they laughed and joked with him. He was beginning to enjoy their company. They were normal blokes simply envying him his situation and having a bit of fun at the same time.

Frank deposited Liz's cheque for three hundred thousand dollars with the startled lady behind the counter and then withdrew two hundred pounds on one of his credit cards. He was now liquid and had some cash. He went back and tipped Jacob and did the same with the two guards. They thanked him politely and escorted him back to his car.

Somehow word had got out and the press were waiting. This startled him and took him off his guard. Flashing cameras, and being jostled by the press with a thousand questions being shouted at him, was not what he was used to. He kept cool and said nothing, he simply climbed into his car telling the chauffer to "Get me the hell out of here." When he got back to the hotel he wandered over to the reception desk. The two girls saw him coming and flashed their best smiles at him.

"Very nice indeed Sir, if I may say so," said one. "That's a lovely jacket. By the way, Mr Blake, there are a few messages for you."

She handed a number of message slips to him. He thanked her. They were mostly from newspaper editors wanting to talk to him regarding serialisation of his story to date. The message he had been waiting for was from Dr Frank Wilkinson of Christies. He phoned him immediately and told him the treasure was on its way to him under escort and should be with him at his secure warehouse by late evening. Dr Wilkinson agreed that he and his staff would immediately start the process of valuation. He sounded very excited.

Putting the phone down Frank phoned another number. One he had been given when on the aircraft carrier by Captain George Wellesley, It was a number in Whitehall.

Upon giving his name he was put straight through to the Home Secretary.

"Hello, Frank," said the Home Secretary. "I have been awaiting your call. I hear you have been out on the town already having fun." There was a note of disapproval in his voice as though Frank should have contacted him first.

"Fuck you," thought Frank. "Yes Home Secretary I had to get some clothes quickly as, having lost everything en route, I only had the clothes I stood up in. The good people here at the hotel kindly suggested that they would cover the cost so I took advantage of them I'm afraid."

"Fine, fine. Frank, I would very much like to meet you, preferably quickly, to talk over the current situation. I understand that your two young ladies have given you power of attorney on discussions, is that right?"

Frank was startled. How did they know that? Josie and Liz had been talking to him on the carrier only a few days ago and they had agreed that he should front all discussions provided that he talked it through with their agent first. The Home Secretary's staff had obviously been listening. This was the sort of thing that made him nervous and pissed him off. Nothing was ever as it seemed.

"Yes Home Secretary that's correct. When would you like to see me? I have several things to do today but apart from seeing my kids I'm free for the rest of the year."

"Yes, mmmmm. Would 10.30am tomorrow morning in my office be convenient Frank? Bearing in mind the trouble you are having with the press at the moment I will, of course, send a car for you."

So he knows about that already too for God's sake. "That will be fine Home Secretary. Thank you. See you then," he said.

"And Frank, be careful. Don't go out on the town without company at the moment. I have reports that there are a number of people who are showing an unhealthy interest in you. Be particularly careful of the press. That's an area whereby certain people will pretend to be members of that occupation so that they can get to see you. Don't open your door to anyone without checking with my man in reception. OK?"

"Sure," said Frank and put the phone down.

Right, the next thing is to get hold of the girls' agent, he thought. He fished in his wallet and brought out a business card that Liz had given him. Joe Rosenthal, Jewish of course. Aren't they all? Frank phoned him.

"Does Mr Rosenthal know you Mr Blake? He is very busy for a couple of days I'm afraid," said his PA.

"Just you tell him Frank Blake is on the phone and that I'm a friend of Liz's. He will know me then," he said.

There was a pause for almost fifteen seconds and then a thick East End/Jewish accent came on the phone.

"Frank, my boy, how are you? I've been waiting for your call for a couple of days. Liz said that you would be in touch. Have you been having some fun or what? Whew. I'm on the golf course at the moment. Wonders of technology eh, so can't talk for long otherwise my chums will get pissed off. Now listen Frank. I'm back in London in about four hours. I suggest that we get together pronto 'cos there's lot's to talk about. What about dinner tonight? Where are you staying?" Frank told him. "That's OK. The food's good there, book a table for us for 8 and I'll meet you in the bar at 7.45. Take this number down, ready? He gave his mobile number. If you have a problem in the mean time phone me immediately, all right? Got to go." The phone went dead.

Frank put the phone down and looked at it. Liz had said that this fella was dynamite. He sure sounded like it.

The phone went again. "Mr Blake? It's the manager here. We are being absolutely inundated with the media who are causing us all sorts of problems. They are insisting that you talk to them. Could you possibly help us out as it is really upsetting a lot of our guests?"

"I'm sorry about that, Graham. Let me have a think about it and I'll come back to you in a moment."

He phoned Joe Rosenthal again. "What," he said. "It's me, Frank Blake, again. You told me to phone if I had a problem. Well I have and it's the press. The manager of the hotel has just asked me to get them out of his foyer now as they are causing mayhem down there. What do you suggest? Come on Joe, start earning your money."

"Christ, hold on a minute, I've just got to putt this for a par." There was silence for a few seconds then a shout of glee. "OK, I'm back. Tell your manager to tell the press that you will hold a press conference in the morning at 10am. I'll be there to guide you through it."

"I can't do that, Joe, the Home Secretary has requested my presence in his office at that time; could probably do it around 1pm."

"The Home Office, what do they want, Frank? Why didn't you tell me? No, don't tell me now. Let me think. I want to be in that meeting, Frank. Phone them back and tell them. Home Office, Christ, what are you up to then my boy? No, don't tell me that either yet. OK. Rig up the press conference for 1pm in one of the suites at the Hilton. That will keep them quiet for a while. Tell the manager that I am now representing you. That will quieten them down as well and get them off your back. See you later. Got to go."

Frank phoned the manager back and repeated Joe's suggestions.

"Thank you Mr Blake, I'll pass on your instructions and I will arrange for a suite to be ready tomorrow at 1pm., anything else I can help you with Mr Blake?" Frank thanked him but said "Thank you, but not at the moment."

He dropped the phone back on its rest and lay back on the bed. "For goodness sake, this is manic," he thought. He could feel his shoulders were tense and thought that some exercise was needed so he phoned down to reception to see if he could borrow some swimwear. He found his way to the pool area, changed, and dived in. He set himself into a rhythm and started to do his usual fifty lengths. He let his brain go into neutral and swam slowly and strongly. He couldn't help noticing when a woman went past him as though he was standing still. He ignored her. Three lengths later she burnt past him again and three laps later she did the same. She was resting at the end of the pool with her arms back on the edge holding herself up and her goggles back on top of her head. She was watching him. Again he ignored her as he turned but couldn't help but notice her breasts pushing out her swimwear. She was very attractive.

Halfway back up the pool she came alongside. "You're Frank Blake aren't you?" she said keeping pace with him. She had a soft lilting Irish accent, which sounded very nice on her.

"Guilty," he said.

"When you've finished can I buy you a drink?" she asked.

"Who are you?" he said.

"Sharon Kemp from The Telegraph," she answered.

He swam on to the end of the length and stopped. She came alongside again and also stopped.

"Sharon, nice to meet you but you are intruding into my private time. No doubt by now you will have heard that I am holding a press conference with you guys tomorrow at 1pm. You can talk to me then. Goodbye."

He rolled back into the water and picked up his rhythm. Completing that length he turned and carried on but noticed that she was still standing at the end of the pool where they had been talking. He watched her as he closed on her. She wasn't looking at him but seemed upset. He turned and carried on. At the other end he turned again and swam towards her again. She hadn't moved and was looking out of the side windows. She appeared to wipe an eye. "For God's sake," he thought. "Bloody woman."

He stopped. "What's the matter with you?" he barked at her.

"Nothing" she said.

He looked around him. Everyone was ignoring them. "Well nothing is that you are crying and it's embarrassing," he said.

"What's it to you? You can foock off if you want to," she said. The way her accent handled the Anglo-Saxon swear word made him laugh.

"Are you seriously telling me that you are upset because I won't give you an interview?"

"It's very important to me. I have been trying to get a break for six months and I know the axe is hanging over my head. If I don't get results soon I'll be out of a job. They don't mess around in the newspaper world. You have to produce or you are out on your ear," she said sniffing.

Frank knew she was probably lying but she did look good and he hadn't had any tail for at least three weeks. "At my age I should grab it wherever I can so what the hell," he thought.

"OK. I'll talk to you but it's going to cost. I'm not doing it for free.

See you in the bar in fifteen minutes." He turned and carried on swimming. He wondered how much time he had. Glancing at the clock at the end of the pool it registered 2.10pm. "That leaves me with at least six hours clear before I have to get ready for dinner. Should be enough time," he thought.

He walked into the bar ten minutes late. She was sitting at the bar talking to two men when he arrived. He wondered if they were press colleagues and moved along side them to order a drink. She turned hearing his voice. "I'll pay for that," she told the barman.

"Hi, Sharon," he said. "Sorry I'm late."

"That's OK, Mr Blake, don't worry about it." She was looking at him in surprise. She hadn't realised how good looking he was. "Hunky man for a Brit," she thought.

She introduced him to the other two men who turned out to be businessmen trying to pick her up. On hearing who he was they immediately tried to get him into conversation about his recent escapades but he apologised saying that he was pushed for time and that he had some business to do with Sharon. Collecting their drinks he took her arm and moved them to a table, which had some privacy.

He looked at her. She had put a lot of effort into looking nice in the short time she had and had long strawberry blonde hair framing a very attractive freckled face. Her figure was superb being a little on the full side but not fat. "Around twenty-seven to thirty-three I should think," he thought. She crossed her legs.

"Mr Blake," she started."

"You can call me Frank if you like," he replied pulling his eyes back from her legs.

"OK Frank," she blushed a little," I have been on to my editor and he has given me permission to offer you £50,000 for an exclusive interview. What do you think?"

He lent back and looked at her, sipping his drink. "Sharon, I'm surprised at you. You know the value of my story and I would have to talk to the girls about it first any way. We are also going to write a book about this and will look into the possibility of making a film as well. That's in the immediate future. If I am to do an exclusive with you then you will have to start talking in six figures quite honestly."

The figure didn't throw her at all. She leant towards him. "Frank," she said glancing around her, "I feel uncomfortable here like this. Couldn't we go to your room where it's more private?"

He wasn't at all surprised at her suggestion. Once inside his room he turned and kissed her. There was no resistance and he hadn't expected any. She returned his kiss pushing herself against him and putting her arms around his neck. He broke off the kiss and taking her hand led her into the bedroom. He peeled off his jacket and took hold of her again moving her over to the bed. Taking his mouth off hers, he started to undress her. He took off her coat and undid her blouse. She glued her mouth to his again while he removed her bra and ran his hands over her large breasts teasing her nipples. She groaned. He eased her down onto the bed and started to remove his shirt and trousers. She watched his every movement and at the same time removed her skirt leaving her stockings and knickers. He moved over her and she pulled his mouth down to her as he slid her knickers off down her legs. She opened her legs for him without saying a thing.

They lay talking for a short while. They had been making love one way or another for almost two hours. He was absolutely bushed and knew he was close to falling asleep. She was a very sexually demanding woman and he had to pull out all the stops to satisfy her. "Either I am getting old or I am simply not fit," he thought. He turned over and kissed her breasts and slowly caressed her body again. He felt very comfortable with her. He told her. "Sweetheart, I am bushed so, if it's all right with you, I'm just going to sleep for a bit. Wake me in half an hour," he said and before he heard a reply he was asleep.

He awoke later to find himself alone. Glancing at his watch he realised that he had been asleep for nearly two hours. There was no sign of the girl. He heaved a sigh of relief. He phoned reception for a tray of sandwiches and tea and set about getting himself ready for dinner later that evening. An hour passed and when the phone rang he was in the bath.

It was Sharon. "Sorry to leave without saying goodbye but I had some work to do. Frank that was a very nice way to spend a couple of hours this afternoon. You're a very nice man and a wonderful lover. I would love to do that again soon. In the meantime I have had another word with my editor and he has suggested that we all get together to talk turkey regarding the exclusive. I know you are busy tomorrow but when can you fit us in? I would like to see you again anyway."

"I would like to see you again as well Sharon. Look I am having dinner tonight with a guy who is probably going to be my agent so I will discuss the situation with him and will talk to you in the morning. Is that OK?"

"That will be fine Frank." There was a pause. She said in a small voice. "Frank can I come and stay the night with you tonight?"

"What the hell am I letting myself in for?" he thought. All his brain could see was the sight of her luscious naked body and his groin spoke.

"I won't be free until about eleven. If you want to come around I shall be very pleased to see you that's for sure. Meet me in the bar again Sharon," he said.

"You're a bloody fool Blake, messing about with this woman," he told himself. He couldn't help himself and decided that this time he would not let the affair linger on for more than a few days. There were too many things to do.

He made long phone calls to his children and discussed coming down at the coming weekend to see them. He missed them badly and they agreed that it would be best if they met at his eldest son's house in Esher. He also phoned a couple of long term chums and made arrangements to visit them as well over the next few weeks. They were all dying to hear his story.

Having done his duties he set about getting ready for dinner.

Reception phoned him and said a Mr Joe Rosenthal was waiting in reception. Joe turned out to be a small portly man around 5' 7" with slicked back black hair, a high rising forehead, and intense dark brown eyes. He had laughter lines around his eyes and he smiled easily. He had a firm handshake and looked Frank straight in the eyes. Frank liked that.

They decided to have a drink in the bar while they got to know each other. Joe was very personable and charming and Frank could quite understand how he had managed to secure so many famous people as his clients. They had just finished their drinks when the waiter came and took them to their table.

As they walked through the dining room Joe said hello to a number of people dining, some of whom Frank recognised from the newspapers. He was obviously well known and well liked. The diners looked at Frank with keen interest. Most of them knew full well who he was. He knew that he looked good in his new clothes and they gave him a feeling of considerable confidence. So much had happened to him in the last few weeks that walking through a famous restaurant full of well known people didn't faze him anymore. He was a big man, good looking to boot, and he walked well. He felt and looked fit. In a nutshell he looked impressive.

"Right Frank," said Joe "Let's get down to business. Why do you think you need my services? Because I'm warning you now, I come expensive."

"Joe I'm a simple man. I've been lucky enough to be involved in an amazing adventure with two famous women and it's caught the imagination of the world media. They, unfortunately, are like predators. I have just experienced a particular situation this afternoon and frankly it is becoming almost too much for someone like me, who has never experienced fame, to handle. On the other hand I want and need to make some money out of all this and I recognise that I need a professional to guide me through the minefields ahead. As you know, I am seeing the Home Secretary about the treasure in the morning. Then there's the press conference that follows and the newspapers that want exclusives. There is also the possibility of a book coming out of all this and, if handled correctly, a film I would have thought. Do you see what I mean?"

He could see that he had Joe's full attention. "Yes I do see what you mean Frank and without expert help you are going to be ripped off right, left, and centre. The jungle drums have already been going, and don't ask me how, but already I have had two television companies onto me asking for you to go on their programmes. I'm not even your agent yet."

Joe asked Frank to fill him in with every detail that had happened from boarding the carrier to two hours ago. By the time Frank had finished Joe knew as much as he did. Well almost. Frank hadn't told him about the diamonds. Joe was quiet for some time while he ate. Frank let him think.

After a few minutes Joe spoke. "I happen to agree with you on every point, Frank. I think that we have something big here; something very big. Boy what a challenge. Everything hinges on Christies' evaluation though. From that point, once we know how much money we are dealing with, we can start to negotiate. I personally think that lawsuits will start to hit you right, left, and centre once the world gets to know that you have the treasure back here. You can be sure every man and his mother will be onto you for their share. You are not only going to need me Frank but you are going to need a top lawyer whether you like it or not. Now, I happen to know a guy who I consider to be one of the best lawyers in the country, and I mean top-drawer stuff. He knows his way around the city and government. Again very expensive, but you are going to need him my boy. Now let's talk money. You are going to take a lot of my time, I can see that so I'm going to cost you 15 per cent of everything you earn year on year and that will be on a five year contract. Is that OK with you?

Frank looked at him and smiled. "Where are you coming from Joe? I'm not a Liz or a Josie. As far as I am concerned, this is a one-off hit for you. Once we have done the treasure, the book and the film that will be it. I'm back to where I was in the first place. So I think 10 per cent will be about right and a two-year contract. The money you'll make from the three of us on those three products alone will make you a multi-millionaire if you're not one already. Hey, in fact you will be on thirty per cent or more of all products. That's not bad in anyone's language. In that case I think you should only charge me five per cent. End of story."

Joe had been listening intently and returned the grin when Frank had finished. "Frank, my boy, the money I am going to save you and make for you will be beyond your wildest dreams. What you have to think about is what is it worth to you for me to take all the hassle off your shoulders and to guide you through the maze that's about to descend upon you. I'll let you off with twelve and a half per cent and a three-year contract and I'm being generous there."

Frank finished his whisky and sat thinking while the waiter replenished his glass. Joe was right. He knows his way around and he could take all the pressure off him. That was his job. Did it really matter whether he earned two or three million out of him? Without him, Frank felt he might, in the end, get nothing. Joe could in fact end up being his guardian angel. "I'll tell you what Joe, and this is final, ten per cent and the three-year contract you suggested," he said.

Joe Rosenthal was generally considered to be the sharpest and most astute agent in London. He knew all the angles and all the people and yet, at the same time, had one of the best reputations in London for honesty. He was a hard man and yet a considerate man both in his private and his business life. In this instance he knew instinctively what money he was going to make out of these three people, the kudos he would enjoy, and the esteem he would be held in if he brought these deals off. That was worth some loss as far as he was concerned especially when such high stakes were to be fought for.

"OK Frank I agree. Let's shake on that." They did so and then toasted each other.

"If you don't mind my saying so Frank, I think you should get the hell out of London as soon as possible; once we have signed the contract that is. I'll have that drawn up by the morning by the way. Once the conference is over you should go somewhere. I'll get you a mobile phone first thing in the morning so that we can keep in touch."

"Yeah I need to see my kids and a few other people and then I might just wander off somewhere for a week or two. I have to check on my business before I go though," he said.

Their conversation covered his business and the fact that Liz had loaned him money to help him out. A waiter came over. "There's a lady who wishes to remind you that you are supposed to meet her at 11pm Sir," he said.

Frank looked at his watch. It was 11.30pm. "Whoops. Where has the time gone Joe? I'm going to have to leave you. It's that bloody girl reporter, Sharon Kemp, from the Telegraph and she wants my body again. What time will you be around in the morning?"

"Did you say Sharon Kemp?" said Joe. "My God, she does get around. That girl uses every trick in the book and then some to get a story. She will fuck you Frank until you are in such a state that you will tell her what she wants to hear. Everybody knows she does that. Now, when you have finished just tell her that you have to go away. Use any excuse but leave and refer her to me. Let me do the negotiating. Then if you want to do some business with them it's up to you."

"Could we string them along until the book is written and then let them do an abridged version for serialisation in their paper?" Frank asked getting up.

Joe raised his eyebrows. "Smart thinking, I'll work to that format." He was thoughtful for a moment. "Frank, no doubt you have learnt from her accent that she is Irish and southern Irish at that. My friends in the Met have hinted that they keep an eye on her because of her old republican links although it has to be said that nothing has ever been proven. Just be a little careful my boy. It's been nice to meet you Frank. I think we are all going to make a bit of money here. See you in the morning and don't wear yourself out tonight."

Frank thanked Joe for the dinner, strode over to the reception counter and asked for Sharon. "I have let her into your room Sir." Frank was not prepared for that. No doubt about it she will be nosing around. He was into the lift in a flash and, as soon as he had reached the right floor, he was out of it and sprinting for his room. He opened the door as quietly as possible and strode into the room. She was lying fully dressed on the bed watching television.

"Hi Frank" she said smiling.

"Sorry to have kept you waiting Sharon."

"That's OK," she said. "You're here now so come over here." He moved over to the bed and she put her arms around his neck whilst opening her mouth around his. He liked kissing this girl. He started to fondle her large breasts at the same time but Joe's warning was niggling at the back of his brain. She was starting to wriggle and she put her hands down between his legs searching for him. She found what she wanted. "You feel as if you're ready for me" she whispered. "Give me a few minutes and I'll be ready too. I don't mind if you get into bed and wait," she laughed over her shoulder as she disappeared into the bathroom.

He was off the bed in a flash and pulled his rucksack from under the bed. The diamonds were still there. He went to put it back but saw the Walther P-38. He hesitated.

Sandy's voice echoed through his head as clear as a bell. "Put the gun close to hand under the bed Frank you may need it."

He physically jumped in alarm and looked around him. Nobody was there. "I'm going bloody mad," he thought. He looked at the gun and then pulled it out of its holster. He checked that the ten round magazine was full and slipped it into the gun, cocked it and then slid it under the bed against the wall. "What the hell am I doing?" he thought. "This is ridiculous." He laughed at himself, feeling embarrassed and a little stupid. He undressed rapidly and slipped beneath the duvet. No more than a minute passed before Sharon came out of the bathroom completely naked. Smiling at him, she switched off all the lights except one bedside lamp and slipped into bed with him. Wrapping her warm soft body around him she began to kiss him.

He was almost asleep, dozing, his breathing deep and regular. They had been making love for the last two hours and he had already slept for fifteen minutes a little while ago. He'd had his fill and simply wanted to sleep 'til morning but he could sense that she was restless. He felt her get up off the bed and opened one eye, he watched her as she tiptoed towards the bathroom. He closed his eye and relaxed. Suddenly all the lights came on and he heard the door burst open. He started and lifted himself up. "What the hell are you doing girl?" he said, trying to focus his dozing brain and then he saw the two hooded men. They moved rapidly to the end of the bed.

"Get the fook up dickhead," the first one said in a thick Irish accent. "Get your fooking clothes on. You're coming with us." Both men were pointing their guns at him and both looked menacing.

Lying naked in the bed Frank felt a bloody fool and very vulnerable. So Joe was right after all and he had fallen for the oldest trick in the book. "Damn it to hell," he thought and started to shove off the bedclothes noticing that Sharon was dressing rapidly behind the two men.

"What are you looking at you fooking old git," she screamed at him, her face contorted with rage and hate. The tall hooded man spoke for the first time. "Just get fooking dressed and shut the fuck up," he said to her.

"You didn't have to fook the fooking old bastard did you?" she screamed, reverting to a thick Belfast accent.

Frank was still half out of bed but had made his decision. He laughed, "My, my, what language. You were loving it and moaning for more. Quite frankly my dear I've had better. You're a pretty useless fuck and I was getting very bored," he said.

The girl screamed in rage and tried to jump at him but the tall one caught her by the hair and flung her onto the floor. "Shut the fook up. He's trying to get you going you stupid bitch. You," he said, pointing his gun at Frank again, "get a fooking move on and I mean now." The short one was waving his gun all over the place. He was clearly very nervous.

"It's the tall one who will be the problem," Frank thought.

"OK, OK, don't shoot for Christ's sake, give me a minute," he said, "Where the hell are my socks? "Here goes nothing," he thought. He half rolled out of bed pretending to look under the bed for them. His right hand felt for the Walther and it fell perfectly into his hand. Completing his roll he hit the floor and pulling the gun up he rolled again to bring the gun to bear on the tall man at the same time cocking the gun and starting to pull the trigger. There was an enormous bang and flash and he felt something hit his face. He flinched at the pain shooting across his jaw. Ignoring it he pointed the gun and pulled the trigger twice. The gun rocked in his hand and the crescendo of sound hurt his ears. Someone was screaming and someone was yelling. Almost in slow motion he watched as the big man, hit in the chest at point blank range by two 9mm bullets, was thrown back against the wall with his own gun firing two shots into the ceiling as he fell. Frank swung around bringing his gun to bear on the smaller man. Again in slow motion he saw that this was the one yelling, his mouth was opening and shutting behind the slit in the mask. He was still pointing the gun but panicking, big time. Frank saw a flash come from the gun but felt nothing and again aiming low he pulled the trigger on his own gun. The small man rocketed back into the corner of the room. Screaming, he dropped his gun and collapsed onto the floor. Frank swung his gun around to cover the girl. She was standing there half dressed with her knickers in her hand and her mouth open. The whole thing seemed to take only a second or two,

He was trembling with emotion, fear, and excitement; adrenalin pumping through him like a torrent. He had just fired a heavy calibre pistol in anger for the first time in twenty years and had hit two men bringing them down. His blood lust was up and killing was in his brain, his finger was itching to pull the trigger again but his old training took control. Slowly the red mist ebbed away. Sharon could see her death in his wild eyes and she dropped to the floor in fear. "Please don't shoot me Frank, please don't shoot me. We didn't mean any harm, only to frighten you a bit. Please, Frank" she pleaded her eyes now wide with fright.

"They shot at me, do you hear you fucking whore, they shot at me." He was so hyped up and angry he wanted to kill her too. "Get into the bathroom you fucking bitch," he shouted at her and picking himself off the floor he kicked and shoved her into the bathroom and pulled the door to and then locked it. He was trembling with emotion and he had to shake himself to get his body under control. He looked at the two men and then went over to them. He carefully collected their guns and dropped them onto the bed. The small one had his eyes screwed shut. He was sobbing and crying, and holding his right thigh but the big man was still. Frank didn't know where he had hit him or whether he was dead or not. He didn't really care and was beginning to get control of himself. "You're in a lot of trouble now me old son, and you had better move fast," he thought. He put on his trousers and a T-shirt whilst watching the men on the floor all the time. He then picked up the phone.

"This is room 219. Frank Blake. There has been a shooting here. I need your security people up here right now." He put the phone down. Picking it up again he dialled 999.

"I want the police first and then the ambulance people," he told the operator. When the police came through he told them where he was and who he was and what had happened. They said they would be with him in minutes and asked whether he had called the ambulance. He said no. They told him they would do it for him and not to move. He told them the hotel security people were about to arrive.

Again he put the phone down. Fishing in his trouser pockets he found what he wanted. Picking up the phone yet again he dialled Joe. After a little while Joe answered in a voice thick with sleep.

"Hi Joe long time no see. It's Frank Blake," he said flippantly.

"Hello Frank what's the problem? Why are you phoning me at this time of night."

"Big one I'm afraid Joe. You were right. The Irish called. Two of them and a woman, and they are either dead or dying. The Walther took them out. I have phoned hotel security, and the police, and they are on their way. I am going to need you though Joe, like now! Can you help?"

"Jesus Christ Frank, can't you keep out of trouble? Ever? I've only just left you," There was a pause, "O.K, I'm on my way," Joe said.

Within a couple of minutes of him putting the phone down, hotel security announced their arrival by banging on the door. The small man was still moaning and semi-conscious. There was silence from the bathroom.

He opened the door. Several people were milling about outside his room looking very apprehensive. Two large men were standing there. "We are hotel security Sir. My name's Frank James and this is Harold Winterbottom. What's the problem Sir? We hear that there have been gunshots coming from in here."

"Yes there has. Come on in. My name is Frank Blake but please don't touch anything. You're absolutely right look," Frank said pointing.

The two men moved into the room and stopped as they looked in disbelief. "Who are they?" asked the man Frank James.

Irish Republicans I suspect, and I have their lady accomplice in there," he said pointing to the bathroom. "I've phoned for the police and they said they would be here shortly but I want you around as witnesses in case these two come round."

They chatted a while about what had happened until the phone rang. The operator asked for Frank James. He nodded a couple of times and then said, "Send them on up."

"This should be interesting," he said. "The police are here already and coming up as well as the ambulance people." There was another knock on the door.

Harold opened the door. Three men pushed their way into the room and stopped dead at the scene. The ambulance men were trying to look over their shoulders. There was dead silence.

The leading man looked around the room and then at Frank. "I know who these two are," he said pointing to the two hotel men. "But who the hell are you and what's this all about? I'm Chief Inspector Gifford by the way."

Frank looked at him. CI Gifford was of the old school. He looked about the same age as Frank and was fairly tall and grey haired. He looked tired but interesting.

Frank introduced himself. "My name is Frank Blake, Chief Inspector. I suspect that these guys are Irish Republicans and were about to kidnap me, but I wouldn't let them." He laughed at his own joke but nobody else did. They just looked at him. "There's another one in the bathroom but that's a girl. I am afraid she's half naked and you had better be careful because she's a reporter for The Telegraph. She's the one that set me up and she's a real bitch."

CI Gifford looked at Frank and then turned to his colleague. "George, first of all get that girl out of the bathroom, make sure she has all her clothes and get her down to the station straight away and keep her on ice until I get there." He turned back to Frank.

"Frank Blake eh? I know you. You're the fella that's been on the television, the one that found all that treasure." He turned to his colleagues. "You know. The fella that turned up with those two film actresses after everyone thought they were dead." He turned to the two hotel men. "I will want a statement from you later. You can leave us now." He turned back to his two colleagues.

"I'll want the whole team down here, and I mean now. This could turn out nasty if we don't do it by the book so tread carefully. Dick, you make the phone call from another room. I don't want anything touched in here. Jim you stay here with me and record everything that's said and done. He turned back to Frank. "Yes Mr Blake. I have heard about you all right, how do you do?" He shook Frank's hand. "You medics get the hell in here and see to these two quick and then look at the girl in the bathroom," he shouted. "First take a look at this man."

His colleague came out of the bathroom red faced and with a hand firmly grasping the girl's arm. She had tried to tidy herself up but the effect wasn't too good. She ignored everyone and grabbed her clothes that were lying on the floor and put them on. She kept glancing at the two men on the floor and when she had finished she turned to Frank.

"You're a dead man Frank Blake. You can't fuck with us like this and live, I'm telling you that. And I will laugh when I hear about it." She tried to spit at Frank but George and another policeman swept her out of the room.

CI Gifford looked at Frank. "There's no doubt she believes that and frankly so do I." Frank shrugged his shoulders. Gifford looked at the two guns on the bed. "Theirs are they?" he asked, raising an eyebrow. Frank nodded. "Did you handle them?" Gifford said.

"Very carefully," Frank said.

"Good, now where is your gun, Sir."

"Over there," Frank said pointing at the bedside table. "I only fired three rounds but it was enough." He felt quite smug.

The Inspector walked over to the bed, lifted Frank's gun with a pencil and checked it. "Yes, I can see that," he said. "So, before the mob arrives, tell me the story." Frank went through the story from when he walked into the bedroom until shoving the girl into the bathroom.

A medic walked over to Frank and held his head. "Nasty," he said. "Wait a moment."

"What's wrong?" asked Frank.

"You have a nasty head wound and there is blood all over your face. Look," he said holding up a mirror. Frank was horrified. There was a gash in his forehead and blood all down his cheek and chest.

"You have a splinter in there, hold on while I pull it out." He did so with a yell from Frank. "Shouldn't be too bad once we stop the bleeding and tidy you up. It may need a stitch or two though. I'll do that here."

"Thanks," Frank said.

There was bedlam at the door. A policeman shouted at Gifford. "Two men here Sir who say they are friends of Mr Blake. They insist in coming in."

"That will be my agent and my lawyer Chief Inspector," Frank said.

"Let them in," said Gifford. "The rest of the bloody world is here anyway."

Joe scrambled into the room and stopped dead at the sight of Frank covered in blood being seen to by a medic and the two men on the floor. There was a tall man behind him. Joe said. "You are a bloody walking disaster zone Frank. Let me introduce you to your new lawyer, Graham Lord."

"Hello Frank," said the tall man. "Nice to meet you." he turned and introduced himself to CI Gifford and they went into a huddle.

"Hells fire Frank. You will have to tell me all the gory details later but we want to get you out of here first before the press catch a whiff of what's going on. Graham is sorting that out now."

"Not until I have finished stitching him up," said the medic. Frank flinched as the medic stuck in his needle. He was soon finished.

"Four stitches I'm afraid Mr Blake, but you will soon look as good as new. Maybe a slight scar but not too bad and certainly not as bad as that old one on your cheek. That must have been nasty at the time. Nice to meet you by the way." The medic turned away to help his colleague with the two men.

CI Gifford broke off talking with Graham and came over to Frank. "You have powerful friends Frank," he said. "I understand that you have an appointment with the Government at 10.30 in the morning. I am letting you go now but I will want to see you tomorrow as soon as you have finished with the Home Secretary. This is a very disturbing situation. You've shot two so called IRA men just when everything on that front had gone quiet and there will be heavy repercussions. I have Mr Lord's personal guarantee that you will call as soon as you have finished tomorrow. Get dressed now while we clear up."

Frank didn't answer but threw some clothes into his backpack; he wasn't going to leave that behind. He went to get the Walther P-38. "You will have to leave that behind I'm afraid and I want to talk to you about that later anyway," said Gifford. The three of them left the room just as CI Gifford was going into the bathroom.

"Nice to meet you Frank. You've got yourself into a merry pickle. We need to sit and talk this through very quickly," said Graham shaking his hand as they entered the lift. "The publicity that comes from this is going to be unbelievable. Let alone the possible legal issues. You could be done for manslaughter and heaven knows what else. When defending yourself you are normally allowed to use 'reasonable force.' Shooting your assailants is considered as going too far by most English courts. They don't like you to have guns. We will have to see. I have to ask the question. Have you got any money, Frank?"

Frank shook his head. "Quite honestly at this point in time I am in debt until we get something for the treasure. No doubt Joe has filled you in on that otherwise you wouldn't be here but that might take months or years. Unless of course we can pull something off with the Government in the morning."

"OK. We will go for Legal Aid if we have to and see what happens.

This is all going to be very expensive, Frank. I hope you have the determination to carry it through," said Graham.

"Don't you worry about that. I see no alternative anyway," said Frank.

"It would be even more important for you to drop out of sight for a month now Frank, with permission from the police of course. I'm sure they would understand under the current circumstances. The press and media in general are going to make hay out of this one. We will put the press off but Graham and I have agreed to do this together. We will simply say that it is now recognised that certain forces are against our client and his life is in danger. In the meantime you are going under cover," said Joe.

They left the lift and started to walk across the foyer. Reporters immediately surrounded them. TV camera lights lit up and suddenly they had nowhere to go.

"Leave this to me Frank and don't say a word," said Joe.

Somehow the press had got word that Frank had been involved in a shooting and they wanted to know with whom.

Joe and Graham fielded all the questions and the press were becoming upset because they were getting no answers.

"All right, all right," said Joe, "All we are prepared to say at this time is that my client, Frank Blake, was attacked in his room by two hooded men with guns a little under an hour ago. There was a gun battle and the two male assailants are now being taking to hospital with gun shot wounds. Any other questions you will have to ask the police who are still upstairs. Now it would be appreciated if you would allow us to take Mr Blake home as he has had a tremendous shock, which I am sure you will appreciate."

At that precise moment the lifts opened and the ambulance men appeared wheeling two stretchers. One stretcher had a blanket covering its full length; the implication being obvious to all. The man on the other stretcher was obviously in severe pain; he was sobbing and shouting at the same time. "You fooking English bastards. Fooking bastards."

"Christ that does it," muttered Graham looking at the stretcher with the dead man on it. For a moment there was silence as the media took in the sight and what the Irish man was saying, and then there was pandemonium as they rushed across the reception foyer to get their photos.

"Our time to get out of here," said Joe grabbing Frank's arm and propelling him towards the door." Let's go," he said.

Frank didn't need any bidding; they all shifted into top gear and almost ran from the building. As the commissionaire summoned a taxi a howl went up inside the hotel as the press realised they were getting away. Frank, Joe, and Graham jumped into the taxi and issued instructions as to where they wanted to go. "And put your bloody foot down or we're in trouble," said Joe to the driver.

"Frank, for the time being I'm taking you to my place but they will soon suss that out so we shall have to move you somewhere else that's safe until later this morning. Graham and I will sort out the press conference, don't worry."

Joe put Frank in one of his spare bedrooms and let him sleep. Despite what had just gone on Frank slipped into a deep sleep as soon as his head hit the pillow. Meanwhile, Joe and Graham withdrew to Joe's lounge to confer on tactics. "This meeting with the Home Secretary this morning Graham is going to be extremely important to us all and will address, in particular, the question as to what is going to happen to the treasure. I imagine that the Government will not want to get their fingers too dirty but will still want their pound of flesh. It will certainly be interesting to see what Christies come up with. They have already told me that results will not be forthcoming for at least a week," said Joe

"Yes, I fully understand that. I would like to thank you for getting me involved with this man Joe" "said Graham "This is going to be a high profile case for me which won't do me any harm at all and I can see that your involvement Joe, if handled well, will most certainly do no harm to your reputation either."

"Strangely enough I'm not too worried about that, I like this chap and find him very personable and interesting. He handles himself well and yet he's not the type of person we normally come across. I can't quite categorise him yet. He is certainly very much a loner. The girls think he's the cat's whiskers and they both said they love him dearly and will do anything for him. That's impressive in my book because girls like Josie and Liz have usually seen it and done it all before and met every type of scumbag on the way. So their endorsement of Frank is quite something as far as I am concerned. I believe we have only seen a small part of his character so far. There is more to him than meets the eye, much more that's for sure. How he got out of that fracas with the hit men this morning I don't know. He was obviously set up by the girl reporter who let her gunmen friends into his room. I have yet to ask him how he managed to get his gun and outshoot them. How on earth did he manage to do that? You and I couldn't do that Graham and also we can't shoot a pistol either. I am going to phone a few people later and do a background check on this fella. He's too good to be true."

"Quite frankly Graham I believe that if we push the 'man of mystery overcomes adversity again' bit, in a statement at lunchtime with the press, he will become a hero throughout the nation. He is already thought to be some sort of Harrison Ford character or something anyway. There is no doubt about it that, if we play it right, this is going to be the stuff of legend as long as we can keep him alive. And, to beat it all, he is sleeping like a baby up there with this entire episode going on all around him. Quite amazing really." Joe said.

The phone rang and Joe answered it. It was the first of many Fleet Street editors wanting to have exclusive interviews. When The Telegraph came on Joe had no hesitation in pointing out that their girl was the potential assassin, which shut them up immediately. Joe pointed out that they'd better get their legal team together that afternoon because Joe and Graham wanted to talk to them, particularly with the obvious problems of bad publicity for The Telegraph. They agreed instantly. They were very worried about the implications. Joe said that they would meet immediately after the press statement at lunchtime.

"That is just one instance of how we can milk these bastards for simply enormous sums. I tell you Graham this is going to be one very interesting gravy train. Believe me," said Joe rubbing his hands together. Graham leaned back in the long deep sofa and grinned at the prospect. "That's all very well Joe, and you're right, just as long as we can keep our man alive," he said.

9

'OUR MAN' WOKE SLOWLY. He glanced sleepily at his wristwatch. It was registering 8.30am.

"Hell's bells," he said and tore the bedclothes off him. He looked around for his clothes but they were not there. He stuck his head out of the bedroom door and yelled "Joe!"

Joe's wife Diane came up the stairs. "What's the matter Frank?" she queried coming towards him. Frank had met her for a short while earlier that morning when he arrived with Joe and Graham and had been impressed with her calmness as though this sort of thing went on all the time. Diane was one of those London ladies who had benefited from a privileged private education. Not only was she a beauty in her own right with her long black hair, deep brown eyes, and perfect creamy skin, but she projected serenity, calm and peace and the ability to handle and solve any problem without a fuss. She was obviously the perfect partner for Joe. Frank had fallen in love immediately as did most other men.

"Where are my clothes Di?" he asked.

She grinned at him. Nobody called her Di anymore. The last time she had been called that was at school and that was a long time ago. Everyone always called her Diane but she liked hearing her name shortened by Frank for some strange reason that she couldn't fathom right now.

"Well, there's a thing. The infamous man of action, Frank Blake, is embarrassed because he has no clothes. Joe tells me that not only did you make love to a horrible terrorist woman, but also you then proceeded to gun down her two assassin friends. And all the time you were in the nude, apparently. And here you are worried about showing yourself to me without clothes, really, Frank, I am disappointed in you." She laughed a delightful tinkling laugh that sent shivers down his spine.

"You're taking the piss Di! " he said. "Come on, where are my clothes?"

She leaned elegantly against the landing wall. "Such language Frank. Your clothes are being cleaned as we speak and should be ready in ten minutes. I have sent for your other clothes from your hotel room. The police have agreed to let them go as you are seeing the Home Secretary this morning. She looked at him poking his head out of the bedroom door. "If only the world could see you now Frank," she laughed handing him a dressing gown and went back down the stairs. "Breakfast is on the table in five minutes Frank," she cried over her shoulder as she disappeared.

What a woman! Frank had never in his life come across this breed of woman; high Society, high breeding, and high living. This was where they resided. "What I couldn't do with that woman. Two hours, no, it would take three before she really fired off and let go. What fun that would be! Now that's the sort of woman I want to end up with but boy would you need money to keep her in the style she's accustomed too." Frank, like most men, often thought in the most basic of terms when thinking about women, especially very attractive women, letting his groin run his head. Under normal circumstances however, he could be quite clinical when making judgements about people and their personalities and usually didn't until he knew someone for a week or two. But Di was another kettle of fish entirely.

In a similar fashion 'Diane' had been thinking of Frank. Talk of his recent exploits had been rife at the bridge parties she attended and every woman she knew wanted to know more about him. Wicked suppositions as to what must have gone on when he was marooned with those two beautiful actresses were also rife. All her bridge set friends had seen photos of him in the press and they all agreed that he looked both ruggedly handsome, dangerous and quite gorgeous at the same time; a heady combination for women who had little or no excitement in their lives. He always seemed to have that naughty grin on his face. "I bet he was bad with those girls," she thought and now he was here in her house. She couldn't wait until her husband gave her the green light. "Just wait until they hear that Joe is his agent and that he was in my house," she thought. "Just wait. Every dining room door will be opened to me, particularly with what went on last night." For the first time in her life she was truly excited. She felt a flush spread to her cheeks and then gently spread over her body. "Yes," she thought. "He does excite me and he's not only a hunk but cheeky as well. He was obviously fucking that girl of half his age when the gunmen came in. I would love to have been a fly on the wall then" she thought wickedly. "The girls will never believe this and now I have him under my roof."

She cruised into the dining room where her husband was having his breakfast. "He will be down in a moment," she said and carried on into the kitchen.

Joe looked after her. They had been married for eighteen years and yet something was different about her. He shook his head and carried on reading the papers. There was nothing about last night. It had been too late for the print runs but he knew the Evening Standard would be the first to hit the streets with the news. He put the papers down and switched on the TV. They were right in the middle of the news item.

A reporter was standing outside the hotel in the semi darkness of morning explaining the events that took place as best he could. There was no mention of the Irish situation but a photo of Frank was superimposed on the screen with details explaining that apparently two hooded men had burst into his room, that shots had been exchanged, and that both gunmen had been taken to hospital with one being declared dead on arrival.

Joe shouted out to his wife. "Diane come and watch this, quickly." She ran in from the kitchen and stood looking in amazement at the TV screen.

The reporter carried on in detail with a switch to the police who gave a potted report on what had gone on. Then there were the three of them. Frank, Joe and Graham being jostled by a melee of press people and Joe explaining briefly what had happened which matched the police report. The camera zoomed in on Frank. His eyes were hooded and he looked like a stag wanting to bolt. He was taller than the other two, he leaned down and whispered something into Joe's ear and at that point the cameras swung around to view the stretchers coming out of the lift.

"At this point Mr Blake and his colleagues left the hotel and sped off in an unmarked car," said the reporter. "He does intend to give a press conference at 1pm today to explain the extraordinary events which have been taking place recently. This is…" Joe turned off the TV.

"You can now expect the phone to ring incessantly darling." At that moment the phone rang. Joe smiled at his wife. "I am relying on you dear to field all questions from everyone because Frank and I have a lot to do today."

"Can I tell my friends that Frank is staying with us darling?" she said.

"Don't tell anyone that you know where he is until we have left to see the Home Secretary. After that I am going to send him into hiding so you can say what you like. His life is now seriously in danger Diane and so would ours be if we let him stay here."

"Is this because of the treasure he found with those two girls?"

"Yes," he said. "That treasure is Second World War Nazi bullion and Frank said that some of it was obviously stolen from the Jews in Poland and the rest of Europe. Strangely enough he is quite ethical. I'm surprised. He is saying that it should be given back to the Jews but I think that's going too far. We will see today."

The phone was still ringing so Diane picked up the phone and answered it.

Joe went to his bedroom and started to dress. When finished he went back downstairs to find Frank eating his breakfast and Graham sitting with him talking earnestly. The phone rang again and Di did what she was destined to do for the rest of the morning and answered it.

She turned to the three men. "It's Liz darling. She wants to know how she can talk to Frank. She is in Paris and has just seen the news item."

"I'll talk to her," said Frank. He got up and walked over to Di who handed the phone to him.

"Hi, sweetheart," he said.

"What have you been up to now Frank you rascal? Can't I leave you alone for just a day or two without you getting in to more trouble?"

"Well there's a lot to tell you Liz but there is no time. We are having meetings with the Government today about the loot and then Joe is sending me into hiding. Now I have your mobile number and Joe is getting me one today as well so I will be able to phone you OK? When are you coming home anyway?"

"I'll be back in three days. I should have finished here by then. The trouble is that my partner is with me now. She caught up with me so we can't do stuff, if you know what I mean."

Frank laughed out loud. "For God's sake, Liz, you don't have to worry about that. Look I will phone you as soon as we know what's happening. Either I will or Joe will. And I look forward to seeing you again Liz. Be good." He put the phone down. It rang again instantly. He gave it to Diane and walked back to the table.

They discussed the coming meeting and what Frank wanted to say.

At 9.30 a.m. precisely a Government car pulled up outside. Already press and TV crews were arriving; they had got wind of the fact that

Frank was staying with Joe. They managed to get to the car without too much trouble due to the fact that the press were not really ready for such a manoeuvre. At 10 a.m. they pulled smoothly into Whitehall and up to the Home Office entrance. Two armed sailors were waiting for them and they were escorted through long corridors to a waiting room.

Joe and Graham were very quiet but Frank was interested in what was going on. He was dressed in his new suit; the first time he had worn a suit in years, but it was so comfortable he didn't feel out of place. He found wearing a tie uncomfortable. He hadn't worn one of those for nearly three months.

"This place could do with bringing up to date," he said to his companions. There was dark wood everywhere and the carpets looked as though they had seen better days. Everything was very sombre with dark red settees matching the dark red carpets. They relaxed into their respective chairs. "Hey Joe, do you know this Home Secretary fella?" Frank asked.

"Never met him but the word from friends who have is that he has succumbed to the usual problem of politicians who have been in office for too long. He thinks he's God's gift to the nation, and the universe, and that the world could not possibly survive without him. Pomposity personified is the term I think that's most often used. That's a point Frank. What ever you do don't lose your temper. It gets you nowhere with these guys," said Joe.

A 'suit' came through the dark oak panelled doors and approached them. He looked about thirty, was pink cheeked and had a light frown on his forehead. He stood before them with his hands together as though praying.

"Good morning gentlemen. The Home Secretary is running a little late but won't be long. Which one of you is Frank Blake?"

The others had stood up but Frank hadn't. He felt like being rude and stubborn. Joe was glaring at him but he ignored him. "I am sonny," he said to the suit.

The boy didn't flinch an inch. In fact the frown went from his face and he smiled at Frank. Ignoring the other two he moved towards Frank with his hand outstretched. Frank couldn't help but get up to take it.

"So nice to meet you, Mr Blake. We have heard so much about you and I have been reading of your exploits; so exciting. Oh I do apologise. My name is James Elliot. I'm the Home Secretary's PPS."

The boy's smile was infectious and Frank couldn't help but like him instantly. He was obviously very bright and his handshake was strong. He looked Frank straight in the eye and smiled. Now that Frank had got to his feet they were both the same height.

Frank introduced Joe and Graham to the young man. James said hello but instantly turned back to Frank.

"While we are waiting, may I ask how you managed to out shoot the two gun men? From what we are to understand you were, uhmmm, without clothes at the time. What puzzles us, and a few others I have to say, is how you did that."

"Oh that's easily explained James," he said airily. "Joe here warned me that the girl was Irish and had a history of Republican sympathies. Bearing in mind that we were becoming paranoid about the possibility of being taken by some sort of strange group who wanted their hands on the treasure, I put my gun, cocked and fully loaded, under the bed, just in case of trouble. If you guys hadn't let me keep the pistol I would be either dead or in a very bad state right now so it's you I have to thank for that. They told me to get dressed so I pretended that my socks were under the bed. I must say the dead fella was pretty quick because he shot at me before I had time to get the gun up. Fortunately he was a bad shot and missed, hence the cut on my cheek. Splinter from the wooden bedpost, I'm afraid."

The boy was nodding all through Frank's answer and then his eyes looked over Frank's shoulder and he straightened.

"That's some story Mr Blake," said a voice behind them, Turning they saw a tall heavily built man with a beard.

"Gentlemen, may I introduce the Home Secretary," said James.

"Please come in," He stood back as James ushered them into the office. It was comfortably furnished and instead of sitting at the desk James sat them down in low leather Chesterfield settees. There were already two other men seated there, drinking coffee. The Home Secretary introduced them as members of his staff who were there on a need to know basis. Three fat files lay on the coffee table between them. Frank, Joe and Graham sat opposite after shaking hands all round. The Home Secretary sat with his people.

"James, rustle up some coffee or something for our guests please," said the Home Secretary. Frank asked for tea and the others plumped for the coffee.

There was silence for a bit. The Home Secretary was studying Frank and Frank looked him straight back in the eyes. It was the Home Secretary who looked away first.

"Mmmmmm. Well gentleman. Our Mr Blake here."

Frank interrupted him. "You can call me Frank Sir."

"Thank you Frank. Our Frank here, appearing from nowhere, suddenly comes to the attention of the world by various extraordinary exploits, the last of which I found initially quite unbelievable. I have to say Frank that the time we have had to spend on your, err, escapades has been quite incredible. What with re-routing HMS Burma to the Falklands, arranging for the flight back and transportation of the, err, goods to London and now this new problem. It is all taking up so much precious time. You may be interested to know Frank that you have even been mentioned in Cabinet, and there aren't many men who could say that. Mind you I don't know whether that's a bad thing or a good thing."

Everyone smiled but they let the Home Secretary have his say.

"Now we can solve the problem of last night Frank don't worry. There may well have to be a court hearing, which you will have to attend, but we have been advised that it's an open and shut case of self-defence. I won't go into too much detail and it will be a little onerous for you but at the end of the day I can categorically say that you will be OK. Our 'friends' from across the water will pitch a very determined case against you, you can be sure of that, and will probably wish to interrogate you on the stand Frank but for certain reasons that I do not wish to go into here we want to shut the door on this one quickly. I am sure that we can persuade the opposition in private that it is in everyone's interest, at this point in time, to make this situation disappear quickly. There are ways of doing this, which I will not bother you with now. We are also talking to the press at this moment asking for their help in this matter." He turned to the other two men. "Is that correct?" They both nodded and agreed.

Graham spoke out. "Home Secretary, I will be representing Frank in this matter. I quite understand that you wish the minimum amount of trouble here but can you tell me who I should be talking to in this instance to ensure that matters run smoothly?"

The minister nodded and gave him a name. Graham's eyebrows almost went off his head. He thanked the Home Secretary. Joe and Frank were impressed too.

"Now we have been informed by our intelligence services that certain elements of what used to be called in the old days the Pro IRA, are looking for you with serious intentions Frank. You shot two brothers from the Mulligan family of South Armagh. They aren't very nice people at all and the word revenge is already being put about. Unfortunately there are another three or four brothers. I am led to understand that they are not very bright but they are persistent and very dangerous. They are well known to us. To put it bluntly they want your hide pinned to a barn door. May I suggest you disappear for a while until we let you know when to surface? We can arrange another passport should you wish to go abroad under another name etc, etc. If you wish we will handle all that either through Graham here or Mr Rosenthal."

"Through Joe, please, Home Secretary," said Frank. "By the way, if it's only the Mulligan family I have to worry about then what is all the fuss about? I was trained to take this type of people with ease. I may be a little older and a little rusty but that can soon be remedied.

"Right, yes, right." The Home Secretary took a sip of coffee and glanced at his watch ignoring the question, and then at his two colleagues. "Next on the agenda is the matter of the treasure that you have brought back from Brazil Frank. I have had a preliminary report from Christies."

Frank interrupted. "Indeed Home Secretary that's very quick and it's more than I have had."

"Yes I needed some idea of its value." I understand that they are quite stunned by what you have brought home. Particularly the paintings, most of which the art world had long thought had disappeared forever. There is apparently great excitement down there to such a degree that even the PM is interested. I am also getting calls from almost anyone who is anyone in the art world, all wishing to see what you have brought back. The media have got a lot to answer for having hyped up the world of art by making false claims on what is there. I am led to believe that there are also some harrowing goods which are extremely sobering."

"Yes there are," said Frank. "You should take a visit and have a look Home Secretary."

"Quite," said the Home Secretary. "Ambassadors from at least six countries are already asking to discuss the situation with me. Somehow or other, they all know that the treasure is here in the United Kingdom. I won't go into details as to who they are right now but you can probably guess. Not the least, of course, is Brazil. They are insisting on the return of the treasure and also wish to indict you Frank for stealing it from their soil." He rose from his seat and walked slowly around his desk pausing to fiddle with something on the desktop as he was obviously thinking about what he was about to say.

"All that aside for a moment, we are curious about one point Frank. We would like to know why their expedition was virtually wiped out and you weren't? The report we have received from our troops who went with you is that there was total carnage, apparently there were bodies everywhere. What intrigues us is that there were no signs of gunfire on the bodies. One of our officers videoed the scene for us and it makes for quite horrible viewing I must say."

He continued. "The Americans have asked me the same question and have asked to see the video. I am reluctant to do that at this point in time but I dare say I will have to relent eventually. I am not at all sure why they have asked but I believe they were probably watching via satellite when it happened. Another strange thing occurred they tell me and this appears to disturb them greatly. They have admitted to me that the arrival and departure of our expedition to that valley was blanked out. In fact they apparently lost total satellite control for some four hours. It's never been known before and they have found no reason as to why that happened. I have to say Frank they are very suspicious and they are exerting exceptional pressure on our office for some answers. Of course I have told them that it was nothing to do with us at all and suggested that they must have had some serious type of computer glitch. They don't agree and have asked me to talk to you to see if you could throw any light on the subject. Of course I told them, on your behalf of course Frank that was silly. Now we know that it wasn't us and they are adamant that they did not have a problem computer wise. Not one they can trace anyway. Taking into account both occurrences and, how can I put it, the strangeness of both situations the finger appears to point towards you Frank in some strange way. Can you throw some light on these matters?"

Frank leaned back into the settee and crossed his arms in an unconscious defence posture. He was very aware that the other suits had leaned forward looking at him. The Home Secretary was also looking at him with keen interest and awaiting his reply.

"I don't have a simple answer for you Home Secretary. All I will say is that I think there is more to that valley than meets the eye. For instance Josie was chased one evening just after we had bathed. All we could see were indistinct shapes and whatever they were they managed to keep up with Josie with ease; and she was shifting I can tell you. I know without a shadow of doubt that I shot one. Even Josie said that she heard the shape grunt and saw it go down but when I later went out in the dark there was no sign of anything. It was all a bit weird. Other than that we saw nothing. Whatever is going on in that valley didn't harm us in all the time we were there. I have, by the way, explained all this to the Captain of HMS Burma. No doubt you have a copy of that conversation somewhere. We saw no sign of footprints or habitation at all. As far as we could tell the valley was deserted and had been for many years. Someone certainly obliterated the General's task force, big time, somehow. As you say, there were bodies everywhere. We weren't touched though and somehow I knew we wouldn't be. As I say, you know as much as I do now."

"Very interesting," said the Home Secretary slowly. The other suits also asked him a few questions about the shapes but Frank pretended to know nothing more. One of them asked if he thought that they came from the pyramid.

"I imagine so, yes," he answered. "That's a possibility I suppose."

"It still doesn't cover the blanking out of the satellites though does it?" one of the suits asked.

Frank was running out of excuses and was becoming exasperated. He leaned forward and stared at the two men who were obviously MI5 or MI6 and decided that attack was to be his best defence. "I'm beginning to get the feeling that we have been summoned here under false pretences. I was under the impression that we were going to discuss the treasure and what was to be done with it." He raised the volume of his voice slightly. "Instead I'm being quizzed on shootings, shadows, and broken down satellites. What the hell do you honestly expect me to know about such things? I'm your average forty-seven year old businessman with average intelligence who happens to have become involved in this incident by pure chance for Christ's sake. Do you honestly think that I am capable of organising shadow killers and destroying satellites? Do you?" He was beginning to shout and Graham had put his hand on his arm to try to slow him down.

The Home Secretary looked quite alarmed but the suits weren't. They simply stared at Frank.

"Why don't you get off your arses and go out there and find out for yourselves?" he said to them. "You might find something really interesting; then again you might not come back, with any luck!"

The suits carried on just looking cold eyed at Frank and Frank glared back at them.

Joe spoke for the first time. "Just shut up for a moment Frank for goodness sake. I'm sorry Home Secretary but with one thing and another Frank is on the ragged edge at the moment. I'm sure you can understand. It isn't everyday of the week that one is shot at and I don't think the shock has really hit him yet." He glanced at Frank. "Perhaps it's beginning to now," he said.

"Yes, of course, Mr Rosenthal. I do apologise Frank. It's just that when the Americans start asking such questions we have to respond and there are a few loose ends regarding that expedition. Now let me see, we did get a bit off track there didn't we?" He opened one of the red files on the table. "Yes, well, let's see; Christies' initial valuation, this is not a final estimate. You have to understand that this is not conclusive and we would not wish to be held to it, but they believe that the value in total is something in the region of half a billion pounds. The pictures alone are coming to almost half that figure!" he said the last sentence quietly.

There was silence. No one moved or said anything for at least thirty seconds.

Joe said. "You did say half a billion Sir, didn't you? Five hundred million pounds?"

"Yes," said the Home Secretary. Frank's brain was reeling. As agreed, he let Joe do the talking on this one. "What is the Government's view on the matter Home Secretary?"

"Well, of course, the situation is difficult. Obviously all of this treasure was stolen and there is no doubt that most of it came from all of the countries occupied by the Germans during the war. Poland, Hungary, Yugoslavia, France and Holland we believe. There will be enormous problems documenting everything and letting the world know what is there so claimants can come forward. Then there is the time span. How long do we go on doing that for? There is, of course, a cost to all this which we haven't budgeted for at all," said the Home Secretary. He was looking at Joe.

"Home Secretary, we are well aware that this would be far beyond our capabilities. We would therefore welcome some suggestion from you to, say perhaps that the Government took over full responsibility for the treasure and the distribution of it to its rightful owners. Obviously, some of it can never be reclaimed. For instance, where did the gold come from? No one would be able to say that it was theirs, as I understand that there are no marks of any kind on any of it. Is that right Frank?"

"My guess is that it was all melted down and is re-cast gold," said Frank.

"That may well be the case. Of course, the other side of the coin Home Secretary is the enormous international credibility the British Government will be seen to project with the humanitarian side of trying to return all of the treasure to their rightful owners. That alone will be impossible to put a price on internationally. Then there are the surplus goods that are never claimed. No doubt you have thought of all this anyway but I just wanted you to know that my clients and I realise this. Now, my clients have been through a considerable amount of personal trauma in finding this treasure and bringing it home. If it is the Government's wish to purchase the treasure from my clients we can save you the trouble of trying to work out a figure. Frank would like to say something here."

"What is it that you want to say Frank?" said the Home Secretary warily.

"Just this Sir. When I first started to open these cases and found boxes of gold teeth, rings, bracelets, silver dinner sets that sort of thing I was upset. But not so upset until I saw what was painted on the outside of the cases, Auschwitz, Dachau; and so on. These were personal items of people who had been massacred and slaughtered. I don't want any of it and the girls don't either. If you are able to get just a small percentage back to the descendants of these people, then everything we have been through will have been worthwhile as far as we are concerned. But, at the same time, we did find the treasure and we feel that it is only right that we should be compensated for finding it and for what we have been through to bring it back." Frank sat down.

The Home Secretary sat looking very thoughtful at Frank. "How much compensation do you want Frank?" he said.

Joe took control again. "I would say Home Secretary, that on the valuation you have been given, and we do realise that it is preliminary, I would say five per cent of the total would be fair. Twenty five million pounds, Sir. On that basis my clients would sign over to the Government all rights and covenants that they legally have on the treasure, lock, stock and barrel."

"Would they indeed?" said the Home Secretary. He sat thinking for a while. "I will have to talk this over with the PM and the Cabinet. I do not have the authority, unfortunately, to make that sort of decision. We are talking about a lot of money here Joe."

"Yes and a lot of money and prestige for the Government as well Sir. I am sure that when your people have done their figures you will see that Her Majesty's Government should end up with at least twenty times the amount my client will have. Plus, of course, the enormous prestige that the situation will give you world wide, which would be priceless. A well worth venture I should think," said Joe.

The Home Secretary gave one of his rare smiles. "Maybe so Joe." He stood up signalling the end of the meeting.

"Gentlemen, I have enjoyed this meeting immensely. Well, most parts anyway. Next time we meet perhaps you will do me the honour of imbibing a glass or two of wine with some rather pleasant food. Until then; good day." James opened the door and they both vanished.

The three of them made their departures and left whilst being shown the way by one of the Home Secretary's secretaries.

"Well, what do you think?" said Graham to them both.

"I wouldn't trust him as far as I could throw him frankly," said Frank.

"Me neither," said Joe. "He's out to make a name for himself both nationally, and internationally, and heaven help anyone who gets in his way. I'm very surprised at the value quite honestly Frank so, with your permission, I'm going to call on Christies. By the way, what was that all about with those two fella's? Who do you think they were?"

"Who do you think?" said Frank. "They were secret service, MI5, MI6, Foreign Office and all that stuff. He's obviously been talking to the Yanks, probably the CIA. In fact he must have done. They wanted some answers but I haven't got any."

"It was quite obvious you know more than you're telling me Frank," said Graham. "If I can tell that you can be darn sure they did. Whatever it is you know Frank; they want to know. It's apparently very important to them. How the hell did you knock out those satellites by the way? If you really did that then you are a very dangerous man to know Frank and I am telling you that worries me."

Frank laughed out loud and put his arms about the two men. "Don't you worry about a thing, this is more complex than you can possibly imagine and, as they say, that's another story and you don't really want to know quite frankly Graham," said Frank. "In fact, it's better if you don't know, either of you. And another thing, I don't believe him about the trial. What do you think Graham? I could easily find myself ending up in clink for five years for manslaughter."

"Leave that with me Frank. I have to make some phone calls and call on a few people before I can be sure as to the eventual results," said Graham.

"Frank. You make yourself scarce. We will handle the press conference. So where do you intend to go then?" asked Joe.

"It depends on what we do now. I have to go back to your house to get my stuff. If you could arrange for a motorcycle courier to pick me up within the hour I can be changed and on my way. The only problem is the press but I'm sure we can dodge them. I will need that mobile phone though Joe."

"I arranged that early this morning and it should be at home now. All I ask is that you keep in touch. Heaven knows there may be other people coming after you. There again they may not. Both of the girls now have minders just in case. Perhaps you should have the same."

"No thanks," said Frank. "I'm sure I can look after myself. Just as long as I have my gun, I'm okay."

They arrived back at Joe's house and Diane had to be filled in on what had happened. She was very proud that Joe had been talking to the Home Secretary. More gossip for the bridge parties. Frank made his way to his room and packed a few clothes in his backpack. He then changed into more suitable clothes for travelling. He also packed away his knife. He took the minimum amount of clothes possible just concentrating on a couple of shirts, underwear and socks. He reasoned that he could buy anything else that he might need as the occasion arose.

There was a knock on the door and Diane came in. "Anything I can get you Frank?" she asked smiling at him. "Anything at all? I hear you are leaving us. That's a shame; we were just getting to know you."

"It's too dangerous for you Di; if I stay here. I have to find somewhere where I can't be found. I might have to go abroad for a while. We haven't worked out the details yet."

She was standing directly in front of him and quite close. He could smell her perfume and almost feel her body heat. "This one is bloody dangerous," he thought and the next thing he knew she was against him kissing him with her mouth wide and pushing him back to the bed. They fell together her mouth glued to his, her tongue probing. She said nothing, her hunger all too apparent, as her right hand slipped down between his legs searching and unzipped his trousers. He was lost once she laid her hand on him. Rolling her on her back he broke his mouth away from hers. Saying nothing but gluing their eyes to each other they silently stripped off each other's clothes until he was naked and all she had on was her panties. She was gasping with excitement now, her eyes were wide and her hips grinding. "Give it to me Frank, please, now," she whispered. He didn't bother taking her pants off simply pulling them aside and inserting himself. This was going to be a quickie all right, he could feel the pressure building as she panted, gasped and writhed underneath him. She pulled his mouth down to hers and whimpered with pleasure as he ground into her. Bursting at last he groaned with the release and she wrapped her legs around him.

For a minute or two they lay quietly getting their breath back. "For Christ's sake Di where did that come from?" he gasped.

"Just wanted to see what it was like having the infamous Frank Blake and I have to say it was very, very, nice." She smiled at him and moved her body slowly from under him until she had released herself.

"As much as I would like to, I can't stay, Frank. They will be wondering what I am doing. You do understand, don't you?" she whispered. She got up slowly from the bed and started to dress. "Mmmmmmm," she said looking down at his naked body. "We will have to do that again soon Frank please, I liked that." She checked herself in the mirror and moved over to the door. "See you downstairs in a minute." she said over her shoulder and shut the door behind her. He lay looking at the ceiling and shook his head slowly in wonderment. What the hell was going on in his life? What was going to happen to him next? He slowly got to his feet and showered, changed his clothes, and went back downstairs to find them all together chatting about the morning's events and the coming press conference.

"Here's your phone Frank," said Joe handing over a small Nokia and charger. "Look after it. The motorbike will be here in ten minutes and then Graham and I have to go to the Hilton for the press conference. We will keep you informed as to what happens or you can see it on the news. They are going to be really pissed off that you're not there."

"Joe, I feel naked without my gun. Can you find out from that policeman chappie when I can have it back? I want to thank you two by the way for looking after my interests and for being my friends. I couldn't have done this without you," he said to Joe and Graham. "I know it's going to cost big money but you are both worth every penny."

"They won't go for the five per cent Frank you know that don't you?" said Joe.

"Yeah, I know that, just get whatever you can, Joe. I know you will,"

Frank said laughing, "Because the more you get for me the more there will be for you." I'm going to leave it to you. Just watch your step with them Joe. I didn't like that fella the Home Secretary, too smarmy for my taste and totally ruthless." There was a knock at the door.

"It's a motorbike man," said Diane looking out through the window. Frank made his goodbyes and taking her by the hand thanked Diane for her hospitality. "If you don't mind I'll leave the stuff here that I can't take with me." He kissed her on both cheeks but near to her lips and she blushed like a schoolgirl. She couldn't speak but simply whispered, "Keep in touch Frank" and gave him a meaningful look. He looked at his friends for a minute and then, shrugging the backpack onto his shoulder, left the house.

Together, with the motorcyclist, he strode quickly down the short drive to where the press were waiting.

10

THREE WEEKS LATER FOUND Frank driving towards Harwich in a hire car. He had been to see his children and had spent valuable time with them. They had been pleased to see him and had appreciated that he'd taken the time to see them; they had missed him and told him so. At the same time they recognised that their father had changed considerably. He was no longer the quiet, conventional, introverted, boring father they had always known. He was now an international celebrity with his face in every paper and on television and, as his children, they had to accept part of the so-called fame that went with that.

He had explained to them the problems he was having with the Mulligan family and that he had been warned by the British Government that they would, in all probability, come looking for him. Therefore he wanted his children to be vigilant at all times, just in case. They told him that their mother had asked that he get in touch with her and they gave him her telephone number. "Not bloody likely," he thought.

He had also made the effort to see his friends. He had several special ones, mostly from his childhood, and had spent several heavy drinking sessions with them in the local village pub near to where he had been born. They had pumped him for details of the recent events, thinking that the newspapers had been uneconomical with the truth. They were stunned, however, to hear that everything they had read about their old school friend was true. The questions were asked, how could all that happen to a friend they had known since they were all five years old? They compared what had happened to him to their days in the village when they used to raid the local vicar's orchard and Frank was always the one who pushed it too far and invariably got caught. They also pointed out to him that he was always the aggressive one in the local football team. Frank laughed at the exaggerated stories they thought up.

He smiled to himself. They were his real friends. There was no naked ambition, spite, jealousy or harm in any of them and they knew him as well as he knew them. They had the innate ability to pull his leg to keep him down on solid earth mentally. They were a breath of fresh air to him after all he had been through. He also set one day aside to visit the local crematorium where the ashes of his mother and father had been scattered and arranged for a rose to be planted to their memory and a plaque to be placed by it so that he, and his children, would always have a definitive place to visit when the mood caught them. His children had asked him to do that and he had thought it a good idea. He still missed his parents desperately as did his children even though it was now some five years since they had both been wiped out in a multiple car accident.

He visited his business only to find that everything was running smoothly. He felt affronted by this at first; as being the owner he naturally thought he was indispensable. He was wrong. Fortunately he had already set up the company to run without him and it had done so very well indeed. He had some very good people on board who were hungry for success. He took all the staff out for lunch and offered to sell the company to them for the share value of £1,000. They jumped at the chance so he set the wheels in motion with his solicitors for that to happen.

Only Joe and the two girls knew where he was and within a few days of his going into hiding a package arrived by personal courier with a note from Joe. It was his gun. The police had reluctantly returned it to Joe under pressure from the Home Office who recognised the possible threat from the Mulligan family. A full licence was also included stating that Frank was allowed to carry it under special circumstances and threat to his life.

He decided to buy a new house. He had been lodging with some old friends in the mean time having sold his old house shortly after his wife had left him. Too many memories, but he felt that now was the time to start afresh. It was then that his ex-wife contacted him.

Not realising that it would be a problem, his friends, being her friends as well, had told her that he was staying with them. Frank had no knowledge of this until she turned up on the doorstep one afternoon and walked into the room.

"Hello Frank." He had heard the doorbell go but had paid little attention, as he was deep into an article in his newspaper. The sound of her voice made him jump and he looked around. Kath was still a good-looking woman, quite tall at 5.9" with long auburn hair to her shoulders and a good figure but now very much on the plump side as she entered middle age. She had quite obviously tried to make an effort to look presentable and almost achieved it but not quite.

He rose to his feet not knowing what to say and feeling slightly betrayed by his friends who were standing grinning. They meant well but as far as Frank was concerned they had made an enormous mistake.

"Hi Kath. What on earth are you doing here?" he asked.

A look of disappointment crossed her face and she frowned. "That's never a good sign," he thought.

"Oh, you know Frank, I was just in the area and thought I would pop by and say hello to Doug and Ann and they told me that you were staying here." She fiddled with her handbag and glanced sideways at their friends who were bustling about making them a cup of tea. They seemed pleased with the fact that, as they saw it, they were reuniting their two friends. It was the last thing Frank wanted.

"But you are living in Suffolk with that plumber fellow now Kath aren't you?" he asked. The whole episode of that period two years ago still upset him. He had resigned himself some time ago to the fact that she had rejected him for another man, their plumber in fact. He had well and truly made up for lost time since. She didn't know it but she had done him one hell of a favour.

"Well yes, but things aren't going too well and anyway Frank I just couldn't believe it when I saw you on the telly, and all that money. What on earth are you going to do with it all? I would have thought that you would have remembered your friends and family first surely, especially the children and maybe me as well, Frank. Especially bearing in mind all the years we spent together. I almost think that I am due some of it anyway as your ex-wife. It's not as if you worked for it is it? No, you went and found it didn't you? How much have you got then? How many millions?" She said all this without taking a breath.

It all came flooding back to him. She had started and usually it almost took an act of God to stop her once she started to talk and got into her stride. Frank couldn't believe what he was hearing; he raised both hands with his palms pointed towards her, which stopped her in her tracks. His temper was building.

"Now you hold it right there Kath. Just who the fucking hell do you think you are coming in here and making these stupid demands? You walked off and left me with all those debts, mostly instigated by you, remember? Went off with that dickhead plumber, who only wanted your money and I haven't heard a word from you since then. Not a birthday card, telephone call, nothing. If you remember we are divorced and a bloody good thing too I say because I have been having an absolute ball since you have been gone, you stupid woman, and that's the way it's going to stay. You're getting nothing because you had everything from me last time but that's all finished now. No, it's not even up for discussion. Watch my lips, Kath. You don't deserve anything and you are going to get nothing. OK?"

She stood looking up at him and had gone deathly white. She had really believed that she was entitled to some of this money. After all, she had been his wife, but she was seeing a different man standing in front of her to the one she had been used to for some twenty years. A seemingly bigger, taller, more self assured and angrier man and with his deep tanned strong looking face and black curly hair he looked very attractive to her. His deep blue eyes had always been his most attractive asset and they were flashing at her in a rare anger, he looked very dangerous and she had never ever seen that in him before. She remembered that she had heard on television that he had apparently killed that Irish man. She shivered. He had never lost his temper with her ever before but she could see he was on the brink of doing so now. The thought excited her and it flashed through her mind that she had made one big mistake in ever leaving him.

"Sorry Frank. I didn't realise that you would be so hard. Dick said that I deserved some money and that's why I'm here. It was his suggestion."

"Why doesn't that surprise me Kath? You are just going to have to go back and tell him that there's not going to be any money. Oh, and by the way, don't you worry about the kids; I have made sure that they are well and truly set up for life. They are just going to have to wait a little, that's all. Now if that's all you have to say to me Kath, you have to excuse me. I'm going away for a while and I have to pack. Have a safe journey home." With that he left the room. He hoped he would never see her again.

* * *

He had always wanted a house by the sea, particularly on the South coast. The sea held a big attraction for him as he'd had various boats for nearly twenty years, so he spent five days scouring estate agents from

Sussex to Dorset. He eventually found a small and very attractive, two bedroom detached chalet bungalow with a small garden overlooking the sea near Lymington in Hampshire and close to the New Forest. It had been converted to a chalet bungalow with a large master bedroom fitted into the roof with two enormous bay windows at each end.

The views were wonderful, facing south towards the southern half of the Isle of Wight and the Solent. Frank relished the thought of re-building his life there, maybe buying a boat again and perhaps taking up golf once more. One of the main attractions for him was the number of good country pubs in the immediate neighbourhood. The cottage had only been on the market twenty-four hours; the existing owners reluctantly had to move abroad because of business. They wanted a quick sale. His generous cash offer on the house, £5,000 over the asking price, was accepted immediately and he instructed his solicitors that he would have the cash available for the cottage within three or four weeks. He put down a deposit of £50,000 to ensure he did not lose it. In the meantime he would be abroad for a short while but could be contacted on his mobile if necessary.

His solicitors did not have a problem about Frank getting the cash together, nor did the owners. Because of the continual media interest in him he was now instantly recognisable and the fact that he was involved with finding treasure helped to grease the wheels of business. The cottage had been beautifully restored and furnished. He agreed with the owners to take everything and negotiated a cash price that was fair to both sides. He was very pleased with the result and looked forward to taking up residence and to being a homeowner again. He invited his children down for the day and they all agreed that it was simply perfect for him.

Joe had been very busy during this time and was already in negotiation with several publishers who had shown a keen interest in the trio's story. He was also talking to the Americans regarding the possibility of a film. Joe was very excited about that project. Things were hotting up. The bad news was that they had been 'shafted' by the Government as they had expected.

Frank, Josie and Liz had been offered seven million pounds each exclusive of tax as a 'finder's fee' as the Home Secretary had put it, on a take it or leave it basis. Joe had been horrified and had tried to argue but that was all that was available they were told. The trio had agreed, from their respective places around the world, and the money was now in their bank accounts. Frank was a wealthy man. They had also signed across to the British Government all of their respective rights to the treasure and in their inimitable way the Government had very quickly made a statement to the world, via the press and television, promising to return as much of the treasure as possible to its original owners. This publicity had not done them any harm at all as it made headline news internationally.

Frank felt massive relief at the news, as did the girls. He now had no pressure on him except for the coming court case, which was at least four months away. He had therefore decided to go to Amsterdam to sell his diamonds.

* * *

The large circular rosewood table gleamed in the reflection from the low lights round the room as the three girls, all dressed in naval uniforms, busied themselves laying out files around the table.

Without warning, five men burst through the double door and strode towards the table. The man leading them, grey haired, tall and distinguished, gestured to the others as to where they should sit. The three girls discreetly removed themselves and stood back in the shadows around the edge of the room waiting to be of service. The grey haired man remained standing as the others sat and looked briefly at the files laid out in front of them.

"We haven't got time for small talk today gentlemen and that's not my way anyway, as you know. What we have to discuss is of course to remain top secret and for your ears only." One of the men glanced at the girls standing discreetly in the shadows. "You don't have to worry about them George they are all grade "A" clearance. If you look at the top file in front of you, coloured green, you will see a photo of a man you will recognise. Don't bother to read the rest; you can do that at a later date. It's the limey who interests us today and who flew into our lives three weeks ago. He brought back the two models from the jungle. You know who I am talking about. So, what's his problem? The truth is we don't know, all we do know is that he is connected to something we consider to be very serious. I was personally watching on the satellite when that crazy Brazilian General sent his Sikorskys into the valley in the attempt to find the alleged treasure that the limey has been spouting on about. I watched in disbelief as I saw his boys virtually wiped out. I was also watching when our satellites went down as we watched the Brits beginning their attempt to fly into this strange valley." He paused and took a breath. "Now, what I want from you guys are some ideas as to what this is all about. It all links together, our satellites going down and the guys getting killed in the valley. I know you have all been hearing stories and that you have seen the film of the massacre, the question we have to ask is why, and how, did the satellites go down and why didn't the Brits get attacked as did the Brazilians? Over to you. The grey haired man slowly sat down as though he had a back problem.

There was silence for ten seconds. Then one of the suited men spoke. "Boss, is there no reasonable explanation for the satellites going down?"

"None."

"What about interference either from space or from the ground?"

"We have discounted space, whatever it was came from earth. They did not malfunction; they simply failed for a period of time. I have it on unimpeachable authority from NASA that nothing was wrong with the satellites and they are as puzzled and worried as we are. I can't emphasis how important this is. This affects national security on a major scale to the point even the President is concerned. He wants answers and so do I, that's how serious this is."

"Sir, we could conjecture for the next hour, the thing is we have to cut through the crap and find the answers." The youngest man present, small, thin and completely bald he couldn't have been more than thirty years of age spoke this quietly.

"What do you propose Graham?"

"That we pick up the limey and persuade him to tell us whatever it is he knows."

Silence spread around the room and everyone sat looking at either the grey haired man or at their files.

"I happen to think you are right Graham, that's also my line of thinking, it would have to be done soon, within the next week and fast. Do you all agree?" The grey haired man raised an eyebrow and looked at the others. Nods of agreement went round the table.

"Well, it's your idea Graham, lay it on and organise it. Watch your step though and use only your best men. From what we have heard he is no push over. The Irish tried pulling something on him and failed to the point where he killed one of them so he's no mug. If you read his file you will see he is very proficient with a gun. It's all in the file." He paused,

"Maybe that's an angle you could use, if you use our Irish friends to get him for us our profile will be nil and they can have their fun with him afterwards. They will appreciate that. Think on it. We will meet at the same time next week and hear how you have progressed. Don't take too long and do whatever it takes; but be discreet. I don't want trouble with the Brits. We have a "special relationship" with them or has no one told you?" There were wry smiles around the table. "OK, that's item one. Let's get onto the next. Please open your Red file."

* * *

Frank had been taking his time driving to Harwich and the traffic on the M25 had been quite reasonable for a change. It was when he diverted off to take the A12 for Harwich that be became aware of the black Mercedes which was keeping contact with him three cars back, regardless as to whether he increased or decreased speed. He wasn't too worried although, having said that, he could not stop himself continually checking his rear view mirror to see if it was still there; and it always was. He didn't like it. Shortly after Colchester he pulled into a petrol station and began to fill up. Looking around casually he noticed the Mercedes had parked on the exit road. Whoever was trailing him must have realised by now that he was heading for Harwich and the boat to Holland and, in that case, would probably follow him onto the boat. That was no place to have enemies; there was nowhere he could go to escape them if trouble was what they were up to. Frank decided that he would forgo the trip at this time and lose his admirers in the streets of Harwich before making his way back to London and home.

The petrol pump kicked and stopped his tank was now full. He made his way to the kiosk to pay and, having done so, made his way back towards his car. Opening the door he sensed someone behind him and before he could glance round he was shoved violently against his car and, at the same time, felt a sharp sting in his shoulder. His legs almost instantly went weak his eyesight blurred and he felt himself being bundled into the car.

He came to his senses slowly; his head thumping and his brain whirling around as though in a deep mist. There was one thing he was pretty sure of. He had been hit and drugged and he felt shitty; his mouth was so furred up that he wanted to spit and his body felt weak and useless. Slowly his brain began to clear. It was best if he kept his eyes closed and feigned sleep, that wasn't difficult to do. His head slumped between his legs and he allowed a low rumbling snore to escape his lips; he let his senses take over. He was definitely back in his car and he felt bodies on both sides of him so he decided that he must be in the back seat. His hands were tied in front of him and yet his legs were free, that was ok so far. Many years ago he had been taught that if captured the best time to escape was shortly after that event. To wait to see what happened next could be disastrous. Whoever his captors were wouldn't be in the habit of being kind. For sure he was in big trouble and even death could be on the menu; certainly very heavy interrogation, and that wouldn't be very much fun either. Had they found his diamonds and what did they want him for, and who the hell were they? So many questions began to ping into his head and his body ached at having to be in this ridiculous position for so long.

"Shut the fooker up, that fooking snoring is doing my head in." An elbow slammed into his ribs and he jerked, pretending to mumble something but continued to feign sleep. There was no doubt about that accent they were Irish. "Jesus that was it" he thought, he wasn't going to hang around with them. He could feel strength pouring back into his body.

"The Yanks said that after they were through with him we could have him. We will make the fooker suffer for Jamie's death; the fooker will wish he had never been born. How far is it to the farm now?"

The Yanks wanted him. "What were they doing working with this lot?" he asked himself. There was no time to worry about that now. He slowly opened his eyes and looked to his left and right as best he could without moving his head. Sure enough there were legs either side clad in old blue jeans and scruffy trainers. He felt that the car was moving fairly swiftly. Too late to worry about the consequences; thank God they hadn't hooded him. He was ready, and ready to kill, if necessary.

He jerked violently upright at the same time slamming his right elbow in to the face of the captor on his right with all the strength he possessed. He felt the nose and mouth give way. The man screamed but Frank was too busy doing exactly the same to his left. The car swerved as the driver looked into his mirror to see what was happening and that was the last thing he saw as Frank jumped forward and wrapped his arms around his neck pulling him back hard into his seat. Frank had a second's view of the road in front turning into a bank. The man on his left slammed a punch into Frank's ribs and he turned and kicked at the man's crutch with all his might. Another scream rang out as his foot connected and then the car was upside down and flying. Frank kept his arms around the driver's neck, choking the air out of him. They were rocketing up the bank through small scrub, Christ they must be doing over eighty, they were going to crash big time and he pulled himself closer into the back of the driver's seat for protection. Then there was just the sound of the engine screaming and he counted to four before the car slammed into terra firma, tumbling and rolling with glass shattering and bodies flying. It came to a halt upside down and then slowly rolled onto its wheels on the slope of the bank. It trundled down until it stopped on the level of a field.

Frank lay still for a moment feeling himself to see if he was OK. He had trouble untangling his arms from around the driver's dead and crumpled body. As soon as he had done so he kicked at the door to his right but there was no movement and there wasn't any from his companions either. He kicked at the nearside door and that refused to budge also. "What am I doing?" he asked himself and leaned over and released the door latch. It fell open. "Christ, I must be in shock, I'm not thinking straight." He scrambled out over the bodies of his captors. He felt OK but quickly checked himself again. He had a cut high on his head somewhere, as blood was running down his face, but that was all. No broken bones but his left shoulder felt bruised and his ribs hurt where he had been hit. His pack, where the fuck was his pack? The boot lid was open and he looked around desperately; he was beginning to panic. His whole financial future was disappearing in his mind at the loss. He found it no more than a few yards away and, breathing a sigh of relief, he quickly checked to see if the diamonds were still there. They were. His hands were still tied together with the plastic strip but he managed to cut it in two on the broken glass of the driver's window. His captors were either all unconscious, or dead, and frankly he couldn't care less which. That had been a close call. He looked around him. The car hire company were going to be really pissed that was for sure.

Where the hell was he? He could hear shouts and voices. It must have been one hell of a sight seeing a car come off the motorway like that. People would be here any minute, and the police too, and maybe these guys had another car following them. His head was spinning but what he knew was that he had to get the hell out of there and find out where he was. He needed to put some distance between himself and these guys. He looked around him; they had come off the motorway, gone up an embankment and dropped down the other side into this field. The smell of petrol was very strong, probably from a burst hose; for certain there was going to be a fire any minute so it was time to leave. Grabbing his pack he left his suitcase. No time to start carrying a suitcase about the country. What was in there was not important and he could always buy new clothes. He stumbled away from the crash scene taking care not to leave too obvious a sign that he had fled the scene. With any luck the police would assume that what they found was all that had ever been in the car. The bad news was that the car had been hired to him. This was getting very messy.

He skirted along a hedge around the first field and then the second. He stopped and looked back. There were people all around the car now and it hadn't burst into flames Pity. It was beginning to get dusk and he could see lights of houses through the trees ahead. Where the hell he was was anyone's guess but the first thing he needed to do was to clean himself up. His shoulder still hurt and he needed to wash the blood off his face. He needed a change of clothes but otherwise he was fine. He stopped and squatted down by the side of the wood. He looked down on a small village tucked into a valley ahead of him. How the hell was he going to get cleaned up? If he knocked on any of those doors they would almost certainly call the police. Having said that, perhaps if he told the truth he would get away with it, it was worth a shot. He shook his head. This was all crazy but there was no time to get too heavy on the thinking. He couldn't be too far from Harwich, maybe between Colchester and Chelmsford. That's it, what he needed was a Taxi. He stood up and walked down towards the small village wiping his face with his handkerchief. There had to be a telephone box somewhere. He walked past the Church and along the length of the small street but couldn't find one anywhere, but the pub looked to be open.

The Shepherd and Flock, it sounded nice and inviting. He gave the door a shove and walked into the bar looking around warily. There was nobody around at all. He saw the sign for the toilets and sighed with relief. Looking at himself in the mirror he didn't look too good and he still had blood down the side of his face. He ran the tap and washed his face with the paper towels. When he was satisfied with the result and he had run his fingers through his hair he reckoned he now looked quite presentable. He walked back into the bar, leaned against it and waited for someone to appear.

"Sorry Sir, didn't hear you come in.," said the young girl coming in from a room behind the bar. "What can I get you?"

"I'd like a double whisky please with plenty of ice."

The girl glanced at him as she hit the measure twice and put the drink on the bar then spooned in four cubes of ice. "I wanted the bloody whisky over the ice" Frank thought but he was in no mood to upset the girl. He downed the drink in two gulps and felt the fire of the spirit roar into his stomach. Boy, he felt better for that and, slapping another tenner on the bar he ordered another. The girl gave him another long quizzical glance.

"Would you mind putting the ice in first and what's your name" he asked the girl.

The young girl took a few seconds to respond. "Jenny." She said.

"Jenny is there anyone in the village who could ferry me to Harwich, my car has broken down and I need to catch the boat" he hesitated looking at his watch, "In about two hours."

The girl was absently wiping the bar top with a cloth and didn't answer for a minute. She took so much time Frank was about to ask the question again.

"Me boyfriend will probably do that for 'yer, I'll go and ask 'im." She said and turned and disappeared out to the back of the bar. Frank sank back onto the bar stool, things were happening a bit quick, If the Yanks, i.e. the CIA, were now involved he was in very serious trouble he knew that. It was probably something to do with the valley he wouldn't wonder. Even so, if they had been following and saw the accident they would know by now that he was missing and alive. None of them would like that very much. Frank stood up suddenly as a thought hit him. Christ, they would be looking for him and being so near to the crash site this village would probably be the first place. Depending on how quickly they could get to it, they were probably on their way now. Frank swore to himself again.

He waited impatiently and suddenly the girl appeared with a white, spotty faced, youth no taller than the girl herself. He had narrow shoulders and a slumped posture. No more than seventeen Frank thought. Wouldn't last ten minutes in the man's army and that's probably an exaggeration. More like five. The boy wouldn't look Frank in the eye.

"Can I help you mister? Jenny says you want a lift to Harwich."

"Yes and I'm in a real hurry, I don't care about the price so what would you say to one hundred pounds?" The boy was really startled and the girl's eyes widened, then she grinned and nudged her boyfriend hard in the rib's. For the first time the boy looked up at Frank towering above him and his eyes narrowed.

"You in trouble mister?"

Frank was surprised; the boy was brighter than he looked. Just shows you shouldn't make snap judgements he thought. "OK, you got me son, you're right of course. I am in a lot of trouble frankly and I think they, the bad boys, are going to arrive within the next five minutes. If I'm right I can honestly say to you that I'm dead meat. So you have to understand that you could be in trouble yourselves if you help me, and I mean big trouble. So how much do you want then?"

The boy looked up at Frank again his little eyes were gleaming with interest. This was probably the first time in his life that anything like this had happened to him. He was going to milk it for all he could.

"Two hundred and fifty pounds mister and we can leave now. Cash up front."

Frank had to laugh at the pure cheek of the boy. "You'll go far son, make it two hundred and we have a deal OK? Let's go." The boy nodded agreement, Frank stooped and picked up his backpack and swung it onto his back, He opened his wallet and counted out two hundred pounds in twenties from his wad. The two youngsters watched with their eyes popping out of their heads. Frank gave the money to the girl who immediately started to count the money again.

"One word of warning Jenny, if they do come in here you will have to deny that anyone had been in at all so far this evening so wash my glass now," Frank finished off his whisky and handed the glass over to the girl. "OK young man what's your name?"

The young man turned away waiting for Frank who vaulted over the bar. "It's Nigel" he said and disappeared into the small hallway. Frank turned and looked at the young girl. "Be very careful Jenny when they arrive, if you get it wrong we will all be in trouble, don't forget you have seen no one OK?" The girl nodded, smiled and whispered "Good luck." Frank nodded and said, "Hide that money somewhere safe," and then followed Nigel down the hallway.

Frank smiled when he saw Nigel's car. It was a Fiat 1100 at least ten years old, battered and bruised, but a heart of a lion. It was a midget of a car. Frank levered his big body into the passenger seat and strapped himself in. Nigel immediately floored the accelerator the rear wheels protesting on the gravel of the car park. The car swung violently onto the road and careered on down the street. Nigel was into his James Bond mode and was out to impress. Frank said nothing and for the next twenty-five miles kept his mouth and, repeatedly, his eyes shut as the young lad pushed the little car as hard as he could, its engine and tyres were protesting and screaming. When they arrived at the ferry terminal Frank had to admit that the boy had done well. He thanked him profusely and gave him another fifty pounds. It was worth every penny to get here without any trouble. The boy simply nodded his thanks and looked Frank in the eyes for a moment.

"Who's after you then mister?"

Frank leaned back into the car through the small side window. "The CIA actually and that's the truth. Do you remember the story recently about the fella who brought back the two models from the Brazilian jungle?"

The boy looked at Frank for a moment and then his eyes slowly widened. "It's you ain't it? It's bloody you that's who it is, it's bloody you. That Frank something or other it's bloody you. Christ almighty mister, if I had known it was you I would have done this for nuffing, honest."

"Get out of here Nigel. Keep your mouth shut for a while and tell Jenny to do the same. Keep it to yourself and say nothing to anyone. I'm serious Nigel; this could be very dangerous for you if they find out that you have helped me. Now get the hell home and good luck."

"Good luck to you Frank," the boy muttered and with squealing tyres he spun the little car around and headed back towards the motorway. Frank watched it go, wondering how long they would be able to keep their mouths shut. Two hours probably but by then he would be well on his way. He shrugged his pack back onto his back and headed for the terminal ticket office. It had been an interesting day.

The overnight ferry to Holland slipped away from the quay on time and Frank slept the night through in the comfort of a cabin with a chair firmly under the door handle. Picking up another hire car on arrival, he drove to Amsterdam and booked himself into the Sheraton Hotel for six nights. He wanted to explore Amsterdam and its many delights after he had completed his business. He kept a careful check on anyone near him and at last felt that he might have thrown off his trackers.

The hire car company in England was on his mind and he phoned them. They were very surprised to hear from him and told him that they would have to claim off his insurers for the loss of the car. He told them to send him their bill to his English address and he would settle it. They also told him that the police had been asking questions.

He phoned Joe. "Frank for God's sake what's going on? The world and its brother are going crazy over here, and the newspapers are full of it. Haven't you looked at one yet? They are all saying you have gone missing leaving two men dead and another half dead in a car hired by you in an accident on the A12. What the bloody hell is going on? Oh, by the way the police want to talk to you as well."

"Sort them all out for me Joe, say I have gone into hiding as I temporarily lost my memory after the accident. I don't care what you tell them just keep them off my back."

"The police have been asking me these strange questions Frank mainly about the three Irish guys who were in the car with you and why one was driving without permission. I won't be able to keep them off your back for long and anyway where the hell are you?"

"Can't tell you right now Joe, if the girls phone put their minds at rest as to how I am. I'm really OK and I promise to come back and face the music soon. More than that I can't tell even you now, I am having to go so that I can talk to my kids so I will phone you tomorrow." Joe started to bluster and demand something or other but Frank put the phone down.

He phoned his three children one after the other to put their minds at rest about his well being. He missed them badly and felt a warm glow at the fact that they were really worried about him. They said that many of his old friends had been phoning them to see if he was alright. That was nice.

He had lost all sense of time somehow and realised that it was a Saturday morning and that the town was bustling and busy. He wandered around the town for a while eventually finding an attractive looking restaurant near to the river and settled down at a table on the pavement to read The Daily Telegraph. This was pure luxury. He had all the time in the world and was determined to wring every last second out of the day in doing precisely nothing. The warm summer sunshine beat down on his neck and seemed to massage all the stress of the past weeks out of him. He was horrified to see that he was a main item of news, albeit that it was on page four, but even so the reporter was making outrageous suggestions about him and what could possibly have happened to him in the car accident. It also covered his recent escapades. It made him out to be an extraordinary character, which Frank knew was a lot of old rubbish. He was still the same Frank Blake. He sat drinking steadily watching the world go by and thinking hard. He felt quite angry with life; it was throwing so much shit at him at the moment that he found it quite unbelievable. After all he was just a normal guy, quite what he had done to deserve all this crap he couldn't imagine. After a while, and a few beers, he decided he felt hungry and called for the menu. He treated himself to a bowl of oysters swimming in a thick white wine sauce and completed the meal with a large, beautifully cooked, steak with an Italian salad and a bottle of full bodied red wine. At the end of that Frank was feeling better, in fact he felt very good.

The wine waiter was particularly helpful and Frank engaged him in conversation whenever the man had a free moment. The waiter introduced himself as Marion, which made Frank smile, and sat down to chat whenever he could. Frank asked him confidentially if he knew who the best diamond merchants in Amsterdam were and who would be willing to buy a few.

Marion looked at Frank for a moment. "I don't myself but I have a friend who would have the answer to that," he said. "I will go and phone him now and ask the question."

He was back in a few moments. "My friend is very interested and would like to meet you Frank," he said. "If it is convenient, he asked if he could meet you here?"

Frank smiled back at Marion. "That would be just fine Marion, get back on the phone and get him down here. In the mean time, let's break open another bottle."

Frank leaned back in his chair and again let the sunshine cover him in its warmth. He was full of good food and wine and he lazily watched the population of Amsterdam going about their business through half-closed eyes. He couldn't help but notice the women, a large number of whom were very attractive. He noticed that a particularly stunning brunette with a face and figure to match plus long hair and long legs passed by at least twice and on the last pass had smiled at him. He smiled back. She veered across the pavement and sat down next to him.

"Whoops, I'm being picked up," he thought. She said something to him, which he presumed, was Dutch. He shrugged. "Sorry I don't understand. I'm English" he replied. Breaking into English she said. "Oh, Engleesh. What is your name?"

"Frank," he replied.

"Mine is Christie. You look as though you are having a good time. Do you mind if I join you?" Frank waved to Marion who came over, frowning. "Another glass for the lady please, Marion," he said.

Marion spoke rapidly to the woman who fired back a salvo of words.

"I do not think she is a good girl Frank. You know what I mean?" The girl fired off some more words and Marion flushed.

"It's OK Marion she's not doing any harm and I'm a big boy now. I shall be seeing your friend in a minute anyway" He poured the girl a drink.

She flashed perfect teeth back at him. "Where are you staying Frank?" she asked raising her glass and taking a large sip all the while watching him. He told her.

"I know that hotel of course, but I have never been inside for one reason or another. Would you mind if I came back with you so that I can have a look around. Do they have a good bar?" she smiled.

"Why yes of course. I have someone I have to see in a minute but if you give me your telephone number I can phone you later and arrange to take you there if you like." He looked her up and down. She was sitting with her long legs crossed and her skirt hitched slightly above the knees. She certainly had great legs. She saw him looking and hitched it a little higher. He raised his eyes to her and they smiled at each other. "She could be useful in several ways," he thought.

She lifted her small handbag and pulled out her purse from which she extracted a business card. He noticed that she had beautiful hands. Long tapering fingers with well manicured scarlet nails. Good-looking hands on a woman always turned him on. "You can reach me on my mobile on that number Frank. I shall be waiting for your call." Her eyes looked over his shoulder and changed. "Thank you for your drink Frank I have to go," she almost whispered the last few words. "Please phone me. I would like that." She smiled at him and glancing behind Frank once more she quickly rose and strode away. He watched her long stride and the way her bottom twitched as she walked. A hand fell on his shoulder.

"What a lovely girl Frank. It is Frank isn't it?" boomed a deep voice.

He had known someone was behind him from the worried look the girl gave so he wasn't that surprised. He turned slowly in his chair and looked up at a mountain of a man. He was huge, well over 6'5" and at least twenty-five stone. Frank rose and took the man's hand. It was a firm grip by a man dressed in a loose fitting white cotton suit that had seen better days and had not seen a cleaner for some considerable time.

He looked at Frank through tiny piggy eyes that were a strange yellow and black colour that Frank had never seen before. They were quite the weirdest eyes and yet the man's big fat grin offset the intensity of them. For some strange reason Frank liked him instantly recognising that the man was one of natures natural rogues with a keen intelligence that he kept well hidden.

"Hello. Yes my name is Frank, what's yours?"

The man laughed a deep booming laugh and his whole body shook. "My name is Gustav, Frank. You don't need to know my surname at this point in time." He turned and roared at Marion who was hovering near by. "Marion, my chair." A very strong looking and very large wooden chair with a well-padded seat appeared as if by magic and was put at Frank's table. Gustav sat down. His breathing sounded wheezy and he coughed into a handkerchief.

"As you can see I'm a little overweight Frank and it's starting to affect my health. I really must lose some weight but the food is so good in this city it just seems to be a crime not to indulge." He spoke perfect English. He paused and leaned forward. "Speaking of crime, I understand that you have some diamonds for sale," he whispered.

Frank leaned back in his chair and looked at the man. "For all I know you could be anybody Gustav. Interpol, CIA, Dutch Secret Service, police anybody. Why should I talk to you?" he said.

The man leaned back in his chair, wiped his face once again and laughed. "Quite right Frank, quite right. Yes, I could be anyone. In fact sometimes I can be all of those things if I wish, depending on the situation. But I do have the advantage you see. I know who you are but you don't know who I am."

"Who am I?" said Frank frowning at the man.

"You, dear boy, are Frank Blake, British hero extraordinaire. Did you seriously think that you could sit out here in public as you have for the last two hours and expect half the population not to recognise you? If you did then that would be very naïve. Your face has been on the front pages of the newspapers and on television for the last five or six weeks for one reason or another and only today you are mentioned again." Gustav wiped his face. "Within five minutes of you sitting here I was told who you were and where you were. Even without Marion phoning me I would have come and introduced myself. You see Frank you are very famous and have been having some interesting times recently. Plus, of course, there is the treasure." The man grinned, licked his lips and wiped his face again. He was sweating profusely in the warm afternoon heat.

"You should read the papers Gustav. We don't have the stuff anymore. The British Government has it and they are giving it away. Haven't you heard?"

"Yes I have heard and no one believes a word of it of course. Did they pay you for it or did they steal it?"

"Both," said Frank.

The man roared with laughter again, his whole body was shaking. He stopped and looked at Frank with his small, strange, yellow and black piggy eyes. For some reason they gave Frank the shivers.

"I like you Frank and why shouldn't I? You are a man after my own heart. Now, let's get down to business and talk about diamonds. You obviously managed to keep a few for yourself."

"Let's just say that I have accidentally found some and they don't have an owner. My aunt left them to me, of course, in her will or I found them in my garden. Whatever. Yes, I do have a few."

Gustav was looking intently at Frank. "How many and what value?" he asked quietly.

"A handful of average quality and a few of very high quality. The latter are mostly pure with one or two being dark red and even blue and all, without exception, over twelve carats. The others range from a few carats to six or seven," Frank said.

Gustav raised his eyebrows. "Really," he said. "May I see?"

"What here?" Frank replied.

"Let me tell you something Frank. This is my area. Nothing goes on here without me knowing and nothing happens without me knowing. You could pour a pocketful of diamonds onto this table and nobody would blink because it is my place. Now let me see one."

Frank put his hand into his inside pocket and pulled out two packages, one a black velvet pouch. Gustav put a napkin in front of him and Frank shook out the first bunch of diamonds destined for the troops. Gustav looked at them briefly, picking out one or two and looking at them through his eyeglass. He sat back and wiped his face again frowning slightly his fat face gleaming with perspiration. "Quite a good selection and very marketable. I will give you, let's see in English pounds, yes, I will give you £80,000 for these in hard cash and that's my best and last offer." Frank looked disappointed. He had hoped for more for the troops but thought that they would be pleased with that under the circumstances. He did a quick mental calculation, that would work out around two and half thousand per man. He decided that he would make it up to three thousand per man himself. It was the least he could do.

"I'm a little disappointed at the price Gustav, but I agree."

Gustav nodded and glanced at Frank. "Now, let me see these others." He ran his tongue across his thick lips in anticipation. Frank shook out four large diamonds from the second packet. He'd polished them that morning and now the sunlight caught them and they burst with colour.

Gustav sucked in his breath and sat looking at them. Frank looked around him. Everyone was studiously ignoring them but he had the feeling that everyone was watching.

The fat man picked up a stone and put the eyeglass to his eye. He lifted one of the larger stones to the glass and sucked in his breath again. "Magnificent, simply magnificent" he muttered. He put that one down and lifted another. "Mine Gott, wunderbar" he looked carefully at all four lingering on the last one. He then put them back in the pouch and pushed them back across the table to Frank.

"You are right. Quite exquisite quality and wonderfully cut. They have been cut by a master craftsman, a fellow countryman I suspect, and some time ago perhaps even some sixty or seventy years ago. They are very rare indeed. How many have you got, Frank?" he said.

"I said earlier, a few," Frank replied.

Gustav was breathing very heavily with what Frank assumed was excitement and he was right. "I want first option on them all. They are magnificent and so pure. I will need to see the rest, of course," said Gustav.

"You can't because they are back in England. I have deliberately scattered them around a bit so that they are not all in one place," he said. He was lying of course as they were in a locker at the main railway station now, and the ticket was in his wallet.

"You may well want them Gustav, but the price has to be right. This is my pension fund. I also want to see some other dealers to compare prices."

Gustav leaned towards him again. "Now listen to me my friend. I can understand what you are saying. That's business. But I still want first refusal. I will pay you top rates. Wait just a minute." Gustav retrieved a small calculator from his jacket pocket and poured over it for a minute or two punching in figures with his fat little fingers. "Frank," he said after a moment, "We will go to my bank now and I will pay you £160,000, by banker's draft, for the large one, and £140,000 each for the others."

Frank studied Gustav's hot, sweaty, implacable face carefully. The man really wanted these stones but was trying not to show any emotion. A slight tick at the corner of one eye gave him away. The price was about right as far as he was concerned; this Gustav must be a very wealthy man indeed to be able to lay his hands on so much money just like that. Frank wondered what other scams he was into, drugs maybe and probably prostitution as well. He deliberately let the silence hang for ten seconds but he had already made up his mind. "OK Gustav, you've got a deal," he said. Gustav sat back in his chair. "You agree?" he said frowning in surprise. "No arguing? What are you up to Frank?"

"I don't believe in hanging around and messing about. I like to make a decision good or bad. So rather than haggle for an hour with you I agree. I think that's a fair price even though you will probably make half as much again," he said.

Gustav let out a long breath. "Let's go then before you change your mind," he said rising from his chair.

Frank called Marion over to pay his bill. "It's on me," boomed Gustav. Frank thanked him and they moved away down the street. Frank noticed two men close in around them.

Gustav put his arm around Frank's shoulders as they walked. "My boys Frank. Don't worry. It can get a little out of order here sometimes as I have competitors so I have to look after myself."

"Armed?" asked Frank.

"Of course, as you are," Gustav replied smiling down at Frank. Frank checked the P38 under his left armpit by squeezing it with his arm. It was a very comforting feeling.

"I have to look after myself as well Gustav, as I proved in London. No doubt you read about my little bit of trouble there?"

"Yes, that was well done but I wouldn't want to be in your shoes when they catch up with you," said Gustav.

They entered his bank, which turned out to be less than two hundred yards down the street. Immediately the manager came out and was almost grovelling to Gustav. He was told what needed to be done and said that it would only take a few moments. They were shown to a private room.

Gustav and Frank chatted for a while. "I should have sufficient funds to make an offer similar to this for about twenty or thirty stones within a week." Gustav said. "That's providing we can agree a sensible price subject to me seeing the other stones."

"Let's just say twenty stones for now," said Frank.

"You have more than twenty Frank? You naughty boy. When can you get them together?" Gustav asked.

"Pay me for these first and we will talk about the others," said Frank grinning at him.

The manager came back in with the bankers draft for signature. As soon as he signed it Gustav held it in the air in front of Frank who slowly withdrew the two pouches and poured the four stones and the bag of smaller stones gently onto the desk. The manager tried to stifle a gasp but couldn't.

Gustav took the four diamonds and gave Frank the draft at the same time. Frank folded it and slipped it into his wallet. Gustav continued to hold the largest diamond in his hand looking up at the light through it. "Perfect, just perfect. Now Frank, let's talk."

"No Gustav, that's not what we agreed. You're trying to steam roller me and I need to talk to some other people first. So why don't we get together in a few day's time?" They agreed.

He made his apologies to Gustav saying he would definitely call him again in a couple of days and made his way back to his hotel after first depositing the bankers' draft and having it transferred to his account in England. When he arrived at the hotel he found two messages for him.

"That's strange," he thought. "Nobody knows I'm here." The calls were from two different diamond merchants in the town. He went to his room and phoned each one in turn. They both made the same excuse, which was that they had heard he was in town and had some business to transact. They would both like to see him as soon as possible. He made appointments with each one for the morning.

"This sure is a small town. Obviously within a few hours the word has gone around," he thought. He stripped and climbed into bed to sleep off his lunch.

Two hours later he woke and had a shower to freshen himself up. He fished in his trouser pockets until he found the card the girl had left with him. He phoned her. She answered within a few seconds.

"Hello Christie, it's Frank,"

"Frank the Englishman. How nice to hear from you. Sorry I left you so quickly today but I don't like that man who came to see you. I hear that he is very bad.

"That's OK Christie. I just thought that if you have some spare time we could go out on the town tonight."

She was surprised. "That would be very nice but wouldn't you like me to come round now?" She offered.

Without hesitation he answered. "Yeah, do that, I'm at the Sheraton. Room 335. Come on over Christie and bring some extra clothes to go out in tonight."

"I'll be there shortly," she said.

The whole business of meeting her and her being so eager to jump in his bed was surreal. "There has to be a hidden agenda," he thought. He picked up the phone and called Gustav.

"Gustav," he said when the phone answered. "It's Frank Blake. One favour Gustav. Do you recall the girl that was sitting with me today at lunch when you came over? Do you know her?"

"Of course I know her Frank. She is what I would call a high-class lady. Very expensive and she picks her own men. But maybe I am being unkind. She has her own business as a freelance photographer and has a good clientele. She is a very beautiful woman with a figure to die for but even I have never scored. I think that's the word you use isn't it? If she doesn't want a man it doesn't matter how much money you offer her she will refuse, as I have found to my cost. She is very selective. Why Frank?"

"She picked me up today and is coming round to see me with obvious intentions. She is deliberately acting like a whore and I just wondered why she has picked me. Does she have any links with any particular group Gustav?"

"Not that I know of. She is independent. Watch out though and take precautions as you did in England. I need to have you around for a while until I have all those diamonds from you. Ha, Ha." The fat man thought that was a very funny joke and chuckled on.

"Very funny Gustav, and thanks for the word. See you in a couple of days."

Frank put the phone down and waited. He then jumped up and ran into the bedroom, and dug out his gun. Checking the magazine he again put it under the bed." Here we go again," he thought. He didn't have to wait long. Within fifteen minutes his phone rang. It was the manager in reception. "There is a young lady coming up to see you Mr Blake. Did you invite her?" There was disapproval in his voice.

"Yes I did Johan. Don't worry I know what I am doing, thank you."

He put the phone down as his bell rang. He walked over and opened the door.

She was standing there looking stunning and she was smiling. "May I come in Frank?" she asked.

He stood aside as she wafted past leaving the scent of her perfume in his nostrils. She turned as he closed the door. She was nearly as tall as him in her high heels. He walked up to her and taking her by the arms kissed her on the mouth for six seconds and then broke away. He walked over to the drinks cupboard. "What would you like to drink Christie?"

She was still standing in the same place. "You can't just walk up to a girl and kiss her like that and walk away Frank," she said in her thick Dutch accent. "A glass of champagne, please."

"Make yourself at home Christie," he replied. He pulled a bottle out of the cabinet cool box and popped the cork. He poured them both a glass then followed her over to his settee where she was sitting. She took the glass and drank half without stopping. "Delicious" she said. She took off her small jacket and leaned towards him; her breasts were straining at her blouse. He couldn't take his eyes off them. He put out his hand and slowly undid the first two buttons just above her breasts. She wasn't wearing a bra. She took another sip of her glass and watched him. He took the glass out of her hand and moved against her with one hand moving inside her blouse to find her breasts. She offered no resistance and slowly fell back into the cushions.

Whatever was in her mind she certainly didn't let it hold her back. She was a skilled lover and used her body to good effect on him. As they made love he looked down at her beautiful body in wonder. She was at the peak of her life physically and her skin was as soft as silk. He became intoxicated with her beauty and her body. All he wanted to do was to take her and take her. After the initial sex, which was what they both needed, she lay stretched out like a cat while he kissed and caressed her. He slowly sexed her until she came with great gasps, her body heaving and straining for the climax. Very little was said throughout the three hours of their lovemaking except for the occasional whispered words of love and pleasure.

A few hours later they bathed and dressed and went out to a local restaurant that she knew.

She sat back in her chair watching him and smiling. "I'm so full," she said stroking her tummy. "Isn't this food wonderful Frank? I come her twice a week, when I can afford it, for a good feed and the people here are so nice."

Frank looked around him. Christie had told him that this was a very fine restaurant and frequented by many people from the theatre and the professions. He had been particularly struck by the attentiveness of their two waiters. The two had introduced themselves as Carlos and Ryan. Eventually they had both asked Frank for his autograph; he had realised they had recognised him. Christie found this all very amusing.

She had woven her web over him as only a beautiful woman can do. He was totally smitten but he fought desperately not to show it. He knew very well that there had to be a reason for all this and made the decision to find out, but not during this night. This was all too good and he was determined to take all the pleasure she was prepared to give him. Life was too short. After all he was forty-seven and believed that at that age you didn't waste time brooding on possibilities. If there was a problem it could wait to the morning.

A small band started to play. He took her hand and led her to the small dance floor. She moved close into his arms putting one arm around his neck and taking his other hand into hers. He could feel her from her breasts to her thighs.

"I didn't think the English could dance like this," she said after a while. "You are a surprisingly good mover Frank."

"Some of us can still dance properly. You, young lady, are just fortunate enough to have in your arms a man old enough to remember how, and who loves this type of music," he said. She laughed throwing her lovely hair back and moved even closer to him so that she could anticipate his movements. She smiled up into his eyes.

"I have to say Frank that I consider myself a very lucky woman to be here with such a handsome man. Do you realise that I am the envy of every woman here tonight? They have all recognised you and know who you are. I have noticed that I am getting some very envious looks. If any woman tries to take you from me tonight they will be in very serious trouble."

Frank gave her a smile. He still hadn't got used to the fact that, because of the international press coverage of his exploits with the girls, he was now so well known. She noticed his slight flush of embarrassment and was deeply impressed. "You are such an Englishman Frank and I love you for it. Enjoy your fame you deserve it," she said. The band changed mood and started to play a slow number.

She moved her head to his shoulder and he felt her relax against him. He couldn't stop his body responding. She giggled into his ear but didn't move away. "That's going to be embarrassing for you when we walk off the floor so I'll just enjoy it while I can," she whispered. A little later when they were dancing she spoke softly in his ear "I'm beginning to fall in love with you Frank Blake." He didn't answer but just gave her a slight squeeze.

The next morning he woke early and put his hand out to stroke her body slowly and gently. She murmured in her sleep.

"What the hell have I got myself into?" he thought. "I'm sleeping with a woman I hardly know and already I'm becoming too fond of her for goodness sake. There's no fool like an old fool and I'm behaving like an old fool. I'm going to get hurt if I'm not careful. What's the matter with you boy? Get a grip of yourself, just fuck her and walk away because that's what she is going to do to you." He lay cocooned in the warmth of the bed and the woman, thinking and watching the light slowly grow stronger through the curtains.

She woke up and went sleepily to the bathroom. When she came back she didn't bother to hide her nakedness. When she realised he was awake she wiggled her breasts at him as she got back into bed. She snuggled up to him and wrapped an arm across his chest. "How long have you been lying there thinking?" she whispered.

"Some time," he replied.

"It's a bad thing to think too much at this time of the morning," she said. "Tell me all about it." Her face was tucked into his neck as she spoke.

"I'm trying to reason with myself and stop myself becoming too attracted to you, if you want to know. I mean, for goodness sake, I have only known you for twenty-four hours and to cap it all you picked me up in the street."

She said nothing for a while. "OK" she said in her deep, thick voice, "let's sort this out." She got up and drew the curtains. Wrapping his dressing gown around her she came back to sit on the bed.

"I'll be honest with you Frank. I haven't had a man for quite a while. I could have any one I wish for if I try but no one has appealed to me. That's until I saw you sitting and drinking at the restaurant. I had to walk past you twice to get a good look. I fancied you immediately because somehow you looked different to any one else. That's why I picked you up. Also, if we are being honest, I recognised you from the newspapers.

I knew who you were Frank, and I was fascinated and intrigued. However, this won't go anywhere unless you want it to, I know that. So let's just enjoy each other while we can."

He was amazed at her frankness. "OK," he said, "You've been frank with me and I'll be frank with you. I thought you were on the make somehow. That doesn't matter now. I agree, let's just enjoy whatever time there's going to be for us. Sod it, life's too short to worry about such things." He reached out and pulled her down to him. She laughed as he pulled her dressing gown aside and began making love to her again.

They went down to the dining room and during breakfast he told her why he was in Amsterdam. "Diamonds, Frank, you have diamonds?" she asked. "Was that why you were talking to that horrible fat man yesterday?"

"Shhh," he said. "Don't shout it out loud. Yes, I have a few, which I am selling. Look." He took the black felt pouch from his pocket and took one out and put it on the table in front of her. She gasped. "Frank, I've never seen anything so lovely in my life. It's enormous, simply so beautiful." His common sense left him completely. "It's yours Christie, because if I don't live another day, I will have trouble matching the fun I'm having with you."

She gave another sharp intake of breath, her big eyes growing even wider. "Mine Frank? Oh don't be so ridiculous. You can't just give that to me like that. Besides," she paused. "It would make me feel cheap. I don't want to feel that you are buying me. Nobody buys me, Frank."

"I'm not buying you Christie," he said "for some stupid reason I want to give it to you. I know I must be mad but there it is. Please take it and enjoy it, or if you want to sell it to buy something, do so."

She laughed tossing her head and throwing her hair back. "OK Frank, I'd be pretty stupid to say no wouldn't I? Thank you. In that case I will." She picked it up. "It's so big, whatever can I have it made into? I will have to get some advice but I will have it made into something Frank, which I will keep forever in memory of a truly wonderful man."

"You're just an old fashioned romantic," he said laughing at her pleasure.

"Let's go back upstairs so I can thank you properly," she grinned at him.

"Only if you carry me," he said. You're wearing me out."

* * *

The phone rang interrupting the grey haired man's conversation. "I said no interruptions Jean."

"It's George calling from England Sir."

The grey haired hesitated, "All right, put him on."

"Good evening Sir."

"It's morning here actually George but what do you want?"

"Just to let you know that our girl has made contact with the limey and we should have him shortly."

The grey haired man sat thinking, "I'm not so sure that it's worth it anymore George, things have moved on and we may not need him. Not at this point in time anyway, maybe later. That was sure a balls up recently and I am looking for your report by the way. Questions have been asked as to why we are involving ourselves with the Irish and the fact that three died attempting to get him only proves what I said to you in the beginning. He's dangerous and I think we should leave him alone. We don't need the hassle now."

"We are close Sir. Just one more try, we are very close."

"One more try then George and then come home. There are more important things for you to do now. The heat has gone out of this one." He put down the phone. "Now gentlemen, where were we."

11

THEY LAY IN BED talking, and he asked her about her life and about her family. She was quite easy with him and spoke at length about her life in the city, her job and about her mother and father.

She asked him what he was doing in Amsterdam and he replied that he was simply selling some very special diamonds that had belonged to his grandmother.

"Initially I was going to do the rounds of the other diamond merchants and sell to the highest bidder, but I've been thinking. If I do that, soon everyone will know what I'm up to and the price will drop. I already have some problems in that direction because of the gun fight in England and also because the British Government wants some answers to a couple of questions, which I'm not prepared to answer. I think what I will do is sell them all to Gustav and leave it at that." There was no way he was going to tell her the truth.

"I don't like that fat man Frank, but you must make the decision," she said. "I have been thinking. Would you like to come and stay at my house? It's only small but it's quite nice."

He turned and looked at her. "That sounds great. It's the best offer I've had today. I'll pack and we can go now. No, wait a minute. In case I'm being followed I think you had better go first. Leave me your address and I'll make my own way there within the hour."

She agreed saying that it made sense. "Better to be safe than sorry," she said. She loved that English expression.

Later she showered, dressed, and left him with a kiss, telling him not to be too long.

He started to get his things together. He collected his gun from beneath the bed, un-cocking it as he did so, and slipped it into the shoulder holster under his left arm. He lounged lazily watching television and when an hour was up he opened the door to the apartment, lifted his case outside, locked the apartment door after him and left to pay his bill.

He decided to walk to the railway station and left his case with the hotel porter for collection later. It was such a beautiful day and it didn't take long. Finding his locker, he opened it and removed the backpack that had followed him around the world. Looking at the map he realised that he could quite easily walk to Christie's apartment, which was by the river. It couldn't be more than two miles away at the most so he could be there within an hour if he got a move on. He needed the exercise anyway. He moved off at a quick pace enjoying the atmosphere of the streets. As he walked he switched on his mobile phone and dialled the fat man's' number. As he waited for a response he smiled to himself at the way that Christie had labelled Gustav as 'The Fat Man.' The name was going to stick now. Gustav answered the phone with a brisk, "Yaw?"

"Hi, fat man, it's Frank."

"Frank, God almighty, just the man. I have been trying to find you. I have phoned the hotel but they said you had left and I do not have your phone number. Where are you?"

"I'm still in Amsterdam, why?"

"The diamonds, Frank, I sold them for a very, very, good price. They were almost snatched out of my hands. Quite remarkable and now strange things are happening. I have had the top diamond merchants in Amsterdam, the Van Hoon family, coming on very strong, demanding to know how I obtained the diamonds. They are the people who purchased the ones you sold to me and now they want more and they want to know where I got them, and they want to know very much indeed. How many have you got, Frank, because I will buy everything from you?"

"Don't get greedy on me, Gustav. I can let you have another twenty tomorrow but that's it. And you must not let anyone know where you got them from either or any future deals are off. Is that understood? If you do, we are both going to be in very deep trouble with quite a lot of heavy people."

"Do not worry my friend, your secret is safe with me. As safe as the Bank of England, isn't that what you say? I am most pleased that you can let me have them, Frank, most pleased. It will put me in very great position with the Van Hoon family. They are very powerful in the diamond area in Amsterdam. Nothing much in precious stones goes on here without them knowing. They are a very old family and very respected and Mr Van Hoon is very formidable. He must be in his late 80s now. Most respected for his resistance during the Second World War. Caught by the Nazis, you know, and tortured. But he survived. Meet me tomorrow at 1pm at the same place as yesterday and we will conclude the deal, Frank. I will have a bankers draft ready. Can we agree on the same price for the remaining stones?"

"Yes, on the whites, but I do have a red and a blue which, I know, are particularly valuable. They have the same cut and almost the same carats. You will have to raise the stakes on those, Gustav."

"I will pay you £200,000 each for those two Frank, and that's my first and last offer."

"That's a deal Gustav, nice to do business with you," Frank said, knowing full well that Gustav would make as much as half again on the deal and switched off.

He looked up at the clear blue sky and then at the sunny tree-lined street filled with happy people. Life was very good here. For the first time in years he had money and was happy. Life was indeed looking good. There was money in the bank and in his pocket and he didn't have his business to worry about. In fact there wasn't much to worry about at all if the truth was known. How wrong can you be? Instinctively he noticed a black BMW saloon cruise past him slowly and stop a few yards down the road.

He was miles away, thinking of Gustav, but his newly developed instincts made him watch the BMW almost casually. He slowed his pace and almost stopped, his senses were warning him but he didn't know why. Three men in masks carrying light machine pistols piled out of the car in a big hurry and they were all looking in his direction.

Screams ran out from people all around him and everything seemed to go into slow motion. They were coming for him fast. There was nowhere to go and the first bullets came spattering across the pavement pinging off the walls behind him. They were shooting wildly. Almost in a dream he realised that they were meant for him. Two women in front of him took the first burst of fire and saved his life. Even so he suddenly found himself rolling backwards across the pavement feeling a violent blow to the body together with a searing pain that had just hit him in his left side. He had never been hit by a bullet before and shock seared around his body. He swore continuously; more in anger than at the initial pain, as the adrenalin was pumping him up and protecting him from it. His brain, though, was as clear as a bell, and knowing that he was going to be dead any second he rolled desperately for the nearest doorway for cover.

Bullets ricocheted off the brickwork around him and, gathering his senses, he remembered that his gun was in his shoulder holster. He drew it, cocking it and flicking off the safety catch at the same time as he raised it. His left arm didn't seem to work properly but he didn't allow himself to think about that. The masked men saw him raising the gun and reacted like the professionals they were. They broke left and right and the middleman dropped to a crouch and raised his gun.

More screams rang out and people began running in front of them in a total panic. The adrenalin continued to pump and all Frank could think about was that he had eight shots left and no spares, and that his side hurt like hell, but there was nothing he could do about that now. He threw himself out of the doorway down onto the pavement gasping as the pain in his side hit him again and he rolled over onto his tummy presenting the smallest of targets cursing as he did so because he had banged his elbow, just as the middleman let off a burst of fire at him. In the back of his mind he was thanking Sergeant Davidson from over twenty years ago. Sergeant Davidson had worked on Frank for a full day on that particular move and now it was going to save his life. It wasn't an orthodox move but it was effective. Davidson had said it would be one day and he knew a thing or two having been a bodyguard to the Queen.

Where the shots went he had no idea but Frank simply pointed and fired two shots in return. The man's head jerked back, his body flopping to the ground. Frank was momentarily surprised at his handiwork because he had been aiming at the upper body, but had no time to dwell on it. The man running to his left had stopped in shock. Frank let off another two shots deliberately aiming lower to allow for the kick. The hooded man spun around dropping his gun and falling to one knee, screaming, and then fell over, still screaming. Frank felt a tug at his shirt and heard two more bangs. "Shit, that's close," he thought as he rolled over again and came up looking for the third man who was now running back for the car as fast as he could go. Frank went to shoot and then thought better of it. The car took off in a rush, wheels screaming with the man scrambling on board.

He heard the sound of running feet behind him and spun round. Three more men, all in dark suits and ties, were running towards him. One of them seemed to be reaching for a gun inside his jacket. Frank's gun pointed straight at them and collectively they stopped and stood still just looking at Frank.

"Just coming to give you a hand boy." The twang of his American, Deep South, accent grated on Frank's frayed nerves.

"Don't need it, boy, so fuck off, NOW." They could see that Frank wasn't joking and he did have the gun, which was pointing at them. Also they could see the look in Frank's eyes. He was very serious and all pumped up. The three men glanced at each other, and turning, walked back to another black car fifty yards away. Frank got onto his feet feeling anything but steady.

The pain in his side burnt like hell. He looked down seeing blood all over his shirt. "Fucking hell, I'm not hanging around here," He was shaking with fear and excitement. People were still screaming and he saw another man lying still on the ground, with blood seeping from his body. Obviously a stray bullet had hit him as well as the two women. Frank bent down slowly grimacing at the pain from his side and collected his backpack. He walked quickly over to the wounded man lying on the pavement, and ripped his hood off. The terrorist was in fact a boy, no more than twenty.

He opened his eyes and looked straight into Frank's. "Fook you, you fooking English bastard. We'll fooking get you next time don't you worry," he gasped with tears of pain pouring down his cheeks.

The howl of police sirens sounded. He needed to get away fast. People were watching him. Damn it to hell, he would be recognised.

"You Mulligans keep telling me that, and look where it's got you, you idiot. Tell your family to give it up for God's sake. I'm fed up with dealing with little boys like you." Frank kicked the boy's gun into the gutter. The youth didn't answer. "Your knee is busted to hell, sonny, and probably your thigh as well. Tell your family that if they try this again I'll kill the fucking lot of you, right?"

"Fook you," sobbed the boy through clenched teeth.

"And fuck you," said Frank. He stood up tucking his gun back in its holster under his left arm and moved rapidly away.

Once round the corner he ran like hell, for what must have been over two hundred yards, clutching his side. Soon he slowed down worried that he might make his wound worse. Apart from the pain in his side he felt very good and fit and thought again about what the Monk said in the Pyramid. He decided that he must get out of the area fast before the Police set up roadblocks, if they hadn't already done so. He could still hear sirens, seemingly all around him. He walked, as quickly as he dared, a full three blocks and turned another corner to find himself by the river. The area was surprisingly quiet. He stopped and slowly pulled his shirt up out of his belt to look at the bullet wound. It wasn't bleeding much anymore but it did look a bit of a mess. The bullet had just creased his side but hadn't penetrated leaving a six inch long wound just as though he had a red hot poker pushed against his skin. Strangely enough it didn't hurt any more. He was lucky, it hadn't done too much damage but it needed treating quickly and the bleeding needed to be stopped.

"Bloody Irish, they can't shoot to save their lives." He thought. Three men should have taken him out quite easily and without too much trouble but the public that had been all around Frank on the pavement must have put them off. He had indeed been very lucky. And those three suited fella's. Must have been the Yankee cavalry. The CIA. They were always just around the corner. The thought worried him. He dropped his pack down onto the pavement and pulled out an old tee shirt. Taking off his shirt he slipped the tee shirt back on yelping several times as he did so. Tearing the old shirt in three he tied the pieces together and wound them tightly around the wound under his tee shirt. He slowly lifted his backpack back onto his right shoulder, crossed the road, and walked along the river until he found a riverboat boarding pontoon. It was full of Japanese tourists jabbering merrily away. They completely ignored him, which suited him just fine. In a few moments a river cruiser came along side and he boarded with the rest of the tourists. A ticket collector came up to him and asked in English how far he wanted to go. Frank told him roughly where he was headed for and the ticket collector told him where he would have to get off. On his map it looked to be no more than a mile to Christie's place.

He settled back in his seat, wincing as he did so, and let himself relax to the sound of the boat's hull swishing through the water and feeling the sun coming through the leaves of the trees. He was curious about himself. He hadn't used a pistol for years until he had acquired this one from the dead German pilot. And yet his old skill was still there. He was still good. "It can only be a fluke but I deliberately tried to shoot the boy in the leg and I did." That was too uncanny for words. "It's as though someone guides my hand," he thought.

The boatman waved to him to indicate that he was at his destination; Frank got off the boat and walked in the opposite direction to where he wanted to go until the boat was out of sight. If the police do talk to the boatman then that hopefully would make them search in the wrong direction. He turned and retraced his steps studying his map. She had an apartment by the river.

He found Christie's apartment fifteen minutes later and rang her bell. "Ya? Is that you Frank?" He admitted it was and she told him the number and floor and let him in.

She was waiting for him looking gorgeous in a white open necked blouse and jeans with her dark hair falling over her shoulders. He loved that hair. He took her into his arms and kissed her long and hard, at the same time backing her into her room and shutting the door with his foot. She kissed him back hungrily. They came up for air. "Where have you been you naughty boy?" she said.

"I had a little trouble on the way," he replied and told her about the gunmen and getting shot. She instantly wanted to see his wound and lifted his shirt gasping at the sight of the old tee shirt drenched in blood. She ran into the bathroom and came back with a bowl of warm water and bandages.

"You will have to see a doctor straight away Frank."

"People have been killed Christie and they will be waiting for me to do just that. I must have left blood on the pavement so they know I have been hit. Just do what you can now and I will have to sit it out and heal myself. I'm sure if you put enough antiseptic on it, it will be just fine."

Christie bathed the deep wound and poured something on it, which hurt like hell. She then put cream onto it and bandaged him around the waist. It felt better immediately though he knew he would be very stiff in the morning.

"The police will be looking for a man dressed like me so I will have to get some more clothes. Will you go to the hotel and collect my suitcase Christie, please?"

She looked shocked. "Of course I will. Who are these men who want to kill you Frank?" she asked. He told her. "But they are crazy and how did they find you here in Amsterdam?" she asked.

"I'm surprised about that myself because very few people know I'm here. This is going to be in the papers that's for sure and some people are going to put two and two together and make four." He paused. "Christie, I'm going to have to conclude my business quickly and get out of Holland I'm afraid."

"No Frank, please." Christie looked concerned.

He took her into his arms and kissed her. She looked tragic. "Let's talk about this later," he said. Christie immediately collected her car from her garage and drove to the hotel to collect Frank's suitcase. Nothing was said to her and no one paid her any attention. On the way back to her apartment she stopped at a public phone box and dialled a number.

"What the hell happened? Can't you idiots do anything right." She listened to the voice at the other end. "He is now at my apartment and is talking about leaving the country somehow. If I can I will find out how and let you know. He was hit by one of the gunmen by the way. Stupid Irish. Didn't you tell them to be careful?" She listened to more conversation and then said. "I don't want him taken at my place see! What are you talking about base isn't interested in him anymore? After all that we have been through with him?" She listened a little more. "That's all well and good but your mistakes aren't mine and I have to go now so I will talk to you in the morning." She drove back quickly ensuring no one followed her.

Some time later they were sitting on her little terrace overlooking the river and drinking wine. The sun was still warm as the day closed to early evening and the tourist boats hummed up and down with the voices of the boatmen drifting up to them in the evening breeze. "How about if I make a suggestion Christie?" he said. She had been very quiet since their lovemaking. "What is that Frank?"

"How about you coming to live in England with me? he said.

She smiled at him and took and held his hand. "That is a great compliment Frank but impossible. I have my life here and my family and my business. My business is very good and I love it. Don't think that I hadn't thought of that," she said.

"In that case I have to hope they don't find out who I am and that I can leave the country easily. I will have to work on that. In the meantime, may I hide here Christie, for a few days and enjoy the local hospitality?"

She got up and carefully sat on his lap whilst trying not to hurt his wound. "You are a bad man taking advantage of your hostess. If you don't take me back to bed and make love to me again I will report you to the police."

"My pleasure," he replied and, very carefully, did just that.

A little while later his mobile rang, Frank rolled over the bed and picked up the phone. "Yes?" he said.

"Frank my boy, its Joe. Am I interrupting anything, perhaps?"

"Yes you are, but we are taking a break. So what's up Joe? Good to hear from you."

"I've had a call from our boy at the Home Office wanting to know what you are doing in Amsterdam and telling me that apparently you shot two more of the Mulligan family in the street? The shooting is on the news here and people have been killed Frank, although they haven't mentioned your name yet. We understand they might, however, once they have a positive identity. They said that a person was seen leaving the scene and was wounded. Is it true Frank, are you OK?"

"Whew, that's quick. Yeah, they creased me but it's not serious. I was lucky. It only happened about four hours ago. Three of them tried to take me out in full view of everyone in a main street and I was just walking along minding my own bloody business. The reason I'm in Amsterdam Joe is that, one, I love the place and you told me to lose myself, and two I happen to know a very lovely lady here who is an old friend I'm visiting. OK? Tell that to the boy. By the way I'm running out of ammunition fast."

"OK Frank, I'll tell them what you said but for goodness sake look after yourself. I think the police over here will want to talk to you so you had better make arrangements to get back here. By the way, the film is beginning to look really hot. We have got a major player who wants to do it. He loves the story but can't do it for a year. Now that would be good because it would allow us to get the book out first. Frank, I really need you back here to help with this. I have a ghost-writer who will do it all but he will need your input. Also the preliminary hearing for the shooting over here is coming up next week so you had better get back for that."

"Joe, I think the Home Office is guessing. While you have been talking I have been thinking about it. Tell them I have said that I am not in Amsterdam and that I am touring England looking for a house. They won't know that I have bought one in Hampshire already because I paid cash and I have the deeds. There is no way they can pick that up just yet. I will trickle back into England without them knowing. Threaten legal action or do whatever it takes but keep my name off the news. I will talk to you later Joe when I get back. Should be a couple of days. Bye." He switched off the phone.

"So you are going?" Christie said.

"I have to sweetheart, but I will be back and I will keep in touch. I have a lot to do but, in the meantime." He pulled her to him and kissed her breasts until she moaned for him. He was feeling a lot better.

They switched on the evening news and the shooting was the second feature. What shocked Frank was a fairly fuzzy picture taken by a tourist of him standing over the IRA boy with his gun still in his hand. Fortunately, because of the poor quality, it was impossible to say who it was. The headline was 'Gang Warfare Has Broken Out Between Local Gang Leaders and Others Unknown'.

He awoke the next morning feeling very stiff and sore. As Christie re-dressed his wound he phoned Gustav and arranged to meet him at one o'clock.

Frank was a little early but 'the fat man' was sitting and drinking coffee already. Frank nodded to Gustav's two henchmen and sat down. "Morning Frank. Main headlines again I see," said Gustav grinning. He was sweating in the eighty-degree heat. "It says that a man was seen running away after the gun fight and he appeared to have been hit. Are you OK Frank?"

"Yeah, I'm OK. They just creased me a little." Frank glanced at the paper's headlines. All the broadsheets were running stories of the gunfight with two of the papers stating that the dead gunman and the wounded one were Irish. It also said that two members of the public had been killed and one was seriously injured. Frank frowned when he saw that item. Because of him, and the greed and avarice of other people, innocent people were now dying. That was simply unacceptable, he didn't know what he could do about it but it was unacceptable.

"You're a good guesser Gustav, although I deny any knowledge of it and don't know what you are talking about," frankly I'm lucky to be alive that's for sure, although some innocent people weren't so lucky." He glanced at Gustav who was watching him closely. "Do me a favour Gustav please, find out who died because of me and see what you can do for them on my behalf. I don't care what it costs but I would feel better if something could be done for the families. It would relieve some of my shame." Gustav nodded.

"Because of that little incident, I am going to have to leave sooner than I thought," he said. "Gustav, I need your help. I need to leave Holland quietly and would prefer to leave by boat. I quite expect that all ports and airports will be watched by whoever is looking for me as well as the police who will be really pissed off. By the look of these papers they will be pulling out all the stops to find out who is responsible for this outrage and I don't blame them. Incidentally, I have just heard that even the British Government is asking why I'm here so I am pretending that I'm not."

"You must have a friend who owns a boat that I can hire for, say, a month. The type of boat I need would be about 40 odd-feet in length, have a good sea going hull and must do at least 15 to 20 knots. In other words, have big diesel engines. I would let them know where it is in England when I have finished with it and they can pick it up and bring it back. Obviously I know that this will cost."

Gustav smiled at his friend. "My dear boy, you are such a fortunate man in knowing me. I can produce anything you require. I have such a boat myself moored at a marina on the coast. I use it occasionally myself on special trips and sometimes for holidays. I also charter it out occasionally. It is an English boat, a Nelson 46 with twin 400hp diesel engines. She is a very good sea boat and would be ideal. Do you know it?"

Frank couldn't believe his luck. "Absolutely perfect, Gustav. I'll need all the correct paper work in case I'm pulled over by customs. You know what they are like now," he thought for a moment. "Gustav would you let me buy it? Under the circumstances I would be prepared to pay over the going rate and I'm in a hurry."

Gustav thought for a moment. "I don't use it very often but it is quite special to me. I have had it for almost ten years, it is in perfect condition and maintained regularly. I suppose I could always buy it from you again later if I find I miss it too much. Could we agree on that Frank because, if we can, simply give me one of your beautiful diamonds and I will sign it over to you now?"

Frank laughed out loud at the man's audacity. "Gustav, you are the biggest rogue in Christendom and will never go to heaven. OK, it's a deal. I will need the boat's registration documents and a bill of sale by this evening because I want to get away as quickly as possible. Could you phone the marina and tell them that you have sold it to a friend and that I am taking it away tonight. I want it thoroughly checked over and fuelled so that I can leave immediately. You can pay for that. I will also need current charts of the North Sea and any new navigational hazards. What has it got on board, Sat-Nav radar?"

"Everything, dear boy, absolutely everything you could possibly need. By the way, fully fuelled it will have a range of some four hundred miles at fifteen knots. Just in case you want to go somewhere else. I will also check on the weather forecast for you. Give me a call around 4pm. Now, have you the diamond?"

"Gustav, I have only known you for a couple of days but feel that I have known you a century. You are a true friend even though you are a wicked old bastard. You're my sort of man. I will give you a special for the boat." He brought the blue diamond out from his pouch. Gustav's mouth dropped open at the pure opulence of the beautiful flashing stone. It sat in the palm of his fat hand, sparkling and spreading its light in all directions. Frank was not to know that he had just given his friend a death sentence.

Gustav spoke Dutch to himself quietly for almost thirty seconds and then reverted to English. "I have never, ever, seen such a beautiful diamond, Frank. I don't know what to say." He looked at Frank with those terrible snake eyes and they where brimming with tears. He reached out and pulled Frank into his enormous bulk patting him gently on the back. "No one has ever given me anything like this in my life. I will not forget your generosity, ever. Take my boat with pleasure and enjoy."

"The man's a soft pudding really. You just have to find his weak point," thought Frank.

"Now, about the remaining diamonds," said Frank. He pulled a larger package out of his pack and slipped them across the table. Gustav opened the pack and looked inside. A grin split his face from ear to ear and he looked at Frank. He then lifted out each jewel in turn and counted nineteen. "My God they are so beautiful but you said twenty, Frank," said Gustav.

"But that includes the blue one you silly sod Gustav," he laughed back. "Hand over the money my friend and stop dicking me around." Gustav did so and at the same time Frank passed over the stones.

Frank took Gustav by the hand and holding it looked into those strange eyes. "Good to do business with you Gustav. Goodbye my friend. Thanks for all your help and make sure you phone me later. We will meet again. I love this city and will be coming back."

Frank rose and left Gustav still gazing at the precious blue stone in his hand. One of Gustav's bodyguards moved in front of Frank and stopped him. He was a very big man when up close. Frank was over 6' but this man towered over him.

The man spoke in a deep guttural voice in poor English. "We know you are a good man Mr Blake and a good friend to our boss. We are very pleased about this. If you ever have trouble again you come to us. We like you." He pressed a piece of paper into Frank's hand, grinned and backed away.

"Well," Frank thought, looking at the phone number on the piece of paper. "This is turning into an interesting day, friends in the strangest places." He put the paper carefully into his wallet and made his way back to Christie's. On the way to her home he bought some provisions, especially chocolate, bread, tea, sugar, milk, bananas, cornflakes, eggs and bacon. That would keep him going for twenty-four hours. He bought another two pairs of jeans, underwear, three tee shirts, a polo neck sweater and a fleece. He also bought a pair of boat shoes. It gets cold at sea during the night. His side gave him a twinge of pain and he winced. He felt that it was getting better though and knew that it would not take too long to heal completely. On his way back he phoned Christie and asked her if she knew the nearest gun shop. She said she knew of one. He told her he needed forty rounds of 9mm ammunition for his pistol. She said she would go and get them for him immediately and would meet him back at the apartment in half and hour.

Later, they talked for the rest of the afternoon trying to keep calm knowing that this was the last time they would be together for a while. The phone rang and it was Gustav.

"I have all you need Frank, including a car, which is clean for you to use to get to the Marina. Meet me in fifteen minutes at the restaurant." Christie drove him to the restaurant but stayed in her car almost a street away. Frank didn't want any trouble.

When he walked into the restaurant Marion met him and took his hand. "Hello Mr Blake, so nice to see you. He is waiting for you over there." Frank walked over to where 'the fat man' was sitting. He rose from his chair and enveloped Frank in his arms making Frank yelp because of his wound. Gustav laughed and apologised.

Gustav handed Frank a packet of papers. "All the boat's papers are there including all repair bills and your bill of sale. I have changed the insurance to your name and have instructed the marina to ensure that the boat is ready for sea. They have filled her with fuel and water and will give you my spare keys. The other set is in the package. Her name is Prowler by the way. You can leave any time you want and in complete secrecy now. Please look after yourself and phone me when you get to England."

Frank waived to Marion, "One last drink Gustav." Marion disappeared with their order and returned within a few minutes. The two men took a glass of Schnapps each and toasted each other. "To the future Gustav," said Frank.

"To the future Frank," said Gustav. They drank.

"I have to go. Cheerio you old bugger." He shook Gustav's hand warmly.

"Cheerio Frank you 'old bugger' yourself whatever that means," Gustav laughed but then became serious. "Bon Voyage Frank."

Frank turned and left, not looking back. He was not to know but he would never see Gustav again. He waved farewell to Marion and the bodyguards. They waved back smiling.

He found the old BMW outside and started the engine and then carefully followed Christie back to her house. He wanted to go now and he was ready. They arrived at her apartment and loaded his goods, plus some food supplies she had also bought for the trip, into the car saying little.

Christie told him she wanted to change his dressing before he left and busied herself doing so. The wound was looking good and healing nicely. She commented that he had been very lucky indeed. When she had finished he turned and took her in his arms. "'Till we meet again Christie." She was starting to cry.

"Please phone me when you get to England Frank, and think of me. These last few days have been so wonderful."

"Just remember what I've said, Christie. If the Gods will it we will be together again soon." He got in the car and started the engine. She leaned through the window and kissed him before disappearing. He drove away.

It took him three hours to find his way to the coast. He didn't rush it as he hadn't driven on the right-hand side of the road for years and he didn't want an accident. Eventually he found the marina without too much difficulty and parked up as close to the boats as possible. It was a very busy Friday evening and the weekend sailors were descending onto their boats. He walked over to the harbour master's office and introduced himself under the false name Gustav and he had agreed.

"I have come to collect 'Prowler,'" he said.

"Yes, we were informed that you were coming. I understand that you have now brought her from Herr Zeithorp. She is a lovely boat and is not used enough unfortunately. We have run up the engines and she is ready to go." He checked the mooring register behind him. "She is lying on No

5 pontoon berth 16. Over there" he pointed out to towards the middle of the marina. It was close to dusk but Frank could just see a blue bow.

Frank thanked the harbour master for his help, collected the keys and, carrying his two boat bags, made his way down the pontoon towards the boat. He was excited. He hadn't been to sea for some years and the challenge was still there. He came to the end of No 5 pontoon and looked at the boat lying at its berth. It looked a strong and purposeful boat, a 'well found' boat they used to call such a boat in days gone by. It was all his.

He unlocked the side door and climbed into the cabin. She was clean and tidy (he had instinctively decided that it was a she) with a faint musty smell typical of boats laid up for some time. He put down his bags and checked the controls. It had a nice-sized steering wheel with dual Mercury throttle and gear controls. He couldn't wait. He jumped back onto the pontoon. He strode back to the car and loaded the rest of his supplies into a trolley. Locking the car he left the keys at the office with instructions that someone would be coming to collect it the next day. He pushed his laden trolley back to the boat and proceeded to store everything away.

The first thing he did was to open a can of beer. For the next hour he acquainted himself with the boat and where everything lay. He first wanted to check the engines and lifted the hatches. Two enormous 400hp Caterpillar diesels lay in quiet solitude. They looked new and had obviously been well looked after. They were the key to his survival. He also checked out the flares, radio, life raft and all the other essentials that he might need in an emergency. He switched on the gas and made himself a cup of tea and ate a bar of chocolate, and a small apple pie from the supplies that Christie had bought for him. He was ready. He switched on the radar and, after checking his charts, entered his starting point and his eventual destination on the Sat/Nav together with the various buoys he would pass in the night. He switched on the ignition keys, flicked up the start buttons and waited for the glow lights to go out. He then pushed each starter button in turn and the big diesels rumbled into life. The temperature gauges immediately registered warm so he jumped ashore and released the warps from the front and back and threw them back on the boat for tidying later. He eased the boat gently away from the pontoon and towards the lock. She felt superb and was very responsive to helm adjustments. He waited in the lock for the sea gates to open and passed the time tidying the warps away safely and ensuring everything was tightly secured on the deck.

The lock gates opened and he was ready to face the North Sea. Leaving the protection of the harbour walls the boat met the swell of a 5/7-sea state and rose to meet them. Frank eased open the throttles and felt the power surge through the boat as it pushed its way forward into the head sea, its speed rising to ten knots.

He let her steady at that speed for five minutes. "OK baby, let's see what you can do," he thought. Bringing the boat round onto its proposed heading he continued to push the throttles forward gently. Gradually the boat picked up speed as the propellers of the powerful engines bit into the water. Spray pumped up from the bows and the speedometer registered 15, 20 then 24 knots. The boat hardly seemed to notice that there was a big sea running. It simply ploughed through it with spray pumping up over the bow and wheelhouse. Frank felt there was more to come if necessary but decided to cruise at a steady 18 knots with the big diesels running easily at 2,000 revs.

"This is the boat for me. She's just plain bloody awesome and those engines. Whew." He revelled in the power of the boat. He felt a sense of relaxation come over him as he looked around at a relentlessly heaving grey North Sea and a clear horizon. It was the first time for many a long day that he had felt like this. Freedom and the ability to have as much space as you wanted, that was the feeling that he had been missing and searching for and didn't know it. "Instead of going all the way to Brazil in a fruitless search for something with the pyramids, all I had to do was buy a boat again. How could I have been so stupid?" he thought. "Then again if I hadn't, look what I would have missed. Having fun with the girls and, of course, meeting Christie. Maybe it was all meant to be. I could have done without the bloody Mulligan family though."

He settled down in the comfortable helm seat watching the radar and checking that the boat stayed on its programmed course. There was a long night ahead. He set the radar to warn him of any hazards that might be within five miles as a precaution, switched over to autopilot, strapped himself in and immediately dozed off. He had only been at sea for half an hour.

Waking later he looked at his watch. He was shocked to discover that he had slept for over ninety minutes. He checked his instruments to ensure that he was still on course with no hazards around him. It was now dark and he was cocooned in his own world. He turned off the cabin lights and switched the instruments over to night travelling. They glowed dull red and would not affect his night vision. He gazed out into the dark night seeing nothing, thinking.

The night passed uneventfully. There was not a lot of traffic and what there was seemed to be going in the same direction as he was, towards the mouth of the river Thames and London. Throughout those long dark hours he had time to think of the events that had overtaken him in recent weeks. He thought most of all about the woman he had just left behind. "Once all the problems are out of the way I can either use this boat to see her or fly out. It's not as if I won't see her again" he reasoned. "If I can only get her over to the house she may not want to go back, but then again am I ready for such a relationship and do I really want that?" He didn't have an answer at that particular moment and decided to leave it for another day.

The other problem that troubled him was Sandy and her ability to contact him at will. Obviously she had been instructed to become his guardian angel and was watching out for him. He reflected on his conversation with the 'Cloud' and began to doubt that it had actually ever happened. Then he realised that it had and that because of that conversation he was now a different man. The problem intrigued and worried him in equal measure. So much had been happening in his life over the last few months and he had so little time to himself that he had not applied his mind to all the strange situations concerning Sandy and the pyramid. Whatever she was now, she had saved his life several times already. If it hadn't been for her he would have been dead long ago. "Probably would have died crashing into the pyramid," he thought. "Don't worry Frank dear, all will be revealed when you need to know," her voice answered out loud in his head. He jumped and almost fell out of his chair in fright. It worried him deeply that he could hear these messages in his head. He reasoned with himself as to whether he was slightly barmy or that 'THEY' could contact him at will. No one would believe him if he ever attempted to explain about Sandy and the pyramid. In fact eyebrows would lift in mild surprise and without a doubt whispers would start to circulate. He could just see the headlines if the press caught a hint of what was going on. It didn't need the greatest intelligence in the world to know what they would do. The press, and particularly the British press took great delight in building heroes up and even greater delight in knocking them down again, everyone knew that. So, he reasoned, the best thing was to come to terms with the situation and accept it. There was no doubt in his mind and it disturbed him that he'd had a conversation with 'something' and that 'something' was not of this damn world, that was for sure. Also he had discovered that 'that something' had certainly interfered with his mental and physical structure somehow. Several times over the last few weeks he'd had the opportunity to test his new found strength and had been surprised at what he could do now. It was nothing fantastic, just about three times the strength he had before that's all. He certainly felt physically great without any effort and the extra strength came in very handy now and again. He realised that he had to be extremely careful whenever he used that new found strength, as he didn't want any more attention being brought onto him than there already was.

It was the strange dreams he had at night that troubled him most. In fact if the truth be told, they would make a damned good film. Science fiction of the likes that had not been thought of as yet. He knew damn well where they came from too and had already decided that when things had quietened down a mite he would buy himself a computer and start putting the dreams down onto paper and get a scriptwriter to knock them into a script. That's if the bloody Mulligans and the British Secret Service ever gave him a break and left him alone.

And that brought him to the other problem in his life that continued to worry him; the Mulligan family. For some reason they had made a mission of taking him out. He would have to ask Joe if he would talk to the Home Secretary again to see if they, the Government, could solve the problem their end as had been promised. "I can't go through the rest of my life looking over my shoulder," he thought.

He watched the grey dawn slowly unfurl before him, he loved this time of day at sea and by 6.30am found himself 10 miles off North Forelands in the mouth of the Thames, running along the English coast towards Ramsgate. His fuel gauges showed just over half full and he still had a hundred and fifty miles to go. He decided to call into Ramsgate and re-fuel. The sea around the harbour was full of fishing boats. He took Prowler into the harbour and pulled over to the fuel pontoon. "Good morning. Are you open yet?" he called out to a man who was obviously just opening up.

"Yes Sir, just" he replied.

Frank brought Prowler gently alongside the jetty and jumped ashore with both warps before the man could move to help him. He quickly tied up and then switched off the engines. "Would you fill her up with diesel please," he asked the fuel man.

"Lovely boat, been far?" asked the man. Praise indeed considering that he probably saw some of the nicest craft around in the marina.

"Just cruising down the coast through the night that's all. Yes, I have only just bought her and am testing her out. She's a dream to handle and hardly noticed that sea out there last night. Is there anywhere open around here at this time of the morning that does a proper breakfast?" he asked.

"Right up there on the quay. Doris runs it and it's the best English breakfast you will get anywhere. I'll swear you won't get back in your cabin once you've eaten there. If you aren't staying long, would you kindly put your boat over there, when we have finished. It will be quite safe and I will keep an eye on her. She sure is a lovely looking boat."

After filling her tanks Frank moved Prowler to where the man had suggested. He moored up and, strapping on his gun under his jacket for safety sake, walked up to the little café. He felt grubby and he rubbed the 12 hours of bristle on his face and massaged the small of his back as he walked towards the small café. Opening the door he was hit in the face with the smell of bacon being grilled and his stomach growled with hunger. The fuel manager was right. Doris; a big, blousy, big-hearted woman, was merrily trading insults with about ten fishing men while at the same time cooking their breakfasts. She looked up as he entered and smiled at him.

"Hello ducky, what can I do for you?" she said. Noisy ribald suggestions came from the men and Frank grinned at them. Turning to the woman he said, "I've been told that you do the best breakfasts around Doris, and I've been out all night. I'm starving so, yes please, can I have the works and a large mug of strong, sweet tea. Oh, and some toast. A couple of rounds will do."

She looked him up and down. "You're a bit of all right aren't yer? A bit tasty I would say, which is more than I can say for this lot here. Right my dear, one full special breakfast coming right up. Would you like a newspaper while you're waiting? "

Frank looked surprised. "Well, yes please, Doris that would be nice."

"Anne," she screamed as she started to break more eggs on the hot plate. A pretty petite girl with waist length black hair came out of the back. "Yes, Mum?" she asked.

"We have a gentleman here for a change, he needs a newspaper; can you find him one and get him a nice mug of tea? Poor man 'as been out all night."

The girl turned her eyes on to Frank. "Hey, you're a beauty," he thought "Just like my daughter." "What paper would you like?" she asked.

"Either The Times or The Telegraph please," he said.

"If you would like to sit yourself down Sir I won't be a moment" she replied.

One of the men nearby said, "You're getting special treatment mister. They don't do that for us 'ere. They're only showing off."

That set Doris off and the ribaldry was up and going again. It was obvious that they did this all the time and everyone enjoyed it. "They are all great friends and she's the lynch pin," he thought.

He settled down to his breakfast, taking his time to read his paper. He noticed that there was no further mention of the shootings. "Old news is no news," he thought. The Government was still milking the treasure story for all it was worth. There was a story that several people had made legitimate claims and were pushing the Government for decisions.

He eventually finished his breakfast and thanked Doris for looking after him. Her face went soft. "Now my boys take note. This 'ere gentleman has manners which you could learn something about. At least he thanks me which is more than you lot ever do." Everyone laughed, Frank included.

"'Ere mister!" One of the men asked. "Is that Nelson yours?" Frank said yes. "Watched you coming in just now from way out. She sure handles the sea nice. What engines you got then?"

"Twin 400hp Caterpillars," he said.

"Thought so," said the man looking out at Prowler, "nice boat."

"Thanks," said Frank and left.

He checked the time. 8.30am, with any luck, he reasoned, he should hit the Solent mid-day and with all the weekend sailors about he should not stand out too much at all amongst the welter of boats that would be out there. The English customs would have spotted him on radar coming across but would have lost him once he was close to land. They would hopefully think he was coming up the Thames to London.

He fired up the engines again, cast off and made his way back out of the harbour and, turning south, headed down the coast towards Dover. The sea was still running quite high with big swells as the wind was coming from the North West for a change so he kept his speed back to a comfortable 15 knots. She rode the swells easily at that speed without too much spray. Rounding Dover he had a few fun moments avoiding the enormous cross channel ferries that were trying to get both into and out of Dover harbour. He set to run close to the coast around three miles out. The sea was calmer this close to the coast as the wind was coming off the land. He increased his speed back up to 20 knots and switched on the autopilot. He then switched on both the normal radio for BBC 2 and also ship-to-ship radio to listen to broadcasts from Niton. He then settled down to finishing his paper. Prowler headed towards Lymington some one hundred and fifty miles distant.

Some four hours later he was back at the helm having just passed Brighton and was entering the Looe channel off Selsey Bill. At the end of the Looe channel was the entrance to the Solent, one of the busiest shipping areas in the world at weekends. You needed to be on your toes at those times as many of the skippers had probably had too much to drink the night before and were not too good at concentrating at that time of the morning.

Prowler cleaved its way past the forts at Portsmouth and then Cowes on his left shortly after. He was making very good time. "Lymington in an hour," he thought, "Home at last."

His mobile rang. It was Joe. "Morning Frank. Where are you and what's that bloody noise in the background?"

"Morning Joe. Where am I? I'm just coming back into England if you must know but I'm not saying where in case we are being listened to. I can't tell you what the noise is either."

"Oh yes, of course, right, several things to report. You have a preliminary hearing on the English shooting next Thursday morning at 9.30am at the Old Bailey. It would be a good idea if you stayed with us on the Wednesday evening I think. Graham has been talking to people and it should be a breeze. Next, really good news. Paramount has agreed to go ahead with the film. Can't confirm who it is yet but a major player is in. Can you believe it? Apparently, once he read the script he phoned them and asked for the part. Lastly, I have a bill for you from me. You ain't going to like it but it is correct so far to date."

"How much?" Frank asked. Joe told him and Frank gulped. "OK Joe, I'll pay you with a cheque when I see you on Wednesday. I'll be with you around midday. You know where I'll be until then of course."

"Of course, Frank. By the way, both the girls, Josie and Liz, are in town at the moment and want to get together with you for a couple of boozy nights on the town. What shall I tell them?"

"Oh, that's great, fantastic. I would love to see them again. Tell them I will talk to them this afternoon, Joe."

"One last thing. We all miss you and Diana sends her love. I think she's a bit in love with you, you Casanova."

"Love to you lot as well," said Frank and hung up. "Christ, I hope she keeps out of my hair," he thought.

He guided Prowler closer to the main land as he approached Lymington and slowed. putting the engines into neutral. He pulled out his binoculars and studied the shoreline. Yes, there it was, his little home close to the shore. He could just see it through the trees. "Can't wait to get back to you," he thought.

Almost to the minute he turned into the Lymington River and slowed to the regulation eight knots as he cruised slowly up river towards the marina near the town centre. He had already looked up the radio channel for that marina and he called them.

"Harbour Master," they replied. He explained that he required a berth for two or three nights and, after, a pause he was given details of the visitors' pontoon to moor to and asked to report to them when he arrived.

As he did so he was conscious of a lot of eyes checking him out. including those of the berthing master. He could see him watching Prowler through his binoculars from his office. Frank executed a perfect dock and, switching off the engines' jumped lightly onto the pontoon. He quickly and expertly warped the boat. Prowler was a pure delight to handle in such tricky circumstances.

He grabbed his particulars and sauntered down the pontoon towards the berthing office with the warm sun on his face. "There's no getting away from it," he thought. "Arriving in port after a while at sea is such a wonderful feeling." He felt good and nodded to those still trying to get their boats ready for a day at sea and received cheery waves in return.

Frank walked into the office. These marina people were of two types, cheerful and helpful, or sullen and unhelpful. The tall bearded man behind the counter was of the former. "Hello, nice boat; been far?"

There was no point in lying to these people. They knew their job too well and Prowler looked as though she had been through some big water. Frank knew that this guy would have noticed that.

"Just bought her in Norwich and brought her down last night. Refuelled at Ramsgate early this morning and just arrived," he explained.

"That's jolly good going if I might say so Sir. "That's well over two hundred miles and it must have been rough off the North Forelands last night, wasn't it?" He didn't wait for an answer. "Mind you, those Nelsons go through anything if you have the right motors and yours sound a bit beefy Sir.

"Twin 400hp Caterpillars," Frank replied, he was very proud of those engines.

"Thought so," the man replied.

Frank introduced himself. "My name is Frank Blake and I recently bought a house just up the coast from here."

"Dick Elson, temporary harbour master, I'm standing in until the permanent harbour master comes back from holiday," said the man. "Whereabouts is your house then Sir? Didn't know anything was for sale up there." Frank told him.

"Oh you bought Mr Sutchard's place then. Where are they going Sir because they have a boat moored here?"

"It's not where they are going Dick. They have gone. To Singapore I think." Frank thought for a bit. "Dick I will be needing a berth long term, now I know you are going to say to me that you have customers waiting for the next three years but I'm desperate to keep my boat here. Why don't we do a deal? I will settle Mr Sutchard's bill to date and pay to have his boat put onto hard standing until he decides what to do, providing you let me have his berth. Plus a thousand or something." Frank said the last few words slowly to give them stronger meaning. Dick raised his eyebrows a little, understanding exactly what Frank was saying. "How about if I pay two years in advance plus an acceptable deposit?" he queried.

There was no two ways about it; this Dick character was as sharp as razor. He might be a Hampshire lad but he was nobody's fool. He looked quizzically at Frank.

"Are you trying to bribe me?" he asked. A slow smile broke across his face.

Frank grinned back at him. "Yes," he said.

Dick looked down at his pad on the counter and pencilled in a few figures. He then looked around to ensure nobody was about to come in.

"I would say that this could cost you quite a lot of money. Pay for Mr Suchard's bill to date plus six months hard standing. Two year mooring fee for what? A 38ft pontoon, plus interest at 10 per cent plus a cash bonus of £1,000 each year for, err, considerations shall we say, and we could be talking turkey Sir." He looked up at Frank and waited.

Frank didn't hesitate. "Sounds reasonable enough to me," he said. "That's a deal," and he stuck his hand out. The man took it and smiling at each other, they shook hands. "I will have all monies ready by Tuesday morning if that is OK Dick," he said.

"Yes Mr Blake, that will be fine and we can conclude everything on your boat if that's OK with you." The man hesitated looking hard at Frank. "You're not the Frank Blake that's been in the papers recently. The one that flew that airplane with those two models are you Sir?"

Frank admitted that he was. "That's even better Sir."

Frank frowned to himself. He could just see this chap telling the whole bloody world that he was there and he didn't want that.

"Dick, I have to tell you something especially as we are being honest with each other. You know I have been involved in a shooting recently. Well, to cut a long story short, there are some people who want to see me dead. Until I have solved this problem, and the Government is trying to help from its end, I have to keep a low profile. What I'm asking is, could you please not tell anyone I'm here? If it gets out, then I'm a dead man. I also have to ask you to keep a wary eye out and report to me if you see anyone suspicious who appears to be hanging around or if anyone makes enquires about me. In effect Dick, my life is in your hands."

"I quite understand Mr Blake. If you get killed I don't get any commission so you can count on me," he said.

After cleaning and washing down his boat Frank found himself a trolley. He unloaded all his gear and trundled it towards the car park. Dick came out of his office.

"Is someone coming to collect you Mr Blake?" he asked.

"No, I'm going to have to order a taxi." Frank replied.

"Leave it with me Sir, I know just the man," he disappeared back into his office.

Within five minutes a 'people carrier' pulled into the car park and drove over to Frank who had just been relaxing in the sunshine. Frank waved his hand in thanks to Dick, loaded the car. and gave instructions to the driver.

"Oh yes I know that place. Lovely little cottage that is, the Sutchard's live there, nice people" he said.

"Not any longer. I do," replied Frank.

"Oh," said the driver and went quiet. He was dying to know more but Frank was too tired to start a conversation this time. Fifteen minutes later they pulled into Frank's driveway. They unloaded all his bits and pieces and Frank paid the taxi driver who then left. He unlocked his door and stepped inside. He walked through to the lounge with its big bay window looking out over the sea where he had passed by an hour ago. "Bloody fantastic," he said out loud. "Bloody fantastic. I'm home."

He checked the house over. It was immaculate. There was a local woman who had cleaned for the previous owners and Frank had taken her on. She had a key and knew the house and what needed to be done. She cleaned for him three mornings a week. It was well worth it. The fridge was well stocked but there was no milk or bread as he had expected. He had brought those items with him from the boat but decided that he would have to slip into Lymington later for other supplies. He opened a bottle of wine and sat looking out to sea watching people having fun on their boats. It was a lovely afternoon for it.

He called Josie on her mobile. They chatted for some time both being really pleased to hear from the other. He did the same with Liz and she was fine too. They all agreed to meet up in London the following week. Both Liz and Josie wanted to come down and see his cottage. After several calls back and forth they agreed a date to do that too. He then phoned Christie only to find she was not in. He phoned her mobile but it was not on either. "I'll try her later," he thought. He checked in with his kids and told them he was back,

The next item on the agenda was the remaining diamonds. "I'm going to have to bury them until I go to London," he thought. He wandered around the garden looking for a suitable place. There was a birdbath in the middle of the lawn. "That's the place for it." Carefully covering the ground around it with newspaper he moved the birdbath aside and dug a small hole. Then wrapping the black velvet pouch holding the diamonds into a plastic bag, he dropped them into the hole and replaced the birdbath.

"Perfect. Nobody would ever know," he thought.

He then walked over to the double garage by the side of the cottage. Unlocking the door he eased it up out of the way. A car sat there with a cover over it. He lifted and pulled away the cover and stood folding it as he gazed in wonder. When he had called on the Sutchard's to discuss the carpets, curtains and all the other things they wanted to leave behind, Douglas Sutchard had taken him by the arm and guided him over towards the garage.

"I have something here that might appeal to a man like you Frank," he said. It's my pride and joy and if you want it you can have it as long as you pay the going rate. Unfortunately I can't take it with me. If I could I would. but it's impractical." Douglas had opened the garage and shown him the beautifully restored white, soft-top Jaguar XK160. "It's fitted with a turbocharger and will do 170mph on the straight. The heads have been adapted to take unleaded and they were ported and polished at the same time. I have had the brakes upgraded to 4 pot discs and she will stand on her nose if necessary if you hit them hard. The turbo is a special from Technics and has no lag. It's beautiful and when you punch the throttle, hold on. This engine is something else. Over and above the fact that she had the suspension modified and also the steering, what is left is perfectly original. I have honestly spent a fortune on it Frank and getting the asking price will only pay for what I have spent on her over the last five years. By the way, she only has 47,000 miles on the clock and that's original."

Douglas had been right and after testing it on the M27 motorway Frank had fallen in love with it. £60,000 changed hands and it was his. He sat in the driving seat and sighed with pleasure. He had a great home, a boat to die for and now this car. "I just want a good woman to go with it and life will be complete again," he thought. But, as we all know, you aren't allowed to have everything in life.

* * *

Sunday morning arrived and by 8am it was obviously going to be a scorcher. He phoned his daughter and asked if she would be free for lunch as he had something to show her. In reality he wanted an excuse to use the car and to show it off to someone. His daughter offered the perfect opportunity. She lived in Sussex now with a nice young man about three years older than her. What he did for a living Frank had no idea. They seemed to be very happy together however and Frank was pleased to see his daughter happy.

He dropped the hood to enjoy the fresh morning air, pressed the starter and felt the straight six cylinders rumble into life. The coast road to Brighton was a fast road and at 10am on a Sunday morning offered little traffic or excitement so he decided to go the long way round by going inland on the M3 motorway and then cutting across country to Horsham and the little village of Amberley. He made the most of it and pushed the Jaguar hard to find its limits. It was an exciting car to drive and very predictable but no problem at all on a dry sunny morning.

He arrived to find one of his sons had also turned up. They gathered around the Jaguar in awe. They had a pleasant day and he felt a warm glow to be back in the bosom of his family. His son quizzed him as to what exactly had happened in the shooting in London. Frank felt that he should put his children in the picture and gave them a brief run down of what had happened and then went on to explain about Amsterdam. He begged them to keep quiet about that as he was not supposed to have been there. He explained how he had managed to get back to England.

His children expressed the opinion that he was completely mad.

"What on earth are you playing at Dad, at your age?" said his daughter; a point her brother agreed with. "If you go on like this you will get yourself killed. You do realise that you are running out of lives don't you. What do you think you are, a bloody cat? And all this travelling across the North Sea in the middle of the night on your own, honestly Dad, have some consideration for us please. It's all very well you being foot loose and fancy-free but you just seem to drift from one incident to another with each one getting more dangerous than the last. Why don't you just find yourself a nice lady and settle down."

They had the ability to make him feel like a child being told off.

"I'm looking all the time little one, but the problem is that now I have a bit of money it's going to be difficult deciding whether they are after me or the loot, don't you think? Anyway, you will both be the first to know if I do."

They talked about each other's lives and problems as all families do, and he questioned the two men on their respective business lives. He suggested to his son that he would be prepared to finance him if he wanted to start a business on his own but his son said that he wasn't ready to do that just yet. "I'll take you up on that another day Dad," he said.

Frank always enjoyed his daughter's cooking. She knew his likes and dislikes and as a treat had made him liver and bacon with mashed potatoes and mushy peas. A dish they always enjoyed together. He was pleased that his children had seemingly forgotten his problems.

Eventually, he made his reluctant goodbyes, promising to talk to both his son and daughter again within the week. Deciding to take the quick way home along the coast, he arrived at the cottage an hour later. He parked the car back in the garage, covered it, and switched off the light.

Over the next two days he pottered around the house and garden enjoying the quiet and solitude. He had been on the go for over three months and this rest was exactly what he needed. So far very few people knew where he was, which was fine by him. On the Monday morning he went to the local branch of his bank and made arrangements to withdraw £10,000 pounds, £2,000 of it in cash with the remainder in a bankers draft. On the Tuesday morning he called again and collected everything. He then drove down to the marina and walked slowly to his boat, knowing full well that Dick was probably watching for him. Sure enough, three minutes later there was a knock on his door. He let Dick in and they completed their business.

They chatted boats for about an hour and Frank asked if Dick could investigate the possibility of increasing the fuel tank capacity so that he could have a longer range.

"I would love to have a thousand mile range but don't know if that is possible," he said.

"There's plenty of room on the boat for bigger tanks. You would simply need to have a switch over facility with extra fuel pumps and gauges. We would also have to be careful as to where we put them. Wouldn't want to upset the balance of the boat. Everything is possible however, especially if you have the money" grinned Dick. "What's the matter, expecting trouble?"

"Listen, with what has been happening to me over the last few months I am no longer surprised at what happens next. I think it would be a very good precaution. So go ahead and get me some quotes Dick."

Dick promised to call him in a couple of days with some information and with that they parted.

Frank phoned Joe and said that he would be leaving that evening and coming up to London a day early to see the girls for a night out. They agreed that Frank should go to Joe's first.

The girls were staying at the Grosvenor Park Hotel and Frank met them in the foyer at 7pm. They were all so pleased to see each other. Frank kissed them, holding and squeezing them both.

"What we need to do is start this evening right and have a bottle of Champagne to celebrate seeing each other again," said Frank. They forgot all about having dinner; Josie took them to one club after another and introduced them to all her friends. The two girls brought Frank up to date with their latest escapades but they both admitted they missed the excitement of their trip together and that they had both been feeling a little flat and depressed after the excitement of their time in Brazil.

"Well, you should have stayed with me," said Frank and told them all that he had been doing for the last two weeks. The girls were silent all through his story, their eyes widening when he told them of the shooting in Amsterdam and of his escape and journey home.

"Damn you Frank," said Liz. She was furious. "You did all that without us. You mean to say that we missed all that fun. Well that does it. I'm sticking to you like glue from now on," Frank laughed.

They continued their reunion until well after midnight with Frank eventually having to call a halt because of his meetings with Joe in the morning. He made sure the girls got back to their hotel and settled in for the night before getting a taxi back to Joe's house.

The next morning, after breakfast, Graham arrived and they sat down together in Joe's lounge.

"I've got some good news for you Frank," said Graham. "The police will not want you there tomorrow as it's just a preliminary hearing before a Magistrate to confirm whether or not the Crown Prosecution Service will decide to prosecute the Irish boy for attempted murder on yourself. They probably will, which means that they will want you for the court hearing at some point in the near future. The police have told me they are not happy that you are wandering around with a loaded weapon but I have convinced them your life is in extreme danger and that carrying a gun will help you defend yourself should such a situation arise again. They said they will be very upset, to say the least, if it does happen again."

Frank was relieved. "Does that mean I can get on with my life?"

"In a fashion. I've also been talking to the Home Office again. They say they have talked to certain elements in Irish society about your problem. They have warned the families against having a go at you in retaliation but apparently it was too late to stop the Amsterdam problem occurring. Now, of course, the cat's among the pigeons with you shooting another one of the family."

"But they were going to kill me then and there," Frank said.

"You may consider that point valid Frank, but in the big picture it isn't. The Government are thoroughly pissed off with the whole affair. They have other more important things to worry about without spending time on yours and the Mulligan family's grievances. That's the word now Frank. Effectively they are saying that there's not a lot they can do for you. They will throw the book at the young Irish lad and probably give him ten years for attempted murder. We all know he will be out in two. The police and the Government at that time will wash their hands of the situation."

"Quite honestly Frank, there's not a lot else you can do. I know it's not very satisfactory as far as you're concerned but I can do no more."

"What those families need is warning off," Frank said.

"Don't cause any more trouble Frank. Just leave it. You will be in serious trouble yourself if you do. You're profile is now so high that the powers that be will not be able to protect you. Then again, why should they? You can't just go around seeking personal revenge because they don't take kindly to anyone doing that vigilante bit."

"Don't worry about it. Whatever I do will be done nice and subtly. When this current problem is all over I will take a look at it."

Frank's mobile rang so he made his excuses and walked into the kitchen to take the call.

"Frank. Is that you? It's Christie here."

"Hi Christie. It's good to talk to you. Where have you been? I've been trying to get hold of you?"

"No time to talk Frank. I will have to phone you again later. A terrible thing has happened and I have someone here who wants to talk to you urgently. Please talk to him Frank. It's Gerhard, Gustav's bodyguard."

There was silence for a few moments. "Hello, Mr Blake," said a hesitant male voice.

"Hi there Gerhard, what's the problem?" asked Frank.

The voice broke a little as he spoke. "Gustav is dead, Mr Blake." The shock of those words roared through Frank's head and he rocked momentarily. "Gustav dead! What the hell? What happened Gerhard? What do you mean?"

"He was murdered last night Mr Blake. Both he and Albion, who was guarding him. Albion was killed first. I have seen where they killed him and he would not have known much. His throat was cut. Mr Gustav died slowly, Mr Blake. He had been shot in each knee and in his lower stomach. Also, all his toes had been mashed. Someone was wanting information Mr Blake."

Frank was shocked and he reeled from the words. Images were shooting around his brain. You take a long time to die when shot in the stomach by a professional and the pain can be terrible.

"Any idea who would have done this Gerhard?" he asked grimly.

Yes, Mr Blake, I do. Yesterday morning four men came around to see Mr Gustav. I recognised the older man. It was Mr Van Hoon, the head of the Van Hoon family. All they do is trade in diamonds and have done so for many, many, years. I was on duty at the time and could hear shouting going on. Someone was shouting questions at Mr Gustav asking where were the other diamonds? This old man was saying that they belonged to him and he wanted them back. Mr Gustav was very rude to them and told him to 'fuck off'". The older man threatened Mr Gustav. As soon as I heard them shouting at him I went into the room. They were waiting for me and jumped me. Eventually they left after making big threats to Mr Gustav. He was very frightened and said to me that should anything happen to him I should contact you. He has left a letter for you. I didn't expect them to come back so quickly." The last sentence was said as his voice cracked.

Frank shook his head in despair. Gustav dead? How could that be? He felt a deep anger rising up within him. He had just got to know Gustav and liked him immensely. Now he was gone. 'The fat man' was gone. Frank made a decision. "I will come over Gerhard. I will be with you in two days. Don't say anything to anyone about this conversation and don't tell anyone that I am coming. Is your other colleague still around?"

"He is here with me Mr Blake."

"Good, what about the police Gerhard?"

"They are not treating the case seriously. They have not asked me many questions. I told them about Mr Van Hoon and his threats. As soon as I mentioned his name they began to ignore me. They will not do anything about this. He is too powerful."

Frank thought for a moment, and then made up his mind. "Gerhard, I am going to need a gun. Preferably something like the one I had with me last time. Walther P-38 or a Mauser, something like that, with at least a ten-round magazine. It will need to be clean. Also I will need a couple of spare clips of 9mm ammunition, OK? Secondly I will want you to do something for me. Find out exactly where this man lives, how many guards he has and when they change. Get me all the information you can on this man, Gerhard and quietly. We will get our revenge don't you worry. Will you and your chum help me?"

"Yes Mr Blake, we will. We loved Mr Gustav, he was very good to us."

"Give me a number where I can contact you when I get to Amsterdam. No, better than that, I will come over in my boat, so I am really coming in through the back door. I will need to be picked up from the marina. You know the one I mean, it was where Gustav kept his boat. Do you know it Gerhard"?

Yes Mr Blake. I will be there waiting for you from 9 a.m. Thursday morning."

Frank did some mental arithmetic. "That will be fine Gerhard. See you then and don't worry." Please put me back onto Christie."

"Frank, did I hear that you are coming back?"

"Yes Christie. But I am worried about you. You have heard what they did to Gustav. He may have said something and incriminated you somehow. I would advise you to go away for two or three weeks, until this is all over, for your own safety. By the way Christie, don't tell anyone I am coming or how I am coming because what I'm doing is obviously illegal. Also, be careful that you are not followed. Tell Gerhard too. They may possibly be watching both of you so take precautions."

"I will do as you say Frank. I will let you know where I am, OK"?

Frank thought for a moment. "Whatever you do, Christie, don't sell or organise anything with the diamond that I gave you. Obviously these diamonds have something to do with Gustav's death and I don't want the same thing happening to you. Please be careful and put it away somewhere safe for another day. Do you understand?"

Christie acknowledged that she did and promised to hide the diamond until such times as she could discuss the problem direct with Frank. He was pleased that Christie would not be at risk. The more he thought about Gustav the angrier he became. He walked back into the room. Joe was watching him.

"You look as though you have heard bad news Frank," he said.

"Yes, a friend of mine has died. I may have to go away for a few days to see the relatives."

Joe studied him. "OK, just stay in touch and don't get into any more trouble. We are beginning to get to know you. You're just a bundle of bloody trouble. You know that don't you? Things seem to happen around you. I have more trouble with you than any of my other clients, that's why I charge you so much." Everyone laughed.

"Frankly my man I don't give a damn. I can't take it with me," said Frank amongst more laughter. "I will be leaving early in the morning if that's all right with you Di. In the meantime can you make one of those wonderful rice puddings for me like you did last time? They are absolutely mouth watering and to die for."

Di's face lit up and she beamed at Frank. "Of course I can Frank. I will make you two so that you can take one away with you." As she walked out of the room Frank watched her hips. "Joe. You have one hell of a woman there."

"Yes, and I mean to keep her, so keep your lecherous eyes off, " laughed Joe.

He left early the next morning, and as promised there were two puddings in a basket for him in the kitchen with a note. 'Hope you will enjoy these as I would have liked to have enjoyed you again. D.'

"Naughty girl," he thought. "I'll have to be careful there." He had noticed the way she looked at him, always with a very direct stare and with a half smile on her lips, challenging. He knew what was going through her mind and although he had enjoyed their brief romp he really didn't think it wise to encourage the affair to continue. After all, she was Joe's wife. It wouldn't be right. Besides, Joe would take him to the cleaners financially if he found out. He would just have to cut down the number of visits he made that's all.

He concentrated on carving his way through the early morning traffic and let the car have its head on the motorway whilst keeping a careful eye out for the cameras and the boys in blue. He phoned Dick at the Marina.

"Hi, Dick, it's Frank Blake."

"Hello Mr Blake, what can I do for you?"

"I'm going on another long trip with Prowler in the morning, Dick, so I'll want her fully fuelled and engines warm when I come down at 8am. Is that all right?"

"As good as done Mr Blake. Any chance of coming along on the trip?"

"Afraid not Dick, another time, O.K?"

"Sure, see you in the morning."

Frank thought about Dick's offer and was sorely tempted but thought the better of it. If things went wrong the chap would only get into trouble. As it was there would only be himself. That was enough anyway. It was to be a major miscalculation.

He arrived back to the tranquillity of his home and the beautiful view of the sea. He made a list of the things he would need and returned to the town. Finding it difficult to park he decided to return to the car park at the marina. He would walk the short distance to the town from there. He parked his car and, as he locked it, he looked over its roof towards the boats. He saw three men talking to Dick near to the Marina reception and there was something about them he couldn't put his finger on. His heart leapt. Damn it; were they on to him already? He was hidden from their view so he stayed where he was and watched. Dick turned and started to walk away towards his office but one of the men caught him up and pulled him round with the other two men coming over as well. He could see that heated words were being exchanged when two marina staff appeared from nowhere and approached the trio. Immediately pushing and shoving started to take place and Frank could hear the raised voices even from where he stood. More people were being attracted to the scene and soon there was a knot of some six or seven people all arguing with the two men. Arms were being waved and voices were raised. "What the hell is going on?" Frank thought, but still stayed where he was.

A siren wailed and a police car came skidding into the car park. The three men broke away and started to run for their car but the small mob stopped them. The police got out of their car and walked over to the scene. There appeared to be a short conversation between Dick, the police, and some of the men from the marina, and then the three men were bundled into the police car, which drove off out of the car park.

With that over everyone went their various ways with some of them walking back to Dick's office with him. Frank decided that he could carry on with his shopping and came back an hour later, loaded his goods into the car and drove back home. He checked his phone for calls. There was one from Dick. Would Frank please phone him soonest?

He called Dick. "Hi Dick, it's Frank. You left a message for me to phone you. Sorry I wasn't here but I have been out shopping," he said innocently.

"Mr Blake, we've had a bit of an upset here this afternoon. You remember saying I should let you know if strangers came around asking after you. Well three Irish fella's came around this afternoon doing just that, and bloody rude they were too. Wouldn't take no for an answer; saying they wanted to see our books. Bloody cheek. I told them where to go in no uncertain terms and they turned nasty in front of everyone. We soon sorted them out. Got the police in who carted them off. Someone is really interested in you Mr Blake and they aren't very nice people. I told them that I would inform the other marinas of their actions and that no information would be given out on customers at all, especially not to them, as we knew who they are. Not that they would anyway. They didn't like that and started to threaten me. That's when it all got nasty."

"Thanks for the warning Dick and your support. I'll keep my eyes open don't you worry. Thanks once again for all your help. I'll remember that. Talk to you in the morning." He started to get everything together for the trip back to Holland.

Arriving at the boat by taxi, the following morning, he found Dick in Prowler checking the engines, which were already running.

They greeted each other and talked for a short while about the previous afternoon's events. Obviously this sort of thing didn't happen around Lymington and the story was already on everyone's lips. Frank was alarmed.

"Don't you worry Mr Blake? This is a small town and we protect our own down here. Your name is not up for discussion anywhere all right? We have given the police the nod and they understand completely. Anyway they are local boys and understand these things. A few bottles of whisky from wherever you are going won't go amiss though."

Frank grinned at what he thought was his new friend. "How many bottles then Dick?" he asked.

"Oohhh, I don't know, perhaps a dozen should do the trick Mr Blake. They do like their whisky down here you know. By the way, you do know that the customs boys can track you if you are more than four miles out, don't you? Perhaps you had better make that two dozen, Mr Blake. That should give you some protection."

Dick accepted two fingers of whisky and leaned against the helm chair. He looked quizzically at Frank and his attitude somehow changed. "We don't like drugs down here Mr Blake. Have to tell you that. I hate all of the bloody stuff with a vengeance. I'll be honest with you. Certain friends of mine have been over this boat with dogs and a fine toothcomb. Fortunately for you there was nothing to find. Because I have to tell you Mr Blake, that if we had found even a sniff you wouldn't be standing here now, you would be sitting in a cell. I feel that strongly about it. So we think you are fairly straight."

Frank was looking at Dick with deep alarm and foreboding. Who was this guy?

"What you are up to is your concern. The fact that a couple of Irish men are asking about you is quite significant. Obviously something to do with that shooting in London wasn't it?"

"Just who the hell are you Dick? Frank asked, ignoring the question.

"Well, you don't have to worry too much about that, Mr Blake. Just be careful that's all. We will do our best to help you though." He paused then hit Frank right between the eyes with the next sentence.

"Going back to Holland are we then, Mr Blake?"

Frank took the whisky bottle from Dick and, glancing at him, poured himself another three fingers. He didn't drink at this time of day but these were unusual circumstance and he needed time to think.

"Well, well, well. I'm not so smart as I thought I was. How did you find that out?"

"Well, you were tracked coming across the North Sea the other night and then you were watched coming along the coast. We also had a report about you from Ramsgate; the man asking about your boat in the café. Our man, and then you, pulled into here. We couldn't believe our luck. You sailed right into the centre of the web Mr Blake. Great wasn't it? We thought you might be bringing in a load of drugs from Holland. But you brought in nothing. Now you are going back because of your friend being killed is that right? Yes, we know about that as well. Pretty nasty stuff. Well, watch your step, they play rough over there. That's why I offered to come. Could be of help you know."

"I'm completely gob smacked and don't know what to say. What side of the Secret Service are you in then Dick?" Frank asked.

"You don't expect me to tell you that do you? We have an idea, more or less, of what you are going back for Mr Blake, and we don't approve, although having said that you will be doing certain people a big favour. The whole of Interpol knows about him. He is an evil and twisted man and it all started from the Second World War. However, people like you can't go around dispensing their own form of justice and behaving like a vigilante from the wild west. Where would we be if everyone started to do that? What a mess we would be in."

Frank turned away, went over to the helm seat and sat down. Damn it, things were happening too fast and now here the MI5 was out-manoeuvring him for God's sake. He looked out of the window at the peaceful scene of the marina. He asked himself where his simple life had gone to, the life before all this started when he was just a simple businessman striving to make a living like everyone else. He decided to bluff it out. He really had no alternative, as he could not admit to becoming an assassin regardless as to how he felt about the situation.

"Look Dick, or whoever you are, you will have to excuse me. I don't know what you are talking about. I am going for a gentle cruise along the coast and will potter about the North Sea for a while before coming back. You could say that I am doing engine trials and doing a little shopping on the continent. Whatever, I will be back in four or five days and will be coming back here at which time you can search me again. I appreciate you throwing the Mulligan family off the scent but I can't take you with me Dick. I simply want to go back for my friend's funeral. I owe him that."

Dick shrugged and finished his whisky. "Well Mr Blake, we will be watching with interest. See you later and have a safe trip." He left the boat and when Frank was ready he threw the warps back onto the boat as he pulled away from the pontoon. As Frank left the marina he looked back to see Dick still standing on the end of the pontoon watching him.

"That was a turn up for the books," he thought. "Bloody bloke is an undercover agent, MI5 drug squad, I shouldn't wonder but at least he is on my side; to a degree," he thought and opening the throttles he set course heading due east back up the Solent.

The first half of the trip would take at least eight hours so once out into the open sea, off Brighton, he relaxed and made himself comfortable with a book while Prowler's powerful engines thrust her into a quartering sea with the auto pilot guiding her to her destination. Frank made several phone calls, two of which were to Josie and Liz telling them exactly where he was going and when he expected to get back. Both girls said they envied him the trip and would have dearly loved to be with him. Strangely enough they all missed each other's company. Their experiences in Brazil had forged a friendship that would last their life times. "We are with you in spirit if not in body," said Liz.

Every half hour or so Frank would check his position knowing full well that the radar would warn him of any vessel coming closer than three miles. He eventually pulled into Ramsgate again to top up his fuel tanks but didn't hang around. As soon as they were full he was off again turning onto a course that would take him directly to Holland, another nine hours across the North Sea.

The night trip was uneventful, and slow work as there was a big sea running. Prowler punched through the beam seas rolling heavily and Frank had to reduce speed to eighteen knots. There was ample time to think during those long dark hours and, even with music on, he couldn't help but think of Gustav and what lay ahead. He would also need all the help possible from the pyramid.

He pondered on his brief friendship with Gustav. It's not often in life that you can meet a person and instantly find empathy, and yet Frank had with Gustav. A more unlikely friend he couldn't imagine. But despite his enormous bulk the man had a razor sharp mind and was always on the look out for a good deal. That was his passion, doing the deal but in the end it had cost him his life. They had very quickly built a friendship on laughter, each gently teasing the other knowing that no harm was meant. Frank knew that Gustav had given his life rather than disclose his source of the diamonds and that made Frank very proud, very sad, and very angry. He was proud of Gustav's bravery, sad that Gustav had to die in such a horrible fashion, and angry that someone could be so ruthless as to hurt another human being in such an awful way for money. At the end of the day, it was all about money. So Frank had decided to take his revenge.

He was surprised at himself. What he was about to do was completely out of character and yet was it? Had this ability to kill without compunction or justification to anyone always been there? Perhaps ever since he had left the service and simply been repressed all this time? He shook his head in puzzlement and with a feeling of regret, yet he was determined to carry through the assassination, for that was what it was. He knew that he was quite capable of doing it with some help from Gustav's two bodyguards.

He judged his landing carefully and joined the Dutch coast some fifty miles south from the marina at around 5am, just as the day was breaking. Hugging the coast as close as he dared he slipped into the marina two hours later. He had been at sea for some twenty hours and apart from a few catnaps he'd had no serious sleep. He felt bushed. The marina people were pleased to see him back and asked how long he would stay this time. He told them only a few days.

He ensured that the boat was clean and tidy with all the electrics and fuel taps switched off before leaving, and requested from the harbour master that his fuel tanks be re-fuelled as quickly as possible. Leaving his keys with them he made his way to the car park carrying his trustworthy backpack only this time without the Walther. Gerhard was standing at the marina main gate waiting patiently and a smile broke across his face when he spotted Frank.

"Mr Blake, good to see you again. Thank you for coming. We were at a loss as to what to do. I hope you can help us."

"Listen Gerhard, we are in this thing together and together we will solve the problem. Have you got all the things I asked for?"

"Yes Mr Blake, in the boot. We were followed as we left Amsterdam. Don't know who, but we shook them off eventually. They will be waiting for us Mr Blake, you know that don't you?"

"Yes I do, Gerhard," Frank said quietly.

"I have borrowed a house that we can use for a few days from a friend. It is nice and quiet with few people around. We will go there now and talk things over Mr Blake, yes?"

He took Frank to an old blue Opal sedan, which must have been fifteen years old or even more. The paintwork was faded and it looked very down at heel but as soon as Gerhard started the engine Frank could tell there was something very powerful under the bonnet. "What's the power unit in this thing Gerhard?"

Gerhard grinned in return. "I have a 300hp V8 Chevy under the hood. Not many cars can get away from me." He said the last sentence proudly.

Gerhard told him the journey would take about an hour so Frank made himself as comfortable as possible in the corner of the back seat and promptly went to sleep.

He awoke to find the two men unloading the car. He got out and stretched looking around him. The whole area was quite heavily wooded; otherwise the countryside was so flat. The house was quite small. It had obviously been a farmhouse in its day. There were several small barns around it, some still filled with hay, and some small stone built shelters with walled areas which were obviously for pigs and goats. Otherwise everything looked empty and quiet. They moved their kit into the house and piled it all into the kitchen. Frank went to make a fire of sorts but Gerhard stopped him.

"We have small gas fired camping units which we can cook on if we need to, Mr Blake. I remember you like your tea so we have brought all the ingredients, tea bags, milk, sugar, and coffee."

Frank made the coffee and tea and they settled down to talk over what they were about to do.

"Right, Gerhard, what's the plan?" asked Frank.

"First of all I have this letter for you from Mr Gustav." Frank looked at the envelope that Gerhard gave him. It had Gustav's scrawl across the front and was addressed to him. Frank put it into his pocket for reading later.

"Thanks for that, now tell me what you found out Gerhard."

"The Van Hoon family does not actually live with the old man. He has quite strict routines and does not go out much anymore. He spends most of his time in an office unit that he has had built on at the rear of the house. He has two minders, ex-army and very good by reputation, who patrol the grounds and look after him. It shouldn't take too much to take them out if you are quick. The office is alarmed of course but not when he is in it. He works there mostly on his own but a woman comes in twice a week. Tuesdays and Thursdays to do his letters and stuff like that. He usually works from about midday until around 7 p.m. and then goes into the big house for dinner. I think the best time would be around dusk, at 5 or 6 o'clock. If we do it at five, it would give us at least two hours to get away."

"What are your plans afterwards?" he asked the two men. They both looked down at the floor. Obviously they hadn't thought that far ahead.

"Do you want to stay here in Amsterdam or do you want to go abroad?" he asked.

"We would like to stay here in Amsterdam. Obviously. It is our home. Our families are here but how can we do that. The police will come to see us first of all because of the trouble we had with them last time," said Gerhard. The other man nodded.

"I've been thinking about that. There is an easy answer," said Frank. "Surround yourself with friends and family for about three or four hours at the crucial time while I do the necessary. That way you will have the perfect alibi, which the police would not be able to break, and I will solve the problem. End of story."

The two men protested loudly but eventually they could see that Frank's suggestion made sense. They made plans for the following Wednesday, two days away. Frank said he would need a car of some sort that couldn't be traced to anyone. Gerhard replied that he knew just such a car, and that he would arrange to 'borrow' it. Everything seemed to be in place.

The two men turned up with the car the next day and then left Frank to his own devices as they began setting their alibis in concrete. They agreed that there was going to be no more contact between them until everything was over.

Gerhard had supplied Frank with a silencer for the Mauser 9mm pistol and he spent some time practising outside the farmhouse. He quickly found his old skill and discovered that he could hit nearly everything he wanted to within a twenty-five foot area. Beyond that he became erratic. He had no qualms about killing this man now. Yet, he could not help thinking that if somebody had said to him twelve months ago that he would be doing this he would have laughed in their face. In fact he doubted that he would have been capable of doing it. It was ironic how circumstances had changed his life in such a short period of time. He shut his mind from any more thought on the matter. He didn't want to think too much about the next day.

Wednesday morning dawned dry and bright. He was going to time himself to arrive near the house within ten minutes of 4.20 p.m. in the afternoon, so that his car would not be too conspicuous. He would need it quite close to the house so that he could make a quick escape. Frank dirtied the rear number plate to make it look as if he had driven through a particularly muddy area and accidentally covered the number plate. It wasn't fantastic but it would have to do. He'd made a hood out of a black balaclava helmet and it looked suitably fearsome when he had it on. He put ten cable straps into his pocket for tying up the guards. Then he checked the tyres, battery, water and oil on the car to ensure nothing silly happened. Finally, he treated himself to a light salad lunch and one glass of wine. He then carefully cleaned up the house leaving no sign, whatsoever, that he had been there. He piled all his kit and other stuff into the car. He tucked the pistol into his shoulder holster, buckled on his knife, and carried the last item from the house; a baseball bat.

He felt a taught excitement across his shoulders and in the pit of his stomach. This was either going to run smoothly or end in total disaster. It would be a fine point between the two. Luck would have to be with him tonight he thought. After all, he wasn't a professional killer; he was just an average man wanting revenge for the killing of his friend. He didn't let himself dwell on the fact that he was about to commit murder. He started the car, checking that he had left nothing behind and set off towards Amsterdam and the Van Hoon house.

He arrived within one minute of his expected time. He parked the car carefully down a lane next to the main wall of the big house and pointed it in the right direction. He sat quietly for five minutes composing himself and quietly asking forgiveness for what he was about to do. Frank wasn't a religious man but he had a feeling someone was looking out for him and so something resembling a prayer quietly tumbled from his lips. He then got out and, slipping on his backpack with its contents, and carrying the baseball bat, he locked the car door and slipped the keys into a handkerchief; he tucked the package away in his thigh pocket. That way they wouldn't "tinkle" or make a noise when he ran.

Looking about him he found that no one was about and there were no cars passing. He was lucky so far. Slipping the baseball bat into his backpack, he moved to the wall, which rose above him to over six feet six inches. He threw over a woollen rug to protect him from the glass embedded in the cement on top. He hauled himself over the wall and was surprised at his agility, and then remembered why. He dropped lightly on the other side pulling the rug with him. As he expected, he was in a small wood. He carefully moved through the wood until he came to the main lawn. He leaned against a tree for ten minutes just inside, and watched and waited. Sure enough, within a few minutes a tall, powerfully built coloured man ambled along the edge of the lawn towards him. Watching him Frank could see that this wasn't going to be easy. The man walked with a casual gliding grace that disguised something else. This man was a professional, fully alert and no slouch. Frank froze into stillness knowing as he did that if he moved an inch now the man's senses would pick up on him and then Frank would be in trouble, serious trouble.

He waited until the guard was three feet past him, he stepped out, and swinging the baseball bat hit the man hard behind the right ear. The man must have heard the swish of air as the bat travelled towards him from behind as he started to turn but as good as he was he was already too late. He didn't even grunt as he fell slowly to his knees and then collapsed onto his face. Frank felt for a pulse. The guard was still alive, thank God, but would have one hell of a headache when he woke up. He tied the guard's hands and feet behind his back with the cable straps and using two more and a wad of cloth, gagged the man. After removing his gun and throwing it into the bushes, Frank dragged the guard into the edge of the wood and, making sure he was as comfortable as possible under the circumstances, left him.

Running smartly across the lawn to the office extension of the building, he positioned himself against the wall and waited another five minutes while he got his breath back. Nothing moved and there was no sound. There was a small window between him and the door and, looking carefully through it he saw another guard sitting reading. He had a pistol in front of him on the table. This one wasn't going to be easy either. Frank moved carefully under the window and then stood in front of the door with the baseball bat, held loosely with both hands, hanging in front of him. He knocked on the door with the bat and waited.

The guard called out something in Dutch.

Frank didn't answer but knocked again. He heard movement and watched the door handle start to move. The door opened smartly and the guard stood in front of him with his feet spread apart, his pistol was pointing straight at Frank's face. He was very good, but not good enough. Frank brought the bat up between the guard's legs with as much force as he could muster and felt the bat connect with the man's genitals. The guard's mouth opened in a silent scream, his face contorted and his eyes bulged out from their sockets as he dropped the gun. Still no sound came out as the man sank to his knees holding himself, and then he collapsed onto the floor into unconsciousness. Frank stepped forward and inserted another cloth pad in the guard's mouth and strapped it in with two more cable ties. He then rolled the guard over on his side and strapped his hands behind his back. He checked the man's pulse; he too was still alive and was also going to have a few aches and pains in the morning. Frank picked up the gun and threw it into one of the large borders close by; he stuffed the bat into his backpack and moved to the door that was behind the guard. He turned the handle and stepped inside.

Frank felt that he had just walked into Evil. The room was full of it. A tall old man was sitting hunched at a very large antique style desk. He was peering through a magnifying glass at something in front of him. He looked up to see Frank striding across the room towards him, and a look of surprise ran across his old face.

"Who're you?" he said in Dutch.

"Don't know what you're saying mate, just shut up and put your hands behind your head Van Hoon or I will shoot you. First in the left shoulder and then in your right." Frank waggled the gun in the old man's face indicating what he wanted him to do. The two of them studied each other. Frank had the full hood covering his face and thought the he must look positively frightening but the tall man showed no fear. He was at least six foot six inches tall and must have weighed well over sixteen stone. He had a high wide forehead which was accentuated by his sparse grey hair and slightly bulbous dark blue, almost black, eyes that peered over a long, broad, very pronounced hooked nose. He had high Slavic cheekbones and a wide, thinly lipped, cruel-looking mouth. 'Cadaverous looking' sprang to Frank's mind but worse than that Frank felt that he had met this man before, in his dreams probably, and he was shocked.

"So, you are the Englishman," said Van Hoon, "I think I know who you are. We have been looking for you." Frank didn't reply, his brain was still reeling from the shock of recognising the man. He fought to pull himself together. In his dreams, his bad dreams, this man was always the devil. How could this be?

There was a silence for a while. Frank continued to simply stand in front of the old man, covering him with his gun. He was working out what he was going to do and how to do it. "You have my diamonds," whispered the old man eventually. It was more of a statement than a question "Give them back to me, this instant." His eyes were now glowing black and he looked the epitome of evil. "This man is bloody dangerous and he has the Devil inside him; and he's looking straight at me," Frank thought. His skin crawled in horror and his hackles rose up on the back of his neck. He prayed silently to himself to have the strength to see it through.

"Van Hoon, you're an evil old man. You killed my friend Gustav unnecessarily after first torturing him, and for what, a few diamonds? I don't know how many men you have either killed yourself or had killed over the years but you are going to die for killing Gustav. Put out your hands old man, hold them together." Van Hoon didn't move but continued to stare Frank in the eye. Frank knew what he was trying to do and could feel the evil of his glare surrounding him. He forced himself to concentrate on why he was here and thought of Gustav's mutilated body until his brain steadied.

He walked slowly around the desk until he stood next to Van Hoon. Reaching out, he pistol-whipped Van Hoon across the face. Once. The gun sight of the barrel tore open the face in a long blood red groove stretching from the eye to the cruel looking mouth. Van Hoon blinked hard and shook his head but said nothing and stuck his hands out in front of him as Frank had asked. Frank, holding his gun with one hand, smartly strapped the old man's hands together with the other.

"I'm not frightened of you Englishman. You should be frightened of me." the old man whispered. The evil was still in his eyes. "I have met and dealt with far worse men than you over the years. I do, however, recognise death when I see it and I see it in your eyes. It is also standing behind you. Waiting. But I am not afraid to die. I have had a long life so let's get on with it."

"Walk slowly round the desk and kneel in front of me." The man didn't move. "Do it!" Frank screamed. The man, surprised by Frank's ferocity, stood up and moved slowly round the desk. He stood in front of him. His eyes, never leaving Frank's, were hypnotic.

"You have diamonds in your possession stolen from my family by the Gestapo during the war. We recognised the one that Gustav tried to sell to us by its cut. We want them all back. They belong to me and my family and they have great value to us," he said.

Frank didn't answer the old man. He felt no pity. From what Gerhard and Ulf had told him this man had been utterly ruthless in his business dealings for the last fifty years, in some circumstances causing men to commit suicide and others to simply disappear. It was rumoured that his strong links with De Beers, the South Africans, had enabled him to virtually control the entire diamond market throughout Europe and the Middle East since the Second World War. Certainly, without their help, that could not have happened.

Frank made his decision. "On your knees and make peace with your master old man, you will not need any bloody diamonds where you are going."

"Before I die tell me where you found my diamonds." Van Hoon said. "I have to know."

Frank looked into those cold black eyes. "Wrapped around a dead German pilot's waist in a crashed Heinkel airplane in the Brazilian jungle, must have been there fifty or more years. Satisfied? Now kneel down."

Van Hoon slowly went down; first on one knee and then the other. He was muttering to himself and looking down at the floor. "Yes, say your last prayers old man, the Devil's waiting for you." Frank moved around behind him and took out another piece of rag. He wrapped it around the old man's eyes and tied it. He then took two steps back, aimed at the back of the old man's head and pulled the trigger, twice.

The silencer did its work producing two dull thuds of sound. Two neat holes appeared in the back of the head in front of him; the old man was dead before he hit the floor. There was a lot of blood from the exiting bullets. Frank walked calmly over to Van Hoon and checked for a pulse. There wasn't one; blood was starting to spread across the carpet. He looked down at the pistol in his hand; it was shaking. He had just killed his first man in cold blood and he didn't like how he felt. He looked around the room checking that everything was tidy and that there was nothing to incriminate him. Over on the desk lay a sheet of black baize cloth covered in diamonds. The old man had obviously been studying and sorting them according to quality. There must have been eighty to a hundred glinting in the strong desk light. Frank wrapped them up in the black cloth and put them in his backpack.

There was a large, old-fashioned, safe to the right of the desk with its door open. He opened the door carefully with his gloved hand. There were a number of trays stacked in there. Frank gulped. There must have been millions of pounds worth of diamonds there. He opened each tray in turn and, ignoring the necklaces, bracelets and rings, took just the very largest and most beautiful stones. Another hundred went into his pack. He hoped that the murder would look like burglary.

He made his way out of the room with great care. He didn't want to leave any clue as to who had been there. The guard was still lying unconscious in the same position, as Frank had left him. Obviously the pain in his groin had been too much. Frank checked the straps holding the guard's wrists and strapped his ankles as well. It would take a lot of time for him to get to a phone and raise the alarm. He picked up the baseball bat and, taking the key out of the door, left and locked it from the outside. First checking that no one else was around he sprinted across the lawn and entered the wood passing the other guard who was also still unconscious but alive. He found the wall and, throwing the blanket over it, hauled himself to the top. He looked left and right down the road. It was clear, so he removed his mask, stuffed it into his pocket and clambered over. He then dropped down the other side taking the blanket with him at the same time. Finding his car, he opened the door and threw his pack onto the back seat. He slumped into the driver's seat. Taking a few deep breaths to calm himself, he drove slowly off.

Two miles down the road he stopped in a lay-by. He checked that he had not left anything behind. He took a flask from a bag that Gerhard had given him and poured himself a hot, sweet cup of tea. He forced himself to drink slowly as his hands were still shaking. Not since landing the plane in Brazil had he felt quite so ill with shock. He would never forget that old man's eyes. Somehow he would have to live with what he had just done. He finished his tea and restarted the engine of the little car. Wearily he set off for the marina.

Two hours later he drove through the marina gates. It was now dark yet the marina was bustling with life as boat owners moved back and forth between their boats and their cars. Frank settled his bill at the marina office and began loading everything on board. When he had finished he wiped down all the controls and handles on the car to ensure he left no trace of himself. He then locked it and left the ignition keys on one of the front tyres for Gerhard to collect later. He got back on the boat and started his engines. Sitting in the helm seat he let them warm for a while and he revelled in their sound. He poured himself a large glass of schnapps and, tossing his head back, sank it in one go. The liquor ran down his throat like fire, hitting his stomach, warming and calming him. He shuddered under the effect of the liquor and poured himself another but took his time in sinking that one. Eventually, he let go of his warps and, easing the boat from its moorings, slipped out through the main marina lock into a cold, dark, North Sea.

After programming in his course he let the auto pilot take over. He found his mobile and dialled in a number. Gerhard answered it. They began a casual conversation with Frank saying "Hi" and saying that they hadn't seen each other in some while and asking how everyone was. That conversation carried on for a few moments and then they said their goodbyes with Frank promising to phone again soon.

"He's got the message," he thought. "Gerhard will now know that everything went off OK, that justice has been served, and that I am off home." He settled down with a book endeavouring not to think about what he had just done. What he had become.

12

THE NEXT MORNING ARRIVED with fair weather. The sun rose blood red into a clear blue sky looking down onto a light sea swell and the sea glinted green in all its beauty. According to the BBC it was going to be a beautiful day.

Frank had an uncomfortable and unsettled night. Hour after hour had passed without sleep, which was not like him. Under normal circumstances he could sleep on a clothesline and catnap whenever he wanted to but sleep, this time, was eluding him and he knew why.

The thought of going home didn't appeal to him as he knew he would get a grilling from Dick or whoever his name really was and then there was Joe of course putting the pressure on, wanting ten per cent of the action all the time. All these thoughts flitted in and out of his head as he watched red eyed at the English coast appearing slowly out of the light morning mist of the early dawn.

He motored slowly into Ramsgate once again and headed for the fuel pontoon. There was no sign of anybody. Glancing at his watch he wasn't surprised. It was only five thirty. Plenty of fishing boats were making their way out to sea but there was no fuel man. Picking up his binoculars he scanned the harbour wall by the town. Yes, Doris's lights were on. He fancied one of her vast breakfasts right now with plenty of soggy fried bread, two eggs, five rashers of bacon, three sausages and some beans. Yes. And a good flirt with the waitress. He locked up the boat and set off along the harbour wall. He felt weary. He was disillusioned with himself and unhappy.

"At this point in time there seems to be no real meaning to my life," he thought and then laughed at himself again. "What's wrong with you chum, you have everything a man could want. There's only one thing missing and she's in Holland. So come on, cheer yourself up, you bloody misery." He felt better for bollocking himself. Taking in deep breaths of the fresh, clean, morning air he looked around him as he walked towards the cafe.

"Strange," he thought. "Everything is so different in daylight. All the demons go away." The many coloured boats glinting in the new morning sun in the harbour made a perfect picture and the warmth of the sun on his face made him feel more human. It took away all the dark thoughts and moods of the previous night and his mood shifted, his soul lifted, and he felt good to be alive.

"I don't need all this shit. Ever since I've been back in England things have been going from bad to worse, and the pressures have been increasing day by day. All because of a few bloody diamonds." He hefted the pack on his back. He wasn't going to let them out of his sight. He took another long deep breath of the clean sea air and looked around him.

"Bloody fantastic my old son. Life can be beautiful after all. OK, let's start living a more normal life. Start taking your life into your own hands Frank and get a grip of yourself."

He walked up to Doris's door and walked in. The smell of cooking bacon, eggs and toast prevailed in the air and the warmth of the place hit him like a wall just as before.

"Well hello there handsome" called Doris. "Have you been missing Doris' breakfast then and decided to come and see us? My God, you look a bit rough this morning, what on earth have you been up to? Explain yourself young man."

"Morning Doris. Oh, I don't know, I've been to places I shouldn't and been doing things I shouldn't I suppose. I sure have missed you but I've missed your breakfasts even more," he grinned sniffing the air. "Do you know Doris, I've been thinking of you for the last four hours."

Jeers went up from the men in the café. "You won't get any free grub talking like that mate," shouted one of the men.

Frank grinned back at the men. "Well, it's worth a try," he said.

"Don't you pay them a mind, mister," Doris said in her broad estuary accent. "It's good to see you again. A bit of class for a change instead of these woofers here." More laughs and jeers from the men.

"What would you like, dearie? Instead of me of course, or would you prefer to be served by me pretty young daughter here?" At that moment her daughter appeared with four plates in her hands and, looking at Frank, blushed furiously.

Frank leaned forward over the counter. "I think I prefer you Doris but don't tell her because she might not understand." Doris burst into loud laughter.

"Oh you are a one mister. It's good to have a laugh with a gent like you really it is. Now, what can I get you? By the look of it you need feeding up a bit."

"Hit me with all the works, Doris, including three slices of fried bread but first I need one of your big mugs of strong sweet tea to start the day."

"Be with you in a tick dearie. Jennie, get this man a paper," she yelled at her daughter.

Frank sat down at a table by the window so that he could see when the fuel man arrived. A notice on the pontoon had said, 'Open at 6 a.m.' so he had a good half an hour at least. The young girl appeared at his elbow with the paper. She looked flustered.

"Thanks Jennie," he said taking the paper. She continued to hover and he felt her touch his hand. He looked back up at her, startled.

"What's you name Mister?" she asked. He could see that it was taking a lot out of her to ask him this but for some reason she needed to know.

"Why, it's Frank, Jennie. Frank Blake."

She fidgeted. "That's a nice name Frank. Where you off to now then?"

"At this point in time I'm not too sure but I feel that I would like to go to St. Malo in France for a while. Why? Would you like to come with me?" he teased her.

"Oh, my goodness," she blushed furiously. "Yes I would Frank but my Mum would never let me. It sounds so romantic, St. Malo."

"It's a beautiful place Jennie, and if you ever get a chance do go there."

She smiled a beautiful little smile at him. "Perhaps, when you come back next time, you will ask me again," she replied.

He looked intently into her eyes. "She means it. Whoops, I'd better be careful here. She wants to break loose," Frank, thought.

"OK Jennie you have a date," he smiled at her. She flushed, glancing down at him through her lashes, and turned away just as her mother called for her. "Jennie, stop flirting with that gorgeous man, he's mine." There was general laughter at that but it seemed to have an edge to it. More than one man fancied young Jennie it appeared.

Knowing full well that he had probably been spotted already by one of Dick's lot, he took his time absorbing the newspaper from end to end. He hadn't had time to read one for the last few days. As usual it was full of political intrigue, rubbish, and what the latest fashion icons were doing with their lives. He couldn't help thinking how shallow life was in England. As a last flourish he wiped his plate with the last of the thick white bread, soaking up the grease and sausage fat, and stuffed his mouth with it with great pleasure. "God that feels good," he thought patting his stomach. "That should last me until tea time at least." He rose and trundled over to the counter.

"Doris that was fantastic. How much do I owe you?" he asked.

"Give me a fiver, luv, and we'll call it quits,'" she replied. "Lovely to see you again Frank. (Jennie must have told her his name) Come back again soon."

Frank told her he would indeed come back again soon and said his goodbyes. He intercepted Jennie on the way to the kitchen and kissed her goodbye. "Bye, Jennie. See you again soon," he whispered. She stood there looking stunned and, when he went out of the door, he looked back through the glass; she was still standing there looking after him. "Poor kid," he thought, "she wants to escape. Maybe she will one day."

Walking back down to the pontoon he noticed two men leaning against the side of his boat talking to the fuel man. He stopped and moved over to the wall so that he couldn't be seen very easily. "Damn it," he thought. "I don't have my gun with me." He thought for a moment. "Wait a minute, I haven't got rid of Gerhard's gun yet. No, I can't use that because it will be matched through Interpol to the Amsterdam incident."

He decided to bluff it out.

He walked down to his boat and recognised the fuel man. The two men, obviously local, so called, toughs continued to lean against his boat as he discussed how much diesel he required with the fuel man. When he finished, and without turning around, he said, "Are these idiots your friends?"

"No," said the fuel man, "they are just passing the time of day I think."

"Who are you calling an idiot?" said one of the men behind him. Frank turned around slowly and looked the taller of the two men in the eye.

"I'm calling you an idiot and you're leaning against my boat so shift your arse now and get off," he said.

"Oh, so this heap of junk is yours, is it old man? Might have known. Well, if you want us to move you will have to say please," said the tall yob.

Frank watched in complete detachment, as his right arm streaked out and grabbed the yob by the throat while his left arm did the same with the other. He banged their two heads together several times very hard and then he felt himself walk the two over to the edge of the pontoon, and he threw them both into the icy water. It all happened in seconds.

"Can you fill her right up to the brim please?" he said to the startled pump man.

"Yes Sir, I sure will but if you don't mind me saying so, they will get their death of cold if we don't get them out of that water now," said the pump man.

Frank turned and looked at the two men scrambling to get back onto the pontoon. They were weighed down with the water in their clothes and were struggling. "Christ, what have I done? That's probably a criminal offence," he thought.

He walked over to the two men who were half in and half out of the water and rapidly turning blue.

"Get us out of here mister. We're freezing!" said one of them.

"Say please first," said Frank.

"Please mister, get us out of here," they said again. Frank and the pump man leaned down and pulled both of them onto the pontoon. A few of the fishermen had gathered by now and were laughing at the two figures sprawled on the pontoon with water pouring from their clothes. "Serves you right you lazy buggers," said one. "Wish I'd done that," laughed another.

A tall grey haired man with an enormous beard and ruddy face came over. "You two had better get off home and change those clothes smartish if I were you," he said. The two young men stumbled off up the quay with water still dribbling from their clothes.

"Did you do that?" asked the grey haired man turning to Frank.

"Yes, they were being plain bloody rude as this man"; Frank pointed to the pump man, "will tell you. I'm afraid I lost my temper and the next thing I knew I had pushed them into the water. Bloody silly thing to do wasn't it?" Frank said.

"I'm afraid it was Sir," said the man. "One of those boys is the son of the local Chief Constable and within thirty minutes he will be down here with a squad car to haul you off to clink, I wouldn't wonder. If I were you mate, I would ship out fast." He cast an eye over the Humber. "Shouldn't wonder if that could get you beyond the twelve mile limit in about that time by the look of her. By the way, you have done us all a favour. Those two have been asking for it for ages and we were all near the limit but we have to live here, unfortunately. What you did will give us a good laugh for some time to come, mister, and no mistake; so thanks a lot and remind me never to cross you."

There was loud agreement by the others standing around.

"That's OK. Thanks for the advice. Right, Mr Pump man, fill me up double quick and let me get the hell out of here," said Frank. Within ten minutes he had paid and was on his way out of the harbour. Several boats hooted their horns as he left and he waved back merrily.

Exiting the harbour walls he steered due south and opened the throttles wide into a force three head sea. Prowler revelled in it and punched her way happily at twenty odd knots towards Dover with spray rising high over her bows.

Frank mused on what had just happened. "It's just as though trouble is following me around. I attract it like a bloody magnet," he thought. But it was never like this up to three or four months ago. He couldn't remember when he had last lost his temper and yet he had seen red mist this morning. He decided to put it to the back of his mind for a while as he had his hands full avoiding the many cross channel ferries that were leaving and entering Dover.

Once clear of that famous harbour, he reset his navigation equipment and punched in the codes to take him to Cherbourg in northern France across the English Channel. He increased his radar warning horns to four miles. He was about to cross sixty or so miles of one of the busiest shipping lanes in the world with ships and tankers of all sizes beating their way up and down the English Channel, and he didn't like the thought of being run down by any of them.

Prowler picked up her skirts and ran straight and fast at twenty-two knots, almost flat out but not quite. Frank increased the volume of the boat's radio leaving it tuned onto channel 16 and went out on the back deck and settled down to read his newspaper under the beautiful morning sun. He put his hand into his pocket and pulled out the letter from Gustav. It read.

My Dear Frank,

If you read this I will be dead. You may remember me telling you that I had sold some of the diamonds to a man called Van Hoon. Well, Van Hoon has turned out to be the very devil himself. He turned up yesterday with his henchmen and was extremely abusive and threatening. He is possessed about where the diamonds came from. He kept yelling that they are his. I sincerely believe that he will kill me if I don't tell him where the diamonds came from and I never will because I made you a promise. We are friends, Frank, you and I, and we always will be friends. We have only known each other a short while and I wish it had been longer because I have enjoyed your company. Because of that and the fact that I have no other real friends, I will never disclose where I got them. I know they will come back again and this time they will be serious.

Have a good life Frank, and keep your head down, I have never known anyone who has the ability to get himself into so much trouble as you.

If the worst does happen, please look after my bodyguards. They have been real friends to me also.

Your very true friend,

Gustav.

Frank slumped in his seat; the letter had a profound effect on him. "And another person dies because of these bloody diamonds," he thought, "but this time it's a friend. Enjoy your time in hell Van Hoon."

He sat on the back deck for some time thinking. No more than twenty minutes had passed when he heard the sound of a helicopter above the noise of his engines. Looking around he saw it coming up behind him fast. It slowed down to his speed and hovered behind. They called him up on his R/T.

"Prowler, Prowler, this is Flybird 776, over."

Frank looked hard at the helicopter; it had CUSTOMS in big black letters on the side. "Oh Shit," he thought. He moved fast down into the cabin and grabbing the microphone he quickly checked his position. He was almost, but not quite, beyond the twelve mile limit with only two miles to go. If he could mess about for a bit he would make it.

"Flybird776, Flybird776, this is Prowler over."

"Prowler, channel 72 over."

Frank took his time dialling up channel 72. When he got there they were already calling him. He replied.

"Frank, just where do you think you are going?" said the voice from the chopper. It was Dick from Lymington. "What the hell does he want?"

thought Frank. "This is an open channel so I'll have to be a little careful."

"Hi Dick, what are you doing out here, aren't you a long way from home?" said Frank.

"What do you think I'm doing? Chasing after you. We saw you come around Dover and then head off across the channel so we thought that we might have a chat."

"Chat away Dick, but it's a free country and I can go where I want," Frank replied. He looked carefully at his position; again he had just gone beyond the limit. He moved out onto the rear deck and picked up the outside microphone. Dick was just finishing saying something.

"Sorry Dick, but I missed that. Say again."

"We need you to proceed to Brighton, Frank, so that we can have a talk. It is very important and relates to certain happenings abroad if you know what I mean. Over."

Frank knew exactly what he meant.

"I have no idea what you are talking about Dick and anyway whatever it is it will have to wait. I am on my way to Cherbourg for a week or two. It's holiday time you know. If it's OK with you, I'll call you when I come back. Over."

"It would really be appreciated if we could have a chat Frank. I can't stress the importance of the matter. Over" There was a trace of annoyance in Dick's voice but he knew he couldn't force Frank to do anything.

"Sorry Dick, I'm not turning back now. Call me on my mobile if you want and we can talk through whatever it is that's worrying you. Over."

There was a pause, and then he saw the chopper peel off to head back towards the mainland. "I'll do that later, Frank, have a safe journey. Over and out."

Frank sighed with relief. He was not in the mood for an inquisition and they knew that it had probably been him who had committed the murder of the diamond merchant and, he also had the diamonds on board. They were well hidden, but they were on board. He had made one bad tactical error. He had been so keen to arrange for an alibi for Gerhard and his friend that he had completely forgotten about himself. He had thought of himself as not being seen to be involved but had forgotten about Dick and his contacts. Dick had put two and two together and had made four.

"You're a bloody idiot Frank, and you're in trouble now, that's for sure." He sat down on the rear deck and watched the sea churn past. "Let's think this out, he thought. "All they know is that I went to Holland and then came back again. No one knows what I did or where I went. I wonder if Christie could give me an alibi?"

He dug out his mobile and rang hers. She answered almost immediately. "Hi, Christie, it's me, Frank," he said.

Her voice lifted and she sounded pleased to hear from him. "Frank, it's wonderful to hear from you. Where are you?" she cried.

"The main thing is, how are you and where are you, Christie?"

"I'm just fine. I'm staying with a cousin just outside Amsterdam, she kindly agreed to put me up for a few days." They chatted for a while and then he told her he had a problem. "At the moment I'm on my way to Cherbourg but I do have this problem Christie and I need your help." He told her the complete sequence of events holding nothing back. She was silent for a while.

"Just how do you get yourself into these situations. You leave dead bodies wherever you go. Poor Gerhard though. I didn't like him, as you know, but he didn't deserve to die like that. Frank, I know that we can't be together, and maybe we never will, but I am in love with you still. Of course I will be your alibi. I spent the whole weekend doing work here at home so if anybody asks me then you were here with me. Just give me the times and I will cover for you and nobody will ever be able to say otherwise."

Frank grinned with relief. "Christie, you're fantastic. I love you too. Thanks for that. Give me a few weeks and I will fly over and spend some time with you. Would you be able to take a few days off and show me around if I do?"

"Oh yes please Frank that would be just wonderful. Please come as soon as you can. I'll look forward to hearing from you. They chatted a little more as Frank gave the times and dates and then he rang off promising to phone again within the next few days.

"Sorted," he said to himself. "You're just a lucky old bugger me boy." He did a little jig on the back deck and then stopped and looked around feeling foolish. There was not another boat in sight. It was a glorious day and Prowler was merrily punching her way through the waves heading for France. He was free and on his own, just how he liked it. He sprang down into the main cabin and searched through the various CDs laying on one of the shelves. Bruce Springsteen. Yes, that suited his mood. He slipped it into the on board stereo unit and switched the speakers to their brothers out on the deck. He turned up the volume to full.

13

Frank felt someone prodding him and he heard a voice saying, "Hey you, stop that snoring for goodness sake."

He opened his eyes and blinked. He couldn't make out who was doing it because all he could see was an image surrounded by the sun. Frank struggled to sit up and the image transformed into a beautiful young woman in a bikini top and shorts.

"That's better. At least you've stopped," she said.

Frank was indignant. He hated being woken out of a deep sleep by someone shouting at him. It was almost a criminal offence as far as he was concerned. His sleepy brain struggled to come to terms with the fact that someone was standing on his deck, on his boat, without his permission and besides all that she had woken him from a wonderful deep sleep. "Just who the hell are you and who said you could get on my boat?" he shouted as he heaved himself up onto one elbow.

"Don't you shout at me mister. We couldn't stand your snoring any longer, you've been going at it for the last hour and we'd had enough so I elected to put a stop to it." She was beginning to look around. "Not bad for a stink boat," she said.

Frank stood up, looked down at the girl and then around him. He was still trying to get his bearings mentally. He remembered getting into Cherbourg late last evening and after arranging for a berth for a couple of days had eaten a light meal and crashed. This morning, after having a hearty breakfast, he had walked into the town, brought a newspaper and wandered back with a few bottles of wine. Drinking half a bottle after breakfast was what had made him fall asleep in the morning sun.

"Well now that I've stopped you snoring I'll go," said the girl. "My goodness you could snore for England."

"Hold on a minute," he said. "You've just woken me out of a deep sleep. Let me at least apologise for making so much noise. That's if I was. Can I get you a glass of wine or something stronger perhaps?" His eyes focused at last and took in the spectacle of the girl standing in front of him with her hands on her hips and her feet wide spaced. "Whew," he thought. "Not bad. Around thirty five to forty I would think." She had her blonde hair pulled back in a ponytail and, combined with a healthy tan, and very attractive features she was a stunning woman all packed into a superb figure.

She looked at him with a small frown puckering her forehead then she glanced over her shoulder. "Well, I'm supposed to be going into town in a minute but I suppose it won't hurt to have just one. "She turned back to him and switched on a devastating smile. "OK, I'll have a small beer please. Now I'm here, can I have a quick look around? It doesn't look bad for a stink boat."

"You've already said that once which probably means that you've come off a stick and rag boat then."

They both laughed at each other. He fetched her a small beer from the fridge. Taking the top off he handed it to her and she took a long swig from the bottle.

"Well, this is the rear deck as you can see with controls up there on the bridge. Then down here is the main cabin." He gestured for her to go ahead. She tripped lightly down the six steps into the cabin and looked around. He didn't say anything just watched her as she brushed her fingers across the chart table and then across the helm seat and steering wheel. She was humming to herself as she nosed into the rear double cabin and then into the kitchen amidships. She opened all the cupboard doors and poked around to see what he kept and then, raising an eyebrow at him, she moved on down into the front cabin areas. He didn't move, he just left her to it but he felt a strange sensation in his stomach. She had a great bottom and wonderful full breasts. He noticed that she was wearing a wedding ring. He couldn't help but notice that she was deliberately teasing him very gently as well. He waited for her to surface, which, after a short while, she did.

"Where are the engines, then," she asked "and how powerful are they?"

He smiled at her and put on all his boyish charm. "They are under the floor here and they are twin 400hp Caterpillars diesels which will push the old girl along at some twenty five knots top speed. She'll cruise for ever at 18/20 knots," he said proudly.

She was about to say that she was impressed when a male voice outside called.

"Kate, we are going into town. Are you coming?"

She smiled an apology at Frank. "Sorry, that's my brother-in-law. Have to go, bye." He followed her out of the cabin with his eyes riveted to her twitching bottom and saw her jump lightly down onto the pontoon to join a couple standing there. They were looking intently at him and then they both smiled. "Can I get you anything in the town old boy?" said the man. He looked about Frank's age, maybe a little older.

Frank shook his head and then looked at the yacht moored alongside him on the other side of the pontoon. "Yours?" he asked,

"'Fraid so old boy. See you when we get back. Maybe have a drink and get to know each other. When in France we Brits must stand together you know."

"Sure," he said." Have a nice time. Bye Kate," he called after the girl. She turned and waved.

"Bye Frank," she said cheekily.

"Now how the hell did she find out my name?" he thought. His phone was ringing. It was Joe.

"Hi, Joe, what the hell do you want?" he asked irritably.

"Well what sort of greeting is that to a man about to pass on good tidings?" said Joe.

"What's the good tidings?" asked Frank.

"The film, dear boy. The film. And, guess what? Spielberg. We have Spielberg wanting to produce and direct. Apparently they have come up with a brilliant script much on the lines of the 'Ark of the Covenant' series of films and they reckon this is the next series. He wants to meet you Frank. Says he has been following your recent career with interest and I told him of a couple of possible other stories. He got very excited and asked where you were now. When I told him you had gone to France on your boat he became even more excited. Said there was another story right there alone. He was very interested in what happened in Brazil Frank. He said that there were a lot of questions going around in the States about you and the problem with the Brazilian army being massacred. Wants to talk to you soonest about that, Frank."

Joe paused for breath so Frank got in a quick question. "How much is he paying Joe?"

He could tell from Joe's voice that he was anxious.

"Well, it's all about customer volumes and all that Frank but he gave us £250,000 up front for the rights to the book and I managed to get 1.5 per cent of the take from the future worldwide sales of the film. Is that all right Frank?"

Frank was in the mood where he couldn't care less anymore. "Yeah, that sounds about right Joe. Whatever. Just let me know when he starts filming. I would like to come and see what they are going to say about me after all, and yes, rig up a time for me to meet him sometime in the next three or four weeks."

"The other great thing, Frank, is that he's taken both Liz and Josie for the parts of the two girls. Can you believe that? They are both very excited about it. By the way they both send their love and said 'keep it in your trousers you dirty old sod'. They said they both had a long chat to Spielberg about you."

"Good for them," Frank said. He just couldn't raise any enthusiasm. "Anything else Joe? I need to get another beer from the fridge."

"If you're not interested Frank then fair enough, but I just want to say that I'm doing my very best for you over here while you are swanning around the bloody sea having fun. A few words of appreciation would not have gone amiss. I'll talk to you another time, you ungrateful sod." Frank could almost hear the phone being slammed down.

"He's right, I am being ungrateful but so bloody what." He felt an enormous irritation curl over his shoulders and wrap itself around him. He shook himself, almost like a dog, trying to shrug it off and did as he said he was going to do and got himself a beer. Three later he was starting to feel better. He knew where the irritation came from. It was this entire bloody money thing. Up until only a few months ago, in fact for forty-seven years, he had always had to watch his spending. Having to be careful not to spend too much. Wanting this and wanting that but not being able to afford it. Like everyone else, working his butt off just to survive to the end of the month. Now money was coming at him thick and fast and he could buy whatever he wanted to and was he happy? No. Something was missing from his life. There was no one to share it all with, no one to talk to about everything. For the first time in his life he realised that he was lonely.

He stood by the rail looking out over the marina at the myriad colours of the yachts and the sheer mass of hulls and masts. It was always a beautiful sight and the sun was so bright reflecting off the water and the hulls that he had to put on his shades.

"The problem, Frank me old lad, is that you are lonely. Twenty odd years with the wife and now there's no one, that's your problem boy. You can go around the world making more money, talking to all these famous people and bonking all these girls but what's it all worth if you're lonely. Diddly squat, mate, that's what it's worth," he said to himself.

He pottered about, occasionally looking at the charts to see the best times for leaving and going to St Malo. There was the Alderney race to negotiate. If you got that one wrong on a bad day then you could be in serious trouble. He wanted to go now but couldn't help thinking about the girl.

"Come on Frank, you can afford to spend another night here and leave in the morning," he told himself. "I know what my other problem really is, I'm frustrated that's what I am. I need a bloody good lay that's what I need."

He climbed back out onto the back deck just in time to see Kate sauntering down the pontoon with bags of goods in her arms. He swung himself off the boat and walked up to her. "Can I help you fair miss?" he asked grinning at her. Her eyes gave nothing away because of her sunglasses but a smile tweaked her generous mouth.

"Sure, Frank that's nice of you thanks." She said nothing more as he followed her to the yacht moored alongside and he helped her climb over the rails to get aboard and then passed the bags of stores to her. All the time he was looking at her long tanned legs and her bottom. He started to fantasise as to where he would like to have those legs wrapped but promptly shut down those ideas. If he carried on with those thoughts it would show in the bulge of his shorts and that would be embarrassing.

"Come aboard Frank, and talk to me. Want a drink?"

"Sure," he said. He jumped over the rails and followed her down into the cabin. It was cool down there. They had the front hatch open and there was a through draft. He was always amazed about these yachts. They were enormous from the outside and yet they always felt cramped inside.

"Beer, wine, or a short, what's your pleasure?" she asked turning and looking at him. She took off her sunglasses. He looked into green eyes that seemed to swamp and absorb him. He was totally bewitched.

"You're staring Frank," she said smiling.

"Sorry, it's your green eyes. Kate they are beautiful. Which side of the family do they come from?" he asked.

"My mother. When Jennie comes back; she's my sister, you will see that she has them as well. You're staring again Frank."

"Mmmmmm," he said. "I have a theory about green eyes." He didn't wait for her to ask the obvious question. "I reckon that they are of Scandinavian origin. I have seen that exact colour many times in Norway and Sweden. So, Viking stock, I guess that's where you come from."

She smiled at him again. She always seemed to be smiling and it made her face light up. She had happy lines around her eyes. "What you mean, Frank, is that one of my ancestors had a good time being ravaged by marauding Viking hordes. Is that what you're saying?"

He laughed at her. "Sure. I guess that's what I mean." She walked past him and as she did so her body brushed his and a wonderful smell hit his nostrils. The scent of a woman and his body reacted in quite a basic fashion. She turned half way up the steps from the cabin to the cockpit to say something and could not help but see. Her eyes widened and travelled up to his face and back down again. Frank didn't do anything, he just stood leaning back against the galley. She blushed and carried on up the steps. He followed trying to adjust himself but he couldn't make the situation much better.

"You had better get that under control before my sister comes back," Kate said half laughing and put her shades back on so he couldn't see her eyes. "It's very impressive," she added.

"Sorry about that just ignore him and he will go away. He just does this whenever I get near a beautiful woman. It's so embarrassing."

"Well, I will take it as a compliment then," she said.

They sat down in the cockpit and raised their glasses to each other. "Tell me all about yourself," he said to Kate. "You are obviously married so what are you doing here?"

"No, I'm not married. My husband died ten months ago of a heart attack and my sister wondered if I would like to get away from everything for a couple of weeks on the boat. I thought it would be a good idea." We had no children, unfortunately, we had been trying for years but nothing ever happened. So here I am." She paused. "I know who you are Frank. My sister recognised you and we were talking about you when we went into town. My brother-in-law is very excited and can't wait to get back to have a chat. I'm interested as well, of course. You seem to lead such an exciting life, Frank."

Frank took a sip of his beer. "Sorry to hear about your husband. I've had much the same experience I suppose but not quite as bad as yours. My wife walked off and left me for another fella two years ago and we had been together for over twenty years. I have three children all in their teens and early twenties. Strangely enough, I was just ruminating a few moments ago about my life." He stopped. He had nearly opened up his heart to a complete stranger. What on earth possessed him to do that? He didn't know. He just clammed up.

Kate pretended not to notice but fully understood what was going through his mind. She had been going through the same distress for the last eight months. She didn't say anything for a while and they just sat there, slowly drinking and thinking.

"Believe it or not, Frank, I know what you were about to say and how you are feeling. I am going through the same scenario myself although I haven't had the good fortune to have the excitement you have had to distract my mind. I think that you are just coming down to earth and hitting the ground with an almighty bump. Am I right?" she asked.

Frank glanced at her. "Yeah, bloody know all" he grinned at her. They both relaxed and chatted about other things until her brother-in-law and sister arrived.

Kate introduced Frank to her sister, Jennie, who was also stunning but maybe five years older and to Jennie's husband Richard.

Jennie had a very bold gaze and said, "Frank, you are much better looking in the flesh, than in the paper or on television. I watched your interview with the press on television when you arrived in Rio and you looked totally different to how you look now. You looked positively dangerous and you frowned and scowled at everybody all the time. What was that all about?"

Frank laughed, "Don't forget Jennie, I had been in the jungle for up to four or five weeks and had just been through a pretty hairy time. I was very tired and pissed off with the media, and by all their questions, and I had a lot on my mind. I was particularly worried about the Brazilian Government planning to steal the treasure we had found, and rightly so because as we were talking they were trying to fly out there to get it."

Richard asked Frank if he had ever sailed. Frank replied that he had a bit and had passed his 'Day Skipper' exams once, many moons ago.

"We have decided to take part in a club race here tomorrow, would you like to join us Frank? We could really do with another crew."

"Sure, I don't have anything else to do. That would be just fine," he replied.

"I'm afraid it's a 6.30am start Frank, so we need to be up and moving by 5.30am You OK for that?" grinned Richard.

Frank said that would be fine and agreed to be on board their boat and ready to go at that time. He wanted the evening to himself so arranged to see them the next morning.

14

B RIGHT AND EARLY, AND on the dot, he jumped onto their boat to find them almost ready to go. Very soon afterwards they joined a fleet of similar yachts all heading out of the harbour for the open sea.

Jennie and Kate busied themselves downstairs in the galley getting food and drink ready for the day because as soon as the gun fired they wouldn't have time for cooking. Richard was very professional and quickly ran through with Frank what he wanted him to be responsible for such as the spinnaker, etc. "When I shout for you to do something Frank, do it instantly without question. OK?"

"Sure Richard, I don't have a problem with that. You're the skipper. Let's see if we can win this one."

"We won't win, there are too many good sailors here with local knowledge. But we will give them a run for their money. See that red and white yacht over there? Number 916. He is usually brilliant and I'm going to shadow him. Not too obviously but I intend to be about a hundred yards behind him all the way. Keep your eye on him and if I lose him I'll be asking you where he is OK?"

"Roger, that," Frank replied and went forward to ensure all his ropes were tidy and to hand.

Promptly, at 6.30 a.m., Frank saw the smoke from the start gun. "Go Richard, the gun's been fired," he shouted and, as they tightened the sails, the boat lurched and increased speed rapidly as they heard the start gun echo out from the marina walls. "Good one Frank," shouted Richard, grinning.

The race was over a triangular course of fifteen miles and they had to complete the course three times. They quickly settled down into a quiet rhythm and found themselves right up with the fast boys because of their quick start. In fact they found themselves in front of 916 by a few yards so they had to do a lot of looking over their shoulders.

"Let him by." Richard shouted, so Jennie lost some wind out of the main sail. The red and white boat pounced immediately and went by them. At the same time Jennie pulled in the sail again, with Kate's help, so that they picked up speed again. "How many knots, Richard?" Frank asked.

"Just over seven and climbing."

"How come she's so fast?" Frank asked.

"I had her taken out and her bottom cleaned and polished two days ago. A faster keel fitted last week. We have the latest Kevlar sails and then there's me, of course," shouted Richard.

"Bloody fast for a weekend cruiser," Frank thought, and settled back to watch the race from his vantage point in the bow. In fact he thought that this boat might even be a little faster than 916. Although Richard tried hard to stay only a hundred yards behind, Frank could see that the girls spilled wind on a regular basis. He made his way to the rear.

"Want some chicken or a drink?" asked Jennie. Frank shook his head and thanked her. They were running with four other yachts all quite close with the rest of the fleet beginning to trail away behind. The first two courses were completed with little excitement with everyone tacking exactly the same as 916. As the wind was staying in the same direction 916 duplicated its first course exactly. As they came to complete the second course and start the third Frank said. "Why don't you take him Richard? You know you can because I've been watching what the girls are doing. When we had to put up the spinnaker on the last leg we could have taken him with ease."

"Can't do it, old boy. They would only protest and then they would find that I am completely illegal below the waterline. The new keel that I had fitted is not allowed in this class. Just wanted to know how much extra speed it would give me and now I know." Richard turned his head away from watching the sails and grinned at Frank. "As it is, the others will be viewing us with great suspicion so we might have to let another one pass us now and roll in third, or something. It's not really about winning Frank; it's about having a good day out and having fun. Look at the girls. Getting tanned, plenty of fresh air and exercise and they are chatting happily away, in all probability about you. Have you enjoyed yourself, Frank?"

"I certainly have. I just don't like to be beaten that's all. I can understand where you are coming from Richard. They have been looking at us for most of the race wondering how you've been managing to keep up with them. Look, that boat behind is edging up on us."

"Yes, I told Jennie to let him gradually catch us so she has been playing a waiting game with them. We only have four miles to go to the finish line outside the harbour so if we are clever they should just beat us by a few yards. I will let them take us on the next tack but will run them very close and not make it too obvious. That will make them very happy." He shouted to the two girls. "To make it realistic Frank is going to fumble changing the jib on the tack. That should just let them through and then we want plenty of action pretending to try to get back at them. OK girls?" The girls waved in reply laughing. "You OK with that Frank. Can you arrange a fumble?" Richard grinned at him.

"I can fumble with the best of them Richard, just watch me."

Sure enough, as they came to the buoy Richard ran a little wide and they dropped speed alarmingly as Frank pretended to slip and fall as he tried to move the sail from one side to the other. Recovering quickly he pulled in the sail as he threw the helm and the yacht heeled over trying to catch the wind on the new tack. Richard was shouting obscenities at Frank and the girls were shouting also. The other boat did exactly what it should have done and took the moment taking Richard on the inside beautifully. The crew were shouting with excitement and as they pulled ahead started to wave and shout jokes at Richard who pretended to scowl with anger. It was all good fun. To give them a fright Richard stayed almost alongside all the way to the line with the girls screaming and shouting at the other crew who worked grimly and quietly all the way to the line. As soon as they crossed the roles were reversed with the other crew shouting and jumping up and down with glee.

"Well done crew. That was just great. At least we know that we could have beaten the lot of them. As it is we will be welcome any time we want to come back. They won't forget that finish in a hurry and we might get a few free drinks in the bar tonight."

Kate sat down next to Frank in the bow as they motored back to the marina. "Well, did you enjoy that, Frank?"

"It was all a bit unusual but yes I did. It was great and what a wonderful day too. You look great too Kate. The fresh air and sun has put a glow to your cheeks." They looked into each other's eyes for a moment. He leaned over and gave her a lingering kiss on the lips. She responded instantly but didn't open her mouth until he had almost stopped and then she flicked her tongue between his lips.

"Naughty," he said.

"But nice," she grinned. Nothing more needed to be said until later.

As soon as they had moored up Richard went to the clubhouse with Frank to record their finish and the two girls made some lunch. As soon as the two men got back they had some food and chatted for a while and then Jennie's husband said, "Frank I have so many questions to ask you if I may. Would you like to join us for dinner on board tonight after the prize giving? I can assure you that Jennie is a superb cook and will make your mouth water. We would be delighted if you could join us wouldn't we ladies?" Jennie and Kate both agreed and Frank readily accepted. He got up to leave. "See you about 7.30 and thanks for a great day," he said and left.

Richard went back on deck to wash the boat down and tidy things up. In the meantime the two girls chatted about Frank.

"So Kate, what do you think of him?" asked her sister casually. She was naturally very concerned about her sister and wanted to see her in another stable relationship as she knew her sister was unhappy.

"Quite honestly, Jennie, he turns my legs to water every time I look at him. I mean, come on, he is a stunning looking man, tall, good looking, tanned and muscular, my God and his wife walked out and left him? She must have been mad. Every time I get near him I can almost smell him and I get hot, I mean he just turns me on; especially when he looks at me with those deep blue eyes. It's the way his eyes linger that does it. I just find him very attractive. I also sense a deep vulnerability which is strange when you look at him as he appears so self assured."

"I noticed that and it's a very attractive side to him. He fancies you too you know. Haven't you noticed that he keeps looking at you and I did notice you two kissing earlier on. Both Richard and I had to giggle but it was so nice to see it. We do worry about you, you know."

The two girls smiled at each other and Kate gave her sister a hug. "If I have my way that's not all he is going to get either," she laughed.

* * *

He didn't have any clothes that would be suitable for the evening so he sauntered into town and, although the afternoon was getting late, managed to find a store. Fitting himself out with several short-sleeved shirts and slacks, plus a pair of smart and very expensive boat shoes and a tie; he felt that he would be a little more presentable than the slob with two days of beard growth and scruffy clothes that he was at present. He called into a barber and asked for the full treatment. He was obviously going to be the last customer of the day so the little French man set to work washing his hair and cutting it back to a more suitable length for the summer. At the same time he attacked Frank's beard whilst tutt-tutting to himself. When he finished Frank looked in the mirror and was startled to see the face of a man who he recognised at last. There were a few more lines around the mouth and eyes that hadn't been there a year ago and the eyes looked older, and slightly haunted, otherwise he didn't look too bad.

He had a problem, nowadays, looking into mirrors. Could "the Monk" from the pyramid see him? That's if he was watching. Frank scowled as he looked at himself. Thinking about that was going to spoil his day so he turned and settled up with the little French barber and thanking him he left the shop. On his way back to the boat he bought a large bunch of roses and two more bottles of wine that he fancied. He crept down the pontoon, not wishing the others to see him, and managed to sneak onto his boat without being seen. Setting to in the shower he gave himself a good scrub and felt all the better for it. When dry he slipped into his new clothes and looked at himself in the door mirror of his cabin. "Not bad," he thought. "I haven't felt this good for many a long day. It's about time to go and wow the ladies with tales of daring do." When he called to the yacht for permission to come aboard, it was exactly 7.30 p.m.

As he was boarding the boat Kate came up the steps from the cabin to welcome him and he froze. She looked stunning. Her blonde hair glowed with health and hung over her tanned bare shoulders. She was wearing a red dress with obviously not much on underneath and her feet were bare.

She stopped too and was looking at him in open admiration. "Is there something I can do for you Sir?" she enquired "Have you lost your way?"

"Stop fooling around Kate, it's only me," said Frank grinning at her.

"No, it can't be. The Frank I know is scruffy and bearded. Anyway I will let you aboard in case the real Frank doesn't come. Jennie," she called, "be prepared for a surprise." She moved gracefully back down the steps and Frank followed her feeling really embarrassed.

"Da dah," she cried presenting Frank as he entered the cabin. Jennie looked at him and gave a long wolf whistle. "Someone kissed the frog and a Prince appeared," she said." Everyone laughed.

"You two ladies look pretty damned gorgeous yourselves. I'm glad you invited me now." Richard gave Frank a large glass of red wine and proposed a toast to lasting friendship. He sat Frank down at the table and Jennie quickly started to serve the first course.

Two hours later Frank was stuffed to the gills. "Jennie that was just one of the tastiest meals I have ever had. The lobster was unbelievable. I think I will always drool just thinking about it." They were now all very relaxed. They had grilled Frank gently on his experiences over the last few months and had been wide eyed at his tales. Obviously he had not told them everything and they were bright enough to know that he hadn't. He had seen some glances from Jennie to Kate and back.

"One last thing on these stories, I have deliberately held back a few because it wouldn't be in your interests to know about them. One or two I am not proud of but that's life. I have changed beyond recognition from the man I was a year ago. However sometimes I wish I were back in my little company having another boring day. At the moment I feel that I am on the run and under a lot of pressure. I have to live with that and learn how to handle it. That's why I'm here. At least I feel that I am amongst friends with you three." Kate leaned over and took Frank's hand and pressed it.

"Don't worry Frank, you are," she said.

Frank turned to Richard who had been absorbing everything like a sponge. "What do you do to keep yourself amused Richard and to keep Jennie in the manner to which she had become accustomed?" He asked.

"Oh, I have several jewellery shops in London. My father started them just after the war and I have sort of taken over and expanded the company to where it is now. Not half as exciting as what you have been doing though Frank. I so envy you. What's the matter, Frank?" he asked.

Frank was looking at Richard with his mouth open and a startled look on his face.

"You sell jewellery, diamonds? Oh Christ, I don't believe it." He got up and sat down again. The two girls watched him in amazement. "What on earth is the matter Frank?" said Jennie.

He banged his forehead with his right hand. What was this all about? It couldn't be simply fate could it or was there something else here? A hidden agenda perhaps. The way they had moored alongside and had so quickly met him and taken him on board, the casual way they had got him to talk, the way that Kate was seducing him. It was so obvious to him now. It was a set up. But by whom?

His brain was whirling with a thousand thoughts at once and he fought to bring himself under control. He could feel the blood thumping through his veins and his whole body was as taught as a bowstring. His eyes came up slowly from beneath his brows to meet the others. Jennie gasped in fright and Kate went white. Frank's face was contorted with suppressed fury and rage and he looked around like a caged animal. He felt like one. Rising slowly to his feet he was ready to spring for the entrance. He had no gun or knife. Knife. He looked around at the galley. There were long carving knives there, which would do. He looked back at the girls, and at Richard; a red mist developing before his eyes.

Jennie spoke first. "What's wrong with you Frank? For goodness sake sit down and relax you are frightening us. You're looking as you did on television. What has happened to do this to you Frank, please? We are your friends, what on earth is the matter?" He looked at Kate. She was plainly terrified of him and sank back in her chair. It was only Richard who appeared unafraid.

"Here, have a brandy old boy. Whatever it was I said I'm sorry. We all know what you have been through and wouldn't do anything to upset you. For goodness sake sit down and let's talk this through. Now, what is this all about? You look as though you would like to murder us all just then. I've never seen anything like it."

The red mist slowly faded away as he listened to what they said. At that moment he had almost lost control of himself and he knew it. He sat down. "Cool it, my boy, play it cool and let's hear what they have to say," he thought. He closed his eyes, counted to ten and opened them again. They were still looking at him. "Maybe I should give them the benefit of the doubt, I have to trust someone at some time and it might as well be these three," he thought. "They seem OK."

Frank asked himself what the cause of all this trouble was. The answer came hammering back at him. "The bloody diamonds" He had an idea and spoke slowly to the three people in front of him. "Sorry about that, the only way I can explain myself is if I go back to the boat and get something which I need to show you," he said. "Excuse me a second."

He left the table and hopped over the railing onto the pontoon before jumping onto his own boat. He dug out his bag of diamonds from their hiding place and, locking the door behind him, went back on the yacht.

They were still sitting in the same position and were obviously talking about him because they stopped when he dropped back in the cabin.

He cleared an area of the table and removed some of the dinner plates. He produced the bag and slowly poured the diamonds onto the table until they all lay there. There was dead silence in the cabin; everyone was gazing in astonishment at the beautiful sight of the gems glinting in the low light.

"Holy Mother of Jesus," said Jennie.

"Unbelievable. Never seen such beautiful stones," said Richard.

"Stunning, absolutely stunning," gasped Kate.

"Richard, they are all yours, I don't want anything for them. There's blood on all those stones and they have brought me nothing but bad luck and trouble ever since I first saw them. I want rid of them. Do what you want with them? They are yours from this moment on and don't worry about a bloody receipt. Having said that I still have some at home which I think I will keep for an emergency." He was thinking of those remaining diamonds still buried in his garden.

Richard looked at the stones and then looked at Frank, "You must be joking of course Frank. Tell me that you are and don't tease me. This is serious stuff. There must be several millions of pounds in value just laying there at cost, let alone retail. Tell me you are joking, Frank" He bent forward, picked up a particularly large stone and held it up to the light. It glinted and gleamed with fire.

"I'm not joking Richard. I've just told you, they are yours. They are no good with me and I'm not comfortable with them. Many people have died because of them and I don't want to be included in that list. See those big ones, the same as the one you are holding. I found them on the skeleton of a dead German pilot in The Brazilian jungle. Nobody knows about them. Fifty years they had been sitting around his waist and a lot of good they did him. They also caused the death of a very dear friend of mine. Do what you want with all of them. Now if you don't mind I desperately need some fresh air." He got up and left the cabin.

"I'll look after him," said Kate and followed Frank out of the cabin.

She found him sitting in the bow on the cabin roof. She sat next to him and leaned lightly against him but didn't say anything. They sat there for about fifteen minutes just looking out into the night and listening to the sound of people talking, their laughter drifting across the marina on the warm night air. Finally Frank said. "It's all for the best Kate. Fate deals some strange hands and finding you three was the strangest.

I'm sorry that I lost it earlier but the coincidence of Richard being in jewellery was too much. I thought I had been trapped."

"Well you frightened me to death. I've never ever seen such anger and hatred in anyone's face as I did in yours. I saw death staring me in the face." She turned his head with her hand and stroked his cheek. "Looking at you now I can't believe that it could show what I saw. This strong handsome face twisted with rage and hate."

"I'm sorry about that Kate, I've been living on the edge for months now. It's all been foreign to me and, frankly, hard to handle. I'm quite a simple man really and have just about had it with all this pressure and problems. Don't worry, it won't happen again. Let's go and see if Richard has had a heart attack yet."

They re-joined the other couple and found them in deep conversation. They both looked up when Frank and Kate came back through the hatchway.

"I just wanted to apologise for my behaviour earlier on," Frank said. "I'm really sorry and I want to apologise to you in particular Jennie, as you had just fed me such an amazing meal."

"It's all understandable now Frank. Don't worry about it just don't ever look at me that way again, not ever. It looks as though you have a few meals in reserve by the look of this lot. Richard reckons there's at least five million pounds worth."

Richard was studying the diamonds closely. "Mmmmmm. There are some with very old cuts and some with much later cuts. Both cuts are Dutch and very similar. You say these bigger ones are old Frank, What about these others?" He looked up at Frank with questions unasked.

Frank sat down. He found that he was still holding Kate's hand. He looked at her and she smiled at him. If he was going to take this further then he was going to have to tell them everything and play it from there.

"OK. What I am going to tell you, only two other people in the world know and quite a few others suspect but it isn't very nice. It doesn't show me in a very good light at all and you will probably be disgusted. I wouldn't be at all surprised if you are. I'm not too pleased with myself either. Anyway, here's the story." He then told them all about Amsterdam and his two trips.

They listened in total silence. Their eyes were wide and were fixed on him throughout. He spoke whilst looking down at the diamonds all the time and his voice dropped to a low monotone. He made no mention of what had happened to him inside the pyramid. As the story unfolded a strange thing happened. He felt himself drifting away from the table and his body. He could see himself sitting there talking and the next second he was standing at the entrance of the second level of the pyramid with his hand on the door.

"Don't try to come in Frank, you are not ready," said the voice of Sandy. "We are aware of your turmoil but be aware that you are being tested and, in the fullness of time, you will be ready to join us but not yet. You have just passed an important test. Well done, Frank. We will talk again." He gasped aloud as his soul hurtled back through space and thumped back into his body.

Kate put her hand on his arm. "Are you OK Frank?"

"I'll be OK in a second, don't worry," he replied.

There was silence in the cabin for a few minutes. He was glad of that as he tried to come to terms with what he had just experienced. "I am beginning to think that I am about to have a nervous breakdown," he thought. "Hearing voices and now this. What the hell is happening to me?" He could hear Richard talking and had to drag his conscious brain back to attention.

"Frank, I'm not worried about the old stones, but I am worried about these new ones. Do you know if the man that you killed had them logged?"

"Yes, he had and I have the log," said Frank. "I found them in his safe at the time and took the book as well. It is now sitting at the bottom of the North Sea somewhere with the gun." He turned and looked at Kate. "Still interested in a man who has cold bloodedly murdered another man?"

Kate glanced at her sister who nodded as though in agreement with a secret message they had transmitted to each other.

"Frank, in front of my brother-in-law and my sister, I have to say that you are the most extraordinary man I have ever met. You are full of contradictions. Obviously brave and determined as you have proven and you have a totally ruthless streak when you think you are being threatened, but at the core you are just a soft pudding. I have no problem with being involved with you Frank and I have only known you for what, thirty-six hours? I am more comfortable in your company than I have ever been with any other man I know frankly. Now, what I suggest is that you take me to your boat and make love to me. We can then all talk more in the morning."

"That's my sister. Good girl, I'm proud of you," laughed Jennie. "Go for it. Don't worry about the washing up. Get off with you and have some fun, Heaven knows you both need it and deserve it."

"Hold on a minute," said Frank. He looked at Kate who was grinning from ear to ear at him. "Don't you know it's the man who likes to do all the chasing? What if I said no?"

"Say no then," said Kate still grinning.

Frank looked frustrated. "OK. Let's try this then. Kate, you are a beautiful woman, obviously in need of love, passion and friendship and possibly sex. How about coming with me to my boat and sleeping with me tonight?"

"You're on," she replied. She took his hand and pulled him to his feet. "Don't spend all night ogling those diamonds Richard. Just remember your wife needs some attention as well and you are on holiday after all so do your duty. Night all." and they left the boat together.

When they got back onto Frank's boat shyness overcame both of them. Frank took the initiative and drew Kate to him. He put his arms right around her and kissed her deeply. Her mouth opened under his and her tongue slipped into his mouth, probing. She moaned and gripped him tighter with her arms. She took her mouth away from his but, still holding him tight, said. "You can kiss me as long as you like but just keep kissing me like that and I'm yours for ever."

He took her hand and walked her into his bedroom in the prow of the boat. It had a large double bed and was very comfortable. Kicking off his shoes he picked her up and put her down on the bed whilst slowly kissing her all the time with his mouth moving to her throat and her breasts. His hands found the zip on the back of her dress and he slowly undid it all the while continuing to kiss her. He drew the dress off her shoulders and buried his mouth onto her now naked breasts. She gasped pushing her hips hard against him. He lifted himself and pulled the dress from her body. She had no underwear on at all and he looked up into her grinning face. "Surprised you, didn't it," she said.

"You little minx. Well, we will see if you like this," he said and promptly started to kiss her body from her neck all the way down to her thighs. She moaned and writhed as his mouth found her and gasped in shock when his hands found her as well. Her hands tore at his clothes seeking to hold him, so he stopped and removed them quickly. Her eyes watched him and when he was naked she reached for him and ran her hands slowly up and down his erection. "Get back down there and finish what you started, mister, and then I'll sort you out too," she laughed. He did.

Later that night they were lying talking with their arms wrapped about each other. "Why don't we slip away early in the morning and head for St Malo and wait for them there or do you think we should tell them first?" said Frank.

"I think we should tell them first and then go, and anyway I haven't any clothes here. Does that mean that you want me to come with you Frank, because if you do I don't mind one bit?"

"I think that's what I'm saying, yes. OK?"

"Only if you promise to make love to me twice a day for ever as you did tonight. God I needed that and hadn't realised it. How about some more then?" she asked crudely, reaching for him, and she giggled with pleasure when she found him already erect.

15

JENNIE AND RICHARD WERE surprised to hear that Kate was going off with Frank. However, they wished them both luck and promised to see them in St Malo within the next few days. Frank was going to make the hop within the day but it would probably take Richard two.

Before they left Richard asked Frank for a moment in private. "Frank, these diamonds are burning a hole in my pocket and I am going to have to send them to my office. I want my team to evaluate them so that I can work out what to do."

"If you are going to start talking about money Richard, forget it. I have all I need and just don't want to be associated with those stones ever again. O.K. So the originals have brought me wealth in a strange way but I still think they emanate from a bad force. So, yes, I would recommend that you send them back to your offices and then get rid of them, one way or another."

"Don't worry Frank, from what you have told me I quite understand how you feel and, of course, this is my industry and I know exactly what I am going to do with them. From the proceeds I will ensure that Kate is well funded financially."

The two men talked for a further fifteen minutes and then made their separate ways back to their boats.

Frank and Kate checked their fuel and stores and, having decided they had enough of each to make the trip, they set off early that morning as the tide was on its final ebb. Once free of the harbour Frank opened the taps to three quarter throttle and let Prowler loose at twenty knots. Kate was fascinated. Not being used to power cruisers she was surprised that there was so little pitching and rolling and that they could make a cup of tea with little problems. The sea was down to a low swell and there was hardly any wind. She sat on the back deck and soaked up the sunshine while Frank fed her a continuous stream of chilled white wine.

He heard his boat's name mentioned on the radio and that there was "Traffic" for him. He switched stations to listen. There were two messages. The first one was from Joe saying that he had some very important news that Frank should hear immediately. It was a life or death problem.

Frank frowned. He didn't like the tone in Joe's voice.

"Do we have a problem?" asked Kate.

"We are about to find out. That's my manager I was telling you about. I had given strict orders not to phone me for the next week so something strange must have come up."

The second call was from Dick requesting that he contact him immediately as well as he had some very serious information that Frank would want to know about.

"What the hell is this all about?" he asked Kate.

"There's only one way to find out and that's to phone them," she said.

He decided to phone Dick first. After all, Joe's information would probably be about money whereas Dick was another kettle of fish.

Frank dug out Dick's number in Lymington and called the harbour office on his mobile. His familiar voice came back down the line. "Marina harbour office"

"Hi, Dick, you wanted me?" Frank said.

There was a slight hesitation and then, "Well, that was quick, I only put the message out an hour ago. I was hoping that you would be listening out. Frank we have a potentially serious problem. The Mulligan family has broken out their boy. The one you shot in the hotel. He was on a routine hospital visit with his guards to have his wounds dressed when they jumped the ambulance and killed one guard in the process. All hell is breaking loose back here about this and even the Home Secretary's office is becoming involved; presumably because of the huge press interest. The front pages are full of it. Everyone knows that he had sworn to come after you because you killed his brother. My message to you, Frank, is to stay away for as long as you can because, without a doubt, they will be coming after you. That's all. How's your holiday going by the way? Found any good women over there?" he quipped.

"Yup. I have one sitting on my lap right now and she is gorgeous. Don't you worry your little head about me Dick; I can look after myself as you may remember. Anyway, thanks for the warning."

"Let me know when you are coming back and I will arrange for some light cover for you" Dick said.

"That's very kind of you Dick. Don't worry; I will talk to you later. Bye"

"He sounds a nice man." Kate said.

Frank got much the same story from Joe.

They spent a month in St Malo with Jennie and Richard relaxing and exploring the surrounding countryside and cruising the local coastline, visiting marinas and small bays, and spent another four weeks visiting Jersey and Guernsey.

Slowly but surely Kate and Frank fell in love, glorying in their friendship and mutual admiration. Frank found that Kate had an impish sense of humour and the laughter and fun they had together made Jennie and Richard smile. Like all good things the holiday had to come to an end and eventually they made the decision to head for home.

Frank had been fretting about Christie. He knew he had been a little in love with the girl but he felt a much deeper attraction to Kate. He decided to talk to Christie about it. Christie was surprised at what Frank had to say but she soon rallied. She had known that their relationship could not really work especially as she had another agenda anyway. That did not stop her liking him though. Christie wished Frank all the best and told him to keep in touch. She promptly picked the phone back up and dialled another number.

Kate had heard so much from Frank about his new home that she asked if she could come to stay. Frank had said yes. Jennie and Richard decided to stay in St Malo for a few more days so they made their way back across the Channel with Frank dying to show his home to Kate. He forgot about the warnings from Joe and Dick and the threat from the Mulligan family.

* * *

He awoke with a start. The voice was calling him urgently. Her voice boomed inside his head. "Frank, wake up, you have men with guns coming into your garden, hurry Frank." It was the unmistakable voice of Sandy and he became wide-awake.

Not even questioning the voice he shook Kate awake and told her there were men entering the garden and to dress quickly. He rolled out of bed and quickly threw on a heavy tee shirt and tracksuit bottoms. He then rummaged at the back of his wardrobe and pulled out an old duffle bag. He pulled out two pistols and two boxes of ammo. He immediately screwed a silencer on one and ensured that the guns were fully loaded. He slipped two more magazines into his tracksuit trousers. By that time Kate had dressed in jeans and jumper and was looking very frightened. "Who can it be Frank?"

"Without a shadow of a doubt it's that bloody Irish family again, and they mean business this time. So, we have to be better than them Kate or we will be dead in about three minutes. Can you shoot?" he asked.

She took the gun and cocked it smartly. "Sure thing," she said. For an instant he wondered where the hell she had learned to handle a pistol like that but there was no time to think of that right now.

"Good girl. If you have to shoot, hit them high in the chest twice. Let's go," he whispered.

He gently eased the curtains aside and peered out. It was a bright moonlit night and the countryside could be easily seen. "A bombers' moon," he thought. They climbed out of the bedroom window onto the sloping roof of the chalet bungalow and hid themselves by the large chimney. "Listen Kate, if anybody pokes his nose out of that window and looks as though he is coming out onto the roof, shoot him. Don't hesitate, don't ask questions, just shoot him, OK?" She nodded. He saw shadowy figures moving in from the woods into the garden. How many he couldn't determine. He nudged her and pointed. She nodded, not saying anything, but her eyes showed a lot. He reasoned that it would take them about two or three minutes to get through the patio doors as they had a pretty smart locking system and then they would be in trouble because the alarms to the police would activate. However that would still mean that they would have to defend themselves for some ten minutes or so. An awful lot could happen in ten minutes with professionals like these loose. He whispered to her to stay where she was at all costs, and told her that he was going hunting. She nodded, grabbed his head and kissed him hard on the mouth. He showed his teeth in a grin, patted her on the shoulder and whispered that he would be back shortly. He pulled a pair of night glasses out of the small pack on his back and put them on. The whole world changed and he could now see everything clearly. He eased himself slowly down the shallow, angled roof of the bungalow until he was at the gutter. There was no sound coming from inside the house. They would be in there by now, looking for him though. Over to his left he could see a man standing by the willow tree, obviously acting as look out and back up. He must be the first to go. He reckoned that he must be over the front door. As far as he was concerned there was only one way out now and that was to attack. He was fed up and angry at having to be on the defensive all the time, anyway how long was this whole thing supposed to go on for? Until they killed him? No way. He had no time to make a firm judgement on an attack procedure; he was going to rely completely on surprise. They wouldn't be expecting him to be awake and coming after them that's for sure. Surprise was going to be his secret weapon, that and his ability with a gun as well as his grim determination to defend his home and his woman.

The mind plays strange tricks when it is under such stress and a slip of a Kipling poem ran across his mind as he watched the man below.

'Its when they stand like an Ox in the furrow,
Their sullen set eyes on you own,
And they say, "This isn't fair dealing,"
My son, leave the English alone.'

He smiled grimly to himself that just about summed it up.

He looked at the drop from the gutter. It must be ten or twelve feet, or there abouts. "God damn it, I'm too old to do all this shit," he thought. There was no alternative however. He jumped and the drop seemed to take for ever. He rolled hard when he hit the ground; his night glasses almost fell off his head. The sound of Frank hitting the ground made the man by the tree whip around. Before he could get his gun up, the hooded man let off a burst at him. It was a recklessly wild reaction to Frank suddenly appearing from nowhere, and the bullets tore past Frank; they didn't touch him. Before the intruder could correct his poor shooting, Frank shot him from twenty feet hitting him twice in the chest. Frank heard a loud groan and a sob from behind him and rolled to his right. He swung around to face the door. There was another one, standing halfway inside the door, gawping at him from only ten or fifteen feet away. He had been hit by his mate's wild shooting and was trying to hold himself up at the door. He was holding some sort of light machine pistol in his hand. Frank didn't hesitate and pumped one round into him. Thrown back against the doorpost by the force of the bullet from such short range, the man twisted and toppled over slowly pulling the trigger of his gun in a long staccato cacophony of sound the bullets shattering the ground in front of the door.

"That's torn it," Frank thought. He knew from his old training that the men inside would not come out the front way now. They would probably either wait for him in the house or run out of the back door, depending on their determination.

"A pound to a penny they will run, now that the surprise factor has been blown," he thought.

He climbed to his feet, put his night vision glasses back on and ran around to the back of the house. He arrived just in time to see two men crouching low and moving fast out through the back door towards the small wood that separated the house from the sea. They saw him at the same time as he saw them. Still running, they emptied their machine pistols vaguely in his direction. Frank dropped to one knee and coolly snapped off shots at the two in much the same way as shooting at ducks at a fun fair. He saw them both drop, one was screaming. The first man sprang back to his feet and disappeared into the shrub as Frank pulled off another shot. He knew as he did so that he had missed. Frank ran towards the downed man when a figure came hurtling out of the house and ran full tilt into Frank, bowling them both to the ground. Shocked, Frank rolled and came to his feet fast, his adrenalin was pumping and he knew that he had let go of his gun somehow in the collision.

The figure in black was even faster and was already coming at him; the light from the moon was glinting on a naked blade. Neither man spoke as, breathing heavily, they came together; Frank's hand was grabbing for the knife arm. He knew that he probably had no more than five seconds. This man was agile, young and strong, and was obviously good at close combat but Frank felt stronger and sharper. He had hold of the knife arm but he knew that it wasn't going to be for very long. He dropped his right shoulder into the man's stomach and, still holding onto the arm, heaved with every ounce of strength in him. He heard the surprised gasp come from the shadowy figure as he flew into the air and Frank, keeping the man's arm straight, dropped him onto the rigged arm and knife. He heard the satisfying snap and then a groan as the man fell like a sack of potatoes and lay still. Frank quickly put one foot on the man's neck and checked for a pulse with his free hand. There wasn't one. He had indeed fallen onto his own knife and it had sunk deep up through the stomach into the heart. Swivelling quickly Frank looked for his gun and finding it close by ran over to one of the men he had shot. He pulled the man's hood off. The assassin was a man about his own age with grey hair. He lay gasping and swearing quietly.

Frank looked down at the man's body and saw that he had caught the bullet low down in the gut. Blood was oozing out between the man's hands and he began to cry with the awful pain. "Oh, Mother of God, it hurts." Opening his eyes for a second he looked into Frank's. "You fooking bastard Blake, you ffffooking, ffffooking bastard. We will get you don't you worry. We will get you." The man sobbed, curling up again with the pain cramping in his stomach.

Frank stood up and looked down at the mortally hit man. Strangely he felt no emotion at seeing this man dying. "I seem to have heard something like that before somewhere. Anyway, it's too late for you, sunshine. You're dying and by the look of you it will take about five or ten minutes, so you have plenty of time to make peace with your maker and ponder on the folly of all this and the knowledge that I have just killed three of your brothers. Have fun."

He turned and ran hard for the beach. He knew that was where the men must have come from. He jumped his hedge and saw a figure on the beach. He could clearly see from the moonlight that the man was struggling to push a large rubber dinghy back into the water but the tide had dropped and the assassin had at least ten feet to go. Frank walked towards the swearing figure and snapped another magazine into the Mauser.

"Going somewhere?" he asked quietly.

The man spun around. He had nothing in his hands, he'd obviously thrown his gun into the boat. He was short and he was now sobbing.

"Take your hood off," said Frank. The man did so.

"Are you the one I shot in the hotel?" asked Frank.

Sobbing and crying the boy dropped to the sand on his knees. "You've shot me in the leg again and it hurts like fuck. Please, mister, it was their idea. I didn't want anything more to do with it but they said it had to be done. Please, mister."

"Get into your boat boy and go. Tell your family that it's finished and to stop this stupid nonsense. They will never get me. Do you understand?"

Still sobbing the boy got up; the tears were streaming down his cheeks. "Yes, mister, I will, I will. I'll tell them what you said." He pulled furiously at the rubber dingy until it was in the surf. He fired the engine, spun the boat around and headed out to sea. He had gone about twenty yards when the engine stopped. The boy stood up.

"What's the matter now," Frank thought and then dived for the sand as a hail of small arms fire hurtled at him from the boat. He could hear the boy screaming something at him. The bullets were hitting the sand uncomfortably close. Frank rolled over, drawing his pistol, and pumped off four shots at the dark figure in the boat.

Silence descended. The boat was drifting with the engine ticking over. There was no sign of the boy. The on shore wind drifted the boat onto the shore. The boy was lying in his own blood in the bottom of the boat. He was dead. Frank's wild shooting had hit the boy in the chest and face; he was almost unrecognisable. Frank switched off the engine and lifted it so that he could drag the boat ashore. There was a small anchor in the front so Frank dropped it into the sand and bedded it so the boat would not drift away. He looked down at the boy and shook his head in despair at the stupidity of it all. His mind switched to Kate. In a panic he turned and ran quickly back up to the house and through the front door looking for her. He stopped. The man he had shot was not there but a long smear of blood on the floor was.

"Kate. Where are you?" he shouted, his heart rising in his mouth as he ran down the hallway.

"Right behind you darling. Is it all over my hero?"

He swung around. She was standing in the kitchen doorway still holding her pistol, smiling her beautiful smile at him and then he saw her eyes widen in horror as they looked over his shoulder. It was a look that he would never ever forget. She was raising her pistol as three holes stitched their way across her chest and her eyes changed to bewilderment and shock as the explosion of the shots drove into his eardrums.

Frank spun around. The hooded man from the doorway, covered in blood, was leaning against the doorway of the hall like a drunk, trying to bring his gun to bear on Frank. Too late. Frank, screaming with rage, emptied the rest of his magazine into the man slamming him back against the wall of the hallway. The man dropped to the floor and lay still. Frank kicked his gun away and turned back to Kate who was lying on her back, her eyes staring vacantly at the ceiling. She had died instantly. He knelt down by her side and slowly put his head on her chest. Groans of despair tore out of him. He began to sob, his heart feeling as though it was dying. He knelt there crying and whispering her name, trying not to acknowledge that this beautiful girl was dead. That, after unconsciously searching for a soul mate for so long she could be so coldly taken from him. He cursed life, he cursed the god's and he cursed the Irish.

He didn't know how long he lay there with her but eventually he heard the sirens coming.

16

He managed to make it through the funeral without cracking, but when they all moved outside to view the flowers, and Jennie put her arms around him, he was nearly done for.

He held onto her as Jennie, crying, whispered private things into his ears about how she knew Kate had been so happy with him. Jennie thanked him for that. Richard stood behind his wife with tears rolling down his cheeks patting Frank on the head like a baby. Frank's children hung back, embarrassed, not knowing what to do or say to their father. They had not known this woman who appeared so important to their him.

He pulled himself together and gathered his children around him, telling Jennie and Richard that he would come over to see them at their home the next day. Eventually he began to walk away with his sons and daughter. Recognising that he was deeply distressed, his sons put their arms about their father.

"Frank, I know it's not the right time but can I have a quiet word with you?" Dick stood in front of him with two other men.

Frank and his family stopped. He'd had enough of this lot recently with their endless questions and accusations. They had been pestering him with questions for days. He glowered at Dick from underneath his eyelids. "You're right, it's not the right time so get out of our fucking way and leave me in peace." His children where shocked. They had never heard their father speak with such venom, let alone swear like that, and the look on his face frightened them. They were beginning to get to know this new man who was their father. This latest episode had rocked them to their very beings. Their father, killing five Irish republicans single-handed, had been an international story for days. Headlines had screamed from the front pages of every daily paper. 'Pro IRA assassinate Blake's girlfriend' read one. 'Blake shoots five Pro IRA assassins' read another. 'Blake in Major gun battle with the Pro IRA' and so on and every account was accompanied with photos of Frank, usually from the Brazilian episode.

Dick was used to Frank and people like him. He stood his ground. "We fully appreciate that you are upset Frank but, we have more questions that have to be answered. There's uproar at higher levels and they want heads. We wish to see you tomorrow morning for questioning again."

"Have you no compassion, can't you see my father is upset? What's wrong with you for goodness sake? Leave him be," shouted his daughter. His sons moved to protect their father.

"Chip off the old block ain't she Frank?" said Dick. "Whether you like it or not we are coming round and will have to take you in if need be."

Frank stood up to his full height and glared at Dick. "Don't you threaten me. I've had enough of you and your kind. All you are interested in is appeasing those Irish bastards who killed my woman. You take me in and I will cause the biggest uproar that you have ever seen. If you think that's a threat believe it, it's true. I will go on television, and to the press, and tell the full bloody story regardless of the cost. You won't be able to muzzle me. They are willing to pay fortunes right now for me to do just that. Co-operation. Forget it. You have no regard for my situation and I have none for yours. So go fuck yourself."

"Good on you Dad, you tell 'em." Said Jason, his eldest son.

The family turned and walked around the three men. "Let him go," said Dick. "We'll give him another couple of days then pick him up. He will have to face a trial whether he likes it or not. No one can go around killing people as he has and get away with it regardless of the situation. The vultures are already gathering."

A small figure bobbed up in front of them. It was Joe. "Sorry about this Frank but I need to talk to you. It's very important. Give me a day. When? I have just about every company on earth wanting a piece of the action now. Millions can be made Frank, millions. Come on, when?"

Without stopping the family marched towards their cars. Frank's children were surrounding and protecting him. "I'll see you in three days time Joe. I have a lot to sort out so that's the soonest I can see you. I'll come to your offices, OK? Oh, and by the way, tell Graham to keep those damn MI5 people off my back and keep me out of clink for as long as possible. I have things that need to be done."

"Of course, Frank, I'm very sorry about the way things have turned out. Very sorry. Talk to you later." Joe dropped out of sight.

The media surrounded them, shouting their questions and, for a moment, they were unable to get into their car but the small group forced their way through without saying anything. Two large men appeared from nowhere and forced the media roughly out of the way with cameras and people flying in all directions. It was his friends from Holland.

Frank smiled at them weakly and they smiled back. "Good to see you Frank. If we can be of any help give us a call. We are staying over here for a few days in case you need us." Gerhard stuffed a piece of paper into Frank's hand. His children looked in awe at these two enormous men. The media went silent for a minute with cameras turning and reporters scribbling. Then chaos broke loose again as they threw questions at Gerhard. Nobody had seen these two big men before and the wanted to know the relationship. "Who were they and how did he know Frank?" Gerhard simply smiled and moved away with his friend.

"Dad, is there no one you don't know?" asked his daughter.

"You don't know the half of it sweetheart," he said. He made a mental note to send money to these two men as Gustav had requested. He had forgotten to do that.

"You're right there Dad" she said. "But I'll tell you this, we three have been talking and before the week is out we want to know everything, and I mean everything. OK? Everything that's been going on since you went on that holiday. You are not going to hide anything from us anymore, right? After all, we are your family Dad." They had arrived at their hired limousine and slid into the comfort and privacy of the back. The chauffeur started the car and started to pull away. Frank waved to the two men and they moved off through the large crowd with the photographer's cameras flashing.

"I can't believe all this," said his son Jason. "Dad, you're like a blinking pop star. Who were those men who stopped us"?

"Security Service. They don't like you shooting the Pro IRA people nowadays you see son. It's simply not done." Frank was extremely bitter and couldn't stop. He didn't want to stop the bitter sarcasm dripping from his voice. "Its very inconvenient for them and it disrupts the process of negotiating. It ruffles feathers and will probably be made illegal before very long. Don't worry; I have them by the balls right now because public opinion is behind me. They wouldn't dare to arrest me now. The row and publicity would be too great I'm pretty sure of that. But I will not be able to keep them at bay for long and when they do come I'm sure they will want to bang me away in prison for a while. That's why I asked the three of you down for a chat. I needed to talk to you without your relevant spouses or friends around. What I want to say to you is deeply personal and is for your ears only. I only have you three and a few others who I can trust now; I have no one else I can rely on. Let's leave it until we get home." He put his finger to his lips, pointed around the car, and then to his ears to ensure that they understood the car might have been bugged.

They looked at their father with varying degrees of astonishment and lapsed into silence.

* * *

The police had in fact arrived at the scene of the gunfight very quickly that night, although Frank hadn't any idea of what was actually happening at the time his mind being completely overtaken by the death of Kate. They had been alerted by the burglar alarm and also they had been contacted by one of Frank's neighbours who had heard the gun fire and, knowing who occupied the bungalow, had put two and two together. They were totally out of their depth having never had to deal with five dead men all in one go. Dick and his men were brought into the situation at once. While they were waiting for Dick to arrive they did their best to comfort Frank but at the same time they viewed him with awe. His name was now familiar to almost everyone within the law environment. They had never met a man who had killed so many people and was not behind bars. Dick was very angry at what had happened. The carnage that had just happened on his patch was particularly embarrassing. Frank had to be pulled off him at one stage.

"You had to kill them, didn't you? Bloody hero, eh? You couldn't just walk away and leave them be, could you? Oh no, you had to come out all guns blazing. Do you realise the trouble you have caused with this rubbish tonight. By the morning the whole world will know about it, which will cause massive problems for us here and abroad. But you don't care do you?"

It was at this point that Frank had leapt at Dick in silent rage, forcing him to the floor and three men had to prise his fingers away from Dick's throat before pulling him off. Dick had never been so close to dying and could not speak for days afterwards, his throat was so badly bruised.

Frank had never felt such rage in himself and recognised that it was all getting a bit out of hand.

Another security officer took over and apologised to Frank for Dick's insensitive actions. He had the foresight to see that Frank was in a traumatised state and he called a doctor for help.

The police took Frank to London to be interviewed and the media very quickly picked up on the story. Someone, somewhere, had leaked the story and the next day it was front page news in all the major national tabloids; as well as around the world. Frank was now a worldwide celebrity and everybody wanted some of the action. Joe's offices were overwhelmed with visitors and phone calls. Joe, being the mercenary person that he was, thought that heaven was now here on earth. Everyone wanted an interview with Frank, his life story, his version of the latest happenings, anything.

Frank had phoned Graham from the cottage for his help and he had promised to be on hand as soon as Frank arrived in London. He then phoned Jennie and Richard on their boat and told them what had happened. He pleaded with them to leave the boat and come home immediately to help him. They responded saying that they would and they were back home in four hours. Frank also phoned his children and had told them the story. They could hardly believe him. It seemed so improbable. He told them to keep their heads down as the media would probably be coming for them as well and advised them that the security people would be along to help to look after them and their children. He told them that he would be back in touch as soon as possible.

As for himself he was distraught. The sight of Kate's smiling face, and then the shock of seeing the bullets stitch across her chest would not leave him. It was all so cruel. He wanted revenge and an idea began to form in his mind.

The police kept him at Scotland Yard for a full twenty four hours, questioning him relentlessly about what happened, and even slipping in questions about Amsterdam. Graham defended Frank telling him not to co-operate as he was in too much of a traumatised state to be able to answer such questions. He eventually managed to have Frank released on a very expensive bail. The police were not happy, as Frank had not been at all co-operative. As Frank was leaving Dick appeared as if from nowhere.

"You do realise that you can't get away with all this don't you Frank. We will have to have you back for more questioning, very soon."

Graham, seeing that Frank was very close to exploding, stepped between them. "I don't know who you are but I can assure you my client will not respond to bullying tactics if I can help it. If you persist in this manner I will most certainly ask questions as to your involvement in this matter of the Minister, all right?" Graham too was angry.

They walked away. "Who the hell was that man Frank? I thought the two of you were going to have a go at each other there and then. He doesn't have any love for you who ever he is."

"I'll tell you later." Frank replied.

The media was relentless in the pursuit of information. Television kept it in the main news programmes for two days and ran surveys and discussion groups as to whether individuals should be able to defend themselves in such a way under the law. Nearly ninety per cent of the answers received from the public supported Frank and his actions that night, although quite a few wanted to know why he had a gun. As far as the media was concerned this was a story that would run and run for days and they were going to milk it for all it was worth. With Joe's permission and supervision, and the reluctant agreement of the police, Frank gave one ten minute interview with Sky television. They paid half a million pounds for the interview and sent it out worldwide. The television company made a major mistake initially and put a well known Irish interviewer in front of Frank to talk to him. Within two minutes they were at loggerheads when the interviewer asked Frank how he felt about the dead men's families.

Something inside Frank snapped. He had risen to his feet, pulled off the microphone and thrown it into the interviewer's face. He then leaned over him making him cower in his chair. "Fuck them boy, how would you feel if you had the one you love killed in front of you by some crazy fucking terrorists. I would stop asking stupid fucking questions like that if I were you. Right? Now, someone round here had better get someone with some common sense and he had better be English otherwise I'm out of here."

The interviewer was changed, much to his embarrassment, as the incident was made public nationally. The questions were altered to reflect the seriousness of the incident and the impact on Frank's life; everything was fine. Frank managed to conduct himself with some dignity and handled the death of the five terrorists with candour, honesty and frankness. His telling of his girlfriend's last few moments was especially poignant and the TV broadcast was a great success for him. There were many messages of sympathy arriving for him. The reaction from the remnants of the Mulligan family in Ireland was not so good; there were further threats of revenge to Frank's life being widely forecast and, in some instances, broadcast as "imminent." When questioned by the media about his reactions to these threats he simply answered. "Let them try. I would just love them to try. I have a score to settle with them and it's not over yet." By the look on his face everyone had no doubt that he meant it.

In between all this, the security forces and the Government tried to quieten down the publicity but failed miserably. The whole thing was a disaster as far as they were concerned. They showed no compassion towards Frank, which made him all the more determined to be reactionary towards them. Questions were asked as to why he had two pistols and where he had got them from and who had authorised them. The fact that if he hadn't had them he would probably have been dead as well as Kate never seemed to occur to anyone except the members of the press and television. Many articles were written about the incident and the fact that teams of Republican hit squads could roam Britain with impunity and with murder on their minds. The Tories asked questions in parliament about the incident with particular emphasis on the fact that this could happen to anyone in authority, and that if it did, the outcome would be entirely different as the person being attacked would not have had the means to defend him or herself as Frank had been able to do.

The Labour Government gave only vague answers in return. This was noted by most of the major newspapers. Frank's cause became stronger and stronger. Joe and Graham instigated a massive public relations campaign with a view to getting the public debate on Frank's side. They were pleased when the Daily Mail took up his cause.

* * *

The limousine arrived at Jennie's and Richard's house in West Sussex; a delightfully converted barn. This was where Frank was hiding away and where he wanted to talk to his children. Jennie and Richard had arrived back before them and had tea and coffee waiting. Jennie fussed around Frank and took them all into the area they had loaned to Frank where there was a decent sized lounge. She settled them all down with cake and biscuits and then withdrew kissing Frank on the cheek as she went.

"She likes you Dad," said his daughter.

"Well, I like her. She's a lot of fun and a great comfort at the moment. I wish you three could have met Kate. In many ways she was like your mother. She had the naughtiest sense of humour and she loved me. Even though we were together for only a few weeks I knew she was going to be the one for me. It's all a great shame and such a waste of a life. That brings me to why I asked you to come with me here today."

"Kids, I'm going away." There was silence as they waited to see what else he was going to say. "The continuing threat from this crazy Mulligan family could get very serious indeed. I don't want you to become involved any more than I am already as they could quite easily come after any of you and I am fed up to the back teeth with looking over my shoulder all the time. It's time to lance the boil. I am probably going to America to learn to fly. During that time you will hear that I have crashed somewhere and died. Well, that's what the media is going to hear. Of course I won't have, I will simply have disappeared. I will find a way to turn myself into someone else with all the necessary bits and pieces such as passports and maybe a slight change of appearance or something. There's one thing I have learned over the last year and that is money will buy you anything so I'm going to get the right advice. The Americans are good at that. Besides, I don't want the British Government to know either. So there will be a period of problems from the press for you guys. Simply confirm to them that as far as you know I disappeared on a training flight but you are sure I will turn up again as I did last time, or something to that effect. That's all you need say and make sure you all tell the same story and don't embellish it either. Keep it simple."

There were gasps from all of them.

"Don't worry, I won't have actually died although the whole world will think I have. I will drop out of sight and will not be able to contact you for some considerable time. In reality, as far as you three are concerned, I might just as well have died. I will be in contact with you by another means and you will know all about it when I do. I love all three of you more than you will ever know. Now, let's get down to business."

"As you would have expected my Will is split three ways with all three of you as executors together with my solicitor. You will have to sell the house and car. I have not had time since I have been back to buy bonds and stuff like that so most of the money, some eight million I think, is quickly available."

His children looked at him in total disbelief.

"How on earth did you manage to get hold of eight million pounds Dad?" asked Jason,

"Proceeds from the sale of the treasure to the Government, interest, and I sold a few illegal diamonds in Holland. There should also be about a million coming from Richard for reasons I can't tell you about just yet and then, of course, there's Joe. He is the little guy who bounced around us as we were leaving the funeral. He is my agent, one of the smartest and most honest in the business. You don't know about it yet but he has convinced Stephen Spielberg to do a film of my life in the 'Raiders of the lost Ark' sort of style. Yeah, they will have even more material now won't they? And then there's the book. He is working on that with a ghost writer as well."

"Am I hearing right, Dad? Spielberg is going to make a film of you and a book is being written as well?" asked his daughter. "Well, I just can't believe it can you?" she asked her brothers. They shook their heads in amazement.

"So, all in all, you should be getting quite a lot of money. I will salt away a couple of million from other sources that again you don't want to know about. I will need that money to live on and to start another personality. Basically though, as far as the whole world is concerned, and you three as well, I will have simply disappeared. It's the only way out kids, I hope you will understand."

He looked at his three children. They were completely bewildered by everything and what he had just said wasn't sinking in.

"When are you going Dad?" asked his daughter.

"In about two weeks I should think," he replied. They just sat there with heads bowed not knowing what to say or do. Very soon after, they left and hugged their father as they went. "Don't go without saying goodbye properly Dad, will you?" said his daughter; tears were streaming down her cheeks. "I have only just got to know you properly and now this. It's just not fair Dad," she sobbed. He held her tightly and told her she must be brave and that he would talk to her again soon. He waved to them as they drove away. Jennie came up to him and put an arm around his shoulder. He had already told the two of them his plans.

"Don't worry, we will keep our eyes on them. They will be all right. Don't worry Frank, come on in and have some food." Food was the answer to nearly everything as far as Jennie was concerned. Frank sat down to talk to Richard. He had come to trust this man who was so different to himself.

"Richard, you have the diamonds and should make good money from them. Now, I will be needing cash now and again and will contact you from various points for monies to be forwarded, do you understand?"

"Yes, Frank, but how do you want me to handle the cash?"

"I'll transfer a couple of million pounds to a certain bank in Barbados and deposit it under another name. That will be my working capital. Anything else I need I will either call you or e-mail you." They agreed on code words for the method of contact, and agreed to talk again before Frank left.

Over the next two days he made his peace with Joe and explained that in future all monies due to him from the book, promotions and the film would go into a trust fund for his children, which Graham was organising. Joe was distraught and tried desperately to get Frank to change his mind but to no avail. Frank was a licence to make money as far as Joe was concerned and for him to leave the country and disappear was going to be calamitous. Joe had so many ideas on how to capitalise on Frank's name and exploits and now it would all go down the drain unless he worked very fast.

"Spielberg's people are insisting that he meets you Frank."

"Then you had better get in touch with him and tell him the game plan. It's within the next few weeks or not at all. I am going to America; maybe I can meet him out there. See what he says," said Frank.

He visited his solicitor and ensured that his Will was in order and that he would act as Frank's trustee. He was an old friend and completely trustworthy. His next call was to his brothers and sister. He spent some time with them explaining the situation and how impossible things had become. He promised to keep in touch from wherever he was and explained that he would probably never be able to see them again. This was a very difficult time as he was very close to all three. After leaving them he started to have his doubts as to what he was about to do. His life was here but he knew he would never be able to live it normally again. Life had thrown some strange balls at him over the last year. He recalled Sandy's words that he was going through a trial period. So what the hell was that all about and why him? Why was his life being so completely turned around? He reasoned that there was no answer to that and to simply follow the path that he felt had been laid out in front of him.

Driving back to Richard and Jennie's place a black depression descended on him. He was deeply unhappy and felt that life was really not worth living. Turning the wheel of his car he headed for Lymington and his boat. He needed solitude and the sea. He phoned Jennie on his mobile and told her where he was going.

Arriving at his home he was pleased to find it deserted. Putting his car in the garage he walked inside to where so much had happened. Richard and Jennie had arranged to have the house cleaned and put in order, and it was immaculate. Rather than brood about seeing Kate killed here he piled his sailing things and his passport into a bag and left, locking the house behind him.

Deciding to walk the three miles to the marina he set off. He was the wrong side of the river but knew he could get a water taxi across; that would save a mile anyway. It was late afternoon and the evenings were starting to draw in as autumn approached. He walked looking about him at the beautiful English countryside with the neat houses with their neat gardens and realised that was never going to be for him. Kate and he had talked about their future and they had chatted happily about gardening together. He had been looking forward to all that. Frank was deep in thought when the sound of a car's horn startled him. An old Wolsey, circa the late 1940s, pulled along side.

"Care for a lift old boy?" The old man wearing a deerstalker hat, tweed jacket and handlebar moustache and leaning across the passenger seat must have been eighty if he was a day He was grinning at Frank. "You look as though you are going to the marina. Well, so am I so I can save you a bit of time. Want to come?" he asked.

Frank smiled at the man and was grateful for the distraction from his morose thoughts and the company. "Yes, thank you, that would be just great," he replied and piled into the passenger seat throwing his bag onto the back seat. The old man selected first gear and the car pulled smoothly away with a howl coming from the gearbox and the back axle. "Car's getting a bit old like me but should see me out without too much money having to be spent on it," he said in way of explanation. "The name's George Cuthbert by the way. I know who you are so don't bother to introduce yourself. You're that fella who shot all those bloody IRA chappies the other night. Bloody good show old boy. Would have loved to have been there to give you a hand. Sorry about your lady though. Everyone around here is. Tragedy, bloody tragedy. Sorry to talk so much, I have a tendency to do that."

Frank was holding on for grim death. The car was being hurtled through the country lane at a ridiculous speed that even he, in a modern sports car, wouldn't consider let alone this old monster with hardly any brakes to speak of. "That's all right, George. It's nice of you to give me a lift. I appreciate it," he shouted above the din. He doubted whether they would ever actually make it to the marina if the old boy kept this speed up.

"So, where are you going today then? You've got that rather lovely 38' Humber haven't you, the blue one? I've always liked those boats. They have wonderful lines and have the reputation of being able to go through anything anywhere."

Frank laughed. The man was a breath of fresh air to him even though he couldn't get a word in edgeways.

"In answer to your questions. George, I haven't made up my mind frankly," he shouted above the noise." I suddenly had the desire to get out to sea and have some peace. I haven't had much of that lately, and yes the boat is an absolute delight."

"Thought so," said George. He glanced across at Frank. "What you need is a bloody good drink, old boy. We will make a slight detour. I belong to a small gentlemen's club near here. It's very select, old boy, very select. No riff raff. Fancy a quick snifter?" He swung the wheel at the next corner and the car slid effortlessly in a four wheel drift into another road, its tyres screaming in protest. The old boy was a very good driver but if there was another car or a tractor coming the other way they would be mincemeat.

Frank laughed out loud at the man. God, it was so good to laugh. He hadn't heard anyone talk like this for years, and it sparked memories of his childhood. He certainly hadn't heard that word 'snifter' since his father had been alive. Why not? He wasn't in any hurry to go anywhere really.

"That sounds just the ticket, George. In fact the more I think about it the more I fancy a couple of good snifters."

A wide smile went across the old man's face and he twirled his moustache with one hand. "Only a couple of miles down this road, won't take long. Introduce you to a few old friends of mine too."

They were now hurtling down a narrow country road, which was only wide enough for one car. Frank could see they were running parallel to the sea, which was just over some sand dunes to their left. He glanced at the old boy who was driving the old car as though it was a racing car. He was relaxed in his seat and stroking the steering wheel with practised hands but his concentration was total. "Some old geezer this one," thought Frank.

"Here we are," said George and he swung the old Wolsey into a driveway with the tyres howling in protest. The driveway opened into a small car park and George braked to a stop sending shingle flying. A lovely old three storey Georgian mansion stood in front of them surrounded by lawns and rhododendrons. In the car park was a selection of cars that made Frank's jaw drop. Jaguars, Lagonda, Daimlers, Bentleys and Porches; all of which were vintage.

"Some of the boys are here. That's good. Want to introduce you. Follow me." Frank got out of the car to follow behind George and smiled to see that George was wearing plus fours as well. The man was straight out of history, he thought. Even with his long legs Frank had to almost trot to keep up with the old man as he strode into the house.

They entered the mansion via the vast front door and into a beautiful long hallway panelled in a dark mahogany. Old dark brown Chesterfield settees lined the walls both side of the hallway. "Where's that bloody fella Gordon?" he roared. A man seemed to glide out from nowhere. "Here, Sir George. Sorry not to have been waiting for you but we have a small crisis in the kitchen." How are you Sir, good to see you?"

Frank was a little startled. "Sir George, eh," he thought.

The man flicked his eyes at Frank who felt that he had just been measured and weighed up in a second. They were the strangest eyes he had ever seen. Jet black and very large with long thin black eyebrows to match; very oriental. The man had slicked back black hair with a very high forehead and prominent cheekbones. Frank logged him as definitely eastern European. He was almost as tall as Frank.

"I'm just fine, thank you, Gordon. You're looking as evil as ever." The man smiled, obviously relishing what to him was a compliment from a man he respected. George continued. "I want to introduce you to a man we may well see a lot of and I want you to treat him with the same respect as you do me. His name is Frank Blake."

The man called Gordon turned, looked straight into Frank's eyes for a moment and then bowed slightly. Frank felt a shiver go down his spine. Those eyes were, without a shadow of a doubt, the strangest he had ever seen. Frank felt as though he had just looked straight into the depths of the unknown. He shrugged off the feeling as the man spoke to him.

"Mr Blake, it's an honour to meet you. Obviously I have heard all about you. You are most welcome here." Gordon turned back to George. "What's your pleasure this evening, Sir?"

"We just want a bloody good drink so get out of my way man and let us get to the bar." George strode off down the hallway shouting, "Come along Frank, this way." Frank nodded to Gordon who bowed again and ran after George who was disappearing around the corner of the hallway.

He followed George into a large lounge. There was an enormous bar running down one side of the room and several men were leaning against it drinking. The room was filled with deep luxurious leather armchairs and low mahogany coffee tables. A roaring wood fire burnt in an enormous fireplace. The room was warm, comfortable, and smelled of whisky. It instantly felt like home to Frank.

George was roaring again. "Listen up, everyone. We have a new friend and I want to introduce him to you. Gather round now, gather round. You, Boyles, get off your fat arse and get over here. You too, Buckles." There were about twenty men in the room, most of whom must have been in their seventies or eighties with a sprinkling in their sixties. Frank felt like a child in their company.

George stood with his back to the bar. He was a very tall man well over Frank's height of 6'1" and still straight backed. "Gentlemen, I have a surprise for you. I want to introduce you to a man after our own heart, a man of whom we were only talking two days ago, and a blood brother. Shake the hand please of a true Englishman, Frank Blake."

Frank felt embarrassed but the look on the men's faces changed all that. There were a couple of whoops and some cheers and they crowded around him, pushing and shoving each other in an effort to shake his hand and to say hello. Every handshake was firm and strong. "All right, all right, that's enough now," shouted George. We have come here for a drink so if any of you fancy buying us one then we won't say no." George winked at Frank. "Free drinks all evening now, my boy," he said.

The drinks came fast and furious. Frank followed George and started on whisky, and it stayed that way all evening. The men behaved like old friends immediately and there was much joking and leg pulling. They were dying to hear the real story of his recent experiences and although he tried to keep it brief they would have none of it and asked so many questions that it was impossible. After about half an hour of this grilling George called a halt to it.

"Let's leave the poor boy alone now, Gentlemen. He's been through a tough time, as we all have, and he needs some peace."

George was the type of man that Frank needed right now, jocular, intelligent and good company. He had apparently been a fighter pilot in the Second World War and stayed in the RAF until the mid-sixties retiring as a wing commander. "Could have gone higher, old boy, but I was always in trouble and refused to 'brown nose' as they wanted you to, as simple as that."

"You flew Spitfires?" Frank asked, his mouth dropping open. This man was a true hero in Frank's eyes if he had.

"Spitfires, Hurricanes, Typhoons; and the best of the lot, the Mustang, bloody good crate that was. Fast, tough and tremendous fire power. Jerry didn't like it when we went after them with the Mustang, did they boys?" Several of the older men around them laughed at the memories. "Quite a lot of us here are from the old days you see Frank."

Frank became lost in the world of these old men and his problems seemed nothing compared to what some of them had been through. In no time at all the evening went by and suddenly he realised it was close to midnight. He was completely stoned.

"George, I'm as drunk as a skunk. For God's sake get me a cab so I can get back to my boat."

"I won't hear of it, old boy, won't hear of it. Will we lads?" He asked the question of the remaining hard core drinkers who could hardly stand. "It's tuck up in bed time Frank. We have spare rooms for such an emergency and certain comforts as well. Gordon," he roared. Gordon came into the room. "Yes, Sir George?"

"Mr Blake needs a room for the night. His bag is in my car if you would be so kind as to attend to that for me, Gordon. I might suggest that certain comforts are laid on for him as well. Thank you Gordon, I will need the same in about thirty minutes."

"What are the certain comforts then, George?" slurred Frank.

"Oh, don't worry about that. Just leave it all to me. See you in the morning, Frank. Sleep well dear boy."

Frank felt Gordon take his arm and support him. For some reason his legs weren't working too well so he let Gordon take him to a small lift by the stairs. He saw the red light inside wink to "1" and the doors opened. Gordon supported him to a door and knocked. The door was opened by a vision in a light pink chiffon dressing gown. She was tall, blonde, and very attractive. Frank tried desperately to focus but couldn't quite make it.

"I have a gentleman for you Lisa. His name is Frank Blake and it's orders from Sir George to look after him as he is a personal friend," said Gordon.

"Frank Blake as in 'the' Frank Blake?" the girl asked.

"Yes, so look after him. It's precious cargo, Lisa," said Gordon handing Frank over to the girl he shut the door.

All Frank could feel was warm soft flesh. He wanted to go to the toilet desperately and told the girl so. When he had finished, she came into the bathroom and washed his face and hands. She virtually carried him back to the bedroom. She made him lay on the bed while she took his clothes off.

He was aware of what was going on but was completely incapable of doing anything about it. He felt very happy. "Lady, just roll me into bed and leave me. I could no more take advantage of you than fly right now."

"Don't you worry about that, Frank, leave everything to me," she said, and that's the last he remembered.

17

HE WOKE THE NEXT morning to see the sun streaming in through the open window. He felt warm and snug in the deep bed. The girl's warm body was tucked along side his. "Morning," she whispered. "How do you feel?"

He turned his spinning head slowly to see the vision lying next to him. Her eyes were hooded and fixed on him.

"Head's throbbing a bit but otherwise I'm fine," he lied.

"I'll fix that. Hold on a minute." She threw the bedcovers back and rose out of the bed and strode naked to the bathroom. He gaped. Her body was fantastic. When she came back holding a glass and some tablets and nothing else, he gaped again.

"Take these and you will be fine in about an hour," she said. She climbed back in the bed and moved her body against his. Her hands moved to his groin and his body reacted like fury.

"Mmmmm, well you can't be too ill if you can rise to the moment as quickly as that," she said.

He let her work him over and make love to him as he simply gave way to the lust.

He was making love to her for the second time when there was a banging on the door. "Frank my boy, get out of bed and leave that girl alone this instant. We have things to do. See you downstairs for some breakfast in thirty minutes."

Lisa wrapped her long legs around his back and wouldn't let him out. "Not until you have sorted me one more time. I haven't had great sex like this for ages so give it to me Frank Blake, now," she said. He didn't really believe her but carried out her instructions. The way she moved and groaned excited him so much that he couldn't hold back and he came with a roaring rush.

He was fifteen minutes late meeting George for breakfast and Lisa was right. He felt a lot better. He heard George before he saw him. The breakfast room was about half full with most of the men he met last night.

"Over here, Frank, over here," bellowed George from across the room. Everyone cheerfully said hello or good morning to him and he felt that he was among old friends. "How strange" he mused. "Only met them last night and they act so pleasantly towards me." He had never experienced anything like it before.

"Had a good night, dear boy? So did I." George always appeared to answer his own questions. He leaned across the table in a conspiratorial manner and whispered loud enough for the whole room to hear. "What do you think of young Lisa then my boy? Lovely lady is young Lisa, can't ever have enough of that young lady. Too much for me I can tell you. I've told her several times; in my youth I would have given her a run for her money. Oh, yes."

Frank was embarrassed and at the same time curious. "I had a wonderful evening and morning. I can't say much about the night because I can't remember a thing, but this morning was pretty damn good. What the hell is this place George anyway?"

"It's a Gentlemen's Club, Frank, for the more discerning and older man. Nobody under sixty comes here. That's a rule so you are very privileged and we have decided to make an exception for you." he roared with laughter. "Eat up, dear boy. You will need your strength today. Thought I would take you out sailing in my little yacht. We must be away in about sixty minutes if we are going to catch the tide."

Frank stuffed down two eggs and five rashers of bacon with mushrooms and two cups of tea before he was literally dragged from the table by George. Gordon was standing in the reception with his sailing bag all packed. "I have put one or two extras in there for you, Sir. I hope you don't mind," he said to Frank. Those eyes pierced into his and again Frank felt a strange feeling. Gordon's face broke into a smile. "I do hope you had a good time Sir, we try our best."

Frank stopped in front of Gordon and accepted his bag. "I can play this guy at his game," he thought. He dropped his bag; he took Gordon's hand in both of his and saw a startled look come into the man's dark eyes. "I would just like to say that it has been a pleasure Gordon. Thank you for your quite exceptional hospitality and would you please extend that to the young lady. I didn't quite have the time to say thank you properly. I have enjoyed myself enormously and look forward to coming back." Frank let go of the man's hand and picked up his sail bag again.

"Yes, yes of course you have Frank. For goodness sake let's go. We can always come back again tonight. May see you then Gordon dear boy." George strode off towards his car with Frank struggling to keep up. As the car sped off down the narrow lane Frank said. "George, it's been a pleasure knowing you, you old reprobate. How do you manage to keep up this incredible pace for God's sake?"

"Death, dear boy, death. As far as I am concerned it's just around the bloody corner and always has been but it's not going to get me yet. Too much to do, too much to do, too many lovely ladies to make love to, too much wonderful food to eat and too much whisky to drink. There's never enough time dear boy, never enough time. Anyway, I want to have a chat with you today. I have a feeling about you and I'm worried. Seen it many times before in the faces of my fighter pilot boys. It's on your face and it shouldn't be. Not with your experiences anyway. You're a one off Frank, a one off." He spun the wheel gently and the old car careered past another coming the other way. There couldn't have been a coat of paint between them but the old man never so much as ruffled a feather.

"We are going to have a good time today and I am going to give you a few words of advice my boy. Yes, a few words of advice. That's what you need." George's voice dropped an octave and he appeared to mumble to himself. "Should have had you in my squadron, Frank my boy, and you are now. You are in my squadron now and it's my duty to ensure that you are able to look after yourself when mixing it with the enemy." He stopped talking and a grim expression set across his face.

"Is this old man completely off his rocker or what? Is there something else here?" Frank thought. "Have I been guided to him and if so why?" He settled himself down into the car seat and smiled to himself as the hedgerows streaked by. His life was obviously in the hands of someone or something else and all he had to do was roll along with it and respond whenever it was necessary. This was going to be very interesting.

18

He looked up at the main sail reaching for the sky and the small white clouds seemed to be playing with the top of the mast. The boat heaved over another large wave and skewered through the next one. A burst of spray came back over the great bow and Frank ducked down in the cockpit.

George laughed. "What a wonderful day for a sail my boy, I'm glad you came. It's nice to have company sometimes."

George's 'little' boat was a 47ft Swan twin masted Yawl. He had it rigged for single handed use and even in his late age was completely comfortable handling this beautiful fast yacht on his own. Frank felt relaxed and sipped at his hot brandy laden coffee that George had brought with him in a flask. The sea flashed by and Frank glanced at the log. He watched the needle hovering on nine knots. It seemed very fast but that was a mystery that always intrigued him. Twenty knots in the Humber didn't seem all that fast but ten knots in this magnificent beast seemed as though they were approaching the speed of sound. He glanced at George. He had his head back as though he was smelling the sea air, and he probably was. It was all quite glorious. Frank watched the Needles off the Isle of Wight come up and slowly recede behind them. "He's heading for Poole," Frank thought.

"What's your pleasure Frank? Where would you like to go dear boy?" George asked.

Frank didn't reply at once. He looked out to the mainland some ten miles away on their starboard side. "I'm not in a hurry to go anywhere, am I?" he thought.

"How long have you got George?" he asked.

"Probably about five years," George quipped.

"Then let's go to Dartmouth. I have always wanted to enter the River

Dart from the sea and there are some great pubs down there. How long should it take? Two days steady sailing?"

"Yes, about that. Dartmouth it is then Frank. I haven't been there for quite a few years myself but it shouldn't be difficult. I'll leave the navigation to you dear boy. I'll just keep the mainland on my right and we can't go wrong. Charts are all down below so when you are ready have a look and give me a straight and steady course. The wind is perfect. Just off the port bow. Go to it my beauty." He said the last sentence to the boat, which seemed to respond and he felt the slight surge of extra power as George tightened the mainsail.

They agreed a four hour on and four hour off watch and Frank left George to it. He slipped down the companionway and searched for the charts. He found the radio and switched it on. Humphrey Littleton had a jazz programme on and was concentrating on the traditional jazz era. Chris Barber pumped out an early classic of his and Frank was off. Boogieing around the cabin he lost himself in the wonderful old music. George stuck his head into the companionway, saw what Frank was doing, shook his head and retreated to the cockpit.

They had a comfortable voyage to Dartmouth and Frank found George to be a great companion telling many funny stories from his past. In a similar fashion Frank opened up and told George all that had happened to him over the last year. George knew some of it, of course, but when he heard the details he was amazed. The killing bits didn't disturb him. He had done all that stuff himself during his time in the RAF.

They arrived in Dartmouth and were instructed by the Dartmouth harbour master to tie up alongside the old town quay. This was indeed an honour as this was where the Mayflower stayed before setting out for America some two hundred years before.

Frank had enjoyed the sail and a new plan began to form in his mind. That evening they were to be found in a small pub near to the quay tucking into bangers and mash with relish, and supping the local ale. The beams were black with age and the ceiling low. It could easily have been two hundred years previously. Small groups of visitors were scattered about eating and drinking while the locals were all tucked up close to the bar. George was experimenting with a particularly strong local beer and Frank had noticed some of the locals nudging each other with quiet glee. He watched George with alarm at the speed with which he drank his beer. It was obviously a game the locals played with visiting yachties and they were waiting for some reaction. They were disappointed because George carried on chatting without a hint of a problem. Four pints later his eyes were still as clear as a bell.

George raised his glass to eye level and squinted at the dark golden liquid. "Bloody good stuff this my boy. This is real beer, not your namby bloody pamby stuff knocked out by the big breweries today. Reminds me of the beer we drank in Kent during the war. Now that was good stuff. Could never drink more than eight of those though. Used to knock me out just like that." George never spoke quietly and Frank saw that the locals had heard. A few heads were shaken. They knew with George they had picked on the wrong one this time.

Frank discussed his new idea with George. "That is one hell of a boat you've got there, George What about if I bought myself one of these Swans, could that take me off to the Canaries and then to the Caribbean. Could I do that on my own?"

George looked at Frank. "My boy, I think you could do anything you set your mind to but what you have to remember is that the sea is a dangerous place and one stupid mistake could cost you your life. You are talking of some 6,000 miles of sailing. Tiredness is the killer if you are on your own out at sea and not used to it. Personally I would hire a skipper and a couple of crew and do it the easy way. They would ensure that you arrived wherever you wanted to go in relative safety. The rest would be up to you." George paused and looked at Frank with his rheumy gimlet eyes.

"Thinking of hiding away in the Caribbean are we, old boy?"

Frank felt a little stupid but replied. "Maybe, George, maybe. There's not much that can get past you, you old bugger is there? Its just that I feel that if I can escape to somewhere such as the Caribbean, I can still have a life and quite a good one without the problems I am having here. I'm warming to the idea, George, I'm warming to the idea, the more I think about it, and the more beer I drink. Let's have another."

For the next three days and nights they talked through Frank's plan and they polished it all the way back to Lymington. By the time they arrived back at their home port they had already located three boats that would do the job, all within a hundred miles of each other. Out of the three Frank eventually chose what was going to be his home for the next few years.

The man really did not want to sell his boat having had it since new eight years ago, but the break up of his marriage was forcing his hand. "Chantelle" was his pride and joy and the condition of the boat showed this. He had spent many thousands of pounds on the boat over the years and it was fitted out with the very latest style Kevlar sails along with every electronic gadget imaginable. Long range fuel tanks and a powerful 150hp Volvo marine engine ensured fast cruising if there was no wind and it had been fitted out in a similar fashion to George's boat for single-handed sailing. Frank loved it at first sight and George's endorsement finally confirmed the deal. Frank paid the man with a banker's draft without quibbling at the price.

They began to provision the boat, and one of the first projects was to have the inside painted white. The heat that would be generated by the dark stained mahogany wood, when in the tropics, would be unbearable but the white would reflect the heat and make life a lot cooler. The boat was hauled out and given two coats of special antifouling. The keel was taken off and filled with a further 100lb of lead to make it stiffer to sail in heavy seas, the base was rounded and thickened with many layers of fibreglass and formed into the design of a pear drop. The thickening was to prevent too much damage when contacting reefs, and the latter to increase speed. Within four weeks the boat was ready.

19

Frank had been keeping as low a profile as possible and had put his house on the market for sale together with his treasured car and Humber powerboat. He had been staying at the club incognito, each night savouring the pleasures of Lisa. He was very lucky. The word quickly spread among his new found friends that he was selling his house, boat and car, and two members approached him saying they were interested. He sold them everything at the asking price. Frank had his suspicions that George's hand might have instigated the sales but he feigned innocence with a hurt expression.

Frank had decided to let his daughter and sons clear out the house and to put everything into store, but against his better judgement decided to clear out the boat himself. Choosing what he thought was a quiet time of the day one lunchtime he slipped quietly into the marina with George keeping him company and walked down the pontoon to the boat. Piling everything into black plastic bags, and then into a trolley, he closed up the boat for the last time and started to wheel the trolley back down the pontoon towards the car park. At the end of the pontoon three men were waiting, one of whom was Dick.

"Now where would you be going on such a lovely day then Frank, and who the hell are you?" the latter being directed at George.

From what Frank had told him over the last few weeks George pretty well knew who these men were.

"Fancy meeting you here Dick," said Frank lightly. "I thought there was a strange smell about the place, haven't seen you since the funeral. Let me introduce you to my friend and colleague Sir George Cuthbert DSO, DFC and KC. George, this is Dick Elson of Her Majesty's Government, some department or other. I have never found out which but he does act as though it is a very important department. Whatever he is supposed to do he's not very good at it. Anything we can do for you Dick"?

The sarcastic tone of Frank's introduction rubbed a raw nerve with Dick. These two men did not like each other one bit now.

"We have been looking for you for some time Frank. We've heard some strange stories about you looking for another boat, a sailing boat no less, and a big one to boot. Going away are we, because you had better think again if you are? There is to be a preliminary hearing regarding the killing of the five men at your house and it would not be appreciated if you disappeared, if you catch my drift! In fact it would be seriously frowned upon, as it was you who did the killing."

"I think you are out of touch, chum. My lawyers have informed me that there is no charge being put to me and that the Crown Prosecution Service is not making a case against me. I understand that this has all been agreed at a high level, so perhaps you had better go back and check it out with your masters sunshine." Said Frank, deliberately being rude.

Dick ignored Frank's taunt. "The Government is not best pleased with you Frank. The repercussions of that night are still reverberating all the way to Ireland and back and have caused all sorts of problems. You're just a psychopathic killer as far as I am concerned and there was no valid reason for you to slaughter those men in that fashion just because of a bloody woman. So, I want you to report to Lymington nick each day until I am satisfied, either way, as to whether charges are being made against you or not. This could well take up to two months. I will want to know where you are staying in the meantime and that you aren't carrying a gun anymore. You're not, Frank are you because if you are it's the nick for you right now? Search him boys and all that stuff he's got there."

The two men moved forward and George stepped between them and Frank before Frank could answer.

George drew himself up to his full height and growled very loudly at Dick in his beautiful cultured voice. "You had better stop right there young man. I know who you are boy. You're one of Richard Gardner's lackeys and I have to tell you that I have very little respect for him or anyone who works for him, he's an absolute wanker of a man, does this country a lot of damage. Now I want you to listen to me very carefully. If you haven't got a warrant then don't take one step closer. All of this equipment is mine and if you so much as touch this trolley without a warrant I will have you skinned alive and then tarred and feathered. I will also pursue the matter to the very top in Whitehall, let alone the newspapers. In the meantime, you have my permission to call Gardner now and mention my name. We will wait while you do so."

Dick was startled at both the tone and volume of Sir George's voice and also by the fact that he knew his boss. That was supposed to be a tightly kept secret. He had heard of Sir George, of course, but had never met him. Everyone knew George locally and it was well known that he could wield tremendous influence and had very powerful connections. He was not a man to trifle with. Dick knew that.

Sir George turned and looked hard into Frank's face and shook his head in warning. He knew and recognised the anger that was boiling there by the way Frank's cheeks were flushed and the darkness of his eyes. He wasn't usually impressed any more by anyone and he had seen many brave men over the years, but this man could send a shiver down his spine. He had no doubt, that when pushed into a corner, Frank could be extremely dangerous and unpredictable. He had proved that he could kill with no thought for the consequences. George had known men like that before. They would be the most charming of companions and great fun to be with but in certain situations not the type of man to be around when provoked into anger. Besides, Dick had just insulted Frank's dead girlfriend and George knew from the look on Frank's face that he was on the edge. It was his considered opinion that this Elson fella was trying to prompt Frank into a fight so that he could then put him away. It was a very dangerous game to play when dealing with Frank. There was also the problem that lying deep in the clothes in the trolley was Frank's personal pistol and 100 rounds of 9mm ammunition.

Dick looked at Sir George and then flicked out his mobile and dialled a number. Telling his men to watch George and Frank he turned away and spoke softly into the phone. The conversation didn't last long.

"It would appear that the feeling is mutual Sir. Sir Richard sends his regards and says that you are free to go. He will however wish to speak to you later and knows how to get hold of you. Now please let Frank speak for himself. Where are you staying Frank?"

Frank had had time to cool down. "With Sir George, actually, so if you want me that's where I'll be; but just send round the police next time. I don't appreciate being threatened by a nonentity like you. Come on George. Let's go." Frank picked up the handles of the trolley and walked straight at the three men. They broke away and let them both through.

"Don't you worry Frank. We are watching your every move and will be calling if you try to make a break." Dick called after him trying to get in the last word.

Frank stopped. George's hand gripped Frank's arm. "He's trying to get you to react, Frank. Keep calm and walk away. Come along, let's go."

Frank gave himself the pleasure of flashing a look of pure hatred over his shoulder at Dick and did as he was told.

"I think that's one very dangerous man Sir," said one of Dick's men. "I thought you had him at one point but I wasn't looking forward to what he might do. How many of those Mulligan boys has he killed now?"

Dick was looking thoughtfully after Frank and Sir George and it was some moments before he answered the question. "Eight I think. I could be wrong it may be more. I can't remember and it's not only the Mulligans he has killed. There are a few questions Interpol would like to ask him about something that went down in Holland but there's no firm evidence that he was there. We just suspect he was. There's something about him that brings out the worst in me. You are quite right Jim, someone who can kill eight armed men without getting hurt himself can only be regarded as bloody dangerous. I think he is hot-headed and totally unpredictable. If he is still carrying a gun he's a bomb waiting to go off. We simply can't have him wandering around like this. He was on the edge, all right, just now when I taunted him about his dead girlfriend. I really thought he was going to go for it and I don't know what would have been the end result either. Certainly someone would have got seriously hurt, that's for sure, but it would have been the end for him. Sir George is a very shrewd old man and certainly saved his bacon. He's lucky to have him around. I wonder how that started. We will have to do a little digging there, methinks."

Frank had no intention of reporting to the local police station and told George so. "What he said cannot be legal George. He is not a policeman and I haven't been served with a court order so that instruction was very strange. I will contact my own lawyer now and clarify things. I think what all this means, George, is that I leave very soon and very quietly."

They were sitting together in front of a roaring fire in the main lounge of the club sipping Scotch. Frank was comfortable in George's company regardless of the thirty-five year age difference. George had a very mature and yet paradoxically a young personality. The girls loved him because he was considerate and kind to them and naughty at the same time. As far as they were concerned he could do no wrong and so, usually, he dallied with one particular girl at the club at least three times a week. When tackled on this point by a very curious Frank he had admitted with a smile that he 'still fired on all eight cylinders'!

They were both sad at their imminent parting. For Frank it was particularly difficult. He did not make male friends easily and yet this man had taken him under his wing and they had become firm friends. George promised to pop over and see him two or three times a year wherever he might be.

"I have employed a young man on your behalf. He is to be your skipper Frank. His brief is to get you to where you want to be, in one piece. He has vast experience and has done the single handed Atlantic crossing as well as the 'Round the World' so he knows a thing or two about boats. Take no notice of his age Frank, he's just very good. He has his girlfriend with him as one crew and a friend of hers is coming too who is to be cook. They will take you to the Caribbean and then leave whenever you want. There are a few surprises on board for you and you will find them in time." George paused. "I will certainly miss you Frank. Things seem to happen when you are around and life is going to be very dull and boring from now on. If you get into any trouble where you are going you will phone me won't you, dear boy? Knowing you, I am pretty darn sure you will find trouble, either that or it will find you."

"Of course I will George. I have to be honest with you though and say that I hope it doesn't find me. I really could do with some quiet times; I have some healing to do. Now, this crew, when can I meet them?"

"The day after tomorrow would be a good idea. They wish to have tomorrow to check the provisions we put on board and to look the boat over as they may wish to make some alterations or something. I thought that was a good idea and agreed on your behalf, of course, Frank. I have informed them that we shall all meet up on the boat at 10 a.m. on Friday morning. How does that suit you?"

"That will be fine, George. Now, I have a surprise for you. I have invited four very dear friends of mine to dinner here tomorrow night. I won't tell you who they are now but be prepared for a nice surprise. They should be here about four tomorrow afternoon and will need to stay the night so just make sure you are here and tell that freaky Gordon that I will want him to pull out all the stops in the kitchen. In fact I will tell him myself. Give him one of your famous calls George."

"One day when it's more appropriate I will tell you all about our

Gordon, dear boy. There's more there than meets the eye. GORDON," George bellowed.

Gordon appeared as though from nowhere. "You wanted me Sir George?"

"Mr Blake wants a word with you Gordon, so pay attention and whatever he wants ensure that he gets it."

Frank got up from the table and took Gordon aside, and explained about the following evening. They stood together in deep conversation for some ten minutes and then Gordon nodded to Frank and moved silently away.

"What's all the secrecy about then Frank my boy?" asked Sir George.

"I can't tell you that or it wouldn't be a surprise, would it? You will just have to wait and see," said Frank.

He spent another hectic night in the arms of Lisa. She was a highly sexed young woman. Frank, even though in his forties, was a relatively young man compared with some of the other guests who stayed there and she relished the fact that Frank was as energetic and interested in sex as she was. She knew she had met her match at last though and told Frank so. He told her he had to leave soon and she cried.

"I want you to promise to keep in contact with me, Frank, even if it's on high days, low days, birthdays or whatever." As he wiped away her tears he suggested that maybe once or twice a year she could come out and stay with him on the yacht, wherever he might be. She smiled at him through her tears and made him promise he would do that.

The next day he played a round of golf with George and two of his buddies, and they joked and laughed their way around the course. After a few beers in the clubhouse, Frank let George drive him back to the club so that they could both freshen up before his visitors arrived.

They were both waiting on the steps. At four thirty precisely, two taxis drove up the drive to the magnificent front doors of the old Georgian mansion. Two very beautiful and excited females erupted from the first one screaming and shouting Frank's name. Liz and Josie were back in town and they tore up the steps and enveloped Frank in kisses. George was looking on in stunned amazement. While they were chattering and hugging Frank, Jennie and Richard climbed a little more sedately from the second taxi; George went down to greet them and introduce himself.

Frank was just as excited to see the two girls as they were to see him and the conversations were running fast and furious between them as they tried to make up for lost time.

"Hold on a minute you two. Wait a bit. I want to introduce you all to a very new and dear friend of mine. This old geezer, with his plus fours and tweedy jacket, is Sir George Cuthbert, known to his friends as George. Take a bow George, and let me introduce you all properly inside over a glass or two." He turned around and jumped. Gordon was standing right behind him and his strange eyes were fixed on the two girls.

"Hi Gordon. Ladies and Gentleman, may I introduce Gordon? He solves all problems and has arranged for you to have a wonderful evening. Say hello, Gordon. This is Liz and that's Josie, and that's Jennie and that's Richard."

The guests all chorused their hellos and for the first time Frank noticed that Gordon was completely thrown.

"Your guests are lovely people Sir, and I am honoured that you have introduced me to them. The ladies are all particularly beautiful."

"Are you including me in that statement young man, because if you are I'm coming up there and giving you a kiss?" said Jennie.

"Of course I am Madam," he said.

"Stop flirting with my ladies and get off and do your stuff Gordon. Come on, George, bring them all in and let's have a drink." Frank looped his arms around the two girls and marched into the hallway, down the long corridor, and into the lounge with them chattering away into his ear. George, Jennie and Richard followed along behind.

The reaction to Liz and Josie when they entered the lounge was predictable. All the old boys jumped to their feet and wanted to be introduced. The two girls were of course instantly recognisable because of their modelling, television and film work.

When the ruckus had died down a little Frank introduced George again.

"This crazy old man saved my bacon when I was at a very low ebb, he has restored my sanity and given me direction. Tonight I have surrounded myself with my most precious friends and just wanted to show you all how much I appreciate your friendship and what you have done for me."

"Don't be such a whingeing shower Frank," said George. "We all like you and recognise what is really there underneath all that action man stuff that you try to project; and we love you all the more because of it."

Liz wrapped herself around Frank and looked up into his eyes. All the old men in the room who were watching, gaped in envy. "This man saved our lives and then brought us back to civilisation again. I will love him forever for how he looked after us in that terrible place in the jungle. We could have died a hundred times but we survived and it's all down to Frank." She kissed him on the cheek again.

"Yup, and if I wasn't married I would be flashing my knickers at him right now because he's my sort of man. The only problem is that he's a bloody Pom," said Josie. Everyone roared with laughter.

That set the tone of the evening and they were soon ushered into the dining room with the girls sitting either side of Frank. They were entranced with George as he turned on the flattery and 'old world' charm. He told them a few of his old stories, which everyone enjoyed. It wasn't what he told them but the way he could weave a story and make everyone feel as though they were actually there. He was a master storyteller.

Gordon and his staff surpassed themselves that night with the food and wine; soon everyone was more than a little merry. The three girls were fascinated with Gordon and the way he looked. Josie especially, who commented that she had never seen anyone like him before in her life and, although he looked quite weird, and dangerous, he was obviously a very nice man. Jennie and Liz pressured Sir George to tell them all about himself but Sir George was surprisingly reticent and declined by saying that the story would have to wait for another day, as it was long and complicated. This made everyone even more curious and the girls, realising there was something fairly serious here, stopped their questioning and changed the subject.

Richard and Jennie watched and listened with great amusement to every story of the trio's escapades. They had never met the two international beauties before and found them refreshing and quite normal. The bond between all five of them was Frank. Jennie and Richard were very sorry to have heard that he was going abroad. They liked him and his company but they had also seen a change in him over the last few weeks and understood completely why he was doing this.

Liz turned and carefully addressed herself to Jennie.

"Josie and I were very sorry indeed when we heard about your sister, Jennie. It was such a tragic situation and at least Frank killed the bastard who did it. When we heard that Frank had found a new lady we were very happy for him. It is all so sad. I do hope you don't mind me saying this because Josie and I are very close to Frank and anything that affects him affects us. We are both so very sorry."

Jennie replied, "That's very kind of you to say so Liz. We miss her desperately, of course, and we know Frank does too although they had such a short time together. Never mind, let's enjoy ourselves tonight and try to forget it."

By the time midnight had arrived everyone was more than a little drunk. George got to his feet and was swaying slightly.

"Ladies and Gentleman, and Frank; I wish to propose a toast, but before I do I want to say something. I am pleasantly inebriated tonight and I am, what you would describe as, an old man. Even so, I have seen many things in this life, both good and bad. Tonight I have made some new friends. It is not many times in one's life that you can say that but, yes by Jove, I have made some new friends. Richard and Jennie. I find your company delightful and I love you both. We will remain good friends. Liz and Josie. What can I say? You are the two most beautiful women I have ever seen and the most wonderful of company. So rude and so refreshing. Frank, you are the luckiest bastard I have ever come across. Being marooned with two such beauties for over a week would be every man's dream. It would certainly be mine, even at my age. I therefore wish to propose the toast that on this day in one year's time we should all meet again at this house and have, once again, a wonderful evening together."

They all rose shouting "One year's time" clinking their glasses together. Frank, who by now was completely drunk, promptly collapsed into a heap on the floor.

The next morning, they slowly emerged in various states of hangover for breakfast. When they had finished the two girls thanked Gordon and Sir George for looking after them so well the previous evening and, when Frank appeared apologised for his behaviour in getting so drunk. Gordon smiled his thanks and Sir George said it was nothing out of the ordinary. Frank said his head hurt, which nobody was surprised about. The two girls took Frank aside and, holding his hands, talked to him quietly for a while before tearfully saying their goodbyes and leaving. Richard and Jennie did likewise with Richard promising to look after whatever money he made on the diamonds. George went to the boat to talk to the crew and to ensure everything was ready. Frank was left to his own devices for the day.

Lost for something to do and with a whole day in which to do it, Frank suddenly had a desire to drive to where he was born. He asked a couple of the members if they would loan him a car for the day and they readily agreed. One of the old boys said that he could have his car and not to damage it. It turned out to be a beautiful dark green 4-litre E Type Jaguar, which was in pristine condition. Promising to be careful with it, he drove slowly through the country lanes until he was able to access the A3 arterial road heading north. He drove for just under the hour and weaved his way through country lanes again until he came to the common.

He had been born close by and had lived for the first twenty years of his life there. The common was part of him; he had spent so many days during his childhood at this place that he knew every inch of it. This was his own personal holy place; it healed him and solved his problems. The common stretched some two miles deep and a mile wide and had deep valleys and a central high ridge, which was almost like a spine running across it. From this high point beautiful views stretched twenty odd miles to the south over green rolling countryside that dipped and then rose to the blue hills in the distance and on a clear day, stretched from the East to the West as far as the eye could see.

He sat in the heather in the warm autumn sunshine letting the quiet and calm of the common run over and through him. He lay back closing his eyes and all he could hear was the sound of bees in the heather and a lark singing high above him in the sky. He fell into a deep sleep and immediately slipped into the incredible dreams that he always used to have when he fell asleep in this ancient place, but that's another story.

Eventually, when his dream travelling was over, and just before he awoke, she came to him. In his deep sub-conscious he had been worried about the pyramid and the strange things that had gone on there in the valley but the roller coaster ride of events since he had left the valley had suppressed his concerns. It was only now, when his mind was relaxed and running free, that he returned to confront that worry.

"I have been worried about you Frank; quite unnecessarily as it has turned out. You are now very well equipped at looking after yourself and now you wish to ask questions. I have permission to answer some of them but only some. We need your assurance that you will not inform anyone of what I am about to tell you. We are quite sure you won't, as we know you now. However, I want your solemn promise Frank."

"You've got that," he said.

"What do you want to know Frank?"

"What form do you take Sandy and why do you exist in that pyramid? What are you doing in there?"

"That's three questions Frank." Her beautiful face looked down at him and she smiled. There was a pause. "Yes, I can answer those questions but that will have to be all and my answers will have to be brief and probably not satisfactory, but I will do my best," she said.

"We are not spirits as you know and understand the term Frank, however in reality we are, but of a human kind. We have powers and abilities the like of which humans could not possibly understand. We are in the pyramid, as we have nowhere else to go on this increasingly hostile and populated planet. My elders have travelled over many continents over the centuries and we have found peace here but we can see that this is now changing. With regard to your last question, as to why are we here Frank? We are the guardians. Guardians of a secret of Biblical proportions, guardians of the story of Christianity, and guardians nominated and approved by The Lord." She paused again for a long moment. "Have you heard of the Knights Templar?"

"Yes, of course I have Sandy, they exist all over the world."

She smiled down on him again. "Yes they do and they have all the right motives and enthusiasm. But they are not of us, we are the true ones, the nominated ones, and that is all I can tell you now."

"But, what you have just told me raises a thousand questions Sandy."

She smiled down at him again; he was in love with that smile. "Dear Frank, it would be impossible for you to understand. I cannot tell you any more but one day you will understand. When you have finished your travelling and have come to terms with all of your problems Frank we will talk again. There may be ways that you can help us further, we think."

Frank's mind floated in his dream, he did not understand any of this. It did not make any sense whatsoever. She was so real he felt that he wanted to reach out and touch her and then something startling happened. She reached down and touched his face with a touch as light as a feather but the touch went to his very soul and he felt a deep calm overcome him, and a feeling of deep love and compassion.

"You will travel safely as I will watch over you. Be at peace Frank, we will talk again soon."

She faded slowly into the deep blue mist of his dream, smiling wistfully as she went.

Waking some two hours later, he found the sun starting to sink in the West. He knew that it would be some considerable time before he would come back here again and said his goodbyes to this place that had looked after him so well over the years. "I will come back," he promised. Making his way to the car, he drove slowly back to the coast thinking deeply about his dream all the way.

On his final day in England, George took him to meet his future crew. At the first sight of Frank and George coming down the pontoon the man and the two women sprang into action and lined up on the deck. Of course, they knew who he was and where they were going to so those preliminaries were quickly over. Martin was the skipper. He was thirty three years of age, 5'10' tall, wide shouldered with a strong handsome face that was well weathered and had clear blue eyes that smiled easily. His hair was bleached almost blonde by the sun. He had a no nonsense air about him and was obviously very capable. Even so he was very nervous when meeting Frank whose reputation had preceded him. His grip was firm and he met Frank's level gaze without flinching. Frank liked him instantly.

As Frank talked to Martin, the two girls glanced at each other, grinning. They liked what they saw.

"Hello Mr Blake, nice to meet you at long last. We have heard so much about you. May I introduce the lady members of the crew? This is my partner, Gill. She will be sharing the watches on the boat and general day-to-day crewing." Frank turned his gaze onto Martin's girlfriend. Blonde hair to her shoulders, Gill was very attractive. She was tall, she must be at least 5'9," thought Frank, with the strong wide shoulders of a swimmer and a superb body fitted out in a tee shirt, shorts and boat shoes. Frank didn't have to look to know she had great legs. She smiled nervously at Frank and held his gaze. Frank took her hand; she had a nice firm grip. "Hi, Gill nice to meet you." "Hello Mr Blake, likewise," she said with a strong Australian accent. Frank didn't say anything more but smiled back at her.

"And this is our friend Mandy who will be part-time crew and full time cook."

"Morning Mr Blake, Sir. How are you?" she said leaning forward to take Frank's hand. Frank couldn't help but notice that she had great breasts and that again she had a strong Aussie accent. Mandy was almost the double of Gill, about an inch shorter and of the same age group, around twenty-eight years old. Frank noticed her eyes first. They were beautiful, a mixture of green and bronze and were wide set. She had a cheeky grin on her face. "This trip is going to be interesting," he thought.

"I'm just fine thanks Mandy, good to meet you all." He addressed all three. "As you know we have a long way to go and we'll be spending plenty of time in each other's company over the next few months. You are probably wondering what this is all about. Well, it's all to do with what you have been reading in the press about my problems with a certain Irish family and such stuff. Over the course of the next few weeks I will tell you the story. Right now I want you to set sail for Guernsey as soon as you can. Martin, in your custom's report simply indicate that you are going to Guernsey, Jersey and St Malo. I will be waiting for you in St Peter Port marina, Guernsey and expect you to be there within the next two days. I have arranged a visitors' berth for you on berth K22 in the Queen Elizabeth Marina. We will not be hanging around in Guernsey, I'm afraid. As soon as I am on board, we set course for the Azores and then Barbados. That's where I want us to go first. Are you all OK with that?" One last thing, Martin, as far as I am concerned you are the skipper and I am just a passenger and crew. I don't want any favours even though I am paying for everything, just treat me as you do the others."

"That's fine by us Mr Blake, it sounds just great. Come and see what we have done with your boat."

* * *

That evening he spent quality time with George. This was the last time they were going to see each other for a while and each was conscious of the time slipping away. It was very late and they were now alone in the room.

"George, I have to say that meeting you has been one of the highlights of my life," said Frank. "You lifted me up when I was down and set me on the right path. I will always be grateful. You are a complete crackpot but I love you dearly."

"It's been nothing if not interesting," said Sir George. "Now, are you going to be OK tomorrow in that little speedboat thing? It's going to be a 2-3 sea state so you should be all right. I won't come down to see you off, but I will wake and lie in bed to see if I can hear your engines. I do indeed wish you all the best dear boy. I wish I could come with you. By the way Frank, I've been wanting to say this to you for some time. You have often mentioned that you couldn't understand why all these extraordinary events have been happening to you in such a short time span. What you don't realise Frank is that you actually only have a small influence over your life. I am firmly of the belief that one's life has already been mapped out for you, me and everyone else. Only the God's decide dear boy, only the God's decide as to the direction of your life and the main events that occur. Remember that. "

Frank said nothing for a while, thinking on what Sir George had just said and of his experiences within the pyramid, which seemed so long ago now. And, of course, there had been the problem, if that is what it should be called, of the voices and warnings in his head. If what Sir George said was actually true then that changed everything in his thinking. Perhaps he should just go with the flow and accept events as they happened, and tackle them one by one as they arose. Perhaps that is what life is really about. Facing down the challenges as they arise to the best of his ability and, in between times, getting on with his life. Interesting concept he thought.

"Well George I'll think about what you said. You may well be right because frankly not much else makes sense. You just fend off the law and keep Graham, my lawyer, informed about everything you hear. Remember, you know nothing. I will phone you probably twice a month under the guise we discussed and chat, or I will e-mail you. By the way George, I slipped back to the house today, as there was something that I had left there which needed collecting. I wanted you to have one of the items." Frank slipped his hand into his pocket and keeping his hand clenched held it out to George.

George looked at Frank for a moment and then extended his own hand so that it hovered under Frank's. Frank opened his hand and a large white diamond dropped into George's hand. George looked at it in silence for a moment and then said simply. "Thank you Frank, what an absolute stunner, thank you very much indeed. You really didn't need to do this old boy but I do appreciate the gift, thank you" His voice cracked slightly on the last two words.

Sir George humped and grumped a little more and then decided that he would leave. Patting Frank on the back he said "Cheerio, dear boy, have a safe trip and thank you for the, err, little gift" he smiled sadly as

Frank rose and took the old man's hand and held it tightly for three to four seconds as they looked each other in the eyes and nodded at each other. No more needed to be said. Frank let the old man go and George ambled slowly from the room with his head bent down. The room felt very empty without old George and Frank felt a sadness descend on him as he slowly finished his drink and watched the flames of the fire leap and dance while he sat thinking.

Gordon stood in the shadows at the end of the room, unseen. He had been watching the two men for the last half hour and had seen and heard all that had passed between the two friends. He was much moved. He continued watching Frank as he sat slumped in front of the fire, standing guard over the man he had grown to respect in such a short time, his black eyes glowing, reflecting the dancing light of the distant fire. Every once in a while he would nod his head as if in agreement to an unheard voice. Eventually Frank rose and walked slowly off to his room not knowing those black eyes watched him intently all the way.

* * *

Some ten hours later Frank was leaning on the grey granite wall that surrounds the Queen Elizabeth Marina close by the ferry terminal in St Peter Port harbour in Guernsey. His mood had changed as, humming happily to himself, he let the warm autumn sunshine envelop him. Through binoculars he watched his yacht come over the horizon between the rocky Guernsey coastline and Herm Island, heading for the port. He felt a certain pride in owning such a beautiful vessel. He had just arrived himself some three hours ago having borrowed a small 25' powerboat the day before from an old friend in Poole, Dorset. Sir George had not been at all happy with the knowledge of what Frank was about to do, however Frank had insisted and said it was the quickest, and quietest, way to get to Guernsey as no one would think that he would attempt it in a small boat. Any interested parties would probably be watching the ferry terminals, airports and the railways.

Frank had already ensured that the boat he proposed using had the fuel range and that the sea state would be OK. At six o'clock that morning he had slipped quietly away from the club by pre-arranged taxi and had been dropped off at the Poole Harbour marina. Dawn had broken two hours previously and, as predicted by the weathermen, he could see that it was going to be a nice day. The rising sun was already warm and there was a cool light wind on his face as he lifted his head and smelt the sea. He strolled along the various pontoons to where the boat lay and grinned with pleasure when he found it. His friend had told him it was a bit quick and capable of well over 60 knots in the right conditions, and that it was a beautiful black thoroughbred; it was certainly all of that. It was long, low and sleek and it lay quietly in the water as though it was waiting for him, with its nose slightly high and its bottom lying low in the water with the weight of its engines and fuel.

Frank stripped off the cockpit cover and stowed it away. He stepped into the cockpit and slid into the driving seat adjusting it to his own length so that his right foot was resting easily on the throttle pedal and his left foot would be able to brace him easily. He looked through the low windshield along the long nose and grinned for the second time, he was going to have some fun with this beastie. Switching on the fuel pumps he heard them click into action and he then swung the steering wheel from lock to lock to ensure that it was OK. He climbed out of the cockpit, collected his sea bags from the pontoon, and threw them onto the back seat. He strapped them down carefully so that they were secure; there were some very valuable items in one which was his future. He slipped back into the driving seat, slipped on an old life jacket and strapped himself in. He then fired up the twin 200hp Yamaha engines. He let them warm for a few minutes whilst keeping their revs low so that the noise didn't attract too much attention. When the temperature gauges showed warm he tossed the mooring line onto the pontoon, pushed himself off, and eased his way quietly out of the marina. With a light touch to the throttle the boat accelerated rapidly until it was planning gently. The big engines were purring quietly and he cruised quietly out of Poole Harbour making sure that he kept to the speed limit. He didn't want to attract any attention to himself whatsoever. Eventually he passed the harbour entrance and pushed down on the foot throttle until he was cruising at forty knots with the engines still purring quietly.

The boat handled beautifully like the thoroughbred it was and he felt at home. Clearing the Old Harry rocks, some three miles from shore, he slowed and, turning the boat, he sat rocking in the waves for a few moments looking with nostalgia at his home country, which was now just a thick grey bulge on the horizon in the early morning mist and he wondered when he would see it again. He shook his head sadly, gunned the powerful engines, spun the boat back on course in a swirl of spray, put his foot to the floor and rocketed the boat up to a cruising speed of fifty knots and did a fast run to Guernsey through the early morning light. He completed the journey in just over two hours. That had been a lot of fun as the boat bucked and jigged all the way through the low Atlantic swell and several times gave him a real fright by hitting an unexpectedly high wave and flying. He kept a good look out for his yacht and thought once that he could see it far over to his left. If it was them they were travelling further out to sea than he was. He arrived at his destination without getting too wet or flipping it over although it had been close at times; even so it had been great fun.

Too soon, Guernsey came up on the horizon, exactly as expected. He slowed as he approached the harbour and quietly eased the powerboat into a visitor's mooring in the main marina. Tying the boat up securely he let the engines cool for a few moments and then switched them off. Removing his sea bags he fitted the cover back over the boat and ensured it was well bedded down. He made his way towards the harbour office and gave the boat a backwards glance, thanking it quietly for a great ride. Reporting to the harbour authorities had to be done, as they were particularly hot on 'strange unknown arrivals' and would have been on top of him in no time if he hadn't done so. They would have spotted him by radar from a long way out and would have been curious about a boat travelling at high speed at that time of the morning. As it was, the customs officials were waiting for him and wanted to know where he had just come from. They were very impressed when he told them and the fact that he had only taken two hours, very impressed indeed. Frank knew that this incident would eventually be reported but by the time anyone had picked it up in England he would be long gone. He then phoned his sleepy friend telling him where the boat was, where he could collect it and he thanked him for allowing him to use it. His friend, knowing Frank of old, wasn't at all surprised to hear that his boat was now some eighty odd miles away in Guernsey.

It was some considerable time since Frank had felt so relaxed and he gazed out towards the horizon knowing that he would soon be out there breathing the clean sea air. Wanting to get on with the next stage in his life and feeling the excitement of a new adventure in strange lands. He fully intended to 'disappear' within the many islands of the Caribbean so that neither the Mulligans, nor anybody else; and that included the British Police, would ever find him. It was a great place to disappear. He had phoned his children and family the day before and told them what he was about to do and that his plans had changed. He had advised them to say nothing and to admit to not knowing where he was if the press or the police came round, which they would. He promised to keep in touch one way or another and told them not to worry about him. He would talk to all of them in a couple of months time and also write. He had ensured that large sums of money were put into the accounts of all three children and warned them not to spend it all but to put some of it away for a rainy day. They said they would but he had his doubts.

A familiar smell filled his nostrils that he couldn't quite fathom and he felt, rather than saw, a man lean on the harbour wall next to him. For a little while neither said anything, both were looking at the magnificent view in the warm early morning sunshine. Frank didn't move until the man spoke.

"Hello Frank thought I would come and see you off."

Frank turned towards the man slowly and, even at his height, he had to look up to look into his ice blue eyes. 'The man' must have been 6' 5" tall with short grey hair. He had wide set eyes and high cheek bones below a high forehead. He was tanned and slim built, immaculately groomed, dressed impeccably in a beautiful cut grey suit with black brogues, a light blue shirt and dark blue tie. He looked and spoke like a very well heeled 'old school' gentleman in his mid 60's, Frank knew instantly who he was. Three other men dressed in a similar fashion were hanging back about thirty feet away.

"That's very nice of you but to what do I owe the pleasure."

"Well." The man's gaze was piercing and disconcerting but Frank held his eyes. "We have been following your exploits with great amusement and interest Frank, and it is generally considered that you have done very well indeed and acted honourably, in some instances that is, which we are very pleased about. We have, as you know, had to help you once or twice but that is our agreement isn't it Frank?" Frank nodded saying nothing and wondered what this visit was all about.

"Of course you do dear boy, of course you do. Consider this to be a simple courtesy call, you are bound on new adventures and we are keen to follow you albeit from afar but we will be with you all the time Frank. You must understand that you will have to rely on your own abilities more and more as you develop but that is the name of the exercise, self-reliability and we are confident that you will succeed. After all Frank you have a long way to go yet in your life and we have great hopes for you. All we ask in return is that you stay true to your values which I am sure you will. Well, that's the end of the sermon Frank; I just wanted to say good luck."

Frank looked back down to where his boat was entering the marina and then looked back into the man's gaze. Before he could speak the man read his thoughts.

"Yes, it is unusual for us to venture beyond our home but we are finding that if we do we can exert some influence if it is done gently. We find your leaders naïve and rather stupid, and easily influenced; in most cases that is. There are a few who are formidable but they are mostly of the criminal fraternity and we know how to handle them. It might be in that area where we could use you, that's if you don't mind Frank?" The man gave Frank a broad smile, which meant that Frank had no alternative.

Frank couldn't help but wonder how on earth this being, for there was no other word that he could think of to describe this man, could imitate so correctly this upper class, so utterly English, public school drawl so beautifully with all the mannerisms that went with the accent.

"So a decision has been made, and I don't think I am giving away too many confidences here as you are a member of the team so to speak. We are gradually, albeit slowly, beginning to infiltrate most of the world's governments so that we can offer guidance to the decisions that are being made, for good or bad, all over the world. It's a very interesting project. We have never had to do this before but your world is changing so quickly that we have decided that it needs to be done. Our policy has always been one of non-interference but we can see that because of the major advances your world is making some direction needs to be given to help your young society survive. Do you understand Frank?"

Frank let the man's words wash over him and he stored them away for another day. "Not quite, however, thank you for telling me all this. From a personal point of view I have to be selfish right now and concentrate on how to get myself out of the difficult situation that I have found myself in so, if you don't mind, I will think about what you have said at a later date but if you will excuse me I must join my ship. Thanks for coming and seeing me off, Sir." Frank found that he automatically called the man Sir.

"Not at all Frank, no doubt we will contact you once you have settled in wherever you intend to go. We will need to talk to you from time to time of course."

Frank looked into those ice blue eyes and nodded. He then bent and picked up his bags, smiled at the man, and set off towards his boat. This was all surreal as far as he was concerned but he was now well used to extraordinary things happening to him. All the same the fact that 'The Man' should honour him by turning up and talking to him was, he felt, quite extraordinary. What the hell, Frank couldn't afford to think about the situation too deeply right now, he had a crew to welcome and needed to get aboard and get the hell out of here. Places to go and people to see were the critical factors right now. He wasn't in the mood to think about spooky people who could crush him with one thought. He had a new life to worry about and there would be plenty of private times during night watches to think about things.

"Bon Voyage Frank," called out the tall man. Frank waved a hand nonchalantly without looking back.

As he walked he watched his boat as she eased her way into the marina and into a visitor's berth. By the time he had made his way there his crew had refuelled and filled her water tanks, and they were lined up on the deck waiting to be off.

They greeted him with smiles and chatter about their trip. He was looking forward to sailing with them and heaved his two sailing bags with all his worldly possessions onto the deck. He had found packing for this trip strange and had realised that, at the end of the day, you don't have many possessions that can be described as essential and necessary. Passport, money, and clothes, a few photos of his family, a number of very high quality beautifully cut diamonds and that was it.

With one foot on the deck and the other on the pontoon, and watched by his crew, he looked slowly around him at what was going to be the last bit of England that he was going to see for some time. He hesitated, looking back up to where he had been a few moments before; he could clearly see the tall man leaning over the railings, watching him. He waved a hand and Frank, after a moment's hesitation, waved back.

The young Captain hadn't missed a thing and looking up at the Marina wall said,

"Friend of yours Sir?"

"Yes, I suppose you could call him that." Frank heaved himself onto the deck of his boat. "Let's get going Martin."

ISBN 141207675-7